The smile grew, even if it didn't quite catch in his eyes.

"Your father was crazy, I hope you know."

This was said so gently, and with so much love, Deanna's eyes burned. But before she could recover, Josh said, "I know why he sent you away, Dee. Or at least, I can guess. And no, he never talked about you all that much afterward. But when he did..." Looking away, he shook his head. "It was obvious how much he loved you." His gaze met hers again. "How much he loved you. *Missed* you—"

"You mind if we don't talk about this right now? About Dad?"

His cheeks pinking slightly, Josh straightened, turning to look out over the pasture. "Sorry. I'm not real good at this."

"At what?"

"Social graces. Knowing when to keep my trap shut. I hear this stuff in my head—" he waved in the general direction of his hat "—and it just falls out of my mouth."

"I remember," Deanna said quietly, then smiled, not looking at him. "I think that's why we were friends."

"Because I have no filter whatsoever?"

"Yes, actually." She let their eyes meet, and her heart thudded against her sternum even harder than the baby kicking her belly button from the inside.

A Gift for the Rancher

Karen Templeton & April Arrington

Previously published as
The Rancher's Expectant Christmas
and *The Rancher's Miracle Baby*

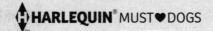

ISBN-13: 978-1-335-04185-2

A Gift for the Rancher

Copyright © 2019 by Harlequin Books S.A.

The Rancher's Expectant Christmas
First published in 2016.
This edition published in 2019.
Copyright © 2016 by Karen Templeton-Berger

The Rancher's Miracle Baby
First published in 2017.
This edition published in 2019.
Copyright © 2017 by April Standard

Recycling programs
for this product may
not exist in your area.

Printed in U.S.A.

www.Harlequin.com

CONTENTS

Karen Templeton is an inductee into the Romance Writers of America Hall of Fame. A three-time RITA® Award–winning author, she has written more than thirty novels for Harlequin. She lives in New Mexico with two hideously spoiled cats. She has raised five sons and lived to tell the tale, and she could not live without dark chocolate, mascara and Netflix.

Books by Karen Templeton

Harlequin Special Edition

Wed in the West

Back in the Saddle
A Soldier's Promise
Husband Under Construction
Adding Up to Marriage
Welcome Home, Cowboy
A Marriage-Minded Man
Reining In the Rancher
A Mother's Wish

Jersey Boys

Meant-to-Be Mom
Santa's Playbook
More Than She Expected
The Real Mr. Right

Summer Sisters

The Marriage Campaign
A Gift for All Seasons
The Doctor's Do-Over

The Fortunes of Texas: Whirlwind Romance

Fortune's Cinderella

Visit the Author Profile page
at Harlequin.com for more titles.

THE RANCHER'S
EXPECTANT CHRISTMAS

Karen Templeton

Once again, I have to give a shout-out to
Kari Lynn Dell
For her patience,
Friendship,
And willingness to answer probably some of the
dumbest horse-related questions she's ever heard.
I hope your eyes don't hurt TOO much
from rolling so hard.

To Carly Silver
Editorial Assistant Extraordinaire
It's with very mixed feelings that I congratulate you
On your promotion.
Because you, my dear, have been a true godsend
To this beleaguered author.
So. Much. Love.

Chapter 1

The baby walloped her full bladder, jerking Deanna Blake out of a mercifully sound sleep and scattering wisps of agitated dreams into the predawn gloom. Her heart hammering, she scooched farther underneath the soft Pendleton blanket, cradling her belly…

"A-*choo!*"

Gasping, Deanna heaved herself around just as the small child fled the room, awkwardly yanking shut the bedroom door behind him.

For what felt like the first time in weeks, she smiled, then clumsily shoved herself upright. Spearing a hand through her short, undoubtedly startled-looking hair, she frowned at her old room, coming more into focus as the weak November sun gradually elbowed aside the remnants of a dark country night. She'd been so wiped out from her cross-country flight, as well as the three-hour drive up from Albuquerque after, she hadn't even turned on the light before crawling into bed. Now, taking in the old *Gilmore Girls* poster, its curled edges grasping at the troweled plaster walls, she wasn't sure which was weirder—how long it'd been since she'd last slept here, or that the room was exactly as she'd left it more than ten years ago. Then again, why would Dad have changed it—?

Deanna squeezed shut her eyes as a double whammy of grief and guilt slammed into her, even stronger than the next kick that finally forced her out of bed and into the adjoining bathroom where she studiously avoided glancing at the mirror over the chipped marble sink. Between the pregnancy puffies and an unending series of sleepless nights, in the past few weeks her complexion had gone from fair to vampiresque. Meaning it was simply best not to look.

Teeth brushed and comb dragged through hair, she wrestled into a pair of very stretchy leggings and a tent-sized sweater before, on a deep breath, opening her door. A child's laughter, the comforting scent of coffee she couldn't drink, tumbled inside.

As if everything were perfectly normal.

Through a fog of sadness and apprehension, Deanna crept down the Saltillo-tiled hallway toward the kitchen, hoping against hope that Gus, her father's old housekeeper, was just looking after the little boy while his daddy tended to some ranch duty or other. Just as Gus had watched Deanna from time to time, as well as Sam Talbot's boys whenever the need arose. In some ways it'd been like having four older brothers, both a blessing and a curse for an only child living out in the New Mexico boonies.

She hesitated, gazing through a French door leading into the courtyard centering the traditional hacienda-style house. A light snow sugared the uneven flagstone, sparkling in the early morning sun. Save for the spurts of laughter, the house was as eerily quiet as she remembered. Especially after the constant thrum of traffic, of life, in DC. A pang of something she couldn't quite identify shuddered through her. Not homesickness, she didn't think. She palmed her belly, where the baby stirred.

Uncertainty? Maybe.

No, definitely.

The cavernous kitchen was empty, save for a huge gray cat sitting on a windowsill, calmly ascertaining Deanna's worthiness to share its breathing space. The room hadn't been vacant long, though, judging from the softly crackling fire in the potbellied stove at the far end of the enormous eat-in area, anchored by a rustic wood table that easily sat twelve. Even though the Vista Encantada's century-old main house had long since been converted to natural gas, Gus had always lit the old stove, every morning from early October through mid-May. The dark cabinets and hand-painted Mexican tiles were the same, as well, even though the vintage six-burner range's lapis finish seemed a little more pitted than she remembered. And for a moment she was a kid again, scarfing down one of Gus's breakfast burritos before catching the school bus in the dark—

"Dee?"

She turned, immediately trapped in a pair of moss-colored eyes that had at one time been very dear to her. Dear enough to prompt her father to send her clear across the country when she was fifteen, to live with her mother's sister. And oh, how she'd initially chafed at Dad's assumption that something was going on between her and Josh Talbot that wasn't. And wouldn't. Because Josh had never been like that, even if Deanna hadn't fully understood at the time what "that" might have been.

Somehow, she doubted he'd appreciate the irony of her current situation.

"Hey," she said, crossing her arms as Josh dumped an armful of firewood into the bucket beside the stove, his mini-me peeking at her from behind his legs. It'd been over a decade since she'd caught more than a glimpse of him on her occasional visits home. And the tall, solid cowboy whose sharp gaze now latched on to her belly, then her hair, was nothing like the skinny, spindly teenager she used to sneak off to see, prompting her father's conclusion-jumping. Although the shy, lonely girl *she'd* been, still reeling after her mother's death, had only been seeking solace. A refuge. Neither of which, looking back, Josh had been under any obligation to give her—

"I didn't expect…" Deanna shoved out a breath. "Where's Gus?"

"Went into town with my mother for groceries. For… tomorrow."

"Oh. Right."

"I'm sorry," he said quietly, but with a decided, *And where the hell have you been?* edge to it.

So much for thinking her heart couldn't be more

shredded than it already was. Irony, again, to find herself facing exactly what she'd avoided by *not* coming home, that look of disappointment. Confusion. Not from her father, no, but still.

"Same goes," she said into the awkward silence. Because she could hardly explain things with a child in the room, could she?

His mouth set, Josh nodded, and pain knifed through her. Josh'd been the only one of the former manager's sons to show any real interest in ranching. Or, later, the horse-breeding operation. Even so, when medical issues forced Sam's early retirement a few years back, her father's asking Josh to take his dad's place had surprised her. At least until she realized how close Josh and her father had become, despite that business when she and Josh had been teenagers. That Dad clearly thought of her childhood friend like a favorite nephew. If not the son he never had.

A feeling she'd gleaned had been mutual.

Blinking away tears, Deanna cleared her throat and smiled for the little boy, who kept peering at her from behind his daddy. Her father had told her about the child, that his mama wasn't in the picture. Her hand went to her belly again, as if to reassure the little one inside.

"Hey, guy," she said softly. "I'm Deanna. Mr. Blake's daughter. Although you can call me Dee if you want. What's your name?"

The child ducked back behind Josh and muttered something unintelligible. Sighing, Josh twisted to haul the boy into his arms. "How about trying that again? Only so she can actually hear you this time."

"Austin," the kid got out, giving her a sweet, heart-squeezing smile. Dark hair, like his daddy. Same eyes, too.

"Pleased to meet you, Austin—"

"How come your tummy's so big?" he said, pointing to her belly, and Josh's face blazed.

"Oh, jeez…"

Deanna laughed, even as she thought, *At least one person in the room is being honest.* "It's okay, I'm used to it." Returning her gaze to Austin, she bent over as much as she could and whispered, "There's a baby growing inside me."

The kid frowned. "Like the horses?"

"Exactly. Except this baby doesn't have hooves."

"Oh. Is it a boy or a girl?"

"A girl."

Austin frowned at her belly again. "What's her name?"

"Haven't decided yet."

The kid gave her a maybe-you-should-get-on-that look that made Deanna's chest tickle as she bit down on a smile. Then, heaving a breathy "Okay," he wriggled out of his father's arms and took off to mess with the cat, who'd thudded to the tiled floor then flopped in the morning's first sunbeam, belly bared to the world. Or in this case, little boys. Brave cat.

"Sorry about the interrogation," Josh said, and Deanna turned to see his mouth pushed into something reasonably close to a smile.

"Hey. At least he didn't ask how the baby got in there."

"Give him a minute," Josh muttered, and for a second she saw the boy who'd kept her from losing it, all those years ago.

The boy she might have loved, if she'd been inclined to such foolishness.

"Austin's adorable. He looks like you."

"So everyone says." He frowned. "Your…the baby's father let you come alone?"

"We're…not together."

There was no denying the judgment in his stony expression. And not only about her pregnancy, she guessed. The baby kicked; stifling a wince, Deanna glanced over at Austin before meeting that penetrating gaze again. "I had no idea Dad was even sick. I swear. Because he'd made *Gus* swear not to tell me. Because if I'd known, nothing would've kept me from being here. And the worst thing is…" Her eyes stung. Tough. "I can't even tell Dad how angry I am. How…hurt."

The staring continued for several seconds before Josh said, "I know he didn't tell you. But if you'd bothered to pay a visit in the last six months—"

"And why would I do that when Dad made it more than clear he didn't particularly want me to?"

And why was she was even trying to explain something she didn't entirely understand herself?

A long, tense moment passed before Josh said, "For what it's worth, it happened pretty fast."

"So Gus said." Deanna glanced over at Austin, now lying beside the cat and apparently telling it a story, before facing Josh again. "Although I gather the only reason he did was because he figured I'd see the death certificate, discover the truth whether Dad wanted me to or not."

Another breath left Josh's lungs. "I suppose he didn't want you to worry—"

"What he did," Deanna said, not even trying to hide the bitterness in her voice, "was unfair and selfish. Kind of a major thing to keep from me."

Josh's eyes once more dropped to her swollen middle, and Deanna's face warmed. Especially when he looked back up.

"Just like I'm guessing Granville had no idea about his granddaughter."

"I didn't intend to keep her a secret forever, for cripe's sake! But I did know…" Her lips pressed tightly together. "That the circumstances surrounding my condition wouldn't exactly make Dad happy. At least not… not before he had a chance to meet her. I had a plan," she said over the stab to her heart. "Unfortunately it didn't jibe with the Universe's."

That got a hard stare before Josh walked away to open the fridge.

"What would you like for breakfast?"

Deanna frowned, confused. "You don't have to—"

"When was the last time you ate?"

"Um…lunch yesterday? But cereal's fine, don't go to any trouble—"

"Not planning on it. But Gus left pancake batter, and even I can scramble eggs. The squirt already ate, an hour ago."

"Eggs, then. If you're sure—"

He shot her another look that shut her up…a look that said they only had to get through the next few days. Then everyone could get back to their regular lives.

Or whatever.

Another wave of grief shunted through her, as she thought about the ramifications of her father's passing, not only for her but for the entire community. Weird, how she'd never thought much about what would happen to the ranch after his death, mainly because that'd always seemed so far in the future. Even though he'd been significantly older than her mother, somehow Deanna had always thought of Dad as immortal, like some Greek god. Especially since he'd never discussed the disposition of the property with her—

A sudden burst of voices from the mudroom shattered her thoughts. "Gramma!" Austin yelled as he abandoned the probably very relieved cat and sprinted across the room, where the woman who'd so often filled the gap in Deanna's life, and heart, after her mother died dumped several recyclable grocery totes on the counter, then swept her grandson into her arms. Gus, the belly cantilevered over his giant belt buckle nearly as big as Deanna's, followed a moment later, hauling several more bags which landed unceremoniously on the floor. Her long ponytail a mass of delicate, staticky silver wires against her back, Billie Talbot turned, her expression softening when she spotted Deanna.

"Oh, sweetheart…" she crooned, and fresh tears sprang to Deanna's eyes. A moment later she was wrapped in the older woman's arms. "I'm so sorry… so, *so* sorry…"

Unable to speak, Deanna nodded against Billie's shoulder, the coarse fabric of the older woman's poncho scratching her cheek. "Such a good man, your daddy," Billie whispered into her hair. "Whole town's gonna miss him like crazy…and oh, my goodness!" Holding Deanna apart, Billie grinned. "Seven months?"

"More or less."

"And they let you fly?"

Scrubbing a tear off her cheek, Deanna smiled, remembering that Josh's mother was a midwife. "Believe me, the flight attendants all breathed a huge sigh of relief when we landed," she said, and Billie chuckled.

"I'll bet they did." Then she sighed. "It's so good to see you, honey. I just wish it weren't under these circumstances."

"Me, too."

Another gentle smile curving her lips, Josh's mom tucked her hands underneath the poncho, seeming to see the rest of her for the first time. "Your hair…adorable. The darker color suits you."

Deanna flushed. "Thanks."

"And on you, the nose stud totally works." A low laugh rumbled from her chest. "Although I can only imagine your daddy's reaction. But listen, you need anything while you're here, anything at all, you let me know. I mean it."

"I know you do. And I'm grateful."

A wordless nod preceded another hug before Billie turned to Josh. "Why don't you let me take Austin back to the house for a while? Y'all don't need a four-year-old underfoot right now."

Josh seemed to hesitate for a moment, then smiled for his son. "Wanna go with Gramma?"

"Yeah!" the kid yelled, wriggling like somebody'd put bugs down his pants, and Deanna smiled, too, over the sadness cramping her heart. For the most part, and despite the events of the past little while, she loved her life back east, a life filled with art and dance and music with more instruments than a couple of guitars and a dude on drums. And no matter what, she had her father to thank for that, for giving her opportunities she would've never had if she'd stayed here. Even so, as she watched Josh softly talking to his mother and little boy, as the love and goodwill she'd always associate with this kitchen, this house, this godforsaken little town, washed over her, she had to admit it didn't exactly feel terrible to be back.

For a little while, anyway.

Although there was no real reason to walk Mom and Austin out to her car, seeing Deanna again—especially an extremely pregnant Deanna with pointy black hair and a diamond in her nose, for godssake—had rattled Josh far more than he wanted to admit. He could only imagine what was going through his mother's head.

"I think we've got everything for tomorrow," Mom said after buckling Austin into one of the three car seats that were permanent fixtures in the back of her SUV. At the rate they were adding kids to the family, though, one of those wonker vans was looking good for the near future. Straightening, Mom swung her gaze to Josh's. "Although Gus said there's already a dozen casseroles and such in the freezer?"

"Wouldn't know."

A chilly breeze tangled his mother's ponytail, pulled off her high-cheekboned face. "What *do* you know?" she asked, and Josh smiled drily.

"Meaning about Deanna?"

"Yep."

"Not a whole lot. Since she's only been back for five minutes. Also, it's none of my business. Or anyone's."

"True. Although I did notice there's no wedding ring."

He paused. "She said she and the father aren't together. And again…none of our business."

"Hmm." Mom squinted out toward the Sangre de Cristo mountains, their snowy tops aglow in the early morning sun, a harbinger of the winter breathing down their necks. Then she looked back at him, a little smile tilting her lips. "I know how much it annoyed you boys, the way your father and I were always up in your business." The smile turned into a grimace. "Especially for Levi and Colin." Both of whom had flown as far from the family nest as they could, even though Josh's twin, Levi, had returned several months ago. "Still," Mom said, "seeing the obvious pain in that little girl's eyes, that she never got to say goodbye to her father…maybe *your* father and I didn't do such a bad job, after all."

"Like I'm gonna give you that much ammunition," Josh said, and she swatted his shoulder.

Then she frowned. "I'm guessing Granville didn't know about the baby?"

"It would appear not."

Looking away, Mom slowly wagged her head. "I don't get it, I really don't. What would make one of the most generous human beings on the face of the planet disconnect from his only child?"

Crossing his arms, Josh sneaked a peek at his son, happily banging two little cars together. A question he'd asked himself many times, though even as a child Dee's discontent with small-town living had been obvious. As though Whispering Pines wasn't big enough to contain all that Deanna Blake was, or wanted to be…a malaise that only increased as she got older, if her periodic bitching to him had been any indication.

And certainly Josh would've never been enough for her, a truth he'd thankfully realized before he'd said or done anything he would've most certainly regretted. So her excitedly telling him on her fifteenth birthday she was moving to DC hadn't come as all that much of a surprise, even if he hadn't let on how much it'd killed him. Especially since he'd known in his gut she'd never come back. Not to live, anyway.

Even so, her father's basically giving her up…it made no sense. Then again Austin's mother hadn't seemed to have an issue with leaving her son behind, had she? So maybe this was simply one of those "there's no accounting for people" things.

Josh realized his mother was giving him her *What are you thinking, boy?* look. A smile flicked over his mouth. "I guess we'll never find out. About her father, I mean."

"Guess not." Mom glanced back at the beautiful old house, which, along with the vast acreage surrounding it, the barns and pastures and guesthouses scattered along the river farther out, had been in the Blake family since before New Mexico was a state. "I suppose this will all go to her."

Josh'd be lying if he said her words didn't slice through him. Yeah, by rights the Vista was Dee's now, she could do whatever she wanted with it. But Josh had never lived anywhere else. Or wanted to. So *by rights* the place was *his* home far more than it had ever really been Dee's.

"I suppose we'll find out tomorrow," he said, trying to sound neutral. "After the memorial, the lawyer said."

"Granville's request?"

"Apparently so." Just as his boss had been adamant he didn't want a funeral, or a burial, or "any of that crap." So he was probably looking down from wherever he was, pissed as all get-out about the memorial service. No way, though, was the town gonna let his passing go without *any* acknowledgment. As much as the old man had done for everybody, it'd be downright disrespectful to pretend as though nothing had happened. Meaning for once Granville Blake wasn't getting his way.

"Well," Mom said, opening her car door, "I'd best be getting back. I've got a couple of mothers to check up on later, but no babies due in the next little while, thank goodness. I told Gus I'd be there early tomorrow to get started on the food for the reception. I'll bring Austin back then."

"You don't have to keep him—"

"I know I don't. But something tells me Deanna's gonna need a friend over the next couple of days." She paused. Squinting. "And I don't mean Gus."

Josh sighed. "That was a long time ago, Mom."

"So? It won't kill you to be nice to the girl."

Thinking, *I wouldn't be so sure about that*, Josh stood in the graveled driveway, waving to Austin as his mother backed out, taking his buffer between him and Dee with her. But when he got back inside, where she was sitting at the table inhaling the breakfast that Gus had whipped up for her in the nanosecond Josh had been gone, it wasn't his mother's pushy words ringing in his ears, but Granville's.

Because two days before he'd died, his boss—the boss who'd guarded his privacy so fiercely he'd refused to discuss his illness—happened to mention his suspicion that Dee was in some kind of trouble but wouldn't tell him what. Mutterings Josh had chalked up to the illness, frankly. Or, more likely, Granville's own guilt and regret that he'd kept his daughter in the dark about his condition. Talk about apples not rolling far from the tree.

Except obviously the old man's intuition had been dead to rights, resurrecting all manner of protective feelings Josh had no wish to resurrect. Especially when she lifted those huge, deep brown eyes to his, and he was sixteen again, sharing one of those soul-baring conversations they used to have when they'd tell each other their dreams and hopes and fears, knowing there'd be no teasing, no judgment…

"If anybody needs me," he said to the room at large, "I'll be out working that new cutter I bought."

Then he got his butt out of there before those wayward thoughts derailed what little common sense he had left.

Chapter 2

Apparently, pregnancy made her nostalgic. At least, that's what Deanna was going with as she waddled outside after breakfast, bundled up against a morning chill laced with the scents of her childhood—fireplace smoke and horseflesh, the sweet breath of piñon overlaying the slightly musty tang of hoof-churned earth. It was always a shock, how clear the air was at this altitude, how the cloudless sky seemed to caress you, make you feel almost weightless. Even when you were hauling around thirty extra pounds that could never quite decide how to distribute itself.

A dog she didn't recognize trotted toward her, something with a lot of Aussie shepherd in him. "And aren't you a handsome boy?" she said softly, and the pooch dissolved into a wriggling mass of speckled love, dancing over to give her hand a cursory lick before trotting off again—*Sorry, can't dawdle, work to do, beasts to herd.*

Other than the dog, little had changed that she could tell. The old, original barn still stood in all its dignified, if slightly battered, glory not far from the house, even though it'd been decades since any actual livestock had been sheltered there. She smiled, remembering the July Fourth barn dances her father had sponsored every year for the entire community, the cookout and potluck that had always preceded them. The fireworks, down by the pond. How much she'd loved all the hoopla as a child, even if she'd grown to dread it after her mother died of a particularly aggressive brain tumor when she was fourteen, when she'd never felt up to being the gracious hostess Mom had been. A role far more suited to someone...else.

Although most of the fencing around the property had been long since converted to wire, the pasture nearest the house was still bordered in good old-fashioned white post and rail...another bane of her existence when she was a kid and Dad had insisted she help repaint it whenever the need arose. Which had seemed like every five minutes at the time. She let her cold fingers skim the top rail, smiling when a nearby pregnant mare softly nickered, then separated herself from a half-dozen or so compadres and plodded over, almost as though she recognized Deanna. And damned if the jagged white blaze on her mahogany face wasn't startlingly familiar.

"You're Starlight's, aren't you?" she said gently, and the horse came close enough for her to sweep her fingers across her sleek muzzle, for the mare to "kiss" her hair. Same sweet nature as her mama, too, Deanna thought, chuckling for a moment before releasing another sigh.

It hadn't been all bad, living out here. Boring, yes. Stifling, definitely. But as quickly as she'd acclimated to—and embraced—living back east, there'd been more than the occasional bout of feeling displaced, too. Even if she'd never admitted it. She'd missed riding, and the sky, and the deep, precious silence of a snowy night. Greasy nachos at the rodeo every fall. The way the mountains seemed to watch over the plains and everything that lived on them. The way everyone kept an eye out for everyone else.

Josh.

She spotted him, working a sleek chestnut gelding in the distance, as homesickness spiked through her, so sharp she lost her breath.

Homesickness, and regret. Choking, humiliating, taunting regret.

Shivering, Deanna wrapped up more tightly in the giant shawl she'd scored for ten bucks at that thrift store near her apartment—

Crap. She had no idea where she belonged anymore, although *here* certainly wasn't it. *Here* was her past, which she'd long since outgrown. But her life *there*, in DC, had collapsed like a house of cards, hadn't it? All she knew was that she'd better figure something out, and soon, before this little person made her appearance. Kinda hard to bring a baby home if you weren't sure where home was.

Still caressing the mare's sun-warmed coat, Deanna looked out toward the other horses grazing the frosted grass, their coats gleaming in the strengthening morning sun as bursts of filmy white puffed from their nostrils. Then she started as she realized Josh was headed her way. His own breath clouding his face, he came up beside her, digging into his pocket for a piece of carrot for the mare.

"I see you two have already met."

Deanna drew back her hand, wrapping up more tightly in the shawl. "She's Starlight's, isn't she?"

"Yep."

"What's her name?"

"Star*fire*. One of the best cutters I've ever ridden. Her babies should fetch a pretty penny. This one's already spoken for, in fact."

"When's she due?"

"Late January or thereabouts."

After a moment, Deanna said, "So she actually gets to carry her foal to term?" and Josh softly chuckled. She knew many "serious" breeders only used their prize mares to jumpstart an embryo, then transplanted them into surrogates. She supposed in some ways it was less stressful on the mare that way, but it'd always seemed to her so…callous. Like the horses were only things to be used.

"Not to worry. Your daddy would've killed me, for one thing. Not to mention *my* daddy. No, we do things the old-fashioned way around here," he said, stroking the mare's shiny neck. "Don't we, sweetheart?"

The horse nodded, the movement knocking off Josh's hat.

"Hey!" The horse actually snickered, making Josh shake his head before scooping the hat off the ground.

Deanna smiled as Josh smacked the old Stetson against his thighs to knock off the dust, then rammed it back on his head. "She looks so much like her mama it's uncanny."

"You seen her yet?"

"Ohmigosh—she's still here?"

Something like aggravation shunted across Josh's features. "Until the day she crosses over. Why would you think she wouldn't be?"

"Because I'd told Dad to sell her, since I wouldn't be riding her anymore. At least, not enough to warrant keeping her. But he kept her anyway?"

Leaning back against the fence, Josh folded his arms over his chest, releasing another little puff of dust from his well-worn barn coat. "He came to talk to her every day. Sometimes twice a day, until…well." A small smile curved his lips. "To tell her all about what you were doing. I even caught him showing the horse your picture on his phone once."

"Get out."

"Of course, then he got all embarrassed when he realized I'd seen him." The smile grew, even if it didn't quite catch in his eyes. "Your father was crazy, I hope you know."

This said so gently, and with so much love, Deanna's eyes burned. But before she could recover, Josh said, "I know why he sent you away, Dee. Or at least, I can guess. And no, he never talked about you all that much afterward. But when he did…" Looking away, he shook his head. "It was obvious how much he loved you." His gaze met hers again. "How much *missed* you—"

"You mind if we don't talk about this right now? About Dad?"

His cheeks pinking slightly, Josh straightened, turning to look out over the pasture. "Sorry. I'm not real good at this."

"At what?"

"Social graces. Knowing when to keep my trap shut. I hear this stuff in my head—" he waved in the general direction of his hat "—and it just falls out of my mouth."

"I remember," Deanna said quietly, then smiled, not looking at him. "I think that's why we were friends."

"Because I have no filter whatsoever?"

"Yes, actually." She let their eyes meet, and her heart thudded against her sternum even harder than the baby kicking her belly button from the inside. "Because I knew you'd always be straight with me. Because...because you never treated me like the boss's daughter."

Confusion flitted across his face for a moment until he punched out a laugh. "Oh, trust me, I always treated you like the boss's daughter."

Now it was Deanna's turn to flush. Partly because she got his drift, partly because she'd had no idea there'd been a drift to get. Or not, in this case.

Another subject she didn't want to talk about, one she'd had no idea was even on the table until thirty seconds ago. However, at this rate they'd have nothing left to discuss except the weather, and wouldn't that be lame?

"Didn't mean to abandon you," he said, and her head jerked to his again. "A little bit ago. For breakfast?"

"Oh. Right. It's okay, Gus took over. As Gus does.

Although I ate so little he threatened to hook me up to an IV."

"So much for eating for two."

"Yeah, well, one of the two has squished my stomach into roughly the size of an acorn. Not to mention my bladder. Anyway, I assured him that since I'd eaten everything that wasn't nailed down in my second trimester I doubted the kid was suffering."

Josh's gaze lingered on her belly for several seconds before he turned to prop his forearms on the top rail. "So how long are you here?"

"Not sure. A couple of weeks? I figured…" Deanna cleared her throat, then clutched the fence, stretching out her aching back. "I figured," she said to the ground as she willed the baby to shift, "there'd be…" Standing upright again, she met Josh's gaze. "There'd be things to discuss. Handle. Whatever. So I left my ticket open-ended. Long as I'm back the week before Thanksgiving, I'm good."

"And what happens then?"

"Among other things, an all Mahler concert at the National Symphony I've been looking forward to for months. But also an installation at my gallery. Well, not my gallery, but where I work. Young Japanese painter. I…" Her face warmed. "Through a weird confluence of events, I sort of 'discovered' him. This will be his first US showing, so we're all very excited…and your eyes just glazed over, didn't they?"

"That's the clouds coming in, they said it might snow later." She chuckled. Josh crossed his arms. "You like it? What you're doing?"

"I adore it. It's what I'm good at. What I love. That

I'm actually employed doing something related to what Dad coughed up four years' tuition for is a bonus."

When she reached behind her to massage her lower back again—because her daughter's favorite position involved ramming her skull into the spot right over Deanna's tailbone—Josh's gaze dropped to her stomach again, then away.

"This must feel weird. Being back."

"You have no idea. Like I'm having a dream where I'm a kid again. Because so little has changed."

Josh gave her a funny look. "Did you expect it to be different?"

"I'm not sure what I expected, truthfully."

"You're not what I expected, either." His eyes narrowed as he scrutinized her hair. "What's up with that, anyway?"

She laughed. "It was decided I needed to look—" she made air quotes "'edgier'. As in, customers are more likely to buy contemporary art from someone who actually looks contemporary to the twenty-first century. So buh-bye long, blah brown hair, hello—"

"Edgy."

"Yep. And this is *not* the pic Dad was showing Starlight. Trust me."

"Since you never sent him one of you looking like this."

"Oh, hell, no."

Josh crossed his arms. "So this is, what? A costume?"

"It's called dressing the part. And everybody does it. Seriously—if you rode into the rodeo ring in a business suit, would people take you seriously?"

Grinning, Josh looked away. "Point taken."

Starfire's breath warmed Deanna's face when she reached up to stroke the mare's nose again. "Gus said Dad had hospice come in, at the end," she said quietly.

"The *very* end," Josh breathed out. "That last week or so. Gus was his main caregiver. The rest of us filled in when we could, of course. Or I should say, when Gus let us. Since according to him we never did things right."

Her jaw tight, Deanna looked back toward the house. "And as I said, Dad could have clued me in, anytime. Or let Gus do it." Her mouth pulled tight. "I can tell how much it sucked for the old guy, caught between loyalty to my father and what he clearly felt he should've done."

"And obviously you were in no condition to be nursing someone—"

"First off, between Gus and me, we would've managed. Secondly, also as I said, Dad didn't know I was pregnant." Her tenuous grasp on a good mood slipped away. "And this is a dumb conversation."

She felt Josh stiffen beside her. "Just like any conversation that gets too close to reality, right? Seriously, if there's some kind of prize for avoiding a subject, you'd win hands down."

"And you might want to think about picking a fight with a pregnant woman."

"I think I can handle it. And have. *And* since I have absolutely nothing to lose here, I may as well say this— whatever's going on with you, whatever kind of relationship you and your father had is none of my concern. I know that. But this keeping secrets crap is for the birds. Especially since your dad knew something was going on with you, even if he didn't know what. And that *was* my concern, since I worked for the man."

Deanna gawked at him for several seconds before averting her eyes again. "That's ridiculous."

"My concern?"

"No. That you think he knew something—"

"Because he told me, Dee. He was worried about you. I'm not making that up."

Annoyance surged through her. "If he was so worried about me, why didn't he say something? Why didn't he simply *ask* me?"

"Oh, I don't know—maybe because he knew you wouldn't've told him, so what would've been the point? Because God forbid the two of you actually talk to each other. And you know what?" he said, pushing away from the fence. "You're right, this is a dumb conversation. And I've had enough of those to last me a lifetime."

"Dammit, Josh—don't be like this!"

"Like what?" he said, a frown digging into his forehead. "Who I've always been? The dude you could *count on* to be straight with you? Fine. You don't wanna talk, I can't make you. But you're not gonna shut me up, either." He shrugged. "Just how it goes."

Then he stalked off, his boots thudding in the dirt, and Deanna sighed.

This was going to be the longest two weeks in the history of the planet.

His toddler stepdaughter balanced on one hip, Josh's twin, Levi, came up beside him in the ranch's formal dining room, where the dark, highly polished table contrasted with the troweled plaster walls and beamed ceiling. But after probably half a century Josh wouldn't have been surprised to find the table's graceful feet had taken root in the pitted grout between the old handmade tiles. He remembered, because his brain was being a real sonuvabitch today, hiding in here with Deanna when they were little—really little, like before he'd even started school—sitting under the table and pointing out "pictures" they'd see in the uneven tiles—

"You doing okay?" Levi asked, frowning at some unidentifiable finger food before picking one up and popping it into his mouth, anyway.

"Sure," Josh muttered, doing some frowning of his own at Deanna through the wide, arched doorway between the dining room and the vast great room where she sat on one of the leather sofas, Mom watchdogging beside her as people offered their condolences.

His brother's gaze followed Josh's, but thankfully he kept his mouth shut. For the moment, anyway. Levi offered the toddler one of the...things, but with a vigorous shake of her dark curls and an emphatic, "No!" Risa shoved away his hand. So Levi ate it for her. As one did.

"Nice service," his brother said, like they were distant cousins who hadn't seen each other in twenty years. Josh glowered; Levi shrugged. "Well, it was. Simple and to the point. Granville would've approved. Don-cha think?"

"Except he didn't want a service at all. People making over him and stuff."

"Yeah, well, we don't always get our druthers, do we? And if you stare any harder at Deanna somebody's gonna melt."

"I'm not—"

Levi snorted. Josh sighed. Levi snorted again.

"You know, I do remember a few things from when we were kids. Like how you two were joined at the hip. Okay, bad choice of words," he said when Josh glared at him again. "But you spent a lot more time with her than you did with any of us."

"Because you all were jerks?"

"There is that." The baby hugged his neck, yawned, and settled her head on his chest, giving Josh a sweet little smile before her dark eyes fluttered closed. Levi smoothed her thick hair away from his chin and said softly, "But I seem to recall you used to be pretty damn protective of her. I'm guessing that hasn't changed."

Blowing out a breath, Josh picked up one of the whatever-they-weres and ate it. Except for the green chile—which found its way into 90 percent of the food around here, with red the other ten—his taste buds weren't really cluing him in. "*Everything's* changed, Leev," he said, chewing. "Seriously—are *you* the same person you were at seventeen?"

"No. Thank God. But I still love the same woman I did then," he said with a glance at his still-very-new wife Val, who gave him a little wave. Softly smiling, Levi met Josh's gaze again. "Only now we're good together. When we were teenagers…" He shook his head. "Would've been a disaster."

"Which has nothing to do with anything."

"Do you even realize how pissed you sound?"

Behind the teasing—and okay, the truth—lay a genuine concern that only proved his brother's words, that Levi wasn't the same live-for-the-moment bad boy he'd been as a kid. Or had seemed to be, anyway. But after six years in the army and taking on a ready-made family, nobility sat a lot more comfortably on his shoulders than anyone could have possibly imagined back then. Which only proved his point that people changed. Sometimes even for the better.

"I don't like unresolved issues, Leev. That's all."

Levi's brows lifted. "Deanna's an unresolved issue?"

"Not for me, no. *No,*" he said to Levi's skeptical look. "But I suspect *she's* got them. And I…" He shoved out another harsh breath.

"You still care. Which makes you feel like an idiot. Hey. We're not twins for nothing," he said, when Josh gave him the side-eye.

"Fraternal. We're not clones, for godssake."

"And you don't share womb space—not to mention a bunk bed—for as long as we did without getting a pretty good feel for what the other person is thinking. Besides, I'm only returning the favor." He nodded toward his wife again. "Considering how you didn't exactly stay out of my face about Val, either."

"And remind me to never say anything to anybody in this family about anything, ever again."

Hiking the toddler higher on his chest, Levi chuckled. "Like that's gonna happen," he said, his gaze swinging toward their father, in conversation with Gus on the other side of the room. "You know what's hell?" he said softly. "Being the child of fixers. Inheriting that gene. Because the truth is, we can't fix everything. Hell, we can't fix most things." From his tone, Josh figured Levi was referring to his tours in Afghanistan, a time he still didn't talk about much. At least, not to Josh. "The trick is," Levi said, facing Josh again, "knowing which battles are yours to fight, and which aren't. And sometimes…" He picked up another appetizer, gesturing with it in Deanna's direction before taking a bite. "And sometimes it's simply about showing up. Being there. Even if you know you're not going to win."

Josh felt another frown bite into his forehead. "Win? Win what?"

"The battle," his brother said, then walked away to rejoin his wife and older stepdaughter across the room.

Yeah, not making him feel better. Especially since, as far as Josh could tell, the battle was in Dee's head. Where it would undoubtedly stay, he thought irritably. And whether or not that made sense—his irritation even more than her reticence—it simply *was*.

Because this wasn't his first rodeo. As it were, he thought grimly.

What was it with women, anyway? At least, every woman he'd ever known. Either they shared every single thought that floated through their brains, or they kept what they were really thinking locked up like it was a state secret. Only it wasn't really a secret, oh, no. Because damned if they didn't expect you to somehow magically *know* what they wanted or what was bugging them. And then what you were supposed to do to make it better. Like you didn't really care unless you could read their minds.

A real stretch considering most men didn't completely understand what a woman was saying when she did tell him. Because there were always these… subtexts. God, he hated subtexts.

Josh took another sip of his beer, not even sure why he was trying to figure this—her—out. Except…

Deanna Blake had been the only female he'd ever known—with the possible exception of his mother—who'd always been open with him. Not rudely, or over-sharing all the girl stuff he really did not want to know about. But he'd always known where they stood with each other. So her clamming up now was pissing him off. Big time.

A rough breath left his lungs around the same time Dee's gaze wandered to his. His mother was nowhere to be seen, meaning Dee was alone, looking very brave. And, weirdly, very small. Since at only a few inches shorter than Josh, she wasn't.

She smiled, after a fashion, and his gut cramped, re-membering how bright that smile had once been. The way it'd light up her whole face…and Josh's insides. How, for every time she'd rant and rave about some-thing, she'd laugh five times more. These huge, com-pletely unladylike belly laughs that sometimes got so out of hand she'd have to cross her legs so she wouldn't pee herself.

But only when she was with him, she'd said.

So he was guessing her obvious unwillingness to talk about what had led to her current predicament—and he had no doubt it was a predicament—was basically a de-fense mechanism for when your life has gone to hell in a handbasket and you're too damn embarrassed to talk to anybody about it. Especially when—he heard his son giggling, playing with his other cousins near the fire-place—it was kind of hard to ignore the consequences of that handbasket ride.

Not to mention the hell part of it.

Tossing his empty bottle in the plastic-lined bin by

the table, Josh marched his sorry ass into the other room and over to Dee, where he dropped onto the sofa beside her like he actually knew what he was doing. Even though, aside from the fact he doubted he could fix things for her any better now than when they were kids, he also imagined they were the worst possible combination of two people in the entire world right now.

And quite possibly the only two people who'd really understand what the other was going through.

He thought this was called working with what you had. Or were given.

Something.

By this point Deanna was so drained, both emotionally and physically, she was basically numb. She'd told herself she wouldn't cry, but that had been a lost cause. Shoot, there were tears when she scored her favorite ice cream in the freezer case; what on earth had she expected at her father's memorial service? Stoicism? And right on cue, her chest fisted. Again.

And Josh was not helping. But asking him to go away would be mean. Not to mention self-defeating. Since as much as she wished he hadn't come over, she didn't want him to leave, either. Actually, what she *really* wanted was to curl into as much of a ball as her massive middle would allow and sleep the merciful sleep of the oblivious. Lord, pregnancy brain was a bitch. However, even if Josh hadn't planted his large self beside her on the couch there was the will reading to get through. Honestly, it was like being in some old black-and-white movie, what with the drama and all—

He'd leaned forward, his elbows planted on his knees. Not looking at her. Just being there, like the old days.

"You doin' okay?"

"Mostly. Sure."

One side of his mouth lifted. "If you say so," he said, and she sort of laughed, rubbing her belly. Babypie was apparently snoozing, thank God, although that hard little head still relentlessly gouged her lower back.

But anyway, Josh. Whose scent immediately brought back a slew of memories—maybe not so numb, at that—that made her think of things she'd refused to let herself think about then, and for darn sure shouldn't be thinking about now. Or ever. God knew not all cowboys smelled that good—and there'd been plenty of times when Josh hadn't, either, to be real—but right now it was all about leather and fresh cotton and something piney and yummy and her extraspecial pregnancy smeller was having a freaking field day.

"You need anything? Food or whatever?"

"No. Thanks. Your mom made sure I ate."

"She's good at that."

Josh sat up a little straighter, scrubbing one palm over his knee. Jeans, of course, although his "good" ones. Paired with a black corduroy shirt with silver buttons, a tan sports jacket, the guy didn't look half-bad. This late in the day a beard haze shadowed his jaw, giving him a sexy male model look, God help her.

Then he laced his hands together between his knees, frowning at the tops of his boots—also his "good" ones, dirt-and dung-free. "When'd Steve say the reading was again?"

"He should be here any minute," Deanna said, and

Josh nodded. The last of the guests—a couple from a nearby ranch, she didn't even remember their names, so sad—stopped to give her the obligatory, "If you need anything, anything at all, please let us know," before walking away, and Deanna huffed a tired little breath. From the time she'd heard until this very moment, everything had felt oddly surreal, familiar and yet not, like being in a play she ought to know her part in but she didn't, really. Now, for some bizarre reason, it felt as though the stage lights were being shut off, one by one, leaving her and Josh on a bare stage, lit only by the eerie glare of a single, stark light. The good news was, she could stop pretending now, if she chose.

The bad news was, she still had no idea what her reality was. Or was supposed to be. But when she looked at Josh's profile, saw that set jaw, the grim set to his mouth, it occurred to her she wasn't the only one whose world was about to turn upside down. Or inside out. Heck, Josh had given his entire life to this ranch. Meaning whatever came next would probably affect him a lot more than it would her.

From the kitchen, a murmur of voices floated into the silent, cavernous room—his parents and Gus, she thought. Austin came over to climb in Josh's lap; Josh wrapped his arms around his son from behind as though nothing, *nothing*, would ever come between them, and suddenly Deanna wanted to know so badly what'd happened between Josh and Austin's mother it almost made her dizzy. She'd asked Gus, actually, but he'd said it wasn't his story to tell.

"Hey," she said softly, and Josh angled his head to look at her, the obvious worry glimmering in those soft goldy-green eyes punching her insides harder than the baby's foot. Even though she knew she shouldn't, she reached over—awkwardly—to lay a hand on his knee, right beside Austin's little sneaker. "It's gonna be okay."

He actually chuckled. "You telling me that? Or yourself?" he said, a moment before the lawyer arrived, looking a little windblown from the short walk from the driveway to the front door.

"Sorry I couldn't make the service," he said breathlessly as Josh stood to shake his hand. "Got summoned to a surprise court appearance in Santa Fe." Sweeping hunks of unruly silver hair off his forehead, Steve Riggs gave Deanna a sympathetic smile. "I'm so sorry, honey, I really am. Your daddy was a good man. We'll all miss him."

The same words she'd heard no less than three dozen times in the past two hours. Still, she knew the sentiment was sincere.

"Thank you."

"Well," the attorney said, looking a little relieved at being able to move on, "I suppose I'm ready when you are. Do you need help?" he asked when she tried to cantilever herself to her feet. But Josh was already on the case, having set Austin down to come around the side of the sofa, bracing one arm across her back to hoist her upright.

The attorney's brows spiked over his glasses. "My goodness. When are you due?"

Because she was not one of those women who only gained fifteen pounds and looked like she was carrying a cantaloupe. "Six weeks or so."

"Well." Steve's favorite word, apparently. "If you

gather the others, I suppose we can do the reading in Granville's office. Unless…" His gaze swung to Deanna's. "You'd rather do it elsewhere?"

"The office is fine."

It didn't take long. Her dad had left modest bequests to various people in the community who'd be notified in a few days. Gus got an annuity, Dad's old Caddy and the right to live in one of the guesthouses as long as he wished. Since Dad had already given Josh's parents a house in town after Sam's retirement, his gifts to them now included a few stocks and bonds and a small Thomas Moran landscape painting Sam had always admired…and which Deanna knew was worth big bucks. Then, aside from a modest savings account which went to Deanna, there were a few disbursements to various charities Dad had always supported, particularly ones that worked with the local Native populations.

"And now," Steve said, peering over his glasses at Deanna, then Josh, before clearing his throat. "'I leave my ranch, known as the Vista Encantada, including the house, the land, any and all outbuildings and whatever livestock on said land at the time of my death, equally to my only daughter, Deanna Marie Blake, and my employee Joshua Michael Talbot.'"

A moment of stunned silence preceded a dual *"What?"* from Deanna and Josh.

"Congratulations, kids," Steven said, angling the will toward them so they could see for themselves. "You're now co-owners of one of the prettiest pieces of property in northern New Mexico."

Chapter 3

"But I don't *want* the ranch," Dee said later, after everyone else had left so she and Josh could ostensibly hash things out. She shifted in the corner of the tufted leather couch in the office, clearly miserable. Physically *and* emotionally, Josh guessed. "I never did. And Dad knew it."

Leaning his butt against the edge of the Depression-era desk, Josh crossed his arms. He'd initially assumed her shock had been because Gran had left half the ranch to him. Apparently not. "You told him that?"

"Yes!" Then, rubbing one temple, she sighed. "Or at least I thought I did. In any case—" her hand dropped to what was left of her lap "—I never made a secret of how much I hated being stuck out here. Why on earth would I want the place?"

"And what'd you think he was gonna do? You're his kid, Dee. The ranch was his most valuable asset. Of course he'd leave it to you. I'm only surprised he didn't leave you the whole thing." Because she hadn't been the only one in shock there. Truth be told, Josh still was. And would be for a good long while, he suspected.

Dee's eyes lifted to his before she shoved out another sigh. "I can't…this isn't my home anymore, Josh."

"Well aware of that." His forehead pinched, he glanced down at the floor, then back at her. "But it's been mine all my life. And the breeding operation… sure, I was only an employee and all, but your dad hadn't had a hand in it for some time. He'd left all the decision making to me—"

"I know, Josh. I know." She paused. "He obviously trusted you. And it's not as if you don't deserve it. But—"

"Look, you don't want to stick around and help me run the Vista, I completely understand. We can still be partners, if *you* trust me enough to handle things on this end, and we can split the profits. There's money to be made with the cabins, too, plenty of hunters would be happy to fork over the bucks during elk season. You know Steve'll look out for your interests, make sure I'm not screwing you over—"

"It's not that," she said, sagging into the couch's deep cushions. "It's…" Her mouth thinned. "Okay. It's not as if I'd really given this much thought, since I didn't figure it'd be an issue for a long, long time. But since he did leave me half the ranch…oh, Lord. I can't even say it."

Josh's veins iced over. "You want to sell it."

A long moment passed before she said, "It's more that I need to."

"You sound like you've got gambling debts."

She almost smiled. "No. But I do have a baby on the way. A baby who's going to be applying to colleges eighteen years down the road." Her mouth twisted. "Would be nice to have one less thing to worry about. Sure, the place might be profitable now. But there's no guarantee it'll stay that way. Not in this economic climate. If we sold it…"

Birds in the hand and all that. Yeah, he got it. Josh sighed, realizing he could hardly argue with her. About that, at least. God knows plenty of ranches went under, through no fault of their owners. And he'd be a fool to guarantee her that the Vista wouldn't. Also, out of curiosity Granville had had the property appraised a couple years back, information he'd apparently shared with Josh because he'd been too stunned to keep it to himself. Even taking into account normal fluctuations in the real estate market, the figure was staggering. To somebody like Josh, at least.

Still, for him, it wasn't about the money. It was about the ranch itself. It was about *home*.

"What about her father? I know you said you're not together, but—"

"He's not even part of the equation," she said quietly, then heaved herself to her feet and walked over to the window facing the mountains. "For reasons I'd really rather not get into right now."

Anger spurted through him. "Or ever, right?"

A frown crumpling her brow, she turned. "My situation is really none of your concern—"

"You want to sell the only place I've ever called home, Dee. A place I'd never, ever in my wildest dreams thought might be mine someday. So now that I'm this close—" he held up one hand, finger and thumb a quarter inch apart "—to seeing those wild dreams come true, you want to yank it from me. So tell me how the reason behind that isn't any of my concern?"

Her arms folded, Dee pivoted back to the window. "You could always buy me out."

"Seriously? Like I've got that kind of cash lying around. For a down payment, maybe, but no way in hell would I ever qualify for a loan big enough for the rest of it—"

"But if we sold it and split the proceeds..." She faced him again, a thin ridge between her brows. "You could buy your own place, right? No, it wouldn't be this big—"

"It wouldn't be the Vista."

"—but you don't need this much acreage to start up your own operation. And you've already got a great reputation, I'm sure everybody knows it's you behind the breeding business. It's *you* who's won all the rodeo titles. And besides, then it'd really be yours. Yours and Austin's. And who knows? Maybe someday down the road you can buy the Vista back from the new owners. Especially since you know as well as I do how few outsiders stick around once the romance of owning a ranch wears off. And you can take whatever livestock you want, nobody's talking about selling the horses. Only the property."

"Except I know for a fact there's nothing available in the area."

"Then broaden your parameters, for heaven's sake!"

Josh's knee-jerk reaction was to say *But I don't want to do that*! Except even he knew he'd sound like Austin having a hissy fit over not wanting to put on a coat, or go to bed, or anything else the kid decided was against his druthers at any given moment. Even so…

Even so.

He swept a palm across his hair, then hooked both his hands on his hips, trying to ignore the plea in her eyes, for him to understand. Probably similar to what was in his.

"I hear what you're saying. I do. But home isn't just about place, it's about people. Family. Although maybe that doesn't mean the same thing to you it does to me."

Deanna jerked. *Sonuvabitch.*

"Crap, Dee, I didn't—"

"No, you're right. I mean, of course I loved Dad, but…" She angled back toward the window, where the stark, late fall light brought the worry and exhaustion on her face into sharp relief. "But we definitely didn't have the kind of relationship you and your brothers did—do—with your parents. My aunt and uncle have always been…concerned for me, and my cousin Emily's a good friend, but…" A tiny, sad smile curved her mouth.

"I'm sorry."

A quick shrug accompanied, "It's what I know. Although…" The smile grew as her hand went to her belly. "Although my plan is to do better by this kid." She almost laughed, but her eyes told an entirely different story. "At least I can dream, right?"

Josh slugged his hands in his front pockets, waiting

out the next, even stronger, wave of sympathy. At least he'd had great examples in his parents, when it came to his own relationship with his son. And that still didn't stop the fear that he'd screw up…

Ah, hell. Because sometimes it wasn't about what you wanted, it was about what was best for everybody. And tying Deanna down to someplace she'd never wanted to be to begin with, simply because Josh had other ideas…

And those eyes…

"Okay," he pushed out.

"Okay, what?"

"You wanna sell, we'll sell." She seemed to sag in relief. "Although…" He glanced around before meeting her eyes again. God, this was shredding him. All of it. "No sense putting it on the market without sprucing it up a bit first. Otherwise we're likely to get a bunch of lowball offers. I'm sure you don't want that." At her wide eyes, a tight grin stretched across his face. "Yeah. Not as dumb as I look. I'd also like to do one last Christmas party. For the community. If that's okay with you."

Like the annual Fourth of July party, Granville had also hosted a Christmas bash at the house every year, even playing Santa for the children. To yank that out from under everybody this close to Christmas…well, it just didn't seem right.

And judging from Deanna's slow nod, she apparently agreed.

"Except…" Her brow knotted. "Who's going to bankroll the fixing up?"

"Doubt we're talking anything major. I can probably do most of the work myself, in fact. Since it's my slow season."

Still frowning, she cupped her hands under her belly, like she was trying to ease the weight of it. "And you do realize my window for getting back home is getting narrower by the second?"

"I figured as much. So if you'll trust me to oversee the reno, let us throw that last party…" Josh waited out the sharp pain in his sternum. "We could list her right after the New Year. Shouldn't take long to sell. Especially since your dad regularly got offers for the ranch—"

"I know," she said on a breath. "That much, he did share." Another beat or two passed. "You're really good with this?"

"Good?" Josh slipped his hands into his pockets again. "Not at all. But you taking care of that little girl," he said, nodding toward her middle, "is far more important than me being nostalgic or whatever. Besides, kinda hard to regret losing what was never really mine."

Her eyes glittered. "I'm so sorry, Josh…"

"Nothing to be sorry for. I swear."

A moment passed before she waddled over to wrap her arms around him and give him as much of a hug as her belly would let her. "Thank you," she said softly, then returned to the desk to rummage through the drawers until she found a legal pad and a pen, after which she awkwardly lowered herself into her father's old swivel desk chair and started making lists.

As Josh felt a dream he hadn't even known he'd had slip from his grasp.

He grabbed his coat and gloves off the hall tree on his

way outside, getting all the way over to the stables before he slammed his gloved fist into the splintered siding, making Starfire turn her head and give him a *What
the* hell *are you doing, boy?* look. Just once in his life,
it'd be nice to have something go—and stay—his way.

And maybe one day he'd discover a hitherto unknown immunity to a pair of sad female eyes.

Today, however, was clearly not that day.

Muttering an ugly curse, Josh slammed the wall
again, then leaned his forehead against the cold, un-
yielding wood, trying desperately to steady his breathing.

"Uncle Granville did *what*?"

Deanna eased back a little more in her father's desk
chair to almost smile at the computer screen. Or rather,
the completely flummoxed expression in her cousin's
bright blue eyes. "You heard me. Left the property to
me and Josh equally."

Emily swept a hunk of soft, sorority-sister-perfect
golden brown hair behind her perfect little ear, looking both curious and concerned. "So what now? You're
hardly going to move back there, are you?"

"Not to worry." Although, strangely, she wasn't
nearly as thrilled with Josh's acquiescence as she
would've expected. Then again, living with a tiny skull
lodged against her spine tended to leech the joy out of
most things these days. She loved this baby more than
life itself, but she'd be extremely glad when they no
longer shared a body. "We're going to sell the ranch
and divide the proceeds. Well, Josh is, I'll be home in
a few days."

Em frowned. "And he's okay with that? Selling, I mean?"

"He…agreed it's for the best."

"Huh." Emily delicately bit off the end of a raw baby carrot. "So how *is* Josh, anyway?"

"Good," Deanna said, deciding not to go into the whole he's-got-a-kid-now thing. Because, pointless?

"I remember him, you know."

Of course she did. As one tended to remember when that first, blinding hormonal rush swarms your brain so hard and hot and fast you can barely breathe. Like a simultaneously thrilling and scary-as-hell amusement park ride.

"He's changed, though," Deanna said.

"I'm sure. It's been…oh, gosh. About eleven years, huh?"

"Yep."

Only once had Emily and her parents visited the ranch after Deanna's mother's death, the summer before Deanna turned fifteen. Why, she never had figured out, since it'd been no secret Aunt Margaret thought her sister insane for hooking up with "that cowboy" after—or so the story went—Deanna's grandparents had taken their two daughters skiing at the nearby resort, and there'd been a dance, or something, where the twenty-one-year-old Katherine Alderman had met a handsome, older rancher and fallen in love. And then chose to live in the middle of nowhere. So to say that last visit had been unexpected was a gross understatement.

In any case, her thirteen-year-old cousin immediately crushed on the sixteen-year-old Josh, following him around like a puppy dog. And Josh had been the epitome of patience and kindness, which had melted Deanna's heart—even as it drove her aunt straight to Crazyville, clearly panicked that her daughter would somehow suffer the same fate as her baby sister. But although Deanna had rolled her eyes—since Emily was an eighth-grader, for heaven's sake—considering her own feelings about living on the ranch, and what she remembered of her mother's chronic wistfulness, she sympathized with her aunt's concerns more than she might've otherwise.

She therefore could only imagine Aunt Margaret's relief that Emily was now engaged to a senator's son, thus realizing the *proper* happy-ever-after so rudely snatched from her younger sister.

"Anyway," Deanna said, "I need to go—" Literally, before she peed right there in the chair. "So I'll be back a week from Sunday, I'll take a taxi in—"

"Like hell. I'm coming to get you. And don't even think about arguing with me."

Deanna smiled. She really did love her cousin. Even if she was… Emily. The poster child for impeccable social graces and never putting a foot wrong. Then again, Emily put up with Deanna, too, so there you were. "Fine," she said, laughing. "I'll see you soon—"

"That *designer* from Santa Fe is here," Gus said from the office door, not even trying to hide his disgust. As far as the housekeeper was concerned, designers and decorators and their ilk were for outsiders who wanted to make sure their ridiculously overpriced houses looked authentically Southwest. Gus thought the place was fine as it was. Gus thought she and Josh were nuts to hire someone to fix something that didn't need fixing.

But mostly, Gus was ticked as hell they were selling. In fact, he'd barely spoken to either her or Josh for a good twenty-four hours after they told him. Yes, *they*. Since even though Deanna tried to take blame for the decision, Josh insisted it was mutual. Never mind that more than once over the past couple days she'd catch him staring at the mountains, or one of the paddocks or barns, with a pensive expression that pulverized her heart. And if she hadn't had this baby to think of—if she wasn't the only person *to* think about the baby—maybe she would've rethought things.

But not only was she her little girl's only champion, she'd let her heart rule her head for far too long. So this time, it was about being logical. Practical. A grownup. And Josh was a big boy, he'd land on his feet. Or someplace even better than the Vista.

If there was such a thing.

"I'll be there in a minute," she said. "Did you offer her coffee?"

"Since I didn' fall down a well in the last little while," Gus said in his heavy New Mexican Spanish accent, "yes, I did. You wan' me to call Mr. Josh? I don' think he's far."

"Please. Thanks. Since the Realtor should be along any minute."

The old guy tromped out on bowed legs that attested to his many years as a ranch hand before opting for inside duty, and Deanna felt a rush of affection for the man who'd done his fair share of mothering her, too, once her own was gone. Another, much sharper rush of feelings followed, as it occurred to her once she left she'd probably never see him again.

Then, as she came out of the powder room she caught Josh in the entryway, brushing fresh, light snow off his shoulders, and she realized she'd probably never see him again, either. Which *logically* shouldn't've bothered her, considering how little she'd seen him, anyway, in the last several years. Hadn't even thought about him all that much, to be truthful. But in the past few days…

Deanna released another breath. Just another hyperemotional preggo, nothing to see here, move along. Sure, being back had stirred a lot of memories—how could it not? And she was vulnerable and shaky and more grief-stricken than she probably even realized, and not only about losing Dad, although that would've been enough by itself. And dammit, Josh was about to sacrifice something *for her* that obviously meant the world to him—

"Dee?" he said, frowning. "You okay?"

"You bet," she said, girding her achy loins. And back. Lord, if the kid would *move*, already, that would be good—

The doorbell rang. Josh let the Realtor in, shaking his hand, polite as hell. Even when the man's cold blue eyes swept over the great room with the practiced ease of a lion checking out the savannah for prey. Honestly, the dude was practically licking his chops.

The designer—a dark-haired beauty swimming in suede and turquoise—stood as they entered, grinning for the Realtor, who'd actually recommended her. "Toby!" she said, opening her arms for the much taller man to walk into. "So nice to see you!" Then, still smiling, she turned to Deanna, and something in her deep brown eyes put Deanna immediately at ease. Unlike her sidekick whose presence sent chills down her spine.

"Ohmigoodness," the other woman said after introductions were made, her gaze landing on Deanna's middle before lifting again. "We don't have much time, do we? Before the baby comes?"

"Oh. No. I mean, yes, she's due soon. But I'll be home long before that happens—"

"And I don't mean to rush you folks," Toby said, making Deanna blink in the glare of his too-white teeth. "But unfortunately I've got a showing at eleven in Taos, so if you don't mind…?"

The smile lit on Josh, standing off to one side with a scowl so deeply etched it took a full two seconds to let go of Josh's face. At which point he smiled—not as brightly, thank God—and gave a little nod. "Of course. Right this way…"

An hour later, his head spinning with words like *comparables* and *resale value* and *vintage charm*, Josh sank onto the sofa in the office, his arms tightly folded over his chest and his mood the darkest since the day he watched Jordan walk out to her truck without even looking back.

On a sigh, he leaned into the cushions to glare up at the hand-forged chandelier, half wishing it would drop on his head and put him out of his misery. Out in the hall he could hear Deanna and Tessa the designer softly laughing. The gal seemed nice enough, and at least she hadn't wanted to "update" every damn thing in the place, although she did have some valid sugges-

tions to make things look a little less like you might find
Billy the Kid's bones behind one of the doors. Even if
he was gonna stay, he'd probably go along with most
of her suggestions.

The Realtor dude, though…jeebus. Like a villain
right out of a Disney cartoon, complete with dollar signs
in his eyes. Said he'd have an appraiser come give them
an accurate number, but the ballpark figure he'd suggested was even more than Josh had figured on. No
wonder the man was practically drooling. Hell, maybe
Josh should ditch the horse business and take up selling real estate. At least houses didn't kick if they got
pissed at you.

Finally he heard the front door close; a moment later
Deanna joined him in the room, carefully lowering herself into a wingback chair a few feet away.

"That went pretty well, don't you think?"

Josh grunted.

Deanna tapped her fingers on the arms of the chair
for a moment, then said, very gently, "At least they
didn't think we needed to change much."

"Not sure what difference that makes if we're selling it, anyway."

"True, I suppose. And why are you looking at me
like that?"

"You really have no attachment to the place? None
at all?"

A long moment passed before she said, "No. I don't.
But even if I did, I'm in no position to let the past bog
me down about decisions I need to make now. For the
future." She smoothed an oversize plaid flannel shirt

over her belly for several seconds before looking over at him again. "For *her* future."

"And I still say her father—"

"He's married," she said softly, and the rest of his sentence logjammed in his throat.

"Oh, jeez, Dee—"

"I didn't know. Obviously. He was—is—French. Older. A diplomat. And yes, that much was true. Why he was in the States, I mean. I sold him a painting, he asked me out…" She blew a short laugh through her nose. "We even talked about marriage at one point. Or maybe it was only me talking about marriage and he didn't have the guts or whatever to stop me. In any case, it was all fun and games until the diaphragm failed."

"And don't you dare blame yourself for this."

Her gaze slammed into his. "He didn't seduce me, Josh."

"No, he just lied. Same thing. So if you think I'm gonna judge you, you are definitely barking up the wrong tree. Seriously. Like I've got room to talk?"

She almost smiled at that. "Austin?"

"Yep. And Jordan and I were being careful, too. Or at least thought we were. Having a kid had definitely not been on the agenda. But at least I wasn't involved with someone else. Let alone married. And when she told me she was pregnant…let's just say I grew up *real* fast."

"And she took advantage of your big heart."

He felt his brows shove together. "What else would I have done?"

She almost laughed. "Really? After what I just said?" Then her eyes watered. "I'm so sorry, Josh. You deserve so much better than that."

Her sincerity, her *kindness*, stole his breath. Not to mention a good chunk of his earlier irritation, if not his disappointment.

"Thanks."

"I'm serious. You're a prince, dude. Own it."

Clearing his throat, Josh leaned forward, linking his hands between his knees. "Hardly a prince. In fact, looking back, it was probably stupid, her and me hooking up to begin with—okay, so no maybe about it, I knew better and I did it anyway—but at least I acknowledged my kid. Took responsibility for him. What that jerk did to you…" He shook his head, unable to finish his sentence.

"Oh, it gets worse."

From her tone alone, he knew what she meant. "He asked you to get rid of it."

"Demanded, actually."

"Before or after he told you he was married?"

"After. But before he admitted he already had three kids. Yep," Dee said to Josh's softly uttered obscenity. "However, no matter how much I might wish I hadn't let myself get caught up in the fairy tale, that I'd been more alert to the signs I now realize were there all along, the fact is I still made my own decisions. And now I have to deal with the consequences of those decisions. Same as you did…crap," she said, her breath suddenly catching.

Josh jerked to attention. "What?"

"Nothing. Well, not nothing, my back's killing me. But it'll pass." Then she frowned when he dug out his phone. "What're you doing?"

"Calling Mom. Because I've heard way too many

going into labor stories not to know a hurting back's not a good sign—"

"Then I've been in labor for the past two weeks. So put your phone away—"

"Hey, Mom," he said when she picked up. "Deanna says her back's hurting pretty bad."

"Oh?" Mom said, her voice kind of echoey. "How bad?"

"Bad enough she's making faces—"

"I'm not in labor, Billie! Your son's overreacting!"

Mom laughed in his ear. "You probably are. But if it makes you feel better, I'm on my way back into town—I had clinic this morning—so I'll swing by, no problem. If that's okay with Dee?"

"You're on the phone while you're driving?"

"Hands-free, not an idiot. And no other cars for probably ten miles. Well?"

He looked up from the phone. "Mom's gonna come check you out, if that's okay."

She glared at him. "If it gets you to shut up, sure. But I'm not. In. Labor."

Mom chuckled again. "I'll be there in fifteen minutes," she said, then disconnected the call.

Billie stuffed her stethoscope back in her bag, then straightened, her hands on her hips. "You're not in labor," she said, and Deanna released a half relieved, half annoyed sigh.

"*Thank* you—"

"You are, however, about fifty percent effaced and a couple centimeters dilated. Not to mention that baby's sitting real low. As in, engaged already. Probably why your back's been giving you grief."

Deanna felt her forehead crunch. "I thought none of that happened with first babies until much closer to the due date."

"So either your date's wrong—"

"Two ultrasounds. Not wrong."

"Or this child has a mind of her own. In which case, steel yourself, because that's not gonna get better once she's out. Which might happen sooner rather than later," she said to Deanna's undoubtedly horrified expression. "In any case—and you're *really* not going to like this— you might want to rethink getting on a plane right now."

The horrified expression instantly morphed into panic. "I can't stay here, Billie."

"You might not have a choice. Unless you want to risk giving birth at thirty thousand feet with a couple hundred strangers as witnesses."

Struggling to her feet, she shook her head. "Non-ononono… I have an installation to oversee, and I haven't finished setting up the baby's space—" Such as it would be, a corner in her dinky little bedroom. "And…" Deanna sagged back onto her bed, defeated. "Really?" she said in a small voice.

Billie sat beside her, wrapping a strong arm around her shoulders and tugging her close, like she used to after Deanna's mom died. "I know, sweetie," she whispered into Deanna's hair. "Like you didn't already have enough on your plate. And it's not like we *know* you'd go into labor—could be you'd make the trip just fine. But it's not a chance I'd want to take. Or want you to take. And if you do give birth early, at least you'll be back home by Christmas, right? Maybe even Thanksgiving, who knows?"

Deanna felt the blood drain from her face. Thanksgiving was less than three weeks away. Suddenly this all seemed very real. As in, in less than a month she could be holding a baby in her arms.

No—her *daughter* in her arms.

Billie rubbed her shoulder, giving her a little squeeze. "It's up to you, sweetie. It's not like I'm saying you can't fly, I'm only saying you probably shouldn't. So let's get a second opinion, and you can think about it." She gave Deanna another quick hug, then stood and collected her things. "But if you do decide to stay, at least there's people here to look after you, right?"

Not as great a selling point as you might think.

Chapter 4

On the other end of the line, a long, aggrieved breath preceded, "You're absolutely sure you can't fly back?"

No sympathy, then. Not that this was a surprise. Her boss was stingier with her compassion than she was with her salaries. But at least Alita—grudgingly—shared commissions. And Deanna was damned good at matching up potential buyers with exactly what they were looking for. Even if they didn't know it when they first walked into the gallery.

"The general consensus—" as in, from the ob-gyn backup at the clinic Billie worked with "—is that it wouldn't be a good idea. I can email you my notes if that'd help—"

"Don't bother—I'm sure somebody else here can get up to speed. However, if you're not back by the be-

ginning of December, you do realize I'll have to replace you?"

Because clearly the woman had never heard of the
Family and Medical Leave Act. Or specialized temp
agencies. "I was planning on going on maternity leave
by then, anyway. I'm only adding a few weeks to it."
Not that it was paid. Although at least the cash part of
her inheritance would see her through for a while. "You
can't fire me for being pregnant, Alita."

"More's the pity," the woman muttered, then disconnected the call.

Yeah, *that* really cheered her up.

And she'd yet to call Emily, let her know what was
going on. Or not.

"But we're supposed to go bridesmaid dress shopping next week!" were the first words out of her cousin's mouth…followed by a sucked-in breath. "Oh, God,
Dee—I'm so sorry! It's just I was counting on you to
keep the other girls on track when we went to the salon.
You know how they can get."

She did, indeed. Although she wondered if it ever
occurred to Emily that perhaps the slew of sorority sisters and fellow debutantes that made up her cousin's
entourage weren't really the "besties" she wanted to
believe they were. Or how they'd react to Emily's heavily pregnant—and unringed—maid of honor. A moot
point now, she supposed.

"You'll be fine," she said, and Emily sighed. Then
chuckled.

"Which I assume is Deespeak for grow a pair?"

"It is. And no, I don't give two figs what you choose.

I totally trust your taste." In fashion, anyway, if not in friends.

"Thanks. But…crap. This means I won't be with you when the baby comes. And that sucks. And ohmigod, I haven't even thrown you a shower yet! Okay, seriously, the instant you get back, you are so getting showered. Like no new mother has ever been showered, ever. I swear."

Deanna had to laugh. What her cousin sometimes lacked in focus, she more than made up for with generosity. Not to mention enthusiasm. And she'd never forget how the younger woman had instantly become Deanna's champion after Phillippe's betrayal, not only insisting she come stay with her in her tiny Georgetown one bedroom so she wouldn't eat her weight in Häagen-Dazs, but also standing up to her mother. Who hadn't exactly gotten behind her daughter's public support of her cousin.

And Emily, bless her sweet heart, hadn't wavered even in the threat of her mama's yanking closed the purse strings on the wedding. "No," she'd said with a knowing smile, "It's Mom who'd be mortified if this wedding doesn't come off. Trust me." And sure enough, Aunt Margaret apparently decided a pregnant niece was far less of a social faux pas than letting her daughter get married at city hall. In rags.

"Dee? Did I lose you?"

"No, no… I was just thinking…" She smiled, listening to little snow BBs clicking against the window. Perfect baking weather, she thought, her mood lifting at the thought. "Okay. You're on. For the shower."

"As if you have any choice?" Emily said, giggling.

Then she said, very gently, "I love you, you know," and something twinged inside Deanna.

"I love you, too, goof," she said, holding the phone to her chest a moment before shoving herself off her bed, then tucking the phone into her back pocket. A miraculous feat in itself, considering how tightly even maternity denim stretched across her prodigious butt these days—

From down the hall she heard Gus's deep laugh, then Austin giggling, the infectious sound banishing the normally suffocating silence to the dark corners tucked behind the rafters, and she smiled, momentarily content. She knew Austin was in the Baptist Church's preschool program three mornings a week for now, meaning Josh had to cobble together day care however he could manage. Although Gus said these days Josh let the kid hang out with him more and more as he went about his chores. Which was how it was with ranchers' kids, many of whom were homeschooled, working their education around the needs of the ranch.

Not in Deanna's case, however, since her mother, clearly worried about Deanna becoming completely cut off from any social life whatsoever, insisted she attend school in town.

Thank God.

"Dee!" Bellowing her name, Austin scrambled off the chair where he was presumably having lunch and ran to her, arms outstretched. Because bonding happened whether it made sense or not. Laughing over the twist to her heart, Deanna lugged him into her arms and kissed the top of his head, earning her a scowl from the housekeeper.

"You really think you should be doin' that?"

"Billie didn't say I couldn't." Grinning, she tickled the child's tummy, breathing in the scents of little boy and burning logs, the fire's crackling glow banishing the late fall gloom. "So we're fine. Aren't we, hotshot?"

His baby-toothed grin warmed her far more than the fire. "Uh-huh. Daddy went somewhere, so I'm stayin' with Gus. And you!"

Chuckling, Deanna looked over to Gus. "Somewhere?"

"To check out a potential buyer. Josh don' sell his stock to jus' anybody. Jus' like your daddy. You want somethin'? Tea, maybe?"

"I'm good, thanks. And I remember. Hey," she said, giving the little boy a squeeze. "Whaddya say we bake something, you and me?"

"Like what?"

"Well… I'll have to see what's on hand, but you can help me decide. Unless…" She looked at Gus. "I'd be in your way?"

"You kiddin'? Trust me, by now I'm more'n ready to hand over the kitchen duties to someone else."

"Oh, Gus…" For the first time, she realized how tired he looked. That the bags under his eyes weren't only from age, but exhaustion. She hiked the little boy higher in her arms, her eyes stinging when he laid his head on her shoulder. *Falling in love is not an option*, she thought, although she suspected that ship had set sail from the first moment she saw him. "Are you okay?"

The housekeeper looked insulted. "Of course I'm okay, I'm probably healthier'n you. But I'm old. Done. Especially with…" He sighed. "With taking care of people. Not you, buddy," he said quickly, reaching over to ruffle Austin's wavy hair. "But everybody else…" His eyes met hers again as he shrugged.

The stinging got five times worse. "I still don't understand why Dad didn't get full-time nursing care. He could've afforded it—"

"Only that would've meant not everyone would've gotten their full inheritance. I swear, that's what he said. And anyway, it would've made me nuts, strangers around all the time, gettin' in my space." His dark eyes glittered. "Only I forgot I'm not seventy anymore…"

Then his gaze scanned the kitchen, and Deanna sucked in a little breath before setting Austin down, giving him a smile. "Why don't you go find Smoky? I think he's on my bed."

"'Kay," the little boy said, sneakers thudding down the hall. Deanna told herself she wouldn't be around long enough for the cat to exact his revenge. Then she turned back to Gus.

"You're leaving, aren't you?" she said, and a sad smile pushed at the housekeeper's wrinkles.

"My niece and her husband down in Cruces, they've been after me for years to come live with them. To come home. Still got a bunch of cousins down there, too, their kids, grandkids…" He scratched the back of his head, making his thick, gray hair stick out like a duck tail. "And it don' snow there but once in a blue moon. After sixty years up here, might be a nice change. So I said I'd give it a shot, see how it goes."

Deanna smiled, even as her eyes burned. "You'll be missed."

Gus shrugged. "I know the will said I could live

in one of the guesthouses, but nothing's gonna be the same, you know? Somebody else ownin' the Vista…" He crossed his arms over his belly, his head wagging. "I figure if change is happening, I should at least have some choice in what that change is, right?"

"Absol-lutely."

"Aw, don' you go gettin' like that," he said, chuckling as he briefly pulled Deanna into his arms, the soft flannel of his shirt smelling like chili powder and Old Spice and her childhood.

Deanna pulled away, wiping at her eyes. "When?"

"Soon as I get packed," he said as Austin stormed back into the kitchen, clearly bummed.

"Smoky got under the bed where I can't reach him." Chuckling, Gus bent at the waist, his hands on his knees.

"So let's go see what we've got in the pantry, huh? Because this pretty lady's right, this is perfect baking weather…"

"So Deanna's really stuck here until after she delivers?"

Josh took his eyes off the road for a microsecond to dart a glance at his older brother Zach, who'd come along to ensure Josh's latest rescue was going to a good home. One of the perks of having a veterinarian in the family. Of course, that also meant another brother up in his business. And they had a good twenty minutes yet before they got back to town.

"Yep," he said, ignoring Thor's hot panting in his ear. Dog had breath like a damn dragon.

He sensed his brother's frown. "She good with that?"

"What do you think?" Because even Zach would probably remember Deanna's glee when she'd been "sprung" from the confines of living in—or at least near—a town too small to even have a movie theater. "Not like she has a choice, though."

"S'pose not." Zach paused. "She got anything for the baby? Like a crib or bassinet or something? Clothes? A car seat?"

"And since when did you become a mother hen?"

"Since the moment I realized I *was* the mother hen," Zach said quietly, and Josh flinched, since Zach's wife had died in a car wreck when his own boys were still small. Heck, Liam had barely been a year old. Granted, his brother was recently, and blissfully, engaged. But there'd been a long time when, despite their parents' hands-on support, Zach had also known what it was like not only to be a single parent, but the *only* parent. Still, Josh felt like an idiot, that the full ramifications of Deanna's forced extended stay hadn't dawned on him sooner. As in, babies needed *stuff*.

The dog slurped his tongue back into his mouth and flopped on the backseat with a huge sigh. "I've got Austin's crib somewhere," Josh said. "I suppose that'd work. Although I gave away his baby clothes—"

"She's having a girl. Girls need pink. And..." His older brother waved his hand. "Frills."

"I doubt the kid will care. Or Dee." Since she'd never been a girly-girl even as a kid. Far as he could tell, that hadn't changed. In that respect the big city hadn't rubbed off on her. But then, what did he know? Maybe the Goth-meets-lumberjack look was all the rage in the nation's capital these days.

"You'd be surprised," Zach said, like he was suddenly some wise old woman, jeebus. "We can ask Val, maybe? See if she's still got Risa's baby clothes?"

While Josh imagined his sister-in-law would be only too happy to donate to the cause—if she still had anything to donate—suddenly that didn't seem right. Or fair. A used crib was one thing. Nothing wrong with used clothes, either—God knew Austin had worn whatever Josh could scrounge, and both he and the kid were good with that, he thought as he pulled up to his brother's little house in town, next door to his veterinary clinic. But somehow…

"So maybe we should give her one of those parties where people bring things for the baby."

"A shower?" Zach said.

"Right. That. Then we could ship most of it back east when she leaves."

Because that's where her life had been for more than ten years, and whatever they'd meant to each other before had only been a childhood thing. Period. Whatever Josh felt for Dee now…it was empathy, most likely. Knowing what it felt like to be abandoned, to get stuck with the full responsibility for something—someone— someone *else* had an equal hand in creating.

Pushing open the truck's door, Zach nodded. "That might work," he said as his own two streaked out the front door and down the steps to rush the truck, while grinning, eleven-year-old Landon—Zach's soon-to-be stepson—hung back on the porch with his hands plugged into his hoodie's pouch, clearly enjoying his new role as big brother. Zach hauled his youngest boy up into his lap, ruffling Liam's bright red curls. "You want to get Mom on it, or you want me to?"

"No, I'll talk to her."

A half hour later, the dog racing ahead, Josh walked through the hacienda's front door to relieve Gus of babysitting duty, fully intending to take the boy back to the foreman's cabin where they'd been living since his father's retirement. Except all manner of cooking smells greeted him, tangling with the most exuberant rendition of "Deck the Halls" he'd ever heard. What he *could* hear, that is, over Deanna's and Austin's laughter.

In fact, the pair were making so much noise they never even noticed Josh leaning against the door frame with his arms crossed, taking in the various pots bubbling on the stove, the loaves of fresh bread cooling on racks on the counter…the six-inch high chocolate cake on a stand beside the bread, the swirled frosting gleaming like satin in the overhead lights.

And in the middle of the kitchen, a very pregnant woman and his little boy, belting their hearts out to the cat, who was lying in front of the woodstove with a pained expression. Never mind nothing was keeping him there other than his own stubbornness.

A million feelings knifed Josh right in the chest, half of which he couldn't even define, the other half of which he didn't want to. But when the music—coming from Deanna's phone propped against the Mexican-tiled backsplash—stopped, Josh slowly applauded the pair, making Deanna clamp a hand to her chest and whirl around, as Austin beelined for him like his nephews had his brother a little bit ago.

"We made dinner!" the kid said, all bright-eyed

and flushed, and some of those feelings twisted a little harder. "An' cake! An' I helped!"

"I can see that," Josh said, giving his son a big, sloppy kiss—the giggles slayed him, every time—before setting him down again and meeting Deanna's equally bright eyes, glittering underneath her crazy, spiky hair almost as much as that tiny diamond stud in her nose. "Where's Gus?"

"I kicked him off the island." At Josh's puzzled expression, she laughed. "For his own good. He finally admitted how hard the last several months have been on him. So I made him go take some Gus time."

"And he actually did?"

"But only after I convinced him I could use the practice. With a kid, I mean. Did you know about his moving back to Las Cruces?"

Josh nodded. "He told me this morning, before I left. Although I figured it was coming."

"Because we're selling the Vista."

"I'm sure that played a big part in his decision."

"I'm sorry—"

"Things are what they are, Dee. Although..." He glanced around the kitchen the designer had pronounced "retro chic." Whatever. "It's hard to imagine the place without Gus. Hell, it's hard to imagine..."

"*You* not being here," she said gently.

God knows he didn't want to do a guilt trip on the woman. But he wasn't gonna lie, either.

"I'm not sure I'm real good with change."

"Don't underestimate yourself," Dee said, nodding toward Austin, down on his knees a few feet away, vroom-vrooming a little truck. "Seems to me you adapted just fine to that little surprise."

Maybe, maybe not, Josh thought, as, after a huge, toothy yawn and a big stretch Smoky finally decided he'd had it, swiping up against Josh's leg before stalking out of the kitchen. Josh halfheartedly brushed fur off his jeans, then faced Dee again. "Thought you were supposed to be taking it easy. Yes, Mom called me," he said to her frown. "Deal."

Dee swatted in his direction, then clump-waddled back to the stove, where she started lifting lids and stirring things and generally making him crazy. In what might've been, under other circumstances, a very good way. The sweater underneath her flannel shirt was less baggy today, hugging her breasts and belly and reminding him how insanely sexy a pregnant woman could be. Even in hiking boots. From her phone, about a thousand people started singing "Joy to the World."

"I think babypie finally shifted—my back's not hurting as much. Besides, I've always found cooking…" She dipped a wooden spoon into the bubbling concoction, lifted it toward Josh to taste. "Very therapeutic. Helps settle my thoughts." Josh came closer, curling his fingers around her wrist to steady the spoon before taking a taste, ignoring the not-so-slight *Oh, yeah*? in his groin when her pulse and his fingertips collided. However, back to the food. He had no idea what it was—although vegetables and a whole mess of spices were involved—but his taste buds were very happy campers right now. Even if other parts of him…weren't.

"Wow. What is it?"

"Just something I whipped up from what was around. Kind of a Southwest ratatouille."

"Rata-what?"

"Never mind." Her brow crumpled. "And your verdict?"

He took the spoon from her to scoop up another bite, nodding and grunting out, "It's okay," and her smile warmed him even more than the spices. Which suddenly kicked in, setting everything on fire between his mouth and his stomach. Perfect.

Handing back the spoon, Josh yanked open the fridge for a bottle of water, gulping half of it down before twisting the cap back on and getting out, "Might be a bit too much for the kid, though."

"There's a milder version on the other burner. Already kid-tested and approved. Huh, sweetie?" she said when Austin sidled up to her and she tugged him close.

"It's dee-LISH-shus!"

Josh looked at her, noticing her flushed cheeks, how her eyes were the color of root beer. So of course now he was craving root beer. "You got him to eat vegetables? What are you, a magician?"

She shrugged, her eyes twinkling. "Maybe." Her gaze followed Austin as he ran off to play with the dog now, then swung back to Josh, a soft smile curving her lips. The music changed, to some carol he couldn't name offhand. "I decided I could either sit and mope about how absolutely nothing is playing out the way I envisioned it, or I could cook a fabulous meal—and eat it—and hang out with the cutest four-year-old, ever…" She grinned. "And decorate the hell out of this house for Christmas."

"Um…you do realize it's two weeks yet until Thanksgiving?"

"Hey, once Halloween's over, I'm good." She reached for three bowls from the cabinet closest to the stove. "Besides, we'll have to decorate for the party, right? Might as well get an early start. Since I'm not going to get *less* pregnant."

His stomach rumbling and his brain churning, Josh silently watched her ladling her concoctions into the bowls. "You're really okay with this, then?"

Dee shot him a funny look, then gestured for Josh to sit at the head of the big table before calling Austin to join them, pouring the kid a glass of milk.

"I'm *making* it okay," she said, lowering herself into her own chair. "Especially since you're right, the community needs this party. I know they probably think I didn't care about them, since I haven't been around much, but…"

She glanced down, a wave of color washing over her cheeks. "My wanting to get away was never about the people." She twisted her fork over her bowl for a moment, then lifted her eyes to his. "Never."

"Then…" Josh winked at a wiggling Austin, who grinned around a mouthful of food, before meeting Dee's gaze again. "Let's go all-out, maybe even hire a band. And, hey, fireworks. It's the end of an era," he said to Dee's lifted brows as Austin yelled, *"Fireworks?"* between them, instantly on board with the idea. "Might as well go out with a bang, right?" He chuckled. "Literally. So whaddya say?"

"I think…" Dee smiled. "I think it sounds perfect. The perfect way to honor Dad—oh, sweetie!" she said

as a tsunami of ice-cold milk washed across the table...
and straight into Josh's lap.

"I'm sorry, Daddy!" Austin said, eyes huge with tears
as Josh jumped to his feet and Thor dashed under the
table, lapping up the puddle faster than it formed.

"It's okay, buddy, not to worry." Never mind that
his nuts were shrinking faster than the polar ice caps.
Damn, that was cold. "I used to spill my milk at least
once a day when I was little." Josh grabbed his napkin to blot at least some of the moisture, palming Austin's shoulder with his other hand. Out of the corner of
his eye he caught the blur that was Deanna, gathering
towels and a sponge, then zoom-waddling back to the
table, kneeing the disappointed dog out of the way to
drop towels on the floor. Then, grunting, she lowered
herself onto her hands and knees. Which couldn't be
good. Could it?

Wringing the sponge into a little bowl, she looked
up at Josh, mischief sparkling in her eyes. "You spilled
a glass of milk every day?"

"I did. Until my mother wised up and found one of
those lidded cups with a straw...*dog*! No!"

Desperately trying to fend off Thor's milky kisses,
Dee toppled over onto her butt, shrieking in laughter,
her howls only egging the dumb dog on and dissolving
his little boy into a torrent of giggles.

"Honestly, mutt—" His own mouth twitching, Josh
grabbed the dog's collar and hauled him off his "vic-
tim," at the same time tugging the front of his jeans to
get the damp away from his junk.

With that, Dee lost it completely, now laughing so
hard she was snorting. An instant later Austin threw

himself in her arms…and like somebody'd flipped a switch the laughter died as suddenly as it'd started. Dee wrapped his little boy close, laying her cheek in his hair and rocking him, and Josh felt like he was being crushed from the inside.

"It's okay, baby," she said. "It was an accident, it's okay."

Except it wasn't okay, was it? At all.

"I need to get out of these wet pants."

A crease wedged between her brows, Dee glanced up at him, giving Austin's noggin a quick kiss before gently pushing him off her lap.

"I'm sure," she said, then lifted her hands so Josh could haul her to her feet, and her belly grazed his, and her crazy-sweet laughter still rang in his ears, and the image of her cradling his son was burned into his brain, and Josh thought, *Hell.* "So why don't you run on back and change," she said, as the dog checked out the floor again in case Dee'd missed a stray molecule or two. "I'll watch the little guy—"

"Actually we should probably go."

Not even a boisterous rendition of "God Rest Ye Merry, Gentlemen" could pierce the silence now throbbing between them. Until Austin's tiny, "Is it because I spilled my milk?" shattered that silence.

Ah, jeez…

"Not at all, guy," Josh said, scooping the kid into his arms.

"Then how come we have to go?"

"Yeah, *Daddy*," Dee said, her expression as confused as his son's. With a generous dose of *pissed* tossed in for good measure. "How come?"

God knew she deserved an explanation. But how could he give her a reason for his sudden about-face with Austin right here? Especially since Austin *was* the reason?

He was pretty sure, anyway.

"By the time I change it'll be close to this guy's bedtime. No point in coming back over only to leave ten minutes later."

Her eyes narrowed. Because he was a lousy liar. And nobody knew that better than Dee.

But all she did was grab their bowls and tromp back to the kitchen, one hopeful dog at her heels. "Let me pack some of this up for you, then—"

"You don't have to—"

"I can't possibly eat it all, Josh. It'll just go to waste."

"Okay." He swallowed. "Thanks."

A few painful minutes later she handed him a bag bulging with plastic containers, as well as a cake carrier with most of the cake, before walking him to the back door, rubbing her belly. A gust of frigid air swept in when he opened it; boy and dog streaked off toward the foreman's house.

"Well. 'Night—"

"All I wanted," Dee then said in a small, brittle voice, "was to be useful. *Helpful.* To do something good for somebody else. For you. And Austin. But mainly for you. Because I'm long overdue saying thank you."

"For…what?"

"Being my friend when we were kids. Because you didn't have to do that." Her eyes veered to his, their brown depths bottomless in the half light. "So what'd I do wrong now?"

"Nothing," he said quietly, looking away.

"You sure?"

"Positive," he said, screwing his hat back on before walking out into cold night, feeling like crap and not having clue one what to do about it. Because whether his fears were valid or not, the idea of somebody else suffering for them wasn't sitting well. Wasn't until later that night, after he'd cleaned more frosting off Austin than there'd been on the cake and gotten him tucked into bed, that he remembered his promise to Zach, to handle the shower.

Standing at the front window looking toward the Big House, Josh sighed, making Thor come up to lick his hand, wanting to make it better. Maybe one of these days, Josh thought as he stroked the dog's smooth head, life would be easy. Or at least, eas*ier*.

But he wasn't counting on it.

Chapter 5

By the week before Thanksgiving, winter was teasing northern New Mexico with longer and more frequent visits. Cold, white stuff had fallen from the sky more days than it hadn't, although rarely hard enough to close school. Just enough to turn the countryside into a sparkly winter wonderland and for the ski resort to open early, much to the town's delight. Since, Deanna remembered, a longer season meant more tourists traipsing through town and subsequently more moola trickling into Whispering Pines' coffers.

So between the weather and the various worker bees readying the house for sale this was the first chance she'd had to reacquaint herself with the little village she'd called home once upon a time, its shops and little galleries, the quaint town plaza that would shortly wear its holiday finery, every pathway and roof lined with luminarias on Christmas Eve.

She'd have a baby by then, she realized, the thought zinging through her like a jolt of electricity. Although whether or not she and Josh would have mended things between them, she had no idea. A thought that, on top of Gus's departure a couple of days before, made her very sad. And lonely, truth be told.

Brushing snow off her head and shoulders, Deanna hurried into Annie's Place, the only eating establishment in town that catered to locals more than *touristas*. The fare was time-honored and hearty and heartily chile-infested—red, green or that combination of both known in New Mexico as "Christmas"—and as soon as Deanna entered she felt catapulted back in time. The classic diner decor, if you could call it that, hadn't changed one iota from when she and Josh would come in as kids, for burgers and fries and shakes as thick as cement. Smells were the same, too, mouthwateringly spicy and greasy and perfect, she thought on a smile as she unwrapped herself from her shawl and slid into a booth next to a window facing the plaza.

She recognized the waitress from the memorial, as the blonde apparently did her, her bright blue eyes sympathetic as she set down a glass of water, along with a straw and a menu large enough to shelter a stadium. "I'm Val," she said with a bright grin, yanking an order pad out of the pocket of the black apron allowing little more than a peek of a boldly striped sweater, tight blue jeans. "Levi's wife?"

"I know, I remember. Although I didn't realize you worked here—"

"Only the lunch rush these days. Although today's crazy slow, for some reason." Still smiling, Val nodded toward the menu. "You need a minute?"

"Actually, no," Deanna said, handing back the menu. "Green chili cheeseburger, well done. Double order of fries, chocolate shake."

Humor danced in Val's eyes. "Anything else?"

"As if I'll ever be able to eat all of that," Deanna said, and Val released the chuckle she'd clearly been holding in.

She called out the order to the bald black dude behind the counter, then turned back to Deanna. "Josh told us, about you being grounded here. I'm so sorry. About everything. I know what it's like, when life throws you for a loop."

Deanna imagined she did, since Val's first husband had died while deployed to Afghanistan, leaving her a widow with two small children. Definitely put her own situation in perspective. But all she said was, "Thanks. I didn't really know Tomas," she said gently. "But Levi's a good guy. Crazy as a loon, but good."

Val chuckled. "True on both counts. My girls and I are very blessed—"

"And it's about time you dragged your skinny butt in here!" Annie called out, sweeping across the restaurant to haul Deanna out of the booth and against her skinny chest, only to then gift her with the Annie Stink Eye underneath a messy updo that was grayer than Deanna remembered. "What? You think you're too good for us now?"

"Not hardly," Deanna said, laughing. "But I've been

insanely busy, getting the house ready to sell. It's taking a lot more time than Josh and I had expected."

It was fleeting, granted, but the disapproval that flashed across both women's faces made her immediately regret mentioning an obviously sore subject. Even though they had to see that without her father, the Vista was only a ranch. A place. A *thing*. Then again, she knew that tradition was often what held little rural communities like this together, that what some people might call progress others saw as a threat. But then, as if reading her thoughts, the older woman took Deanna's hands in hers, her freckled skin so pale as to be almost translucent.

"Change is never easy," she said softly as Val left to tend to her other customers. "But I know you and Josh will do what's best. Well. That husband of mine'll have your food ready in a jiffy. It's so good to see you, Dee." She gave Deanna's hands a quick squeeze. "You've been missed."

Missed? Deanna thought as she wedged herself and her little passenger back in the booth. Since she'd never felt much like a real part of the community as a kid, she somehow doubted it. She did wonder, though, why she'd never really felt connected to the place her father had obviously loved with his whole heart and soul. What made her feel so itchy now, fighting that same trapped feeling that had plagued her adolescence?

And yet—her gaze drifted out the window, toward the little square where a half-dozen toddlers, under the watchful eye of their caregivers, were having a ball in a small playground that hadn't been there before—her life back east this past little while hadn't exactly been all that, either, had it? Obviously not, if she'd been so quick to grab at a Something More that turned out to be nothing at all.

As her other customers headed out, Val brought Deanna her order. Along with, apparently, a side order of conflicted, since the waitress seemed hesitant to leave after setting down Deanna's food. Grasping her burger, Deanna looked up at Josh's sister-in-law.

"Is something wrong?"

"No, not at all. It's just…well, I was wondering if you'd like company. Except then I thought if I asked and you didn't, then you might feel obligated to say yes, just to be polite. And how awkward would that be?"

"I'd love company," Deanna said, smiling. "And no, I'm not just saying that to be polite."

"You sure?"

"Positive. The funny thing is," she said as Val slid into the booth across from her, "I used to think I was a loner. Probably because I was an only child so I was used to it—"

"Yeah? Me, too. And please, dig in. Before the fries get cold."

Deanna took a bite of her burger, savoring the exquisite little explosions of green chile bliss on her tongue. "But there's a difference between needing alone time and feeling cut off from the world."

"You talking about then? Or now?"

Heh. She'd set herself up for that one, hadn't she? Never mind how gently Val had asked the question. Angry with herself for coming perilously close to dumping on someone she didn't even know, for godssake,

Deanna stabbed her fry into that puddle of ketchup, hot tears pricking at her eyes.

"Sorry."

"For what?"

Unable to speak—let alone eat—Deanna shook her head.

"Hey." Val stretched across the table to clamp a warm hand around Deanna's wrist, her eyes full of *Don't mess*. "You're pregnant and your daddy just passed and you're stuck someplace I'm guessing you don't really want to be. I'm also guessing you have no idea what comes next. So you clearly need to talk to somebody." She leaned back again, crossing her arms over her stomach. "And right now that somebody's me."

"But—"

"Oh, hell, honey—why'd you think I came over here?"

Fighting a smile and tears, both, Deanna grabbed her napkin and blew her nose. "Because you're nosy?"

At that, the blonde belted out a laugh far too loud for somebody that tiny. "I'd be lying if I said no. But like I said, I've also been where you are. Not exactly the same circumstances, but feeling like your whole world's just imploded? Hell, yeah. And I was pretty cut off, too, as a kid. Again, different reasons. Still. I know what it's like, needing to talk to *somebody* before your brain melts. For me it was Annie," she said, nodding over her shoulder at the older woman, chatting with a slightly grizzled-looking, bearded man at the counter. "In fact, if it hadn't been for her I doubt I would've survived my teen years. Before I met Tommy, anyway. And of course now poor Levi gets the brunt of my emotional upchucking—" smiling a little, Deanna finally stuffed that fry in her mouth "—but it rolls right off his back. Then again, that's how the Talbots are. All of 'em. Listeners. Real good ones, too."

Deanna tried the shake, but it needed to melt a little before she could actually drink it. "True. In fact, I used to bend poor Josh's ear something awful when we were kids."

"So Levi said. And now?"

Blowing a short laugh through her nose, Deanna poked a crisp fry in the blonde's direction. "And now we come to the real reason for this little chat," she said, which got another brief chuckle.

"What I said, about knowing how you feel? Meant every word of it. But, you're right, Levi's also concerned about Josh. It's a twin thing, apparently."

"No, it's a Talbot thing."

"That, too."

Deanna's own smile faded as she sighed. "I know Josh doesn't really want to sell the Vista. And I completely understand why. So now I get to add guilt to all the other crap in my head."

A moment passed before Val got up to get herself a cup of coffee from behind the counter, then brought it back, stirring in enough cream and sugar to turn it into basically hot ice cream. "Actually Josh hasn't said much to Levi about it, although we can guess how he feels. But to be honest, I'm of two minds about all of this. On the one hand, heck, he's never lived anyplace else. So of course he's attached to the Vista. On the other…"

Val sipped her coffee, then squinted out the window, cradling the stoneware mug in her hands before facing Deanna again. "It wouldn't be a bad thing, either, for him to start over somewhere that would be completely his from the get-go. Make his own name from his own operation, rather than continuing to live in your father's shadow. Although this is strictly between you and me, since it's not exactly a popular opinion."

"Pretty much what I said to him, actually. But why are you telling me this?"

After another sip, Val set down the mug, staring at it for a long moment before lifting her eyes again. "Because I think this is fixing to blow up in everybody's face, and since my husband is part of that 'everybody' I'd like it all to work out without *too* many hurt feelings."

"In other words, they all think I'm the bad guy for wanting to sell."

"Didn't say that—"

"Didn't have to." Deanna pushed out a sigh. "I can't afford to hang on to some place where I'm not even going to live. As wobbly as my life might feel right now, I know I can rebuild it. There, not here. Because I simply can't see…" Her gaze returning to the square, with all those little kids running around and laughing, she huffed out another, much more aggravated breath. "I almost wish Dad had left it all to Josh."

"No, you don't," Val said, so sharply Deanna looked back at her. "Your first duty is to that child. If selling the ranch means ensuring *her* future, then nothing else matters. Being a single mom is *hard*. I should know. And what anybody else thinks…tough."

Deanna was stunned. "You're really not on their side?"

Val smirked. "I'm on the side of whatever happening that's best for all concerned. Especially when a baby's involved. Besides, Josh is a big boy, he'll figure it out. And get over it. Speaking of whom…he said the renovation's gotten more involved than you guys had hoped? Something about the home inspection turning up a bunch of problems?"

Still reeling from the idea of having possibly found an ally, Deanna's mouth pulled tight. A few little tweaks, the designer had said. The vintage look will work to your advantage, she'd said. Some paint, some furniture rearrangements, boom.

Boom was right.

"Lead pipes," Deanna breathed out. "'Nuff said."

"Ouch. But the more that gets fixed, the higher price you'll get. Right?"

"In theory, anyway."

"So there you go. And again, Josh will deal. Since it's not like he has any choice."

Maybe not. However…

Crap. Everything told her not to go where her brain was yanking her like an overeager puppy. But talking about Josh and the house naturally led to her thinking about his bizarre reaction the night of the dinner fiasco, as if he'd come face-to-face with something he hadn't realized was lurking in the shadows, ready to pounce. Whether Val was the right person to talk to about it, Deanna wasn't entirely sure, but she was here and seemingly available. As opposed to Josh, who for obvious reasons couldn't be her go-to person anymore. Not about this, anyway. Or Emily, up to her eyeballs in wedding planning—

"Do you have any idea what happened between Josh and Austin's mother?"

Val's brows lifted. "He hasn't told you?"

"No. Which is weird since he's all about being honest and open and stuff."

That got another laugh. "When it suits his purpose, most likely. Like most men. Unfortunately I'm not sure how many blanks I can fill in. I know what Levi told me, but I don't really know how much Josh shared with him. Or how much of that Levi shared with me." Val crossed her arms again. "Why? What's going on with you two? Aside from the house stuff, I mean."

So Deanna told Val about Josh's abrupt departure the other night, about how every time she'd offered to watch Austin since then, he'd give her a polite but insistent, "Thanks, but I've got it covered."

Frowning, Val snitched a fry from Deanna's plate. "Okay..." she said slowly, "after I came back to Whispering Pines with the girls, and Josie immediately latched on to Levi when he started hanging around..." Chewing, she glanced out the window, then back at Deanna. "I might've lit into him at one point, so afraid she'd get attached and then he'd decide he'd fulfilled his duty to Tommy—they were best friends, did you know?" Deanna shook her head. "Yeah. Anyway, they enlisted at the same time, and Tommy made Levi promise..." She swallowed. "He made Levi promise to check up on me and the girls if anything happened. Which I didn't know. So when he showed up, I wasn't entirely sure what his motive was. And frankly I don't think Levi did either, at the time. In any case, my daughter had been through enough, losing her daddy. That last thing I wanted was for her to get hurt. Again."

"So you think Josh feels the same way about Austin."

"I don't know for sure. Obviously. But it makes sense, right?"

It did. Especially since the very thought had occurred to Deanna one night when she'd gotten up for the umpteenth time to pee and her defenses were down along with her panties. She did remember, however, letting out a little "Oh…" and the cat meowing back at her in reply, as if to say, *Took you long enough, dimwit.*

Deanna sighed. Since God knew she understood how it felt to have all the responsibility for another human being dumped in your lap. "Although Austin wouldn't even remember his mother leaving, would he? Gus said he was still a baby—"

"No," Val said slowly, snagging another fry when Deanna pushed the plate toward her. "But Josh remembers. Besides, the little guy's older now…"

The last part of Val's sentence faded into the roar inside Deanna's head, where the first part painfully, and persistently, echoed.

That *Josh* remembered.

"So this isn't about Austin at all."

Val smiled, then slid across the booth's faux leather seat, grabbing her mug as she stood. "You wanna take the leftovers? I'll bring you a box."

"Um…sure. Only…what's Josh's favorite thing on the menu?"

That got a funny look. "You really want to go there?"

"No. But anything's better than this impasse between us."

"Got it. Then same as you, pretty much. Except he likes onion rings on his burger. And he usually tacks on a piece of my peach pie at the end."

"Then pack up an extra order to go," she said, handing over her credit card. "With two pieces of pie. Oh, and whatever Austin might like, too."

"Coming right up."

A few minutes later, Val returned with a stuffed plastic bag, as well as a foam box for Deanna and the credit card slip.

"You know what's crazy?" Val said as Deanna signed the slip, then packed her leftovers into the box. "That you and I were both raised right here in Whispering Pines, and yet we never knew each other."

Slipping the box into the bag with the rest of the food, Deanna looked up. "You never came to any of the parties out at the ranch? The Fourth? Christmas?"

"Not until after I met Tommy, nope. And you were gone by that time."

"Too bad." Deanna gathered her purse and the bag, grunting a little as she heaved herself out of the booth and onto her feet. "I could've used a girlfriend back then."

"Same here," Val said, then gave her a hug, whispering, "Well, you got one now, honey," before letting her go. "I love the Talbots, I really do, but they are definitely a force to be reckoned with."

"I remember," Deanna said, gathering the bag. "Thanks again. For everything." Then she cocked her head. "So how'd you handle the situation with Levi and your daughter?"

A slow smile spread across Val's mouth. "I married

him," she said, then crossed the restaurant to take care of a couple who'd just come in.

Josh almost jumped when he opened his door to a snow-flecked, grinning Dee, her cheeks flushed from the cold as she held up the diner's take-out bag. Thor, naturally, swarmed her like she was carrying balloons and a check for five million dollars. Or hamburgers. Thor's needs were simple.

"It's…three thirty." Because the *time* was the most remarkable thing about all of this.

"Which is exactly when we used to eat these after school, as I recall."

On the odd occasion when Gus would pick Deanna up from the private school in Taos where she went after the sixth grade, then Josh and Levi from theirs in town, before dropping them all off at Annie's. Not every day, no—Granville was more likely to chauffer his daughter himself—but often enough that memories now flooded back. Especially of those days when Levi would claim he had other/better things to do, leaving Josh and Dee sitting across from each other, Dee talking his ear off as they inhaled their burgers, oozing with gobs of melted cheese and piled high with green chili and onion rings. His lips twitched, remembering how even at twelve, thirteen, beanpole Deanna could pack it away as well as any cowboy.

How at that point he'd thought of her as a sister.

Josh caught a whiff of what was in the bag and his mouth watered; he caught another whiff of something sweeter, her perfume or hair stuff or whatever, and his hormones wept. Then he remembered how he'd treated her that night and he shut his eyes, listening to his son playing in his room down the hall.

"Josh—?"

Sighing, he opened his eyes again, almost cringing at the confusion in hers. "You shouldn't've done this."

"Because you really don't want to hang out? Or because you were basically a jerk?"

He grimaced. "Do I have to answer that?"

"No. Although you do need to let me in before I freeze. And I promise," she said as she came inside, shedding that blanketlike thing she wore, "I won't speak to Austin, let alone touch him."

"Dammit, Dee—"

"I'm serious." She turned around, her eyes wide. Innocent. Except anything but. "I totally get why you wouldn't want us to bond. Because it wouldn't be fair to him, since I'm not staying. I can hardly be mad at you for wanting to protect your son, can I?"

And again, reality slammed into him, that once the house was sold she'd have no reason to return. Ever. Funny, how even though he'd only seen her a handful of times since she was fifteen, he now realized how he'd never really let go of that tiny flicker of possibility, way in the back of his brain, that they wouldn't lose contact entirely.

And, yes, his knee-jerk reaction—also again—was to put distance between them. But for one thing, he was starving, middle of the afternoon or not. And for another, maybe it was time he grew up already, and stopped getting mad every time something didn't go his way, or when life got bumpy. Because there would always be bumps, there would always be challenges and disappointments and aggravations, and what kind of father would he be if he didn't show his son how to handle the crap with at least a *little* grace?

"I think we can work it out," he said, going into the tiny kitchen where his mother had prepared countless meals for four growing boys and a husband, now basically reduced to the place where coffee, cold cereal and Hamburger Helper happened. "As long as he knows you're only visiting, we're good."

"You sure?"

"No. Then again, he's got his grandmother, and two new aunts now—"

"So plenty of maternal influences," she said, awkwardly levering herself up onto one of the two stools in front of the peninsula dividing the kitchen from the living space. "So I won't be missed. Got it."

His stomach jolted. But Josh turned to see humor sparkling in her eyes, and he thought, *Like hell, you won't be missed*, immediately followed by *Dammit*.

Because he remembered, how much he'd missed her when she'd left before. How he'd missed her dry humor and energy, even her excitement about her upcoming adventure. How her absence had left a huge, honking hole in his life he eventually realized he'd tried to fill in all the wrong ways, with all the wrong females.

Except even then he knew he had nothing to offer that could possibly compete with a world he couldn't even begin to fathom, let alone understand. Because they'd texted, at first, her messages filled with details of her new life, about museums and art galleries and concerts, about seeing this ballet company or that opera. Eventually, though, the texts had stopped. When, exactly, he couldn't remember. But he sure as hell knew why—because whatever they might have had in common before pretty quickly got whittled down to nothing. And now? After almost a dozen years?

He somehow doubted the chasm between them had *shrunk*.

"I guess," he said, pulling plates down out of the cupboard, "we can look at things one of two ways." He carried the dishes—survivors from his parents' "old" set—over to the small dining table behind her, making her swivel on the stool. "Either from the standpoint of what we lost..." He set down the plates, then turned to her, sliding one hand into his front pocket. "Or what we've gained from that person being part of our lives."

Her eyebrows lifted. "Wow. Not what I would've expected, considering—"

"How I acted the other night? Me, either. And to be frank, that's a fairly recent revelation."

"How recent?"

"Thirty seconds ago?" he said, and she laughed, her smile softening a moment later.

"It's a good philosophy. I like it. Seize the moment and all that."

"I guess." He sighed. "I apologize for being a punk, Dee. Really."

Her gaze wrestled with his for a long moment. "And I doubt anybody would blame you, considering everything that's happened in the last little while. I sure as heck don't. But I'm glad..." The smile came back, brighter. Steadier, maybe. "I'm glad we're friends again."

"Yeah. Me, too."

She gave him a thumbs-up, then finally seemed to really see the house, methodically rubbing her belly. Between her hair, the tunic-like thing stretched over the bulge and her cuffed boots, now she looked like a pregnant elf. Except her ears were a lot cuter. "Holy moly. And I thought the Big House was in a time warp."

"The way I see it," Josh said as he opened the bag of food, nearly passing out from the heavenly smells, "if it still works, why replace it? I swear the sofa's upholstered in steel." Thor whined, slurping his slobber back in when Josh glared at him. He pointed to the dog's bed in the far corner of the living room; hanging his head, the dog trudged off, collapsing with a huge, dramatic sigh and giving Josh eyes to match.

"True," Dee said. "But dude, the stove is poop-colored."

He laughed, and for a moment it was like it used to be between them, before his voice lowered and Deanna grew breasts and he was suddenly very, very aware of said breasts. And even more aware that Granville noticed Josh's awareness, no matter how hard he tried to pretend nothing had changed, that he and Dee were still just friends.

And the thing was, on the surface it was true. Josh had never tried anything—he wouldn't have dared—and she'd never indicated she wanted him to. But if she'd stayed…

"Austin!" he called out. "Come see who's here!"

"Who?" his son called as he ran down the bungalow's short hall, actually gasping when he saw Dee, his entire little face lighting up. How on earth had she made that much of an impression on the boy, that quickly? And yet, when he ran into her arms—she'd somehow slid off the stool to squat in front of them, laughing when his enthusiasm and her shifted center of gravity collided—it was obvious she had.

That thing he'd said, about being cool with the moment?

Easier said than done.

Her puffy feet propped on the banged-up ottoman in front of the deeply cushioned chair from which she was probably going to have to be excavated, Deanna watched the flickering flames in Josh's fireplace, smiling at the blended giggles and laughter floating down the hall from Austin's bedroom. Although, despite a tummy blissfully crammed with the rest of her lunch and a huge piece of the best peach pie she'd ever eaten—as well as no small relief that she and Josh had apparently mended a few fences between them—neither could she deny the melancholy scratching at the door of her consciousness, whining for attention.

Because as gratifying as it was to see how much Josh clearly loved his son, watching and listening to their interaction only brought her own situation into even sharper focus. In a few weeks' time she'd be a single parent herself, with all the complications that entailed, piled on top of a life that was already a tangled mess. Hell, she seriously doubted her father would have been nearly as disappointed in her as she was in herself.

Except—her mouth pulled flat, Deanna stroked her belly, only to smile when a little foot pushed against her hand—she could either see this as a failure, or an opportunity. So let's hear it for Door #2, right? Somehow, she'd land on her feet, give her baby girl the life she deserved. And you know what? She'd be stronger for figuring it all out on her own. Maybe this wasn't how she'd ever envisioned becoming a parent, but since this was the hand she'd been dealt, at least she could be the best damn possible example to her daughter she could.

So there, world.

Josh came back into the living room, chuckling and shaking his head at her before squatting in front of the fire to poke at the logs, sending a cheerful spray of sparks up the chimney.

"What's so funny?" she asked, trying not to stare at the way all those muscles bunched and shifted underneath his flannel shirt. Because Skinny Dude had definitely left the building.

More muscles shifted—just kill her now—when he stood to set the poker back in its stand by the hearth. Swiping his palms across his bum, he turned, his grin warming her far more than the fire. "You look like you might not move until spring."

"I *feel* like I might not move until spring." Ripping her gaze away, she stroked the chair's soft, worn arms. "Was this always so comfortable?"

Josh went into the kitchen to pour himself a cup of coffee from the old-school Mr. Coffee. "You don't remember, then?" he said, taking a sip before setting down his mug on the peninsula, and she found herself considering that a pair of soft, kind eyes set into a hard-angled, beard-shadowed face was quite possibly the deadliest combination, ever.

"Remember what?"

He hesitated, then said, "It was right after your mama died, and Granville was…well, kind of a mess."

Her eyes burned. "That, I do remember. Then again, so was I."

"Exactly. So Mom brought you over here to give you a break. Dad made a fire, and you crawled up into that chair, all wrapped up in that very afghan…and you cried yourself to sleep. Nobody wanted to move you, so we didn't." His gaze lowered to the cup for a moment before lifting again to her. "For the next, I don't know, several weeks, maybe? That was your chair. You'd come straight here when you got home from school, crawl up in it and pass out."

"You're kidding?"

"Nope." He picked up the mug and came into the living room, lowering himself into the middle of that godawful plaid sofa a few feet away. Thor immediately crawled up to curl into a ball on the cushion next to Josh, smashed up against his thigh, sighing when Josh's hand absently went to his ruff. "Doesn't even ring a bell?"

"Vaguely. Maybe." Deanna blew out a breath to rival the dog's, hiking the afghan higher on her chest. Not because she was cold, but because…oh, hell—who knew? "I guess I blotted a lot of that out." Then she pulled a face. "That must've been when it started. Or ended, actually."

"What?"

"My relationship with my dad." Frowning, she looked away, picking at a piece of grass or straw or something on the afghan. "We never talked about my mother, really. And certainly not her death." She expelled a harsh half laugh. "A family trait, obviously. In any case..." Her eyes went all tingly. "I used to wonder if Dad sent me away because he simply didn't want to deal with me. Or couldn't, anyway." Another strangled sound erupted from her throat. "And I've never said that to another living soul."

Deanna sensed more than saw Josh take another sip of his coffee before leaning sideways to set down his mug on the end table, his brows drawn. "You seemed happy enough to leave."

"Shoot, Josh—I was fifteen and bored out of my skull here. Which you know. I'd only been back east a couple of times but compared with Whispering Pines? DC was like Oz. Full of wonder and possibilities."

A small smile twitched at his mouth. "And this was Kansas."

"Exactly. But now...well. I'm thinking maybe my problem with feeling isolated had more layers than I could have possibly realized, let alone understood, when I was a kid. I know I was only fourteen when Mom died, but I'd like to think I still could've helped Dad through our grief. Somehow. That we could've helped each other. I mean, I tried my best to be a good girl, to make him proud of me..." She shook her head. "But if he wouldn't let me be there for him..."

"He was proud of you, Dee," Josh said softly. "That I can promise you."

"It would've been nice to hear it, though. At least sometimes. You know?" Her hand went to her cheek, swiping away a tear. "I just wish I could ask him what he was thinking. Why he pushed me away when we needed each other the most. We should have grown closer. Not even more apart than we had been."

Josh shifted on the sofa to cross his arms high on his chest, the move making the dog grunt, then sigh back to sleep. "I guess I didn't realize it was that bad."

"That makes two of us. Don't get me wrong, I never doubted Dad loved me. But why he seemed to have such a hard time showing me how he felt…" Her forehead pinched; she shook her head. "He was so generous to the community, to everyone else…" A tear escaped the corner of one eye; Deanna swiped it away. "I also don't know why I never tried to break down whatever the barrier was between us. Because it wasn't as if I didn't have a great example, right under my nose, of what a normal family looked like."

"And who was that?"

She barked out a laugh. "You guys, doofus. Yes, I know there were issues with Colin, with Levi. Later, anyway. But not for lack of your parents' trying. Not for lack of them *loving* you guys. So why was I so afraid to claim that for myself?"

Josh's eyes darkened. "You were a *kid*, Dee. It wasn't up to you, it was up to your father. You—"

He surged to his feet, making the dog jerk. "God knows I loved your dad. He was very good to me. To all of us, like you said. But I'm gonna say something I've never said to anyone else, either, which is that…" Looking up at the ceiling, he sucked in a breath, then brought his gaze back to hers. "That when it came to you, he screwed up. Epically. And I'm sorry…"

His mouth thinned. "When you first got back…it wasn't you I was mad at, it was him. Only I couldn't tell him why I was mad, so I took it out on you. Because you're right, I wasn't raised to give up on the people I love. Or am supposed to love, anyway. And my parents drummed it into our heads that a person's obligation to those people went way beyond making sure their physical needs were met. Which is why…"

He dropped back onto the couch, and Deanna's heart turned over in her chest.

"Which is why it still hurts that Austin's mom walked away?"

His eyes bored into hers. "How much do you know?"

"That your son's here with you. And she's obviously not."

A ragged sigh left his lungs. "Did you know Jordan's never, not once, even bothered to check up on him, ask how he's doing?"

"Never?"

"Nope."

"And you had no idea this was coming? Her walking out, I mean."

"I knew she wasn't exactly happy, that she felt like we were in limbo. Or she was, anyway. Not really together," he said, cupping the back of his neck as he sat forward again, "but forced to deal with each other because of the kid."

The dog, clearly annoyed at Josh's constant shifting, abandoned him for Deanna, wagging his tail as he laid his chin on her knee and gave her the most pitiful brown eyes in the history of dogdom.

Josh watched the beast for a moment, then said, "Still. I thought the arrangement was working as well as it could. And sure as hell I would've thought her own son might've been worth more to her than a mumbled *Sorry, I can't do this anymore*, when she dropped him off that last time." His gaze met Deanna's as she stroked Thor's head. "So when you told me about your baby's daddy...swear to God, if he'd been standing there? I would've punched his lights out." At her laugh, a smile tugged at his mouth. "Okay, maybe not. But I sure as hell would've told him off."

"I would've paid good money to see that," she said, and he snorted. From down the hall, they heard Austin laughing at something. Josh frowned.

"Is it weird, how much he likes to play by himself? I swear he'll go in there and I won't hear from him for hours. Seems like it, anyway."

"It's an only child thing," Deanna said quietly, rubbing her tummy. "We're good at entertaining ourselves. We also need alone time, to recharge."

"I guess." He didn't sound convinced. Deanna smiled.

"You didn't lock him in there, for goodness' sake. When he wants you, he'll come out, right?"

"True."

"So...the thing between you and Austin's mother... it wasn't serious, then?" Josh's puzzled gaze swung to hers, and she shrugged. "Just wondered."

He pushed a sigh through his nose. "What it was, was a mistake. Plain and simple." A half smile played around his mouth. "But I expect you know how that goes."

"Lord, yes," she sighed out, and the smile stretched a little...followed by one of those no-big-deal guy shrugs that means anything but.

"Not exactly how I'd planned on becoming a father,

though. Especially at twenty-four. And my folks…" He sagged back into the couch's cushions, his hands linked behind his head. "Oh, they rallied, of course they did. For Austin's sake. But I know they weren't happy. Dad, especially."

"And maybe you're being too hard on yourself. Or them—"

"Dad literally didn't speak to me for a week after I told them."

"Oh."

"Yeah. Although at least I did tell them," he said, nodding toward her belly.

Guess he had her there. The dog jumped onto her lap, even though there was no room—

"Thor!" Josh snapped his fingers, pointing to the floor. *"Down."*

"No, it's okay," Deanna said, laughing, as the dog shoved his hindquarters in her face, clumsily trying to find purchase until they figured it out: dog butt wedged between her hip and the chair's arm, dog front draped across her knees, baby belly shoved against dog head. Whatever worked.

"I'm not sure which of you is crazier," Josh said, shaking his head. But at least he was smiling. Sort of. "What about you? Was it serious between you and what's-his-name?"

"Phillippe. And it was on my end. Obviously. Although obviously not on his."

"And let me guess—you're beating yourself up over not being able to spot his douchebaggery."

"Pretty much, yep. I assume you've dated since

then?" she said, desperate to shove the conversation back into his court.

His eyes narrowed—nice to see his BS meter was still in good working order—before his mouth turned down at the corners. "I'm a single dad who works twelve hours a day most days. When would I do that?"

"Oh, and like you couldn't find a babysitter. Please. That's an excuse, Josh. And you know it."

That got several seconds of hard staring before he said, "Maybe. But if nothing else, the whole thing—with Austin, with his mother—woke me up. Because life sure as hell got real, didn't it? What I was doing before—and believe me, I'm not proud of it—wasn't going to work anymore. It wasn't right. Especially now that there's this little person who one day is gonna be a big person who's gonna need to look up to his dad. Only thing is, I'm still not sure what *is* right. Or at least, how to go about making *right* happen."

"I know what you mean," she said with a tight smile. "Oh, boy, do I know what you mean."

"Is this the beginning of a whole 'men are scum' tirade?"

Scratching the space between the dog's shoulders, she smiled. "No. Not really. Although I guess Phillippe was. Is. God, I feel so bad for his wife. Since I doubt I was his first...dalliance. And I seriously doubt I'll be his last. Although who knows?" She frowned down at the now softly snoring dog. "Maybe they have an 'understanding'—"

"Daddy! Look what I made!"

Austin thundered into the room—the dog didn't even twitch—holding out a plastic block masterpiece that was rather…impressionistic. Josh hauled the child onto his lap, suitably—and seriously—admiring the creation. "That is so cool, dude. Can you tell me about it?"

With that, the child launched into a rapid-fire description of what was apparently a robot-weapon-vehicle hybrid, then snatched it from his father's hands to demonstrate its many amazing features. A second later Austin turned, holding it out to Deanna with that adorable baby-toothed grin.

"It's for you."

Deanna's heart stuttered. "Me?"

The child shook his head so hard his waves wobbled. "Uh-huh. 'Cause you brought me food."

"Jeez, the woman'll think I never feed you," Josh muttered, and a laugh bubbled up inside Deanna's chest. Especially as Austin's face turned into one big frown as he tried to process this information. Then he brightened.

"*Good* food."

The laugh exploded, startling the poor dog awake and off her lap. Still chuckling, Deanna held out her arms so the boy could take the dog's place. She shifted him on what was left of her lap, admiring her gift. And thinking how this would be her with her own child soon. *So* soon. "Thank you, sweetie," she pushed past what felt like a rock in her chest. "I love it."

"Really?"

"Really truly cross-my-heart."

"Okay, good. Hey—maybe the baby c'n play with it, after she's borned."

"Well, maybe not right after—she'll be too little. But later, absolutely." Deanna tugged Austin to her and planted a kiss in his curls. "I'm sure she'll love it."

"*Ex*cellent," he said, then wriggled off her lap and scampered back to his room. Deanna watched him zoom down the hall, then shoved one hand into the chair's arm to push herself to her feet, carefully holding the Duplo creation with her other. Josh rose as well.

"You don't have to keep that if you don't want—"

"Are you kidding?" she said, clutching the blocks to her bosom. "When a four-year-old gives you a present, you treasure it forever. Jeez…what rock were *you* born under?"

And the grin that slowly, steadily, spread across Josh's cheeks nearly did her in.

"You need me to walk you back?"

"I think I know the way. Besides which that would mean either leaving Austin here alone or dragging him with you, neither of which I'm about to let happen. But thanks. Good to know chivalry isn't completely dead."

There went that darkening thing in his eyes again. "I've always known how to treat a lady. It's how to have an actual relationship with one I seem to be a little sketchy on."

"And maybe that would depend on the lady?"

"You might have a point at that." He slid his fingers into his front pockets. "I know the reason you're home really sucks. But it's good to have you back, Dee. Even if only for a little while."

"Thanks," she said, then hauled her double-wide butt out of there before he could see the ambivalence in her eyes. Because while he was right, the reason she was back sucked, *being* back didn't. At least not nearly as much as she might've figured it would. Except…that wasn't necessarily a good thing.

Since what *would* suck, would be getting sucked into something neither she nor Josh wanted or needed or could even remotely deal with right now.

Or ever, actually.

Chapter 6

"So how do you want to do this?" Billie said, re-draping her stethoscope around her neck before hoisting Deanna back up to a sitting position on the exam table. "Home, hospital—which means a trek into Taos—or here at the center?"

Tugging down her getting-tighter-by-the-second top over her enormous middle, Deanna screwed up her face. "You're not going to yell at me about my blood pressure?"

"Since yelling at you, as you put it, would hardly reduce your stress…no. And in any case, being as it's not insanely high, I'm not worried. So. Decision time, sweetie. What's it gonna be?"

Dee smiled. She'd toured the facility, which easily rivaled the one in DC she'd planned on using. "I guess…here."

"Good," the midwife said, then helped Deanna down before sitting at her desk to add notes to Deanna's chart. Lowering her prodigious form onto the molded plastic chair beside Billie's desk, she caught the poster on the opposite wall, illustrating—in great detail—the birth process. At least the baby looked happy enough.

"Aside from that slightly elevated BP," Billie was saying, "everything else looks fine, no obvious risk factors, baby's in perfect position. And you'll be at thirty-seven weeks right before Thanksgiving." She looked up, her brown eyes twinkling behind her glasses, the lenses reflecting a dozen colors from her brightly patterned cardigan. "So you're good to go."

At Deanna's nervous laugh, Billie smiled.

"You scared?"

"Of giving birth? Not really." A flat-out lie, but whatever. "Of knowing what to do after? I've never even held a newborn before, let alone taken care of one. What if I screw up?"

"Oh, you can count on it. The good news is, the baby won't notice. Or care."

"Greaaat."

The midwife's eyes softened. "You having second thoughts? About keeping her?"

"Billie! Ohmigod, no! Of course I'm keeping her! Okay, so maybe doing this on my own hadn't been part of my game plan. And I have no illusions about how hard it's going to be. But..." Her eyes filled. "But I already love her."

"Then wait until you meet her," Billie said gently. "And once you do? That intuition will kick in harder than you have any idea. Of course you'll make mistakes. Sometimes even insanely stupid ones. Like the time I was so sleep deprived with the twins I forgot to strap Josh into his baby seat and he squirmed right out of it onto the floor. I bawled for a solid hour, convinced the Baby Police were going to come take my children away. He survived, *I* survived, and so will you. And as long as you're here, you'll have all the support you need. I promise."

Words that arrowed Deanna right between the eyes. Because who would've helped her in DC? Heaven knew not her aunt. And Emily was even more clueless than Deanna—

"Josh said at least the house is all done?"

"Um…yes," Deanna said on a released breath. "As of a couple of days ago." And Josh had been as good as his word, patching and painting walls and whatnot while Deanna kept Austin amused, mostly watching the baby's in utero interpretive dance routine. Man, what she wouldn't give to bottle those little boy belly laughs.

Not to mention the image of a paint-speckled, soft-eyed Josh, chuckling at his laughing son.

"And how's the nursery coming along?"

Nursery. A way too permanent-sounding word for a room she didn't dare let herself think of as *her* baby's. Then again, how permanent was anything in her life, really?

"Josh set up Austin's old crib the other day. So at least I have some place to put Katie after she's…out."

"Katie?"

"Or Kate, maybe. Whichever seems to fit."

"Your mama's name. That's lovely. Your dad would be so touched."

Deanna's thoughts, exactly. Except wasn't it ridiculous that she was still trying to please him, even though he wasn't around to appreciate it?

Josh's mom handed her the chart, then clasped her hands together on the corner of the desk. "So the shower is coming up…"

"Listen, about that…" Because there was support, and there was suffocating. A thin line Deanna worried was about to be crossed. Even though she'd been speechless for several seconds after Billie told her. "Seems like a lot of trouble to go to for someone who's not sticking around."

"And clearly you've forgotten what it means to live in a small town," Billie said, complete with the sharp look of a woman who's raised sons. "And the baby's going to need at least a few things while you are here. So unwad your panties, girl and feel the looove."

Deanna chuckled, then sighed. "Except my cousin's going to throw me one when I get back. Two showers just seems…excessive."

"Your cousin…" Billie adjusted her glasses to peer at Deanna's chart again. "That's who you put down as next of kin, right? Emily Taylor?"

"Yes."

"She came out here to visit a couple of times, didn't she? When you were still kids?"

"She did. She's…" Deanna cleared her throat. "She and I are very different, but she's been my rock through this. I've been very blessed."

A gentle smile brought Billie's high cheekbones into full relief. "So why limit those blessings? Don't see any reason why this munchkin can't be showered twice, do you? And by the way," she said, standing. "You're coming over for Thanksgiving—no, no arguments. Because no way are you gonna be in that big house all by yourself on the holiday." She gave a little laugh. "Although it'll be crowded this year, what with all these new people coming into the family." The midwife frowned. "And why are you giving me that look?"

"Because…"

Because she was clearly insane. Although that was a given, wasn't it?

"Why not have Thanksgiving at the Vista?" Deanna said, struggling to her feet. "It's all fixed up, for one thing. And the dining table could seat half the town, for crying out loud."

Even though it'd never been more than her parents and her for holiday meals. Except for that single Christmas when Emily and her parents had come out, when she was ten. The Holiday from Hell, as she recalled.

Billie's head tilted. "You sure?"

"Absolutely." And the longer she thought about it, the more the thought of experiencing a huge, Norman Rockwell–style holiday dinner made her giddy.

Especially since this might be her only shot at such a thing.

"Seriously—why cram everyone into your little house when there's this great big one just begging to be properly used, for once? Besides, it's Josh's house, too." At least, for a while. "And please," she said as her face heated, "let me help with the cooking. Unless you get off on doing the whole thing?"

"Are you kidding? I've been threatening for years to buy one of those ready-made meals from the grocery store. If for no other reason than to see everybody's appalled expressions. But you're very pregnant, in case you hadn't noticed—"

"What's the worst that can happen? I go into labor with a dozen people around who can get me to the birthing center. One of whom could actually deliver the baby."

Billie gave Deanna a speculative look before saying, "Okay. You're on. Now, I'm sure Val will bring pies—"

"Ohmigosh, I had a piece of her peach pie the other day. I'm still on a high from it."

"Then wait until you taste her pumpkin. And apple. And coconut cream. We can talk in a day or two about who does what with the rest. Although I call dibs on the sweet potatoes."

Deanna laughed. "They're all yours."

Then Billie's eyes softened. "After you moved to DC, Sam and I tried I don't know how many times to get your daddy to join us for the holidays. He never would."

"Even though he threw that big Christmas party for the town?"

"Even though. Just never wanted anything for himself." Her brows dipped. "Pardon me for saying this, but your daddy was a strange man. A good man, all told. But strange."

"You're not telling me anything I don't already know."

"Even so, it was obvious how badly he wanted to make everything perfect for you." Another smile touched the midwife's lips. "Same as he did for your mother."

Deanna hiked her purse higher up on her shoulder. "Only it didn't work, did it?"

"Not that I could tell, no," the older woman sighed out. "Then again, Katherine and I weren't exactly besties. No one's fault," she added quickly. "And she was never less than kind to me. But we really were from different worlds, we simply didn't have much in common. And she seemed to prefer keeping to herself. Well," she said, seeming to shake off the thought. "I guess I'll see you Saturday at the shower. In the meantime, stay off your feet!"

As if, Deanna thought, letting Billie hug her again before trudging back to the reception desk to make her next appointment, then out to the small parking lot to heave herself up into the truck's cab.

Where she sat, thinking about her mother. Her sweet, doting mother who hadn't done nearly as good a job at hiding her malcontent as she probably thought she had. Even though Katherine Blake had obviously loved Deanna's father, Deanna guessed she'd never adjusted to life in a small New Mexican town, either.

The day was as brilliantly sunny as it was bitingly cold, the frosted mountain tops glittering against the cloudless, impossibly blue sky. The aspens and cottonwoods were bare now, of course, but as she drove back to the ranch it struck Deanna how simultaneously vulnerable and brave the skeletal branches were, stripped down to their essence.

As she approached the house, she spotted a tall male figure alongside the post and rail fence, clearly focused on the horses inside it, including the pregnant mare. Then the man turned and she recognized Sam Talbot, the boys' father…and she sighed. Because truth be told, the appointment—not to mention all the musings it had provoked—had left Deanna feeling like a toddler in desperate need of a nap. Why on earth was he here?

Not stopping, however, would've been rude. So she pulled up alongside the fence, praying, as she got out of the truck, she didn't look as much like a walrus as she felt.

His smile now splitting his face in two, Sam Talbot opened his arms as she approached, engulfing her in a brief, hard hug that almost brought tears to her eyes. Like most men around here he smelled of horse and earth, overlaid with an aftershave scent that would always remind her of her childhood. It wasn't until he let go, however, that she realized the hulking man she remembered had lost probably half his weight since she'd last seen him. But while his size was diminished, the sparkle in eyes more silver than gray hadn't dimmed in the least.

Except…

"Not sure I deserve that hug," Deanna said, facing the pasture herself, her hands stuffed into the pockets of her own down vest. Which she hadn't been able to zip for weeks.

"Because you want to sell the place, you mean?" When she snorted a laugh, Sam chuckled in return, then leaned his folded arms on the fence's top rail. "You raise four kids, you get pretty good at cutting to the chase. Makes for much more efficient conversations."

A frigid but surprisingly gentle breeze stirred the piñons bordering one side of the pasture before floating across the pale grass to soothe her hot face. "I know how much the ranch means to all of you—"

"Actually I'm not sure you do," Sam said, not unkindly. "But if that's the start of an apology, you can stop right now. You don't want it, and it's far more than Josh needs. Which I think deep down he knows. Whether he wants to admit that or not." When she gawked at him, he chuckled. "Surprised?"

"You might say."

Sam squinted out over the pasture, his hands knotting in front of him. Gearing up to say something Deanna guessed she didn't want to hear, most likely. Although what that might be, she had no idea.

"What gets me, though," Sam said, "is that Granville knew that, too. All of it."

Frowning, Deanna turned to the older man. "I don't understand."

"Neither do I, to be honest. Since a major reason Gran sent you away was to separate you and Josh—"

"Because he thought something was happening between us. I know."

"You saying it wasn't?"

Deanna picked at a splinter in the wood for a moment before shaking her head. "Josh and I were friends. Good friends, yes, but that's all. I swear."

Another soft laugh preceded, "Yeah, that's what Josh said, too. Even so, your dad wasn't taking any chances that things might change on that score. Since it was pretty obvious the two of you had completely different goals in life. Last thing he wanted was for you…" His mouth drawn in a tight line, Sam looked away again. "For you to end up as miserable as your mother was…"

Clearly the subject du jour. For whatever reason.

"…only somewhere along the line…" The older man's gaze bored into hers. "He apparently changed his mind."

Deanna's head jerked around, her forehead pinched. "Wait. Are you saying my father left the place to both of us—"

"To bring you together. Yep."

In a lame attempt to stop the world from spinning, Deanna grabbed the fence's top rail. "He told you that?"

"More or less."

"More or less?"

Sam released a breath that frosted around his mouth. "The last time I spoke with him, all he talked about was wanting to fix at least some of the mistakes he'd made."

"And you somehow deduced from that he wanted Josh and me to get together." Deanna barked out a laugh. "Seems a bit of a stretch, don't you think? Especially considering—"

"I know, I know. But why else would he leave the ranch to both of you?"

A question she couldn't answer. Or at least didn't want to.

"I knew your father my entire life, remember. We both grew up here, on the ranch. And what I noticed, even when we were kids, was that while God knew Granville could be stubborn as all get-out when he latched on to an idea, he also had no trouble switching loyalties if what seemed like a better idea came along. Not that it happened often," Sam said with a half smile, "but it did happen. So my guess is, as time went on, he regretted coming between you and Josh. Especially once Josh got over his wild oats phase after Austin came along, and your daddy could see what a responsible young man he'd turned into." The man's gentle gaze met hers again. "And I think he suspected you weren't all that happy after you left. And for sure Josh wasn't."

Now it was Deanna's turn to look away. She had no idea how her leaving had affected Josh, since they'd hardly discussed it. But she'd also never had another friend like him. Not even Emily, even though she loved her cousin to death.

None of which changed the fact that her father had, once again, obviously attempted to strong-arm events to his own ends. Or that she was in no position to do whatever her father had expected of Josh and her. Or, apparently, the man standing beside her. However, one meddling parent at a time...

"So Dad thought that by leaving the Vista to both of us we'd fall madly in love and get married and that way the ranch would stay in the family?"

"Stranger things have happened." Sam's voice softened. "Although I do think it was about more than the ranch. He really was trying to make amends, in his own way—"

"Or manipulate my happiness. My *life*." She scoffed. "Except that's what he'd tried to do all along, wasn't it? And what if she—" she pointed to her belly "—had come with a daddy to throw a monkey wrench into his plans?"

"Since he didn't know about that, not sure how that's even part of the equation."

God, she hated when people were logical. Still...

"Wow," she said again, then blew out a breath. "So how come Billie didn't mention it?"

"We decided she'd handle the pregnancy. I'd handle this. Teamwork," he said, and Deanna released a soft laugh. Then she sighed.

"I assume Josh has no idea."

"Only what I told you. And that was maybe two or three days ago. So I take it he hasn't said anything?"

She wagged her head. "But why even bring this up? Since we've already decided to sell. No, wait…let me guess—you wouldn't mind seeing Josh and me together, either."

That got a quiet chuckle. "Mind? Not at all. Except even I know that parents rarely get a say in these matters. One of the downsides to kids having minds of their own. So no expectations here, trust me. But…"

A sleek black mare plodded over to the fence to nudge at Sam's chest. He obliged, fishing a piece of apple from his pocket. "But it occurs to me," he said over the horse's crunching, "there's been too damn many secrets around here over the years. Too much truth-dodging. Not that I've got a lot of room to talk when it comes to keeping the lines of communication open with my own boys. I'm not perfect. But…"

His eyes went soft. "It nearly killed Josh's mother and me to watch the chasm grow between you and your father, after your mother died. But what could we do? It wasn't our place to take *his* place. Or even your mother's. That doesn't mean we didn't love you like one of our own." His lips curved. "The daughter we never had."

"Hence the not-minding thing about Josh and me getting together."

Sam chuckled, then sobered. "Even more than that, though… I guess there's nothing standing in our way now, to show how much we care. And always have."

Deanna's eyes filled. And this time it had nothing whatsoever to do with hormones. Of course she'd always felt a connection with the Talbots that went way beyond simply being the boss's daughter. That whole thing about her falling asleep in their armchair, for example. But the thing was, she now realized she'd never fully let herself feel the connection with them she so desperately wanted to forge with her own father. Because yielding to what was obviously a natural pull would've felt way too much like giving up.

And yielding to it now would feel an awful lot like giving in. To what, she wasn't entirely sure. But after a lifetime of being buffeted by external forces beyond her control, was it so wrong to want to claim at least *some* dominion over her destiny?

Although since Josh hadn't brought up the subject she was probably worrying—if she could even call it that—over nothing. Then again, nobody knew better than she how dangerous assumptions could be.

"Well," she said, pushing away from the fence. "Thanks, I guess? I mean, it's not as if this changes anything—"

"Didn't expect it to. Just thought you should know."

Nodding, Deanna gave Josh's father another short hug, then returned to the truck, wondering what, exactly, she was supposed to do with this information. Not to mention what Josh thought about all of it. So the question was…did she have the cojones to bring up the subject? Or the even bigger cojones not to? One thing she did know, however, which was that as much as she ached for her father, she was now even madder at him than she had been.

She slammed shut the truck's door and revved the engine, hot tears biting at her eyes.

At the sound of the old Chevy's tires crunching into the driveway, Josh glanced out the living room's picture window to see Deanna bang back the door and clumsily disembark. Even from here, he could tell she was upset. And knowing she'd had an appointment with his mom, his heart bolted into his throat: was there something wrong with the baby? Or her? But then, wouldn't his mother have said something when he talked with her a little while ago? Then again, maybe not—

"Dee looks mad," Austin said beside him, practically lost in a sea of old, dusty Christmas garlands.

"It's okay, buddy, ladies who are going to have babies sometimes get like that."

A tiny, scrunched up face lifted to his. "How come?"

"I guess because it gets uncomfortable with the baby inside. Like when you eat way too much and your stomach feels all tight?"

"You mean like when it feels like you gotta poop only it's not ready to come out yet?"

Josh nearly strangled on his laugh. "Maybe. But you probably shouldn't say that to Dee, okay?"

"How come?"

"Because girls don't generally like talking about stuff like that."

"You mean poop?"

"Yeah."

"Oh. Okay," he said. Although with one of those grownups-are-just-weird faces that made more and more regular appearances these days. "But maybe this'll make her feel better, huh?"

Josh glanced around at the chewed-up-looking bags and boxes scattered around the room, most of which Austin had already opened and pawed through. Now Josh wondered if that had been the best idea. Not because of Austin, but maybe it would've been better to let Dee have first crack at it, since it had been her idea—?

The front door opened; Dee actually jerked to a stop, her expression a millimeter away from thunderous. "What the he...ck?"

Grinning—and mercifully oblivious—Austin ran up to her, draped in fake pine garland. "We got out the Christmas stuff! Daddy said we could! There's a *lot*!"

At that, some of the clouds dispersed. Maybe not enough to see the sun, but at least the immediate storm threat had apparently passed. "There certainly is, sweetie." Shrugging off the vest that covered very little, actually, Dee dumped her purse on a table by the front door. Josh could have sworn her belly was twice as big now as it had been a couple of days ago, but no way was he pointing that out. How on earth women even *walked* when they were that pregnant was a mystery. At least horses could spread the load over four legs instead of two.

"So how'd the appointment go?" he asked, and her mouth twisted.

"Fine. More or less. What's all this about?"

"You said you wanted to get a leg up on the decorations. So since the shower's the day after tomorrow…" He shrugged.

Her eyes lifted to his. In which he saw questions. And not, he didn't think, about the decorations. Or the shower. Especially since his father had given him a heads-up roughly thirty seconds ago about their little chat. Which probably explained the pissedness, being as his own reaction, when Dad told him his suspicions about Granville's motives behind the will, had been pretty much the same. Although truth be told her venomous expression when she'd first walked in hadn't done his ego any favors. And wasn't *that* nuts? Because for damn sure the whole idea of them getting together was. For *damn* sure.

However, she then lifted those query-laden eyes to the rafters ten feet overhead, and he assumed the questions would wait. If they ever got voiced at all. Because no way was he bringing up the subject, nope.

"You don't think it's too early?"

"Just following your lead," he said, and a few more of the clouds dispersed.

"I guess I could use some help," she said—reluctantly, he thought—her hand going to her lower back. "Since your mother would kill me if I got on any ladders right now."

"She'd have to go through me first," Josh said, and something close to a laugh popped out of her mouth… the kind of laugh a smart man knew often preceded a meltdown. You know, a little too high-pitched, a smidgen too forced.

But she didn't melt down, even if the gaze that now

swung once more to his radiated with a sadness so deep it took his breath. A sadness that solidified the idea that had been shimmering in his thoughts ever since he'd talked to Mom from *maybe* to *do it*. Whether it would work out or not, of course, Josh had no idea. Dee's lips curved up at the corners. Barely.

"Besides," she said softly, "it's your house, too."

The words almost stuck at the base of his throat. "For the moment, anyway."

"Yes. For the moment."

A weird, sticky silence shuddered between them for a second before Josh said, "You know what you want to do about the tree? There's that big fake thing in a box in the toolshed—"

"Oh, God, no." She looked positively appalled. "Real, definitely. Later, though. Closer to the big party. So." She smiled, trying *so* hard to make it look genuine Josh's heart twanged. "Who wants hot chocolate?"

"Me!" Austin bellowed, his screechy little voice echoing off the rafters, ouch, and making Thor bark. Because clearly *something* was afoot the dog needed to stay on top of. Rubbing her belly, Deanna laughed, then cocked her head at Josh. "And yourself?"

"Sure. Then you can sit—" he pointed to the over-stuffed chair closest to the ceiling-high fireplace "—and tell me where you want stuff to go."

"You're on," she said, then shuffled off down the hall to the kitchen…only to return a second later.

"Do you remember how my mother used to drape the garlands around the chandeliers?" She pointed up to the pair of huge black wrought iron chandeliers that Josh and she had decided, a million years ago, looked like giant prehistoric skeletons. Both the realtor and the designer had been adamant they stay. And since neither Josh nor Dee had really cared, there they were, looking all rustic and "authentic" and crap.

"Enough. That what you want?"

Her eyes squinched, slightly, when she looked up again. Then she shook her head. "Actually…no. I don't. I trust you," she said, then disappeared again.

Josh seriously doubted she had any idea how much those three words had just affected him. Hell, when was the last time a woman had said she trusted him? That's right. Never.

However.

Whatever Deanna needed, he wasn't it. Not any more now than he had been when they were kids. Less, probably, since they'd grown up. Or, more to the point, grown apart.

So. Decorations, he could put up, sure. A real tree, he could get her. A secret phone call, he could make. Anything more than that…

No.

Because the first time she'd left, at least it hadn't been her choice. This time, however, it would.

And that was a hell he wasn't about to put himself through again.

Chapter 7

Even though Josh had outdone himself with the decorations—without even a hint of man-grousing, bless his heart—something had clearly shifted between them. Again. And it was probably not much of a stretch to pin that "something" on what they both obviously now knew about Dad's will. Of course, they *could* get the whole thing out in the open and simply talk about it, like actual grownups. Then again, what would be the point—?

"Ohmigosh," Val said from her perch by a garland-swagged window when Deanna pulled out an adorable, ruffled-bottom sleeper from one of the many, many gift bags stacked at her feet. "I'm hearby putting y'all on notice, if I have another girl, I want one of those. And no, I'm not pregnant, so you can lower the eyebrows already."

But the twinkle in the blonde's eyes said she and Josh's twin were doing everything they could to make that happen. And, yes, Deanna had to tamp down the spurt of envy, at how freaking adorable the newly married couple was, their happiness whenever they were together spilling all over the place like glitter.

Not that she wasn't grateful for the outpouring of affection—and gifts, oh, my, goodness, the gifts, including a bassinet to tuck right beside her bed—this little group was showering her with today, Annie from the diner and Billie and Josh's two sisters-in-law. Or soon to be, in the case of Zach's fiancée, Mallory. But honestly, she didn't even know Val except for that one conversation in the diner. And Mallory not at all. Still, being made to feel like she was actually one of them, even if only for this little while, warmed Deanna's heart. So the green-eyed monster could go screw itself.

As could the unexpected heartache from missing her mother far more than she thought she would. After all, she'd had thirteen years to reconcile herself to the fact that Mom wouldn't be around for any of those milestones a girl expects to share with her mother, and she'd managed just fine up till now. More or less. But something about opening presents for what would have been Katherine Blake's first grandbaby was doing a real number on Deanna's head. That her father wouldn't see little Katie, either...

Hell. It was a wonder she wasn't blubbering into a wad of pink tissue paper by now.

Sitting beside her, Billie squeezed Deanna's wrist, as if knowing what she was thinking. Deanna clutched the tiny pajamas to her chest, her breath hitching when it hit her that in a few weeks the tiny person inside her would be *wearing* the pajamas.

Her eyes burning, she smiled for Annie. "This is *so* stinkin' cute—thanks so much."

The menfolk—yes, this was a forward-thinking bunch—were scattered throughout the house, refilling munchie trays and tending to assorted small children, keeping the mayhem in reasonable check. Except for Josh, who'd had to go into Albuquerque for reasons he hadn't made entirely clear, either because baby showers really weren't his thing, or he was simply trying to avoid her. Considering how little they'd seen each other in the past couple of days, she was going with Option 2. However, Deanna was just as glad none of the men were present when she opened Mallory's gift—a top-of-the-line breast pump.

"That's the brand I used when I had Landon and had to express between takes when I was on the set," the former actress said, pushing her wheelchair a little closer. "Works like a charm. Although..." She chuckled. "Do you even plan on breast-feeding?"

"Yes, absolutely." At least, she figured she'd give it a shot. Deanna opened up the box and lifted out the gadget, trying to imagine fitting the contraption on her boob—

"What's that?"

At the sound of Austin's reedy little voice, Deanna hurriedly stuffed the pump back in the box. "It's, um..." She smiled for the kid, who was wearing an expression so much like his daddy's her heart knocked against her ribs. "A horn."

Val belted out a laugh, only to cover her mouth, muttering, "Good save," from behind her hand.

Big green eyes met hers. "C'n I try it?"

"No, sweetie, sorry…it's for the baby."

Oblivious to the laughter floating around him, the little boy came closer, frowning, to inspect the box. Which thank *God* did not have a picture of how to use the thing. Over the crackling fire in the stone hearth, she heard Josh's truck pull up out front. Great. Just in time to witness her contributing to his four-year-old's delinquency. "What's she gonna do with it? If she's gonna be too little to play with toys when she's born—?"

"Can't wait to hear you answer that one," came a very familiar voice from the entryway. Deanna jerked and twisted around, releasing a little gasp when she saw a grinning Emily, decked out in gray cashmere and designer jeans.

"Ohmigosh—Em!" Bags and tissue flying everywhere, Deanna shoved herself to her feet to meet her cousin halfway, throwing her arms around her. "How did you…? I don't understand—"

"This guy," Em said, nodding back toward Josh, standing a few feet off with his hands in his pockets and mischief in his eyes, clearly pleased with himself.

And instantly turning Deanna into the most confused pregnant woman on the face of the planet.

"You're staying for Thanksgiving, right?"

Reclining on the guest room's four-poster bed with Smoky snuggled up beside her, Emily laughed and bit off the end of another cream-cheese-stuffed jalapeño pepper.

"I'd love to, but I can't," she said, pulling a face as she plucked a blob of the gooey mixture from the front of her satin pajamas. "Command appearance, Mom and Dad and me with Michael's parents. I tried to get out of it, but Michael nearly had a fit. As it was I was lucky to snag a flight back on Wednesday…hey. You okay?"

"Just uncomfortable," Deanna said, shifting in the nearby overstuffed armchair. "The baby's already engaged."

"What?"

Deanna laughed. "As in, ready to launch. It's a good thing. And I still can't believe you're here," she said, and her cousin smiled, then bumped noses with the cat, who'd decided to see if whatever the human was eating was worth begging for.

They'd talked virtually nonstop since the shower ended hours before, mostly while Em helped Deanna unpack half of Deanna's clothes. *Because when an airline allows you two free bags*, Emily had said, chuckling, *you take advantage of that*. Which apparently meant also bringing a few things for after the baby came, although Deanna seriously doubted she'd fit into her fave pair of skinny jeans right off the bat. But she'd been beyond touched by her cousin's thoughtfulness… even as she still hadn't wrapped her head around Josh's getting her here. Even paying for her plane ticket—although according to Em, Deanna wasn't supposed to know that—since getting one this close to Thanksgiving, and on such short notice, was beyond pricey. Especially for a kindergarten teacher. Yes, a kindergarten teacher whose parents subsidized her apartment, but whatever.

"Well, I am, so deal," Em said, sitting up and reaching for her diet soda on the bedside table, her hair a deep gold in the flickering firelight. A great selling point, the Realtor had said—fireplaces in all the bedrooms.

"But…why?"

Setting down the can, her cousin gave her a pitying look as the cat thudded onto the Navajo rug by the bed. "Because Josh asked me to come?"

Deanna shifted again, willing the baby to move. No dice. "That's what I'm why…ing. I mean, what did he say? Exactly."

Emily's mouth twitched. "I didn't record the conversation, Dee. But as I recall, he said you seemed…unsettled. Being stuck here and all. And he thought it might be nice to have something or someone from home to make you feel better. Even if for only a couple of days."

Only, as thrilled as Deanna was to have her cousin here, Josh's bringing that about sure as heck wasn't making her feel *less* unsettled—

Em took another bite of the pepper. Because clearly the threat of late-night heartburn held no terror. Tougher than she looked, that one. "So what's going on between you two?"

Yeah, she'd figured that was coming. "Nothing. At least, nothing different. Josh and I are friends. Same as before."

"A *friend* who just laid out a not insubstantial wad of cash to get me here."

Deanna turned to stare into the flames, figuring the glow from the fire would mask her blush. "The Talbots are a generous lot." At Emily's chuckle, she faced her cousin again. "What?"

Em shrugged, then glanced around the room. "This was where I stayed all those years ago, isn't it? Is it me, or has nothing changed?"

"The sheets, maybe," she said, and her cousin chuckled again. "Because rustic charm is apparently all the rage these days."

That got another short laugh before Em's deep blue eyes met Deanna's. "Josh said he'd take me riding tomorrow, if I want. Unless you can't bear me to leave you for an hour or two." Deanna threw a pillow at her; on another laugh, Emily threw it back. "Seems a shame to sell it, now that it's really yours. Especially since you have no idea how much I envied you, getting to live out here. All this space. All this..." Emily glanced around, sighing. *"Quiet."*

Deanna snorted. "I think the word you're looking for is *solitude*."

"What's wrong with that?"

"Nothing. In measured doses. Twenty-four/seven, however..." Her shoulders bumped. "But in any case, it's not all mine, remember? Besides, what on earth would I do with it?" And no, she had no intention of telling her cousin about her father's "plan." "And my half of the sale will go a long way toward taking care of this little girl until she's not so little anymore."

"But it's your heritage—"

"I'm not a rancher, Em. And did you hear what I said?"

"Then let Josh do his ranching thing and you could open a gallery. Taos isn't that far, right?"

"And where on earth did that come from?"

"Oh, I don't know...maybe from the eleventy billion

conversations we've had about it?" Emily grabbed a down pillow and hugged it to her middle. "You've got the eye, that's not even a question. And you know that's what you want to do."

"Eventually, sure," Deanna said, tamping down a spurt of something that felt more like panic than she wanted to admit. "In DC, maybe. Or some other city with an actual population. In New Mexico—?"

"Only it would be a helluva lot easier to start one out here than in a big city, wouldn't it?"

"Except without selling the ranch, how on earth would I do that? Even here. It's not as if your parents would bankroll me, is it? I didn't think so," she said at her cousin's sigh. "And anyway… I'm not nearly ready to take on my own gallery. And I don't know when I will be. So…"

"Fine, so maybe the logistics need some tweaking. The timing. But honey…" Emily ditched the pillow to reach for Deanna's hand, all those soft brown waves tumbling over her shoulders. "It's perfectly obvious you need a change. Because you're not happy in DC. And you haven't been in a long time."

"Cripes, Em—I was just dumped—"

"Yes, I know," her cousin said gently. "And you're pregnant. But you weren't happy before Phillippe, either." Her mouth twisted. "Or *during* Phillippe, for that matter."

"I never said—"

"You never had to. I know you, Dee. And I know…" Sitting straight again, Emily bit her bottom lip for a moment before saying, "You were…dazzled by Phillippe. Not that anyone would blame you, God knows.

Older, charming…the man is pretty damned dazzling. A douchecanoe, but dazzling. But obviously what you had with him…it wasn't real. And be honest—did you ever really trust him? Completely?"

Blinking away the sting in her eyes, Deanna sagged back in the chair, half smiling when the cat jumped up on the arm to give her a penetrating look. *Yeah, can't wait to hear how you answer* that *one.* And if this had been anyone other than Emily, or if her defenses hadn't been worn to nubs, she might've taken offense. But how could she, since it wasn't as if she hadn't asked herself the same thing a hundred times since the breakup? The thing was, though…

"Yes," she said, a tear slipping down her cheek. Emily plucked a tissue out of the little square box on the nightstand and handed it over. "I did trust him. And that was my mistake. Like you said, I was dazzled. And so, so flattered that he thought…" She blew her nose, then let out a strangled little laugh. "Okay, that I *thought* he thought I was…special."

"Oh, jeez, Dee…" Emily got off the bed to kneel in front of her, taking both Deanna's hands in hers, soggy tissue and all. "You *are* special. He was the jerk. Obviously."

"Then why couldn't I see that? Why couldn't I…" She blew out a breath. "How do I know I won't make the same mistake again?"

Now she noticed her cousin's eyes were wet, too. But instead of spewing more platitudes, Emily only got to her knees to pull Deanna into her arms, rubbing her back when she finally let the tears come.

* * *

One of the problems with doing a good deed, Josh thought on Thanksgiving night after most everybody had left and he found Deanna in the kitchen chowing down on the remains of Val's pumpkin cheesecake pie, was that you never knew what the consequences of that good deed might be. Or when it might come back to bite you in the butt. In this case, the good deed being getting Dee's cousin here, the consequences being Emily's talking his ear off on the long, *long* drive back to Albuquerque yesterday morning. Yeah, he strongly suspected Dee would kill her cousin if she'd known how loose-lipped she'd been.

Of course, it was obvious Emily was only worried about Dee, so he couldn't exactly take issue with her lack of discretion. Especially since God forbid Dee would ever open up to him. These days, anyway—

"Oh!" she said, catching him and Thor watching her. Well, Josh was watching her, the dog was most likely watching food disappear into her mouth. "You're still here!"

"I am."

With a sheepish grin, she waved her fork at the mangled pie. "So come keep me from making a total pig of myself."

See, that was the thing, Josh mused as he dug another fork out of the "everyday" drawer and sat next to her, the dog joining them as though he'd been issued a personal invitation. As he'd already noticed, Dee wasn't a bitcher. Not anymore, at least. Although if half of what Emily had said was true, the woman had more than enough to bitch about.

And whether he was still mellow from being stuffed to the gills, or simply couldn't face returning to his empty house—since his parents had taken all the grandkids for the night—suddenly the thought of sharing a pie with the woman who'd once been his best friend sounded like a damn fine idea. He also supposed, despite his earlier reluctance, they needed to address the business about her father's will, if for no other reason than to clear the air. Move on.

After pouring himself a glass of milk, Josh sat at a right angle to Dee, smiling when she inched the pie closer to him. By his knee, Thor whimpered.

"You don't like the crust?" he said, noticing she'd eaten the filling right up to the ruffled edge.

"Not really much of a crust person. Have at it."

"Done," he said, breaking off a big chunk. His sister-in-law used butter in her crusts, so they melted in your mouth like the world's best cookie. Although he shared with the dog, just to be fair. "Don't tell my mother, but your turkey? Best I've ever eaten."

Forking another bite into her mouth, Deanna burped out a little laugh. Her eyes were practically glowing tonight, like maybe she was feeling pretty mellow herself. "Thanks. I got the recipe online someplace. It was brined overnight in apple cider and all sorts of spices and stuff. Although if you hadn't've put it in the oven for me it wouldn't've happened."

"Glad to be of service."

Smiling slightly, Dee sucked on her fork for a moment, then set it in the plate and leaned back, her arms crossed over the bump.

"You done?" Josh asked. Hopefully.

"My mouth says no, but my stomach has other ideas. It's a little crowded in there. So it's all yours." Thor laid his chin on Josh's knee, and Dee laughed, then sighed. "And we need to talk, don't we?"

"About?"

"Why Dad left the house to both of us."

Even though she'd spoken softly, there was no missing the edge to her voice. Wasn't directed at him, though, he didn't think.

"I agree." Josh took a swallow of milk, then shoved in another bite. "What'd my dad tell you?"

Her mouth twisted. "That my father wanted to 'fix things.' The implication being, that he was sorry he broke us up—even though we weren't really 'together'—by sending me away. And now…" She shrugged, then almost laughed. "God, I can't even say it."

Because, Josh assumed, the whole thing was too preposterous to even consider. Of course.

"If it makes you feel any better," he said, matching her position as he chewed, "your father sure as hell never mentioned his *plan*, if that's what it was, to me. And two, since it's not actually a condition of the inheritance—which probably wouldn't stand up in court, anyway—I think we're good to keep on the way we are. Or, aren't."

After a good two, three seconds of steady staring, Dee finally nodded. "That's what I figured."

"So your dad never said anything to you, either?"

"Not a word." Frowning, she stroked her hand over her belly—he could see the baby moving underneath her sweater—then released a breath that was more laugh than sigh. "You don't think...oh, this is crazy—"

"What?"

"What if *your* father made it up? Because *he'd* like to see us get together?"

"What?"

She shrugged. "Just a thought."

"If a totally off-the-wall one. Because Dad...no," Josh said, shaking his head. "In any case, even if he did, neither one of us is...well. It just wouldn't work, that's all. For so many reasons."

"*So* many," she said, nodding. "So we can just forget about all of that, right?"

"Absolutely."

Dee gave him a funny smile, then picked up the fork again, only to wince, her other hand going to her back. Josh frowned.

"You okay?"

"Probably on my feet too much today. Nothing a hot bath won't fix. And a good night's sleep. Although not holding out much hope for that. And why is your face all pinched like that?"

"Because I don't like the idea of you being here by yourself."

"Um... I've been alone since Gus left?"

"And you're not getting *less* pregnant, are you?" He tapped his fingers on the table, then pointed at her. "So Austin and I are moving over here tomorrow."

"Excuse me—"

He got to his feet. "Actually, make that tonight."

"Now hold on, buster—"

"Yeah? What? You gonna tell me I can't move into my own house?"

That got her, apparently. "Oh. Well. No, of course not. But—"

"Don't worry, not gonna encroach on your space."

An actual eye roll preceded, "What I meant was, I don't want to put you out on my account." She plucked her phone off the table, wagged it at him. "That's why God made these handy little devices."

"And you've clearly forgotten how sketchy the service can get up here. Especially if the weather's bad. And there's no landline at my place. At least if I'm here I can hear you scream when you go into labor."

She gawked at him for a long moment, then burst into laughter. "One, there will be no screaming—"

"Yeah, ask Mom how that works out for most of her patients," he said, which got a glower in response.

"And *two*," she said, "unless you're planning on gluing yourself to my side, whether or not we have cell service when the time comes is moot. So thanks for the offer, it's very sweet. But I'll be fine. Really."

His arms still crossed over his chest, Josh narrowed his eyes, trying to decide which path to take as he watched that stubborn little mouth. Oh, sure, he was well aware that sometimes the best thing was to step back and let a gal make her own decisions. He wasn't a total moron. But neither was he gonna let pride—hers more than his, he thought—get in the way of doing what was smart. And wouldn't it be nice, at least once in his life, to be around a woman who'd just let him be a man, for the love of God? To be protective like his daddy had taught all his sons they were supposed to be?

Of course the irony was that his mother wasn't exactly a delicate little flower, either. This was not a woman who freaked out and called her man to come rescue her from spiders and snakes and bears and such. On the other hand, his father had enough White Knight genes coursing through his veins for three people. So Josh wondered how Mom and Dad had worked that particular little issue out.

But what his parents had or had not done wasn't the issue. What Josh was going to do, however, was. Whether Dee was on board or not. "This isn't about me being 'sweet,' or whatever you want to call it. It's about common sense. Besides which, Mom said I should keep an eye on you." A sort-of lie, but whatever worked, he wasn't proud.

Judging from the ravine gouged between her eyebrows, he guessed there was some pretty intense wrestling going on underneath those spikes. She picked up her fork again, even though the pie was long gone. As long as she wasn't planning on using it on him, he was good.

"It's just…" A breath left her lungs. "It wasn't until this last…fiasco that it occurred to me that…" She sighed again. "That all my life I've looked to some man or other to take care of me. Make the decisions for me. And I finally realized if I ever expected to actually be an adult someday I had to start thinking for myself. Taking care of myself. Instead of the easy way out. Whatever Dad's reasons for sending me away, the fact remains that in his attempt to rescue me, to keep me safe, he kept me from learning how to handle…life."

"But you've been on your own for how long in DC?"

"In reality? Not so much. God, Aunt Margaret and Uncle John were even worse than Dad. They wouldn't even let me live on campus, for pity's sake. So when I finally worked up the gumption to move into my own place after graduation—and they were not pleased, believe me—I guess the freedom sort of went to my head. And I made some bad choices." One side of her mouth lifted. "Although at least they were my choices."

"I take it we're talking about Phillippe?"

"And did you not catch the plural, there? Choic*es*. You are looking at a serial screwup. At least when it comes to picking men. Although the irony was that, after some of the dirtwads I'd dated? I felt like I'd won the jackpot with Phillippe. Because he was all urbane and crap, I guess," she said on a humorless chuckle. "A *man* instead of a boy. Someone who'd actually look at *me* when we went out to dinner instead of his cell phone. Of course the problem was I was so naive I didn't realize what a fake he was."

"We've all been there, Dee."

"Maybe. Except…" She grimaced at her belly before once more lifting her gaze to Josh's. "Some of us get taken in more than others."

At that, Josh had to laugh. "And it's about the cute four-year-old I live with? I love the kid to death, you know that. But he wasn't 'supposed' to happen, either. So you don't exactly have the market cornered on stupid."

"And you do realize you're probably the only person in the world who could say that to me and live?"

"Only echoing your words, darlin'," he said, and she sighed.

"Even so…" Her mouth twisted again. "What became really clear to me, after Phillippe dropped his little bombshell and winged back to his wife and kidlets in the French countryside, is that it's way past time I learn to love my own company. I don't mean living by myself—I can do that, no problem. I mean, really being okay with not being part of a couple. Or defining myself by my relationships. Or expecting someone else to rescue me when things get tough."

"Wow. You've been thinking about this a lot, huh?"

Her hand passed over her belly. "Ever since the stick turned pink. Although to be honest the seeds were planted a while ago. Just took them some time to germinate." Her eyes glittered. "I want to be tough, you know? And I want, more than anything in the world, to be an example to this little girl. For her to be the ballsiest kid in nursery school," she said, and Josh smiled.

Only to sober a moment later. "So let me get this straight—me wanting to move in is somehow a threat to *you* wanting to be your own woman?"

Dee blew a short laugh through her nose. "Woman, hell. *Person*." She finally put down the fork. Thank God. "You know what's funny? When we were kids, what I most hated about living out here was how cut off from the rest of the world I was. How…incomplete I felt. Or at least, how incomplete my life felt. As if I knew there was more 'out there,' even if I didn't know what that was. Now I realize it's only when we stop being afraid of being alone that we find completeness the only place we ever really can—within ourselves."

Josh frowned. "And that's way too heavy for a simple country boy like me." Even though, if he thought about it for longer than two seconds, she was right.

"It's true. Although don't kid yourself, bud—" Her mouth curved. "There is nothing even remotely simple about you. There never was."

"That supposed to be a compliment?"

Dee angled her head, her eyes narrowing slightly, like she was studying him. "It's just…you. Who you are." She hesitated, then said, "For what it's worth? You were the only thing about here I regretted leaving."

Her words ringing in his ears, Josh frowned some more at the decimated pie tin before asking, "Even though I was one of the people who overprotected you?"

A second or two passed before she pushed herself to her feet, a soft smile pushing at her lips. "You were there for me. And I'll always be grateful for that. For the way you put up with me. For *you*. But…"

"What?"

"Let's just say Dad wasn't coming entirely out of left field when he sent me away. Because you were definitely something I needed to be protected from."

He felt like the breath had been punched out of him. "You were always safe with me, Dee. Always. I would've never—"

"Oh, I know."

Josh's forehead creased. "Then—"

"Figure it out, country boy," she said, then started slowly out of the kitchen.

"So does that mean Austin and I can move in or not?"

One hand braced on the door frame, she turned. "It's not as if I can stop you," she said softly, but with a steely undertone that definitely made him sit up and take notice. Because damned if he didn't feel like he'd just been issued a challenge.

Even if he wasn't entirely sure what that challenge was.

Chapter 8

As she stood at the stove flipping grilled cheese sandwiches, Deanna heard, coming from the hallway, the
little boy's high-pitched giggles tangling with Josh's
pretend dinosaur roar. She smiled, despite feeling pretty
tangled up herself. About, well, everything. Josh moving in and her being stuck here and feeling like she was
about to explode and all those jumbled feelings about
her father—

"Something smells incredible," Josh said, and she
turned to see his still-giggling son clamped like a koala
bear around one calf as Josh dragged him along the
tiled floor.

"Just grilled cheese." Josh tried shaking Austin off
his leg. More giggling ensued. Deanna smiled. "And
don't look now, but there's something stuck to your leg."

"You're kidding?" All wide-eyed, Josh raised his leg enough to bump the kid's rump on the floor, making Austin laugh even harder. "I thought that leg felt awfully heavy," he said, scooping his son into his arms and growling into his neck before grinning at him. "Where'd you come from?"

"Right here!"

"You sure about that?"

"Uh-huh. You're so silly, Daddy!"

Chuckling, Josh kissed the top of Austin's head, then set him down again. "Looks like Dee's got your sandwich done. Go get up in your seat."

But as long as that let's-mess-with-Deanna's-head list was, Josh and her living under the same roof definitely topped it. Precisely because of stuff like this, watching him be unabashedly goofy with his little boy, effortlessly straddling the line between responsible adulthood and childlike innocence. No wonder Austin adored his daddy. Because it was equally obvious how much Josh adored his son.

And the more she witnessed all this mutual adoration, the more her heart ached for something that had always felt just out of reach. How tempting it was to see Josh with Austin and think, *Maybe...?*

Which is precisely why she needed to stick to her guns about claiming her own selfhood and independence and ability to make her own decisions. About ratcheting down her expectations, bringing them more in line with that thing called reality. Because her very survival depended on it. Then again, for all she knew Josh was looking at her and thinking, *Oh*, hell, *no*. For sure he was thinking *something*, if those weird glances he shot her every so often were anything to go by. So moot point, most likely.

By now Austin had scrambled into his chair, grinning up at her when she set the sandwich in front of him, cut into four triangles, crusts on the side. Another Talbot charmer in training; God help every female in the county with a beating heart. "Thank you, DeeDee!"

It'd grabbed her breath when the child started calling her that yesterday, out of the blue. No one but her mother had ever called her that.

"You're welcome, big guy," she said, ruffling his hair, then turned to see Josh grab his denim jacket off the hook by the back door, shrugging it on over a black fleece hoodie she'd like to burn, frankly.

"I won't be gone but two, two-and-a-half hours at most," he said with a brief glance to her super-sized middle. He'd sold a horse the week before, to a young barrel racer right over the Colorado border, and—as usual—was delivering the horse himself to personally check out the prospective accommodations. Although he was clearly conflicted about leaving Austin with her.

"And we've been through all this," she said, handing him a paper sack with his own sandwich, a bottle of water, a bag of chips. It wasn't much, but tonight's steak-and-potato casserole would make up for it. "It doesn't make sense taking Austin all the way to your folks when you're going in the opposite direction. And as you said, it's only for a couple of hours. The chances of my popping out a baby in that time span are slim to none. Didn't your mother teach you anything?"

"But you have her number, right? Of course you do, what am I saying? But I'll leave Thor, just in case."

In case of what? she wondered, even as she said, "I'm fine, Josh. We're all fine. And will be fine. Honestly, you'd think no pregnant woman ever had another child to look after. Right?" And she even sounded confident. Yay, her. "Besides, Val said she's coming over in a bit, so we won't even be alone for all that long. So go, get out of here."

He still hesitated—jeez—but finally walked over to Austin to drop another kiss on the boy's head before giving Deanna a funny little smile. And for a moment—not even that, a millisecond—she almost thought he was going to kiss her goodbye, too. And wasn't that totally nuts?

Then he was gone, taking what felt like half the air in the room with him. Not to mention a good chunk of her bravado. Because the only other time she'd been alone with a little kid was that day when she'd shooed Gus off, when the old man hadn't been more than a few minutes away and she knew Josh would be back soon and she hadn't been this pregnant.

Yeesh, overthinking much? she thought on a sigh, then carted her own sandwich over to the table, along with a glass of milk and a bowl of red grapes. Which Josh had specifically told her Austin wouldn't eat. Never mind the kid had eaten vegetable stew, for godssake. And loved it.

"What're those?" Austin asked, suspicion colliding with curiosity in his scrunched up face. Somehow, Deanna swallowed her laugh.

"Grapes."

"Oh. I don't like those."

"Yeah, your dad told me. That's too bad," she said,

popping one in her mouth and mentally patting herself on the back for not pushing him to take a taste. Because, for one thing, she remembered when she'd visit Aunt Margaret when she was little, and her aunt would force her to take at least two bites of everything on her plate, even if it made her gag. *Yeah, I'm looking at you, liver.* And for another, if she'd learned nothing else from five years of selling artwork, it was that you never gave the potential buyer the chance to say no.

She might've, however, made a few these-are-*so*-yummy noises as she munched.

Austin frowned at her. Then the grapes. Then her again. "Are they good?"

"Well, I like them. But I thought you said you didn't."

"Actually... I don't think I ever tasted one." Which would naturally beg the question, *Then how do you know *you* don't like them?*

"I see." Deanna tossed another grape into her mouth. Austin frowned harder.

"C'n I have one?"

Deanna looked at the grapes. "Huh. I don't know..."

"But we're supposed to share. Daddy says. Grandma, too. Please?"

Oh, God—were those *tears*? For heaven's sake, she'd only meant to see if she could get the kid to try a grape, not break his spirit. Deanna practically shoved the bowl toward him. "Of course, sweetie. I'm sorry, I was only teasing."

After shooting her a way too grown-up look, Austin twisted a grape off the cluster and took the tiniest nibble imaginable. Then he nodded. "I guess it's all right." He took another, only marginally bigger, nibble. "But it's not nice to tease."

Deanna's face flamed. "No, it's not. I'm sorry."

"It's okay," Austin said with a shrug as he finally shoved the rest of the grape into his mouth. And took another one. "Daddy said you're not used to being around little kids, so I should go easy on you."

And if she'd had any food in her own mouth, she would've choked on it. "He actually said that?"

"Uh-huh. C'n I have more milk, please?"

"Sure, sweetie." Feeling slightly dizzy, Deanna pushed herself to her feet—yes, by bracing both hands on the table and shoving with all her might—grabbed his plastic cup and lumbered to the fridge. Four, hell. Kid was sharp enough to hold office. And probably more so than most people who did—

"Knock, knock—anybody home?"

"It's Aunt Val!" Austin yelled, morphing back into a little kid as he practically fell out of his chair to streak out of the kitchen, his sneakered feet thundering down the hallway. Judging from the high-pitched jabbering that followed, Val had her two munchkins in tow. Probably why the cat, who'd been asleep in his bed beside the woodstove, took off for parts unknown. Because you never knew with toddlers. Especially that one, Deanna thought, smiling, remembering Val's youngest's non-stop energy and curiosity two days before on Thanksgiving. *And that's gonna be this one in a year or so*, she thought, and she gulped down her smile.

She was so not ready for this. That. Her.

And she should probably get over that *real* quick.

"In the kitchen," she yelled as she cleared Austin's plate, shoving in one of his leftover crusts as she trudged from table to sink, trying not to wince. But damn, her daughter had the hardest head in the history of hard heads, which Deanna prayed was not prophetic for the kind of teenager she'd be.

And maybe she should worry about knowing when to feed and change her before fretting about adolescent angst—

"Oh, my goodness—did you decorate even more?" Val said from the doorway, grinning, her long staticky hair floating around the shoulders of a denim jacket worn over a heavyweight hoodie.

"I might have a slight…problem," Deanna said, and Val laughed.

"So I see. But the house looks incredible. Even in here. That tiny tree on the buffet is seriously adorable. Although you do realize how high you've set the bar for the rest of us?"

"Sorry. But the waiting suuuucks. You guys want me to come decorate your places, just let me know."

"I might just take you up on that, considering how busy I am these days baking pies for the resort." Although Val's glowing expression said she was clearly thrilled. "Might even have to scrounge up an assistant sometime soon. Since child labor is frowned upon, go figure. But the reason we're here is…" She held up two overstuffed plastic bags. "More baby clothes, ta-da! Because there will be those days when between the urps and the poops, there aren't enough onesies in the world…hey. You okay?"

"Back," Deanna got out, pointing, and Val nodded.

"Yeah, Risa was like that. I swear if I could've

reached inside to shift her, I would've. But…" The blonde's pale brows dipped. "You sure that's all it is?"

"Unfortunately, yes. The pain is constant and dull, not—"

"Like a blowtorch to the crotch?"

Deanna burbled a little laugh, then realized that would be *her* crotch, in the not too distant future. Fun. "Is it really that bad?"

"It ain't no hayride, honey. Although at least there's a kid at the end of it. Unlike, say, acute appendicitis. And thank *God* for epidurals. So I'm guessing you pulled babysitting detail today?"

"I did. Because Josh is schlepping a horse across the border."

"Which you realize sounds vaguely illegal," Val said. "But how's it going with the kid?"

"Other than feeling like I'm keeping company with a six-hundred-year-old gnome? Fine."

"Get used to it, kids definitely say whatever they're thinking. And they think a *lot*, jeebus. Josie comes up with this stuff that regularly makes me wonder, Who *are* you?" Then she swung the bags toward the table. "So sit, sit, lemme show you what I brought—"

From the great room came shrieking. And bellowing. And giggles. And more bellowing.

"You sure it's okay to leave the kids on their own?" Deanna said, lowering herself to one of the chairs about as gracefully as an elephant with piles.

Plopping into the seat closest to Deanna, Val upended the bags on the table between them and a million wee baby things came tumbling out. "You kidding? I sometimes think Josie's a better mama at eight than

I've ever been. Kid doesn't let 'em get away with any-thing. And Austin thinks she walks on water. Any-way…" She spread out the loot, patting one particularly faded, splotched sleeper. "This stuff is not pretty. Which is why I didn't bring it to the shower. But like I said, there will be many, many times when clean and avail-able definitely trumps ugly."

Her heart crunching at her new friend's kindness, Deanna fingered a little pair of frilly socks patterned like ballet slippers. "I'd get up and give you a hug but you probably have some place to be before next week."

Chuckling, Val did the honors instead, bending over to wrap her arms around Deanna for a moment before settling again in her seat. Smoky ventured back into the kitchen, craning his head to listen down the hall before scooting away again. "But…" Deanna pressed one of the sleepers—a grayish pink with white polka dots—to her chest. "What if you need these again?" Val blushed, and Deanna gasped. "Oh, my God. You're pregnant."

"I'm *late*," the blonde whispered. "As in, way too early to announce. Which is why I backpedaled at the shower, because I was afraid to believe it myself. And nobody else knows except Levi."

Oh. Wow. Warmth spreading through her, Deanna reached for Val's hand. "I take it you're thrilled?"

A smile slowly crept across the blonde's mouth. "If it sticks? You have no idea."

"Then I am, too. And I won't breathe a word, I prom-ise."

"Thanks. And don't even worry about the stuff," Val said, waving her hand over the messy stacks on the table. "You can always give it back when Katie outgrows it, if it's even still usable at that point. Besides, it might not even be a girl…" Her eyes glistened. "There is no doubt in my mind whatsoever that Levi loves Josie and Risa every bit as much as their father did. But when I told him I might be pregnant, the look on his face…"

Now Deanna's smile felt frozen in place. Not that she wasn't delighted for Josh's brother and sister-in-law, but damned if she didn't feel cheated, that the look on *Phillippe's* face had been more a cross between panicked and furious. Still, before the self-pity demons got their clutches in her, it struck Deanna she was only the second person to know about this baby. True, she'd guessed, but Val could've kept her secret if she'd wanted to. And wasn't it crazy, how good that made her feel? How…included.

Val and the girls stuck around for maybe a half hour or so, at which point Josie—and Val—insisted on taking Austin home with them. Even though the silence left in their wake was so profound Deanna could practically feel it. But the solitude, the stillness, also enveloped her every bit as cozily as her old shawl, which she wrapped up in before walking out onto the hacienda's garland-draped veranda. Not to mention the sparkling clear light, the crisp mountain air, on this icy afternoon.

The memories. Of other early winter days, when her mother was still alive and the house *reeked* of Christmas, when she and Josh would saddle up their horses and ride out probably farther than their parents ever realized, not even caring when their butts went numb from the cold. She certainly hadn't felt hamstrung then, had she? If anything, she remembered a kind of contentment she hadn't felt since.

The thought brought her up short. As did the rustle of wings from the top of a nearby piñon—a hawk, its harsh keen knifing the quiet, prompting Thor to jerk awake from his spot on the veranda's sun-drenched lip to bark at the bird.

She'd missed this. All of it. Dogs and hawks and the sky, dotted with great big fluffy clouds. The peace.

Her breath catching in her throat, Deanna shut her eyes, letting the admission wash over her. Embracing it, even if she didn't have the foggiest notion what to do with it. Much as she still had no idea why she'd as good as admitted to Josh two days ago what she'd felt when they were kids. Seriously, why even bring up something neither one of them could have done anything about then? That still had absolutely nothing to do with *now*.

Never mind that she'd barely slept the past few nights, since he and Austin moved in. Although who could sleep with an octopus inside her? So much for the baby settling down once the head was engaged. Except the thing was, Octobaby's hyperactivity also gave Deanna way too much time to think about stuff. Okay, Josh. More to the point, how manly and funny and caring and crazy he was. The same as she remembered, only the grown-up version, which was proving a whole lot harder to ignore than she'd thought. Hoped.

How her poor sleep-deprived hormones had clearly made it their mission to torment her with images of Josh sleeping right down the hall. Or, far worse, wondering what his reaction would be if she asked him to give her a back rub. Yeah, those hormones were being stinkers of the highest order. Although would somebody please explain to her why in the *hell* she'd feel this hot to trot when she couldn't even walk from her bedroom to the john without getting winded?

Jeezy Pete, her thoughts were whistling through her brain like the wind through the trees.

Thor nudged Deanna's hand, his ice-cold nose making her jump. Chuckling, she bent over to give him some loving, a move which made her back twinge. She ignored it. Tried to, anyway. Really, she should waddle back inside, put away all the clothes Val had brought. Except then she'd think about Josh putting together the crib, or horsing around with his son, or thanking her for making dinner…

Sighing at her own silliness, Deanna and the dog trudged out to the barn—well, she trudged, he did more of a fox-trot—where her old horse was stabled, thinking maybe she'd let her out to enjoy the air. Or she could at least open a stall, right?

The cold only made the barn smell sweeter—Josh was meticulous about keeping the stalls as clean as possible—of hay and horse, overlaid with the slight tang of piñon smoke that permeated the air this time of year. Starlight immediately came over when Deanna got closer to the stall, the space bigger than her bedroom in her "fun"-sized DC apartment. Her father had always taken damn good care of his horses, too, another poignant memory that only spiked her grief. For things she'd had and lost, for things that had never been hers. Not really. Not entirely.

For things she'd like to be hers, even if she had no earthly idea how to get them.

"Hey, girl," she crooned to the mare, who laid her muzzle in the crook of Deanna's shoulder, her horsey scent intensifying the yearning. All she wanted, she realized, was home. But where was that? *What* was that—

"Oh!" she breathed out on a short gasp when the twinging suddenly morphed into something…different. Releasing the horse, she stepped away to grasp the top of the stall door and bend forward, trying to ease the pressure in her back…

She felt a weird, painless prick…followed by roughly five thousand gallons of water rushing down her legs.

Well, crap.

"Stay calm," she muttered to herself, fumbling for her phone. Never mind she was shaking so much she could barely see it. "It's all good, nothing to worry about…" She took a breath. Then another. Then looked at the phone again.

Focus, focus, it's okay…

Except for one tiny problem:

There was no signal.

Josh had been back on the road maybe twenty minutes when his sister-in-law's call came through on his truck's Bluetooth device.

"Hey, Val," he said, keeping an eagle eye on the rusted-out clunker a couple hundred yards up the road. A light snow had begun to fall. No biggie, though. "What's up—"

"I've been trying to get you for the past fifteen minutes," she said, and his heart went ba-da-*boom* against his ribs.

"Sorry, signal's pretty sketchy up here—"

"So Deanna hasn't called you? Well, if she couldn't get through—"

"Val! What's going on?"

"Probably nothing, really. But when the kids and I were out at the Vista a little bit ago she was complaining about her back hurting."

Josh relaxed. Some. "Yeah, she's been doing that a lot. Since before Thanksgiving."

"That's what she said. Still. I've got a feeling."

"But you didn't think she was in labor."

"Then? No. I wouldn't've left if I thought she was. Except then I got home, and…" He heard a soft, slightly nervous laugh. "Sorry, I'm probably sounding crazy."

"Not hardly," Josh said, knowing from experience that when a woman said she had a "feeling," a smart man paid attention. "I take it you tried calling her?"

"Of course. Only she's not answering, either."

Damn. Josh glowered at the dude ahead of him, moseying along the road like he owned it. And of course this was the stretch where it was nearly impossible to pass. Especially with a stupid horse trailer hitched to his truck. "What about my mom? EMS?"

"Billie was about an hour away from the Vista when I called, she's on her way. And we're out of luck with the ambulance, they're out on another call." Unfortunately one of the major disadvantages to living in the boonies was that small-town volunteer emergency crews weren't always readily available. "And I'd go back over, but I've got the kids. Including yours—"

"No, no—it's okay. When did you last see her?"

"Maybe forty-five minutes? Oh, and it's started to snow."

Josh sucked in a steadying breath, releasing it on a rush of gratitude when the slowpoke finally turned off the road and he could step on the gas. Only a few miles left before the highway.

"I'm about a half hour out. At the most," he said, hoping to hell no state trooper was lurking in the bushes. Because right now the speed limit was only a suggestion. Unless the snow decided not to play nice…

"Keep trying to get her, and I will, too. But I'm sure she's fine," he said, more to reassure himself than Val. But the instant he disconnected the call he started praying harder than he ever had in his life.

And God laughed and ripped open the sky, instantly coating the countryside in white.

The first contraction hit while Deanna was still staring at her phone in disbelief, the pain almost enough to distract her from the absurdity of standing in soaking-wet leggings, in a freezing barn, with no other human being for miles. One of those things she'd probably find funny, ten, twenty years down the road.

At the moment, however…

At least, she thought when the pain let up enough *to* think, she'd be able reach someone on the landline.

Back at the house.

Way, *way*, back at the house.

That is, if she didn't die of hypothermia first, she mused as she inched out of the barn and that first wave of ice-cold air smacked the bejeebers out of her. At precisely the moment another contraction viced her lower belly like a sonuvabitch, pretty much bringing anything even vaguely resembling forward motion to a dead halt. And…wait.

Snow?

Okay, not exactly a blizzard, but still. Judging from the bigger, badder clouds rapidly moving in from the north, blizzarding was definitely a possibility. Soon. As in, probably sooner than she was going to make it to the house. Honestly, she didn't know whether to laugh or cry—or maybe both, what the hell—but since one was inappropriate and the other self-defeating, she nixed emotion altogether.

And, since she couldn't move, anyway, checked her phone. One bar. She'd take it. Only now, feeling like a jailbird who only got a single call, she was momentarily stymied as to who she should call first. A quandary she pondered as she took advantage of the break between contractions to continue her agonizingly slow trek toward the house, Thor now snapping at snowflakes as though he'd never seen them before—

"Jeebus!" she yelled when the phone rang, making her jump out of her goose-bumpy skin.

"Thank God," Josh said when she answered. "You okay?"

"Not even remotely."

"Wrong answer."

"Tough." Deanna looked up at the sky, which was now spitting snow in earnest. "Where are you?"

"Close."

"Woman in labor, here. Need specifics."

"Ten minutes, maybe—"

"It's snowing," she said, inanely, holding out her hand to catch a few flakes, like she used to do as a child.

"I know. You'll probably want to crank up the heat. How far apart are the contractions?"

"You don't wanna know."

She heard him sigh. "What're we talking? Every ten minutes? Five?"

"Um…two? Ish?"

The next word out of his mouth was colorful, to say the least. "I thought it wasn't supposed to happen that fast."

"Yeah, well, this kid clearly doesn't know from 'supposed to.' But the good news is…" Finally, *finally*, she made it to the veranda, which under other circumstances she might've knelt down to kiss. Although under other circumstances, she wouldn't have wanted to. She stopped, her eyes squeezing shut as she grabbed the nearest post to hang on.

"The good news is…?"

"I'm not…in the barn…anymore…"

Silence. Then: "Hang on, honey… I'm almost there…"

But she didn't answer him, because that blowtorch thing? Yep.

Too bad the heat wouldn't dry out her pants.

Chapter 9

Over his hammering heart, Josh desperately tried not to think about how he might have to deliver this baby. So of course that was the only thing he could think about. Sure, he knew all about foaling horses, but for the most part his participation had been limited to watching. Or arriving on the scene after the blessed event had already happened. Horses were efficient like that. And since Jordan hadn't bothered to let him know Austin was coming until he'd already arrived, he hadn't even witnessed his own son's birth.

And not seeing his mother's pickup in front of the house wasn't exactly making him calmer. Although rising to the occasion was clearly his lot in life, so...

The trailer rattled like thunder when he slammed into the dirt drive. Thor bounced up to his door, barking his head off. *Geez, human, what took you so long? Lady person foaling, here, get the lead out!* Josh tumbled out of the truck, the dog beating him to the door.

"Dee?" he bellowed, his voice echoing off the great room's rafters. "Where are you, honey?"

"Bathroom!"

Hers, he assumed, his boots skidding on the tile when he hit her doorway. Breathing hard, he stopped at the entrance to her bath, where she stood in the tub, of all places.

"I'm here," he said…and Dee took one look at him and completely lost it.

"Hey, hey…" Climbing into the tub with her, what the hell, Josh wrapped her close and kicked his own panic to the curb. "It's okay, honey, it's okay…"

"Those are t-tears of re-relief, doofus," she said, hiccupping a little laugh as she scrubbed her face, then tried to push away. "Eww, I'm all wet—"

"So I noticed," he said, which got a shaky little smile before she grabbed his arms like she was about to fall off a cliff. The moan started low and soft, only to rapidly escalate into something like out of a horror movie.

"Look at me, honey," Josh said, ignoring his own quaking stomach when her eyes squinched shut. "Dee! Look at me!"

"Can't," she panted out. "Hurts."

"I know, baby. Okay, I can guess," he said when she shot him a death glare. "But the breathing will help. Trust me."

Somehow, she obeyed, and he hooked his gaze in hers and started breathing slowly, deeply, encouraging her to follow his example, even as it nearly killed him to see how much pain she was in. How scared she was. And not, he didn't think, only about giving birth.

And at that moment, he hated the jerkwad who'd done this to her with the heat of a thousand suns. The jerkwad who obviously didn't give a damn about her or his daughter.

Even stronger than the heat, though, feelings Josh couldn't even identify rippled through him, that the woman the jerkwad had done this *to* had chosen to have this baby, raise this baby, *love* this baby…

That Dee had more courage than the jerkwad could even dream about, a thought that made a knot swell in Josh's throat.

After what seemed like a year, the contraction let up, and Josh figured he had a pretty narrow opportunity to get her someplace other than the damn tub to have this baby.

Which begged the question, "Why are you standing in the tub, anyway?"

"Trying to figure out how to get these wet pants off. Seemed as logical a place as any. Except now…" She shrugged. He got it.

"You okay with me doing the honors?"

"You really have to ask? And how do you know about breathing?"

"Mom has these movies, Levi and I got curious one day. Okay. I won't look, I promise."

"Believe me—right now, I do not care who sees what. I just want this kid out of me."

"We can do that," he said, proud of how confident he sounded, even as worry replaced the pain in those big brown eyes.

"I'm not gonna make it to the birthing center, am I?"

"That would be my guess," he said, crouching to help her remove the soggy pants. "Roads are already pretty slick."

"And it was such a great birth plan, too," she muttered, and he smiled.

"Although the good news is my mother's on her way."

Dee's forehead bunched as her hands tightened around his shoulders. "What? How? When—"

"Val." He tugged as gently as he could, but the only experience he'd had with getting wet bottoms off a wet bottom was with skinny little boys. Not curvy non-boys. With giant, baby-filled bellies. "She had an inkling something was going on, so she called you after she left, to check. But—" the soaked pants landed with a plop in the bottom of the tub "—you weren't answering your phone. So she called me. And my mother. And apparently half the county. Okay, put your arms around my neck and hang on," he said, scooping her up into his arms before she had a chance to realize those arms were against her bare bottom. And for him to fully register how heavy a full-term pregnant woman was. Damn.

His phone went off again, buzzing against his chest. "Get it out of my pocket," he said, trying not to grunt as he carried Dee over to her bed.

"It's your mother."

"Who you probably need to talk to more right now than I do."

"Good point. Hey, Billie," she said as Josh lowered her to the bed as gently as his muscles would let him. "Uh-huh…yep, he made it…a little while ago…every two minutes, maybe…no, not yet." Sitting on the edge of the bed, she handed him the phone. "She wants to talk to you."

"So the roads are total crap," Mom said in his ear as Dee's face crumpled again. Josh mimed steady breathing, but she wasn't paying a whole lot of attention. "Although I'm doing my best to get there. How close do you think she is—"

"Oh! *Oh!*" Dee grabbed for his hand, nearly cutting off his circulation. "Oh, *man*, do I want to push!"

"Never mind, I heard. Okay, listen to me. It could still be a while yet. Although considering how fast things are already moving, maybe not." Yeah, not encouraging. "So put your phone on speaker," Mom said, "I'm gonna talk you through it. Josh? You hear me?"

He did as she asked. "Got it. Okay, on speaker now."

"Good. Now go get a bunch of towels to put underneath Dee and wash your hands. Y'all got a baby to welcome into the world!"

At Dee's halfhearted giggle, something shifted inside Josh, replacing the last scraps of fear with something far more powerful. More important. He thought about all times in her life men had let her down or abandoned her or shut her out or whatever.

Damned if his name was about to get added to that list.

Sitting on the edge of the bed, he reached out to cup her jaw, earning him a very startled glance.

"Let's do this, sweetheart," he said, and her trembling smile broke his heart.

Listening to the snow softly snick against the bedroom window, Deanna shifted the solid little bundle in her arms to kiss her silky forehead for probably the hundredth time since her birth two hours before.

She couldn't stop looking at her perfect little daughter.

She couldn't stop thinking about Josh.

But most of all she couldn't unknot her thoughts long enough to figure out which of them were worth hanging on to and which needed to be ditched. Like cleaning out the closet in her head.

Especially now, when Josh sat on the edge of the bed, softly chuckling when Katie screwed up her tiny face, her mouth puckering into an itty bitty O. Billie had finally arrived an hour after Katie did, basically to "tidy up," she said, since the birth had been textbook perfect, and was now in the kitchen tending to that casserole Deanna hadn't gotten around to making. But right here, right now, it was just the three of them cocooned in her bedroom while the out-of-nowhere storm continued its assault on the landscape outside.

As her memories of this amazing experience—of Josh—assaulted her from within.

He'd been her rock through the whole thing, not even flinching when the sensation of pushing out a cannonball might've made her scream, a little. Okay, a lot. Not to mention childbirth was a messy business. Hadn't even fazed him. Then again, he was a rancher, the man knew from messy. Also, she supposed this was fitting payback for the time she'd had to mop up *his* blood after he'd whacked his head on an unseen tree branch when they'd been out riding. Gosh, she'd forgotten all about that. How old had she been? Twelve? Thirteen—

"I've seen you make faces exactly like that," he said,

and she looked at him looking at the baby, her little spidery fingers curled around his index finger, and thought, *Hell.*

"Hey," Josh said gently, his gaze shifting to hers. "What's with the tears?"

"Hormones, probably," Deanna said, trying to smile, even as a whole new slew of feelings threatened to take her under. Because in that sweet, tough gaze she saw... everything. Everything she'd ever wanted, everything she didn't dare let herself want. Because what good ever came from looking to someone else to fill the blanks in your life? Your heart. Even someone who'd been there for her in a way no man, no *one*, ever had.

Even if for only this moment—

"I think I'm transfixed," he said, and Deanna smiled.

"Tell me about it."

Grinning, Josh propped his fist against the mattress on the other side of Deanna's legs, cupping the baby's capped head with his free hand. A hand that gripped reins and tickled little boys and hammered fence rails into place, banged up and scarred and callused, the nails jagged. *Real.* Like the rest of him—

"I missed this with Austin," he said quietly.

Deanna swallowed, then frowned. "How old was he when you first saw him?"

"Two weeks? Something like that."

"You're kidding?"

"Nope. Apparently Jordan had been having second thoughts."

"About?"

"Including me in our child's life," he said, tenderly

stroking Katie's downy cheek. "Until she realized she was in way over her head, trying to do it by herself."

Deanna felt her face warm. "Some women can, you know."

His gaze flicked to hers, then away. "Some women, yeah. Not Jordan. Of course I had no idea when she showed up with this wailing baby that 'not doing it all by herself' would eventually turn into 'not doing any of it.' Although to be truthful I wasn't surprised. Gal definitely wasn't the maternal type."

"And you are," Deanna said, and Josh chuckled.

"Apparently so. Still. For a long time it irked me, that I missed seeing my son's entrance. That Jordan stole that from me."

"You still angry with her?"

"For leaving?" His head wagged. "Not so much anymore. Although I was at first. For Austin's sake, though, not mine. Frankly it was a relief, not having to deal with all that negativity." He sat up straighter to face her, his half smile masking his pain even less than his words. "But people are who they are. No sense hanging on to bad feelings about stuff you can't change. *People* you can't change." A soft laugh puffed through his lips. "I may've been stupid as hell, but at least I learned something from the experience."

"Which was?"

"To be a lot more careful about who I get involved with. Making sure we're on the same page about stuff. Or at least compatible. Honesty, too. That's a biggie. If not *the* biggie. If Jordan and I had been up front with each other from the beginning…" He humphed. "Of course I wouldn't have Austin, so there is that."

Deanna was quiet for a long moment, watching her sleeping daughter. Thinking about what Josh had just said about compatibility. Being on the same page.

Honesty.

"I'm glad you were here," she said softly, her gaze flicking over the freshly painted wall, now devoid of Lorelai's and Rory's grinning faces. "Not just grateful, I don't mean that. Although I am. But…" Her insides melted at his slightly puzzled smile. "But that you were here to share this with me. That it *was* you."

And she meant it. Sure, it hurt that neither of her parents were still alive to meet their granddaughter. But not once, not even for a split second, had she found herself regretting Phillippe's absence. Not even right after the baby's birth and it was Josh, not the baby's father, wrapping her up and putting her on Deanna's chest. That it was Josh grinning like hot stuff at the two of them, not the man who'd gotten her pregnant. Yes, what'd happened with Phillippe was ten kinds of wrong, no getting around that. And she doubted she'd ever forgive herself for being so naive. But Josh being here couldn't have been more right.

Another second or so passed before he said, "I'm glad I was here, too. But not nearly as glad that you didn't have this kid in the barn."

Deanna laughed. "*You're* glad? Believe me, the Mary-in-the-stable scenario was definitely not on my agenda. Hey, buddy," she said when Thor cautiously clicked into the room, his tail wagging when he came over to the bed, sniffing. He'd stayed well out of the way until now, most likely because her yelling had scared the bejeebers out of the poor dog. "It's okay, puppy, come see the new person. That's right, come on…"

When the dog inched closer, Josh carefully scooped Katie out of Deanna's arms—and yes, she felt the loss immediately—to lower the baby so the dog could check her out.

"Whaddya think, guy? Cute, huh?"

The baby squeaked and the dog cocked his head… then bowed, butt in air, and barked, his tail madly wagging.

"Sorry, dude," Josh said, chuckling as he gave the baby back to Deanna, his breath soft in her hair, his scent making her heart stutter. "She's too little to play." The dog barked again. "Yes, seriously—"

"So how're we doing in here?" Billie said from the doorway.

"Good." Deanna smiled down at her daughter, her heart turning over in her chest. "Really good."

"I can see that. Josh, why don't you take little bit for a moment so I can check out mama? Dinner will be ready in a few minutes."

"Glad to," he said, gathering Katie in his arms again, and Deanna watched Josh leave the room with her daughter, her heart constricting at how carefully he held her, his gentle smile as he talked silly to her the same way he did with his son. Billie sat on the edge of the bed to take Deanna's blood pressure, nodding in apparent approval at the reading.

"See? All you needed to do was give birth."

Deanna chuckled, then sighed. "Your son was… amazing."

"No surprise there. Boy never has been shy about stepping up, doing whatever needed doing."

"Like with Austin, you mean?"

"With anything." She stuffed the blood pressure cuff back in the bag she'd left earlier on the nightstand. "He even helped with Granville's nursing care, there at the end. Before poor Gus keeled over from exhaustion. Spent every night with him, sleeping in the chair beside your daddy's bed."

"He did? I didn't know that."

"That doesn't surprise me, either. Okay, let me just check to make sure everything's as it should be, then Josh can bring your daughter back…"

A minute later—all was well—Deanna repositioned herself and said, "How is it even possible to love something—some*one*—that much?"

Billie gave her a weird look. "Funny how that happens, huh? Now let's get some food in you, mama…"

A few days later, Josh came through the back door after picking up Austin from his folks' house to find Dee standing at the stove with the baby strapped to her front, stirring something that smelled like angels had been cooking. As usual her phone was docked to the Bluetooth adapter on the counter, filling the kitchen with a huge chorus belting out some Christmas carol. As was she, pausing every so often to "conduct" with the wooden spoon. She stopped midnote, though, when Austin giggled, grinning for the boy when he ran over to her to wrap his arms around her hips.

Her expression soft as an angel's, she cupped Austin's snow-flecked hair. "You have a good day, cutie-pie?"

"Uh-huh," he said, then pulled away to stand on tip-toe, trying to see into the pot. "What's that?"

"Soup," she said, gently tugging him away from the stove. "With all kinds of yummy things in it."

"Like what?"

"Oh…chicken and corn and carrots. Among other things. Whatever I could find. There's also corn bread. And brownies for dessert."

Austin made a face. "With nuts?"

Dee laughed. "Only on top. I'll be happy to eat yours if you don't want 'em."

"'Kay—"

"But only if you try the soup," Josh said, hanging up his barn coat on the hook by the door. "And go wash your hands."

"But I washed 'em at Grandma's!"

"When?"

Screwing up his face, he scratched his head. "Before lunch?"

"Then you get to wash them again. Go on, scoot."

Sighing mightily, the kid slogged off to the half bath and Josh came nearer to get a better smell. Of dinner, Dee, whatever. Yeah, the soup wasn't the only thing getting stirred, that was for sure. And wasn't it crazy, how much he wanted to slip his arm around her waist, nestle his chin on her shoulder to see the baby. Who was sound asleep, all cuddled next to mama like that.

Instead he settled for grabbing a clean spoon out of the drawer and snitching a sample taste.

"Hey!"

"Damn, this is good."

Even though she didn't look at him, he could see the

smile toying with her mouth. "Thanks. Like I said, it's just stuff I found in the pantry or whatever. You can make soup out of pretty much anything."

"*You* can make soup out of pretty much anything. But might I remind you, you just gave birth three days ago?"

The look she shot him had *Seriously?* written all over it. "It's dinner, Josh. Not plowing the back forty. I think I'm good. Also I was bored out of my ever-loving mind. Newborn babies aren't exactly great conversationalists."

Smiling, Josh cupped Katie's little head, cocooned in a knit cap barely big enough to cover his fist, a move that brought him even closer to her mother. A move that apparently made Dee suck in a sharp little breath, like he was breaching some boundary or other. Although if you asked him any and all boundaries had already been breached three nights ago when he'd helped guide this little person into the world.

But, you know. Women.

"I have news," she said quietly, staring at the bubbling soup, and Josh removed his hand, stuffing it in his pocket. "Oh?"

"I sort of got a job offer today."

"I thought you had a job."

"Okay, a better job offer." She rattled the lid back on the soup pot. "Much better, actually."

Josh frowned. "What? Where?"

Finally her gaze met his. "From another gallery in DC. One of those crazy things, someone knew someone who'd attended one of our showings, of an artist who was apparently very appreciative of my work, and long story short…totally out of the blue, this gallery owner emailed me, asking me if I'd consider coming to work for him. As in, big-time gallery owner, someone who showcases artists who've *already* arrived."

Quashing what felt ridiculously like disappointment, Josh gripped the counter edge behind him and said evenly, "You gonna take it?"

Dee turned to reach for soup bowls in the cupboard next to the stove. "Aside from the salary, which is already twice what I'm making, the commission potential…it's really good. Theoretically I could make as much from the sale of one work as I now do from selling three or four."

"Wow."

"I know, right? I was totally up front with him, though, said I had a new baby, wouldn't even be back until probably sometime in January, and wanted to work flexible hours." She set the bowls on the table. "He seemed fine with all of it."

And she seemed…not that excited, actually. "So… what's the problem?"

The baby squirmed; Dee palmed her daughter's head, kissed it through the hat. Then she laughed. If you could call it that. "This is absolutely the perfect fit for me. And it's mine for the taking. And yet…" Her shoulders lifted, gently bumping the baby.

"You sound like you need convincing."

That got a sigh. "Which is nuts, because the last thing I want—or need—is anybody trying to talk me into anything. Or out of it, whichever."

Josh frowned: what the hell was up with the waffling routine? But you know what? After her speech the other day about needing to figure stuff out for herself, damned if he was gonna pry. Even if it nearly killed him not to.

"So it's a good thing, then," he said, "that I'm the last person who'd do that. Since I learned a long time ago that people are gonna do what they want, anyway."

Her mouth tucked up on one side. "So basically you're no help whatsoever."

Josh crossed his arms, waiting out the mule kick to his gut. "A friend's job is to listen. Be a sounding board. But anything more? That's just asking for trouble."

"Friends?" Dee's eyes narrowed. "Like we were before, you mean?"

Okay, why did he feel like somebody'd just switched the channel on him? "And will always be," he said cautiously, desperately trying to figure out what was going on. If anything. Because God knew he was no stranger to imagining things that weren't there. "I'll always have your back, Dee. But I'll never push you into something you don't want. Or try to talk you out of something I think you really do."

Chuckling, she turned to the fridge for a jug of milk, a pitcher of tea. "I need more friends like you," she said, setting the containers on the counter, then surprising him by curving one cold hand over his where it still gripped the edge. A nontouch, really, with little to no meaning behind it. Certainly nothing that should've scorched his skin the way it did. Not to mention a few other things. "Thanks," she said, and he smiled.

"Anytime."

Although once she left his *friendship* would be moot, wouldn't it?

The first three nights Katie had only woken up once, leading Deanna to foolishly believe she'd gotten one of those dream babies who'd be sleeping through the night in no time, and she'd breeze through this new mother-hood thing like a champ.

Then Night Number Four arrived, and with it her daughter's apparent newfound goal to never let her mother sleep, ever again. The problem was, Deanna had always been a Sleeper, never even being able to pull an all-nighter in college because her body had simply said, *Um…no.* So when this little critter woke up at midnight…and two…and four…screaming as though she'd never eaten in her entire short life…

Muttering things loving mothers probably weren't supposed to mutter, Deanna somehow roused herself from what felt like a drugged sleep to turn on the low-wattage lamp on the dresser, then lean over the bas-sinet. How on earth could something that small be so fricking *loud*? And hungry? Close to tears as she tried to shake herself awake enough to change her, Deanna fumbled for a clean diaper and the wipes, only to jump a foot when she heard her door squeak open.

"Somebody giving you trouble?" Josh whispered be-hind her, and she swallowed, hard. Because wussiness was not an option.

"Sorry."

"For what?"

"Waking you?"

"You didn't," Josh said, gently shoving her aside and taking over the diaper changing duty. "She did. It's what babies do."

"You don't have to—"

"Hey. You made dinner. Fair exchange."

Far too gone to argue, Deanna stood with her arms

crossed under her leaking, achy breasts, watching Josh efficiently clean and rediaper Katie's bottom in the chilly room. The old heating system never had worked very well in the bedrooms, and Deanna was too paranoid to use a space heater, no matter how safe they were supposed to be. Billie had only laughed and pointed out that's what sleep sacks were for, the kid would be fine.

"You're good at this," she said, watching him snap up the baby's sleeper, then stuff assorted limbs into a little fleece sack big enough to hold three of her.

Josh hmmed. "Between Austin and my nephews, I've had a lot of practice. It doesn't really get gross until they start eating solids, though."

"Thanks for the heads-up." Deanna yawned, then raked a hand through hair that felt like a freshly scythed wheatfield. Charming. Somehow, the wailing got louder. "What if she wakes Austin—"

"She won't." Josh stuffed the dirty diaper into the lidded garbage can by the table, then hauled Katie against his chest. Even in the dim light—and through the fog of exhaustion—that soft T-shirt left little to the imagination. Hers, anyway. "Kid sleeps through anything. Where do you want to feed her? Chair or bed?"

"Bed. It's warmer."

"Then get back in, I'll bring her to you."

Yawning again, she did, stuffing two pillows behind her back and hiking the covers up to her waist before reaching for Katie. But instead of Josh handing her the kid and returning to his own bed, he set about making a fire in the fireplace. A small one that would burn out fairly quickly, but still. Deanna's eyes burned. And not from the fire.

"That's…" She swallowed. "Lovely. Thanks."

"You're welcome." Apparently satisfied with his handiwork, Josh stood, staring at the flames for a moment before facing her, his forehead crunched. "I could hang out here until you're done—"

"You don't have to do that—"

"And I'm not taking any chances on you falling asleep before putting her back to bed."

Deanna had to smile. "And you won't?"

"Nope. I'll just sit over here…" He settled into her mother's old rocking chair, crossing his arms over his chest. Tightly. "You got an extra blanket or something, though?"

Oh, for pity's sake… "Why don't you get into the bed with us?"

Brows crashed. "You sure?"

As if. Especially since the double bed wasn't exactly roomy. "Of course."

Josh still hesitated, then crossed the few feet to the bed and climbed in beside them, his scent, his body heat immediately swamping the space, making Deanna feel small and warm and safe and scared out of her wits. Because she had this ambivalence thing *down*, boy. Josh crammed the other two pillows behind his own back, then his arm behind his head.

"We should have a movie to watch or something."

Deanna chuckled. "Aside from there being no TV in here…what would that be?"

He shrugged. "Dunno. Anything but a chick flick. Or one of those things where everybody's talking in a weird accent."

"God, you are such a rube."

"Yep," he said, shifting a little in the bed, much too close. Much too *there*. "This is kind of nice, actually."

"If weird."

"Weird is subjective. And that's as profound as I get at four in the morning."

Then he scrunched down under the covers on his side, his head propped in his hand, and it occurred to her that her whole idea of having a man in bed with her had just gotten turned on its head. That in this moment, under piles of bedclothes and fully dressed—well, except for the half-exposed boob so her daughter could feed—she felt closer to this man than she ever had naked with anyone else.

Weird? Heh. Not even close.

"So you decided yet about that job?"

She managed a weary laugh. "Can I get back to you on that after I've had some sleep?"

"I'm serious. Because it sounds perfect for you."

"And you sound pretty sure about something you basically know squat about."

"I don't need to. But I'm guessing you do." He poked her hip. Through three layers of bedding. "Which is why that dude is so hot to get you on board. So you need to ask yourself—is this what you really want? Would it make you happy?"

Deanna looked down into that dear, sexy, aggravating face, forgetting for a moment how wiped out she was. "And what happened to not taking a position one way or the other?"

"Doesn't mean I can't encourage you to do something I really think you want to do. Or…am I wrong about that?"

"No, but…" Focusing again on her daughter, she tucked the blankets more tightly around her, shoving aside a disappointment she didn't even fully understand. "You make it sound so simple."

A moment passed before Josh said, very quietly, "I think the problem is, most people make things too hard. Harder than they need to be, anyway. But then, that's always been the difference between us, huh? Even when we were kids, you'd think things half to death before making a decision, while I'd go with my gut." He paused again. "Mostly, anyway. Since my gut and I didn't always agree. I'd hear it, sure. But I didn't always listen."

"Sounds like there's a story there," Deanna said, trying to lighten a suddenly heavy mood.

The covers went every-which-way when he sat up again, leaning much too close. And not nearly close enough. "All I know is," he whispered, looking at the baby, who'd sacked out in Deanna's arms, "people have a right to be happy. Otherwise, what's the point of living? She done?"

"Um…yeah. It's just…" Tired as she was, she smiled at her precious little girl, then barely touched her soft, soft cheek. "She feels so good, right where she is. It's hard to give her up."

Josh's rumbled chuckle vibrated through her, gentle and warm. "I can see that. But you're not going to be much good to her if you're dead on your feet. So hand her over, cupcake. I'm the best burper in these parts."

So, reluctantly, she did, her heart doing a slow turn in her chest as she watched him snuggle her child against that broad chest, as though she were the most precious, fragile thing in the entire world. Her eyes stinging, Deanna rehooked her nursing bra, her eyes immediately going heavy as she sank back underneath the warm bedcovers, barely hearing Josh getting up to put Katie back into her bassinet. And for a moment she felt the way home was supposed to make you feel, safe and loved and peaceful.

For a moment, she thought as tears pushed at her eyelids, she could almost believe in fairy tales.

"Now can I put stuff on the tree?"

His hands full of silver tinsel garland, Josh grinned down at Austin, a half dozen ornaments dangling from the kid's grimy fingers. It'd nearly killed the boy to wait while Josh strung the lights on the nine-foot fir. Especially since this was the first year Austin really understood that Christmas—and cookies and Christmas trees and *presents*—was an annual event.

"Go for it," he said, figuring he'd work the garland around his son's enthusiasm. Which would probably fade after five minutes, anyway. If that. Focusing wasn't a huge part of a preschooler's skill set.

He'd managed to hold off on getting the tree until two weekends before Christmas, although Josh wasn't sure who'd bugged him more about it—Austin or Dee. But even through the holiday excitement, not to mention the preparations for the party, Josh couldn't completely shake the dread of knowing what came after, that the ranch would go on the market, and most likely sell to some random stranger who'd do God knew what with it.

That he and Austin would have to find someplace else to live.

That in all likelihood Dee would take that new job

back east. And very likely never return. Because why would she?

Josh glanced over at her, sitting cross-legged in leggings and a baggy, sparkly sweater on the couch, chattering to her daughter as Thor guarded them both, his head on her knee—

"I don't know where to put this one, Daddy. There's no room!"

Hauling his head out of his butt, Josh chuckled. The kid had hung five of the six ornaments on the same branch. "Come over where I am. Yeah, like that. See? Plenty of holes to fill up."

Austin flashed him the dimpled grin that shredded his gut every time. Then Dee called Austin over to where dozens of boxes of glittery decorations lay all over the floor, the coffee table, the other sofa.

"Did you see the box of birds, sweetie?"

"Where?" he said, looking every which way. Smiling, Dee touched his shoulder, gently steering.

"Right…there, that's it. Those were my mother's favorites. Mine, too, actually. Mom told me she brought them home from a trip to Germany when she was a teenager."

Austin had already carefully pried one of the jewel-like ornaments from its tissue paper nest, cradling it in both hands like it was a real bird. "Where's Germany?"

"It's a country in Europe. Far away from here."

"Like Albuquerque?"

"Even farther. We can look it up together on the globe later, how's that?"

Meaning the giant antique globe in the study, where Josh had caught Dee and his son "exploring" more than once in the past few days, their heads touching, her arm around his waist...

"'Kay," Austin said, gingerly carrying the bird across the room, where—after several seconds' serious consideration—the child who routinely broke every toy he'd ever received reverently placed it on the perfect branch.

"Good job! Only eleven more to go!" Dee said, and Josh realized she hadn't told the child to be careful, even though the delicate ornaments had to hold a special place in her heart. What kind of woman trusted a four-year-old like that?

The same kind of woman who showed little boys where to find countries on a globe. Who calmly explained breastfeeding like it was no big deal. Who never lost her cool when Austin did spill or break or mess up something. Who understood he was a child without ever treating him like one.

In other words, he thought as his son solemnly found a "home" for the next bird, the woman was seriously messing with Josh's head. And that's not even counting that night he'd spent in her bed. Okay, not a whole night, and not exactly in a way most people would define that sentence. Still. Who knew there could be such intimacy in innocence? That seeing how tender Dee was with her new daughter, that watching her sleep after he'd put Katie back in her little crib, had aroused him in ways he wouldn't've thought possible? Hell, all he'd wanted to do was crawl back under the covers with her and wrap himself in her warmth, wrap her in *his*, keeping her safe from whatever made her forehead crease as she slept.

Whatever had caused that single tear to trickle down her cheek.

Even though he'd meant what he'd said, his own brow creasing as he moved to the back side of the tree—that she needed to do whatever made her happy. Made *her* happy, not anybody else. Certainly not him. And for damn sure not the ghosts still lingering in the house. No, he didn't believe in all that supernatural mumbo jumbo, spirits moving stuff around, making doors slam shut and all like that. But memories, expectations—the crap inside a person's head—could haunt a person every bit as bad. If not worse.

And he could tell, Deanna was haunted. By what, he wasn't sure. Nor was he sure he was the one to shine the light on her fears, convince her they weren't real.

Never mind that's exactly what he wanted to do. As in, so badly it almost hurt. Even though he wasn't sure about why that was, either.

Releasing a breath, Josh turned back to the tree to twist the garland around the next soft, sweet-smelling branch, finally admitting to himself how much he ached to be what he knew she'd never let him be. What Jordan had never let him be, either. Oh, sure, his ex had done all but shove the baby at him—she'd had no qualms about letting him take care of their kid. Not that he'd minded. Especially since the alternative—that she might've taken him from Josh entirely—would've been far worse. Any more than that, though…

Of course, Jordan just didn't want the obligation that came with being in a real relationship, the give-and-take of it. Dee, he strongly suspected, was simply flat-out scared.

And Josh had no idea how to get past that. Or even, frankly, if he should try. Since when all was said and done, they wanted very different things from life. On the same page? Hell, they weren't even in the same *library*.

Austin's laughter blending with Dee's made Josh peek from behind the tree as he tucked the garland's end into a branch. The kid had smushed up against her, giggling when Katie screwed up her face as her mama talked to her, like she was trying so hard to figure out what Dee was saying…and it was this frickin' picture-perfect moment like he'd always dreamed of, even if he didn't know it until *this* moment. His throat got all tight, that history was repeating itself, that he was falling in love with a woman he knew was all wrong for him, even as he watched her with his son and saw how right it could be.

For all of them.

Josh shoved out a soundless laugh—clearly the fumes from this damn tree had hallucinogenic properties. But he really did have to wonder why, in the name of all that was holy, that God, or Granville, or who*ever*, would plant Deanna Blake smack in front of him, like the grapes the fox could never reach in that dumb story he read to his son the other day.

Although, unlike the stupid fox who decided he was wasting his time trying to reach a bunch of probably sour grapes, Josh knew full well these grapes were sweet as could be.

Which made not being able to reach them all the more frustrating.

Chapter 10

Inordinately pleased with herself, Deanna leaned against the archway separating the great room from the dining room, a glass of sparkling cider nestled in her hand and a smile touching her lips. To be sure, between the band's no-holds-barred rendition of "A Holly Jolly Christmas" and the laughter, the madness of God knew how many kids running around and thousands of twinkling lights and shimmering decorations, her senses had given up trying to cope an hour ago.

In other words, it was a perfect party. For everyone else, anyway.

And that was all that mattered, wasn't it?

"Lookin' good, Mama," Val shouted over the din as she came up beside Deanna, a zonked-out baby Katie in her arms. More people had held this kid tonight than had probably held Deanna in her entire life. "That dress is the bomb. Especially with that necklace."

Black velvet. Straight, short and a little more snug than it had been prebaby. And the bib necklace had been a birthday gift from Emily, the chunky red stones appropriately festive for the occasion.

"Thanks. You, too."

"Is it okay? I'm not one for dressing up much."

"It" was a lovely lace top worn over a pair of jeans, loose enough to hide the merest suggestion of a baby bump. A pair of dangly, glittery earrings and a messy updo had the little blonde looking every bit as chic as anyone Deanna had ever seen at one of the gallery openings. Which she told her.

Val laughed. "Levi just said I looked hot."

"Then what more do you need?"

"True," Val said, gazing over the crowd. And a crowd, it definitely was, bigger than Deanna ever remembered from when she was a kid. The band leader, a Willie Nelson clone if ever there was one, asked if anyone wanted to do a sing-along, which got an instant chorus of approval. Val turned to Deanna, her eyes soft underneath newly cut bangs.

"*Now* they're saying goodbye. To your dad, I mean. In a way he would've wanted."

"I know," Deanna breathed out. "Which is why I agreed when Josh suggested it. Why…" Her gaze took in the giant, stately tree at the far end of the great room, glittering with the hundreds of glass ornaments her mother had loved so much, most of which Dad had bought for her. "Why I did all this. To soften the blow."

"Oh, honey…" Val shifted the baby to one arm to

tug Deanna to her side. As much as she could, anyway, since in her heels Deanna was nearly a head taller than her new friend. "I think they all understand a lot more than you're giving them credit for. Tradition might be the thing that holds this town together, but adaptability is what keeps everyone going when tradition falls on its sorry butt. And since my husband is giving me that look, I guess I need to give you back your child..."

A moment later, gently bouncing her daughter, Deanna retreated from the raucousness to the marginally quieter dining room. The goody laden table—she sent up yet another prayer of thanks for Annie and AJ, who'd happily catered the affair—glowed not only from the candlelight of her mother's treasured wrought iron candelabras, but from the luminarias lining the edge of the veranda outside. Not to mention the driveway and roof, a labor of love from all the Talbot men.

"You want to look outside?" she whispered to her daughter, kissing her downy head as she carried the baby over to the ceiling-high paned window, the shutters open to what could only be called a magical view. Another light snow had fallen, golden in the hushed, softly flickering light from hundreds of candle-filled paper bags. Deanna blinked back tears, practically *seeing* her parents, her mother with her head on her father's shoulders as they watched the last of their guests leave after a party much like this, their entwined figures limned in the same burnished glow.

And oh, how Deanna would practically shimmer with her own expectation for the holiday to follow, infected by her mother's love for the season. More images floated past her mind's eye—the almost worshipful look in Dad's eyes when Mom would set the Christmas roast on the table, their laughter as they cleaned up afterward.

Together. Always together.

A silent, shuddering sigh left her lungs. Her parents' love for each other was never a question. But that wasn't enough, was it, to overcome her mother's crippling loneliness—?

"Hey," Josh said behind her, his voice barely audible over the singing in the other room. "You okay?"

Nodding, Deanna hastily wiped her cheek, startled to realize she'd been crying.

"Just…remembering."

"That good or bad?" Josh said, taking the baby from her, his smile gentle when Katie did her funny little frowny face before settling back to sleep.

"Not sure. Don't suppose it's surprising, though, stuff popping into my head I haven't thought about in years." She smiled at him. "I'm glad we did this. Thank you."

Tucking Katie's head under his chin, Josh gave Deanna a look she couldn't quite define. "Closure?"

"Oh. I hadn't thought of it like that, but…maybe. Speaking of which…my current boss called today, badgering me again about when I was coming back to work."

"And?"

"And I quit."

"Ballsy," Josh said, and Deanna laughed.

"You have no idea. But I realized… I deserve better than that. No matter what happens."

A long pause preceded, "Does this mean you've decided to take the other job?"

"It means I'm free to take the other job, if I want—"

From the great room, a great roar went up from the crowd. Josh turned to her, grinning.

"I'm guessing Santa's here. Come on," he said, his hand going to her waist to steer her back to the party. Never mind that she hadn't finished her sentence.

Then again, maybe it was just as well. Since she wasn't entirely sure she could.

"So did you have fun tonight?" Josh asked, finally getting his son into bed nearly two hours past his bedtime. Nodding, Austin yawned, grabbing for his ratty Kanga, a gift from Josh's parents two years ago that had inexplicably become The Toy, although Roo had gone missing ages ago.

"Uh-huh," his sleepy little boy said, yawning again. "'Cept I know that was Grampa playing Santa."

Josh chuckled. "Oh, yeah?"

"Yeah. But don't tell 'im I know, 'cause I don't wanna hurt his feelings."

"Got it. Okay, buddy, I need to get back to help Dee clean up—"

"Are Dee and the baby really gonna leave after Christmas?"

Remembering their conversation—not to mention the pain in her eyes all those memories had obviously dredged up—Josh felt his chest go tight. "As far as I know, yeah."

Austin's forehead pinched. "How come?"

"Because she doesn't live here, guy. She was only visiting."

The little boy tugged the kangaroo closer, and Josh

could practically hear the wheels turning. "But she *feels* like she lives here. Like this is her house. She feels like…"

Gently, Josh brushed his son's hair away from his face. "Like what?"

"A mom."

Josh started, thinking, *And how do you know what a mom feels like?* But he'd had enough examples, hadn't he? His grandmother, for one thing. And more recently Val with her girls. Not to mention the other mothers in town who brought their kids to the church day care. The kid was four, not blind. Or immune to the concept of feeling like something was missing.

Something Josh knew all about, didn't he?

"I know, squirt—"

"You need to make her stay."

Oh, jeez… "Can't do that, buddy."

"How come?"

"Because trying to make people do something they don't want to do isn't good. Dee would have to want to stay. Otherwise she'd be unhappy." Never mind how easily she fit in tonight, crouching to talk to kids she'd never met, completely tuned in to whatever they were saying; laughing at old people's jokes; freely dispensing hugs. Giving Josh a grin and a thumbs-up at one point when it was obvious the party was a hit. "And you wouldn't want that, would you?"

"Noooo, but…" The frown got deeper. "So how do we make her want to stay?"

"We don't. Sorry. But maybe—" Because he was not above grasping at straws. "Maybe after Dee goes back to DC, we can go visit her sometime. And you can see where the president lives. And there's a great big museum there where they have all kinds of neat stuff, like a whole bunch of really old airplanes. And dinosaur skeletons. Wouldn't that be cool, to go see all that?"

That got several seconds' worth of *Not buyin' it, dude*, before the kid's eyes got wet, and Josh remembered that for a four-year-old, *today* was the only thing that mattered. The only thing you could count on. Even *tomorrow*, in most cases, was sketchy. Even so, it wrecked Josh something fierce, that some things, you couldn't promise a kid. No matter how much the kid might want them, or how much you might want to make those promises.

Or want those things yourself.

Yeah, sometimes being a parent sucked. Especially when you could see in your kid's eyes questions he didn't even know how to ask, that you couldn't answer even if he did. Questions that would probably surface one day or another, questions like *How come my mother left?*

Or *Why does loving somebody hurt so much?*

"Hey," Josh said, gently tickling Austin's tummy and getting a tiny smile for his efforts. "You got any idea how much I love you?"

The smile got a little bit bigger. "Lots?"

"Oh, way beyond *lots*. Like, so much more than *lots* it can't even be measured."

"More than God loves me?"

Josh smiled. "Maybe not more than that, He's pretty big. But as close to that as a person can get, how's that? And I'm not going anywhere. Or Grandma and Grandpa. Or a whole bunch of other people who love you like nobody's business. So. Are we good?"

A moment passed before Austin lurched onto his knees to throw his arms around Josh's neck, and Josh wasn't sure which one was holding on harder. Or whose heart was being squeezed more.

"I take it that's a yes?" he said, and his son nodded against Josh's neck, then slipped back down onto his pillow, Kanga strangled in his arm.

"How many sleeps until Christmas?" he asked.

"Let me see…six."

"That's *way* too many."

Chuckling, Josh stood, his fingers in his front pockets. "It'll be here before you know it. Now go to sleep, and when you wake up, guess what?"

"What?"

"It'll only be five."

Grinning, Austin squeezed shut his eyes and was somehow instantly asleep, and Josh sent up a short prayer of thanks: *one crisis averted, a million and three to go.*

The house, as he walked back down the hall toward the kitchen, shimmered with the calm-after-the-storm silence that had always followed these shindigs as long as Josh could remember. The elves—as in, his family—had already cleaned up and, apparently, left. But he found Dee and Katie in the kitchen, the infant asleep in a baby seat a safe distance away from the woodstove, the cat on one side, the dog—who looked up when Josh came in to thump his tail—on the other. Dee stood at the counter, wrapping up leftovers, softly singing along to the "Hallelujah Chorus." That, he knew. Not well enough to join in, no, but at least he recognized it. And even liked it. Kind of.

But instead of announcing his presence, Josh stood in the doorway, his hands slugged in his back pockets, watching. Listening.

Longing.

How do we make her want to stay?

Damned if he knew. What he did know was how effortlessly she meshed with the town, his family. His life. That the way she'd interacted with everybody tonight, her smiles and laughter, the way she'd *glowed*—that'd been the real Dee, whether she realized it or not. Sure, there was still *stuff*, if her subdued mood when he'd found her in the dining room was any indication. But everybody had *stuff*. That didn't mean—

Dee turned, her face flushed and her lips tilted in a questioning smile, and the longing turned into something more…insistent.

Foolhardy.

"Hey," she said, the smile softening. "Didn't know you were there."

"Everybody else gone?" Josh asked, his heart rate picking up speed. Like a freaking runaway train.

"Yep. It's just us," she said, forking a hand through now limp spikes, and the train ran right off the damn track. "Josh?" she asked, questions swarming in her eyes as he approached her…cupped her face in his hands…kissed her…

And damned if she didn't kiss him back.

Hallelujah, was right.

Not until that very moment, when Josh's lips touched hers and his tongue slipped into her mouth—cowboy was not shy, that was for sure—had Deanna realized she'd been wondering what it would be like to kiss Josh Talbot since she was fourteen years old.

Well, now she knew.

And all she could think was, when he claimed her mouth again with a second kiss so deep it threatened to eviscerate her soul, *And aren't we in a whole heap of trouble now, missy?*

As in, nipple-prickling, clutching-his-shirt, please-don't-stop kind of trouble.

Except—big sigh, here—*somebody* had to, and that particular ball would seem to have landed in her court. Before other balls landed in other courts and, well, yeah. But no.

Because at least this time, she *knew* she was needy.

At least this time, Deanna knew from the outset there wasn't a chance in hell this could work. The same as she always had with Josh, for pretty much the same reasons—that they were too different, wanted different things from life. And it would kill her, to break his heart. Let alone Austin's.

Not to mention she wasn't all that wild about getting hers broken again, either. Especially since she wasn't all that sure it was fully healed after the last debacle.

So, with an oh-so-mighty effort, she unclutched his shirt to press her hands to his chest, refusing to look at him as his heart hammered against her palms, and took a very…deep…breath.

"Oh, Josh," she said, in this stringy little voice that didn't even sound like her.

He let her go as though she'd just caught fire.

And laughed.

Frowning, Dee finally met his eyes, full of Joshness.

And still, if she wasn't mistaken, arousal. Even though he briefly clamped his hands around her shoulders to place a quick, brotherly smooch on the top of her head before releasing her again.

"You're not…mad?"

His brows dipped. "After a kiss like that? Why would I be mad?"

"Because… I…" She blew out a short sigh. "Because we can't. Okay, *I* can't."

"Yeah, I figured that's what you'd say," he said with a shrug, then lifted the plastic lid off the nearest container to snag a stuffed mushroom, which he popped into his mouth. "But to be honest I've been wanting to do that since I was fifteen. And I figured, since I might not get the opportunity again, to go for it while I had the chance. Can't say as I'm sorry." He filched another mushroom. "Damn, Dee…where'd you learn to kiss like that?"

Her face warmed. "Is that your usual modus operandi? Kissing someone whether or not she's indicated she's good with that?"

The mushroom hung suspended six inches from his mouth before he lowered it again. "No, Dee," he said softly. "It's not. And frankly I never have before this. Before *you*. But you know what?" Tossing the mushroom in the trash, he backed away, hands up. "I take it back, I am sorry. More sorry than you have any idea. Because you're right, that was a real dumb move on my part. And I promise you, it won't happen again."

Then he left the kitchen before her tongue came unglued from the roof of her mouth long enough for her to point out the obvious, which was that she had kissed him back—with more enthusiasm than she'd ever kissed anyone back in her entire life, actually—so she was every bit as complicit in what had just happened as he.

And he would've been totally justified in calling her on it.

That he hadn't only balled up everything in her head even more.

Even though Deanna apologized to Josh the next day for her reaction—an apology he seemed to accept graciously enough—there was no denying the tension now present in every conversation, every interaction, that hadn't been there before that kiss. Honestly, it was ridiculous, how hard they were trying not to offend each other. And this…carefulness between them hurt far more than she could have imagined. As though one little make-out session had somehow turned them into different people. Into strangers.

So she was beyond grateful when Val invited her to meet up with her and Mallory and all the kids in town to do some last-minute Christmas shopping. Despite the heaviness clogging her heart, Deanna had to smile at the same tacky decorations she remembered from when she was a kid, how several businesses still decorated the spruces in the town square with everything from miniature chile *ristras* to traditional cornhusk figures to giant, glittery globes the size of basketballs. And the air was crisp and clean and smelled of woodsmoke and evergreens, and the frosted mountains sparkled against the deep blue sky, and little kids sprinted from tree to tree, laughing, their innocent joy wrapping around Deanna's heart, soothing it. Healing it.

Confusing the hell out of it.

They'd gotten churros and hot chocolate from Annie's and were sitting on one of the battered benches in the square—well, Val and Deanna were on the bench, Mallory was in her wheelchair—bundled against the cold, although at this altitude the glaring midday sunshine kept the frostbite at bay. Mallory had commandeered Katie, practically invisible inside a snowsuit that used to belong to the toddler now shrieking back to a crow pretending to be a tree topper. They'd brought Austin, too—of course—and it almost frightened Deanna how much she'd grown to love the sweet, funny little kid in only a few weeks.

Although that wasn't nearly as frightening as how she felt about his father—

"Ohmigosh, Dee," Mallory said, sweeping her long red hair back over her shoulders as she grinned at the baby. "She is so freaking gorgeous. And don't you love how they can sleep through—" Risa shrieked at the crow again, the sound echoing around the square "—anything?"

"Except at night," Deanna said on a sigh. "Kid wakes up if I breathe too loudly."

"Because, hey," Val said beside her. "Twenty-four-hour dairy bar. Right?"

Deanna looked at the blonde, hunched into a pile-lined hoodie worn under a down vest, her cowboy-booted feet crossed at the ankles. "So you breastfed, too?"

"I did. Probably will this time, too." This said with a smug grin, bless her heart. The secret was no longer a secret, since keeping the news to himself was apparently beyond Josh's twin.

"One question." Deanna lowered her voice. "When does the dripping stop?"

Val laughed. "Yeah, the fun part. I swear I felt like an automatic sprinkler system for weeks. But it does get better. Eventually." She chomped off the end of her churro, then wiped the pastry's cinnamon sugar from her chin with a napkin. "Does make things awkward for a while, though."

"Things?"

"As in sex," Mallory said, still staring at the baby. "Bras and nursing pads—not exactly alluring."

Val snorted a laugh through her nose. "You kidding? *Willingness* is alluring. At least in my experience."

Deanna blushed so hard her cheeks actually hurt. "Not an issue for me," she muttered, biting a hunk from her own churro in the ensuing, deafening silence.

"So," Val said brightly, "you're staying through the holidays?"

"Might as well," Deanna said as nonchalantly as she could manage. Although after that kiss? She'd considered leaving as soon as she could book a flight home. But while on the surface that might've been the easiest solution, it was also the most cowardly one. And if ever a time called for big girl panties, this was it. "Since it'll be easier to get a flight after the New Year…"

God, did that sound as lame to everyone else as it did to her?

Austin ran over to throw himself across Deanna's lap, grinning, cheeks pink underneath a triple-cuffed beanie, and Deanna's heart nearly burst out of her chest.

"Jeremy an' Landon and me are playing airplanes! It's so fun! Watch!"

Then the little boy zoomed off, arms outstretched, to join Josh's oldest nephew and Mallory's son, the natural leader of the pack. Deanna had missed this as a kid, not having siblings or cousins close by, living too far outside of town to hang out with the local kids very much. Except for Josh, of course—

"He clearly adores you," Mallory said softly, making Deanna start. Val popped up off the bench to see to Risa, who'd tripped over nothing and landed hard on her tummy. "I remember those days of being worshipped."

Oh. She'd meant Austin. Of course. Except...

"Only Austin's not mine."

Instead of responding, Mallory shifted the baby in her lap, sweeping a strand of coppery hair off her cheek. "So no nibbles yet on the Vista?"

Mallory's attempt to shift the subject to safer, more neutral territory, Deanna assumed. Oddly, it wasn't. "It's not even going on the market until after the New Year—"

"Oh, please. Realtors are masters at letting things 'slip.' And the Vista is prime property."

Her forehead bunched, Deanna turned to the woman holding her daughter. Prime property indeed. Especially for Hollywood types hankering to play rancher during their downtime. And the used-to-be film star undoubtedly still had connections.

"You have a buyer."

Amusement danced in Mallory's soft gray eyes. "I do. Me."

Deanna blinked. "What? Why? You already have a place—"

"Not to live in, for a therapy facility. I've been thinking about looking for a place for a while now, actually. Ever since Zach took me to the one that got me riding again. And Zach understood..."

The other woman cleared her throat. Deanna already knew Mallory had been a champion barrel racer as a teenager back in Texas, before Hollywood. And long before the skiing accident that had left her in a wheelchair and derailed her acting career. And that Josh's older brother had been instrumental in helping Mallory reembrace something that'd clearly meant the world to her at one time.

"He understood what you needed?" Deanna ventured.

Smiling softly, the redhead met Deanna's gaze. "Even if I didn't." She looked back over the square, her breath misting around her face. "Which is how it so often goes, isn't it? Somebody else seeing what you can't? I came here to escape. Didn't work out that way."

And clearly she was not in the least unhappy about that. Mallory's words prickling her consciousness, Deanna took a sip of her hot chocolate. Except it'd gone cold and cloying, nearly choking her. She cleared her throat. "Escape? From what?"

"Life? Myself? A pity party that'd gone on five years too long?" Mallory shrugged. "But Zach knew it wasn't escaping I needed. What I needed, what he *knew* I needed, was to reclaim my...dominion. And now...well. Wouldn't it be lovely, helping other people get past their fears like I did?"

"It would," Deanna got out. Somehow.

"Also, from what little I knew of your dad, I think

he'd be pleased, don't you? Knowing his family home was being put to good use?"

Would he? Even though those weren't the plans *he'd* envisioned for it?

For Josh and her?

Deanna's eyes cut to Mallory's. "So whose idea is this, really? Yours? Or Zach's?"

Mallory laughed. "As it happens, I was about to bring it up to Zach when he beat me to the punch. I swear, sometimes it totally freaks me out, how much we think alike." Her smile softened. "Almost as much as how against all odds this incredibly good man landed in my life. And I thank God every day that he didn't give up on me—on us—when *giving up* would have seemed the most logical choice."

Deanna smiled, even though Mallory's words, not to mention her I-don't-give-a-damn-who-knows-it happiness, made her even squirmier than she already was. "I didn't know Zach all that well when I was a kid, since he's so much older. But I do remember he was a good guy, even then."

"I gather all the Talbot boys were. Are."

"Well, the jury was out on Levi for a long time," Deanna said, ignoring Mallory's subtext as she smiled at Levi's newly pregnant wife playing hide-and-seek with all the little kids behind the sparkly trees. "In fact, you'd've never known he and Josh were twins, they were so different. And who knows about Colin."

"Ah, yes. The mystery man. Zach's not even sure he'll come to the wedding." Set for some time in the spring, Josh had said. "But back to my proposal…it's a serious offer, Dee."

"Didn't think it wasn't. But Josh doesn't know about it yet?"

"I thought I'd feel you out first," Mallory said gently. "Since it's your home—"

"Only half mine, now." She faced Mallory again, her heart pounding painfully against her sternum. "But even before, the Vista was every bit as much Josh's as mine. In every way that really counts. Especially since I haven't even lived here in more than ten years."

"So what if I buy *you* out," the redhead said, excitement making her cheeks brighter than the cold already had, "and Josh could keep his half interest and keep living there with Austin, since Zach and I are perfectly happy where we are. The therapy end would be entirely separate. It could definitely be a win-win for both of you."

Deanna looked away, her stomach churning, even as she knew this could be a perfect solution. Josh could stay right where his heart had always been, and Deanna would still have plenty to invest for Katie's education. Not to mention this would be a painless way to sever her ties without hurting Josh—

Josh? Or yourself—

"This way the Talbots could still keep all the traditions alive," Mallory said, as though assuming Deanna's silence meant she needed to up her sales pitch. "Whispering Pines…"

Mallory smiled down at Katie, making cute little baby faces in her sleep. "What I loved most about this town, the whole area, when I first came here years ago, was that sense of real community I remembered from when I was a kid in Texas. And the people here…from the get-go they made Mom and me feel like one of them. We were…"

She smiled. "Embraced. Welcomed. A lot more than I would've expected, since I do know small towns aren't always like that. But this one is. After so many years of not actually feeling connected to anything real, to have finally found home again…there's no price to be put on that. So if I can in some way help keep intact whatever makes Whispering Pines so special—and I think the Vista plays a huge part in that…" Her eyes touched Deanna's again. "I'd be very honored."

Katie woke up, started to whimper. Deanna stood to take her daughter from Mallory, almost overwhelmed by the wave of protectiveness that washed over her.

"I'll have to talk it over with Josh, of course."

"No rush. Really. Only promise me you'll give me first rights of refusal?"

The baby tucked against her chest, Deanna smiled down at Zach's fiancée. "But you don't even know what we're asking for the property."

"Not an issue," Mallory said, a smile teasing the corners of her mouth. "Now—" she pivoted the wheelchair to face the square. And the small herd of children in it. "I suppose we should corral these little critters before they freeze…"

Deanna hugged her daughter more closely as it occurred to her that everything she'd worked toward the last few weeks was almost effortlessly falling into place. She'd have funds for Katie's education, Josh would get to keep the ranch…a perfect solution, really.

So why didn't she feel happier about that?

Chapter 11

"Hey, squirt," Josh said, grinning for his kid when he came storming into the kitchen, where Josh was fixing himself a sandwich. He grabbed the kid to swing him up on his hip, kiss his cold cheeks. "You have a good time?"

"It was *so* fun," Austin said, linking his hands around the back of Josh's neck. "An' DeeDee and me bought you a present, 'cause she said Santa only brings 'em for kids, not for grown-ups." His smooth little forehead pleated. "That true?"

"Mostly, yeah," Josh said, trying to keep a straight face. "But I don't think you're supposed to say you got something for me."

"DeeDee only said I couldn't tell you what it is. And I'm not gonna. 'Cause it's a secret."

"Good. Where is she, anyway?"

"She went to feed the baby in her room. C'n I go play with Thor out back? I already ate."

"Okay, but only as far as the Big Tree."

"I *know*," the boy said as Josh lowered him to the floor. "I'm not a baby, sheesh."

Josh sighed as kid and dog ran out the back door, then chomped off a big chunk of the sandwich before going down to Dee's room, where he stood at the door warily spying on her. Seated in her mother's old rocking chair wedged into a corner of her bedroom, she softly chattered to Katie while the baby nursed, her hand batting at Dee's chest. Chuckling, Dee caught the tiny hand and kissed it, holding it to her lips as the baby continued to suckle.

And Josh's gut knotted, that no matter what choice he made when it came to Dee, it never seemed to be the right one. Instead of maybe giving her a reason to reconsider her move, to reconsider him, all he'd given her was even more reason to leave.

More reason to remember *all* the reasons why they wouldn't work.

And yet, for all Dee's insistence on returning "home," he couldn't help wondering what, exactly, she was returning *to*. Since Emily had let it slip that Dee's social life hadn't been exactly hopping *before* the pregnancy. That for various reasons Emily had become her only real friend, and her aunt and uncle…well, who knew what was going on there. Nothing good, as far as he could tell. She had her little apartment, and what could be a good job, he supposed. But that wasn't exactly a life, was it?

Still. Although he was obviously a fool, he wasn't so much of one as to bring that subject up with her. Because God knows he'd had enough of those "talks" with Jordan that no way was he going down that particular road again. Like he'd said to Austin, Dee had to want to stay here. *Want* a life with him and his son. Clearly she didn't. And never let it be said he couldn't learn from his mistakes.

Apparently sensing his presence, Dee looked over with a slightly nervous smile curving her mouth, and Josh wanted to smack himself, for letting a single, stupid impulse ruin what had been good and right and honest between them. That he hadn't let well enough alone.

"Ah. You're here." Dee nodded toward her unmade bed. "Have a seat."

"That sounds ominous."

She sort of laughed. "Not at all. In fact, it's good news. At least I think so."

The old Navajo rug absorbed his boots' clomping as Josh crossed to the bed and lowered himself to the edge, then leaned forward to link his hands between his knees. He caught a whiff of those rumpled sheets, smelling of baby and fabric softener, faintly of her perfume, and his libido stirred, intrigued. He told it to go back to sleep.

"So Mallory and I got to talking while we were in town," Dee said, "and…she'd like to buy my half of the Vista."

It took a second for her words to register. "You serious?"

"Well, she certainly seems to be. To turn it into a therapy ranch. Partly, anyway, since she fully expects you to keep your enterprise going, too."

He couldn't tell from the tone of her voice how she really felt about this turn of events, although her refusal to look at him told him something. What, exactly, he wasn't entirely sure.

The thing was, on the surface it wasn't a bad idea. At least, a helluva lot better one than selling the ranch outright to some stranger, of Josh losing his home as well as whatever chance he'd convinced himself he might have with Dee. Even if that second thing was now obviously a nonissue. The minute he started peeking below the surface, however, things started feeling sketchy.

"I suppose," he said carefully, "we could consider it."

"That's what I told her." Dee shifted the baby up onto her shoulder to burp her, smiling when the kid released a belch loud enough to hear across the state line. "Not until after the holidays, though. If you're okay with that." When he didn't say anything—because he honestly wasn't sure what that would be—she went on. "This could be the perfect solution, don't you think? Especially since it would keep the ranch in the family."

His frown gouged his forehead. "Whose family, Dee? The ranch belonged to the Blakes. Not the Talbots."

"Technically, maybe. Although you know as well as I do your family's connection to the Vista runs every bit as deep as mine did." She fiddled with her top to put the baby to her other breast, and Josh felt another kind of pull that went way beyond sex. She paused, looking out her bedroom window, where they could see Austin romping with the dog. "Your connection, especially."

For the first time he heard something he hadn't before, although he supposed it'd always been there: sadness. Not bitterness, or boredom, but something more like grief, if he had to put a name to it.

As in, the Vista held some pretty bad memories for her. Memories he now finally, fully realized trumped whatever good ones there might've been, whatever glimmers of hope he might've thought he'd seen in her interaction with his family, the community. Hell, her mother had died here; her father had more or less ignored her before sending her away. Those two things, on top of the isolation she'd already felt...no wonder she wanted to get away. Again.

"You really were miserable here, weren't you?"

A huge sigh left her lungs before she smiled again, forced though it might've been.

"Not all the time," she said. "There were...moments. But there was a reason I glommed on to you. Because you made it bearable." The smile brightened, slightly. "Even fun, sometimes. Still. The moment I returned I remembered..." Glancing around, she sighed again. "How abandoned I'd felt here. Yes, you did your best. And Gus, God bless 'im. But none of that changed how I felt, even if those moments temporarily alleviated it. And then... *then*..." She looked down at the baby, her mouth pulled tight. "There's that whole manipulation business."

"Your father, you mean."

She grimaced. "All I wanted, when I was a kid, was for him to really pay attention to me. A real connection. Like you have with Austin. Like I pray I do with this one," she said, smiling for her daughter. "Not to be made to feel like a chess piece to be moved at will."

"The same way you felt manipulated by Katie's father."

A pause preceded, "Because what else do I know, right?"

And, oh, how Josh wanted to plead that he wasn't like that. And wouldn't be. But even he knew if you had to argue your case, you didn't really have one to begin with. If she didn't know who he was by now... well. Nothing he could do about that.

"Except if Granville sent you away because you were unhappy here—"

"He sent me away," she said flatly, "so he wouldn't have to deal with me. Because..." Josh saw her swallow. "Because I wasn't Mom and he couldn't deal with that. So *now* he wants to fix things?" She scoffed, then lifted her face to his, apology swimming along with the tears in her eyes. "And please don't take offense, because none of this has anything to do with you."

"Good to know," he said, and she pushed out a tiny laugh.

"It's only, when you think of home," she said, looking out the window again, "you should get a warm, fuzzy feeling, you know? Good memories, good associations—"

"And what's in DC for you?" Josh blurted out, earning him a justifiably startled glance. But dammit, somebody had to say it. "Seriously? Because it sure as hell doesn't sound like you've got a whole lot of good memories from there, either—"

"A *future*," she lobbed back. "Or at least a promise of one. Opportunity—"

"That job offer, you mean?"

A second, then another, preceded, "Yes."

"And there's more to life than work."

"There's nothing for me here, Josh," she said, sadly. But more than that, as though the very thought exhausted her. "Maybe if I felt more nostalgic—"

"Screw nostalgia," Josh said, angrier than he probably should be. "We're talking about now, dammit. And *now* there are people here who care about you, who could help *take* care of you—"

The words were no sooner out of his mouth than he realized how deeply he'd put his foot in it. Especially when she gave him almost a pitying look.

"People?" she said at last. "Meaning you? The person who said he refused to get involved with anyone else unless he was sure he and that hypothetical someone else were on the same page?"

Did she even realize what she was saying? Or was he sorely misinterpreting things? Which was entirely possible. See, this was what he hated about trying to talk to women, how they never came right out and said what they meant, but danced around the subject like it was up to you to figure out the coded message.

Except, even if he wasn't, no way in hell was he going to push. Because that had worked out so well before, hadn't it?

"As a friend, Dee. A *friend*. Like I said. And what's so awful about that? About letting somebody be there for you?"

Their gazes tangled for a good, long moment before she said, very gently, "That wasn't just a *friendly* kiss, Josh. And aside from all the other stuff, I can't..." Her throat worked again. "I can't be what you and Austin need. Who you need."

"And that's just crazy talk—"

"Which only proves my point, that there's way too much stuff in my head to sort out for me to be in a relationship with anybody. If nothing else…" She looked down at the baby, then released a breath. "My last experience with this one's father was a wake-up call. Just like yours was with Austin's mom. Only in my case…"

Her gaze brushed his again. "God knows I still have a lot of growing up to do, but at least my eyes are a little more open than they were before. And for Katie's sake, for yours and Austin's, I'm not about to take a risk on something where the odds aren't exactly in our favor to begin with. I can't come back, Josh. Because I can't *go* back to being who I was before."

"And who is that?" Josh said through a tight throat.

Her smile was soft. "The little girl still looking for somebody to connect with. To…complete her." He saw her eyes fill, and his own burned in response. "And it would be way too easy to let you be that person."

Holy hell. The room positively reeked of her fear, rolling off her in waves. She was right about one thing, though—whatever was going on in her head had nothing to do with him. Not deep down. So maybe he should be grateful she was giving him an out.

"Well," Josh finally said, "I expect Mallory will be pleased."

Dee shut her eyes for a moment, then nodded. "So you're good with her proposal?"

"I think that's what they call the best of a bad lot," he said, then left the room, yanking his barn coat back on to walk outside, listening to his son's laughter, the dog's barking, as his gaze swept over the land he'd never imagined might be his one day. That now, after coming close to losing it altogether, would be his forever. Or at least half of it. Which was more than he could have ever hoped for a few months ago.

So how come he'd never felt more empty in his life?

When Josh returned, Deanna suggested she and Katie move to the foreman's cabin. Josh, however, not only pointed out that moving all of the baby's stuff would be a pain in the butt, but if Deanna needed him in the middle of the night he could hardly leave Austin alone in the Big House, could he?

"Anyway," he'd said, not looking at her as he loaded the dishwasher after a meal that redefined *awkward silence* once Austin left the table, "it's only for a few days. I think we can muddle through this like grown-ups."

In other words, this was stacking up to be one helluva crappy Christmas. Although God knew she wasn't any stranger to those.

As least Austin's infectious excitement took the edge off Deanna's increasing regret. Not that she'd made the wrong decision, but that she couldn't figure out how to make it right with Josh. Or Austin, who clearly hadn't yet reconciled himself to the inevitable.

"But I want you to stay!" he'd say, over and over, until Deanna thought her heart would crack right in two and fall out of her chest. As if the look in Josh's eyes, whenever she was foolish enough to let their gazes mingle, wasn't doing that already.

Most of which—leaving out the gaze-mingling-with-Josh-part—she shared with Val as they pushed their daughters' strollers along Main Street on Christmas Eve eve, barely glancing in windows they'd both seen a dozen times before. But then, shopping wasn't the point, as Val pointed out when she'd called that morning simply to chat, and after barely a minute declared Deanna clearly needed to get out of that house before she lost it. Of course, it was obvious she'd only called to begin with because Deanna was guessing Josh had said something to his twin, who'd then said something to his wife, because that's how small towns worked. Not to mention families, Val said with a shrug when Deanna had confronted her about her motives behind the invitation.

"Trust me," the blonde said when they stopped in front of a bookstore/gift shop to put Risa's mittens back on for the third time in five minutes, "No one is immune to that it-takes-a-village thing they've got going on here. As in, nailed." Straightening, Val got behind the stroller and resumed pushing.

"And you're not part of that?"

"Oh, hell, yeah," the blonde said, tossing Deanna a grin. "Except I'd like to think, because I've been on the receiving end of all that helpfulness, that I can be an impartial listener. Which I'm guessing is what you need most right now. And unlike a guy, I won't offer any advice."

Deanna glanced down at Katie, sacked out in her own stroller, her precious little cheeks stained pink from the cold. "They do tend to do that, don't they?"

"You kidding? Loose ends tend to make men real twitchy. Especially those men."

A frown bit into Deanna's forehead. "Loose ends?"

Her new friend chuckled. "I get that you feel leaving's the best thing for you. Not about to argue the

point, because who am I to say? But I will say you don't
sound all that happy about it, either. So, yeah. Loose
ends. Trust me," Val said on a sigh. "I've been there.
So I know what you're saying, that you have to figure
out your own life, nobody else can do that for you. That
doesn't make the limbo period before you do any easier." She paused. "Don't know if this helps or not, but
with Levi and me…" Val's breath frosted in front of her
face when she blew out. "Knowing what I wanted didn't
make me any less afraid of it. In fact, it petrified me."

"What makes you think—?"

"Oh, honey…" Val turned to her, something close to
pity shimmering in her pretty blue eyes, and Deanna
sighed.

"Is it that obvious?" she said, and now Val laughed,
only to sober a moment later, her forehead scrunched.

"Like I said, not gonna offer any advice. Don't know
you well enough to do that, for one thing. But in my
case, I finally had to ask myself whether I'd be happier with Levi or without him. If protecting whatever I
thought needed protecting was worth giving up what I
thought I needed protecting from."

"And is it weird, that I actually understood that?"

Val chuckled again as they approached a storefront
with a For Sale sign in the grimy window. "Being
happy…it's really not about where you are, is it? It's
about *who* you are. Who you're with. At least, that's
what I finally figured out." Tenting her mittened hand
over her eyes, Val peered inside for a moment before
meeting Deanna's gaze again.

"I've got everything I need," she said, "right here in
this two-bit town. Although I sure didn't feel that way

when I was a kid, when I couldn't imagine ever being happy here. Now I couldn't imagine being happier anywhere else." Underneath her heavy hoodie, her shoulders bumped. "Things change. *People* change. And I'm a firm believer that happiness—or misery—is more of a choice than we sometimes think. And that's all I'm gonna say about that."

Then she tilted back her head, looking up at the store's faded sign. "I remember this place from when I was a kid."

"Same here. They sold tacky tourist crap." Deanna grinned. "Coolest store, ever."

"Seriously. I heard the owners moved to Tucson, the kids aren't interested in keeping the business going." Laughter from a couple of bag-laden nonlocals emerging from a nearby gift shop briefly diverted the blonde's attention. "You ask me, though, the place won't stay vacant for long. Not the way those ski resort types spend the big bucks, according to Annie. And wouldn't it make a perfect gallery?" Her gaze slid back to Deanna's, a smile snaking across her mouth. "Snag 'em before they find their way down to Taos—"

From her pocket, Val's phone chimed. "Shoot, I didn't realize it'd gotten so late, I need to pick up Josie from school and get back to my pies for tomorrow—"

"No problem." Deanna smiled. "But it was nice to get out of my own head for a bit. So, go." She shooed Val away. "Fetch. Bake. I'm good."

"You sure?"

"Of course."

"Okay. But if you need to talk more," she said over

her shoulder as she started down the street, "call me. Or text, whatever."

Then she was gone, leaving Deanna standing in front of the empty store. Following Val's lead, she peeked inside...

Her phone rang, scaring the bejeebers out of her. She smiled, though, when she saw Gus's number on the display.

"Just callin' to check up on my girl," the old housekeeper said. "Both of you, actually. So how's it going?"

The phone to her ear, Deanna squatted in front of the stroller to rearrange the baby's little cap, which had somehow fallen down over her eyes. Another clump of tourists wandered by, shopping totes in hand, smiling at Katie as they passed.

"It's going okay," Deanna said over the knot in her throat as she got to her feet again.

Gus paused, then said, "Josh tells me you're gonna sell your half of the Vista to Zach and Mallory?"

"Mallory, yes. To use as a therapy facility."

Another pause. "Win-win, huh?"

"Yep. So how's things by you?" she said, staring inside the vacant shop again.

"Good. Really good, in fact. Like I'm finally where I belong."

Deanna frowned. "You didn't feel like you belonged in Whispering Pines?"

"When your daddy was still alive, sure. And you know I always felt like an honorary Talbot," he said on another short laugh. "But it really didn't feel like home anymore. This does."

"Get out."

Another belly laugh preceded, "Crazy, huh? Especially after a million years of thinkin' I'd rather jab a stick in my eye than come back down here. But you know what? God has a way of puttin' us where we belong, not where we think we're supposed to be. So I'm glad I listened. Although if you'd asked me six months ago if I could see myself living down here again..." He laughed again. "I'd've said you were loco. So. When you going back east?"

"Um...right after the New Year."

"That soon? Okay, keep in touch, honey—"

"Mom hated the Vista, you know," Deanna blurted out, not even knowing why. "And eventually it killed her, being so unhappy. I remember, how trapped she felt. Same as I did—"

"No," Gus said, his voice surprisingly strong. "Not the same at all. Holy hell—is that what you've thought all these years? That your mama hated the ranch?"

"Kinda hard to miss, Gus."

"Meanin' your father never told you the truth about that, either." On a huge sigh, the old man muttered something in Spanish Deanna didn't entirely get. "If that sweet lady was trapped by anything, it was her illness. Not the tumor, what she lived with for years before that. The doctors, your daddy—they tried everything, but—"

"Gus—what are you talking about?"

"Depression. You really didn't know? From the time she was a girl, they said. Although it apparently got worse after you were born. She had good days, sure, but..."

Deanna pressed her gloved hand to her chest as images, incidents, that had always felt fuzzy around the edges flooded her thoughts, suddenly in almost painfully sharp focus. Of course now, as an adult, it made sense—her mother's withdrawals and not wanting to get out of bed, her false cheer when she was awake. But then…

"I remember," she said softly. "Oh, God… I remember."

Gus pushed out another breath. "Your daddy—he wasn't thinking straight, after your mama died. And for a long time after. Never did get over feeling like he'd failed, somehow. Even though it wasn't his fault. And then your aunt came out, and she convinced him—"

Deanna's blood ran cold. "I'd be better off with her."

"Or at least better off not there," Gus said in a tone that strongly suggested there was no love lost there. "And your father was grasping at straws. The Talbots tried telling him it was only you being a teenager that made you moody, then grief after your mama died. And that even if you had been ill like Mrs. Blake, sending you away wouldn't've 'cured' it. But your daddy did what he thought was right. And nothing and nobody was gonna change his mind."

"I thought…" She cleared her throat. "So it wasn't about Josh?"

"Oh, that played a part in it, sure it did. Because your father was definitely scared you'd end up falling for each other, and then…well."

"History would repeat itself. Which is what I'd always figured, about why he'd sent me away."

"Except there was more to it than that. A lot more."

Tears blurring her vision, Deanna sagged against the

grimy window. "Holy crap. Only…eventually he realized he'd made a mistake?"

Gus sighed again. "Lookin' death in the face does that to a person, I guess. But you gotta know, honey— your mama loved the Vista, she really did. Just like she loved your daddy. And she loved you like I've never seen another mother love her child."

Blinking, Deanna looked down at her own daughter, feeling her heart shatter. "I know she did."

"And your daddy loved you, too. Even if he had a weird way of showing it."

She snuffed a little laugh. "By pushing me away, you mean."

"By doin' what he could to protect you."

A sudden, sharp wind zipped down the street, making her shiver, even as she felt as though a boulder had finally rolled off her chest. "Thanks, Gus. For telling me all that. Seriously—"

"An' there's something else you need to know. When you were little, I never saw anything but a happy little girl who loved to be outdoors and ride horses and go tubing in the snow. If you were lonely…well. I sure as hell never saw it. An' I think I would've. Since you never were any good about keeping whatever you were thinking or feeling from showing in that sweet face of yours. And *Dios mio*," he said with a chuckle, "you weren't afraid of a damn thing back then. Some of the stuff you pulled scared the crap out of all of us. I remember thinkin' to myself, there's a gal who's gonna get whatever she puts her mind to."

And now she could hardly breathe. Or hear, for all those words crashing and clanging in her brain.

Words she'd clearly needed to hear, crashing and clanging aside.

Swiping a hot tear off her nearly frozen cheek, Deanna said softly, "I love you, Gus. Merry Christmas."

"Aw, I love you, too, honey. And send me lots of pictures of that baby, you hear?"

"Absolutely," Deanna said, then disconnected the call, turning away from the next round of passersby so there'd be no witnesses to her losing it right out in public.

Which meant she was facing the empty store again...

Her breath hitched. Oh, hell, no.

No.

Because Gus's words didn't change anything, really. Her life wasn't here, hadn't *been* here in years...

Because it wasn't enough, simply *wanting* something.

Was it?

She leaned closer to the window, like some Dickensian orphan seeing hope and promise and dreams-come-true inside, and she sputtered a laugh.

"Get real," she mumbled to herself, steering her sleeping baby back toward where she'd parked the truck, as the strains of "O Come All Ye Faithful" spilled out over the square from the Catholic church's PA system, a block away.

Joyful and triumphant? *Not so much*, Deanna thought as she hauled little Miss Dead Weight out of the stroller and strapped her into her car seat, telling herself it was the cold making her eyes sting.

Although she couldn't blame the temperature for her heartache.

Chapter 12

"Looks like she's doing great," Zach said, patting the horse's rump before frowning at Josh. "Which is more than I can say for you."

"Me? I'm fine."

The stall door banging closed behind him, Zach snorted. "Please. You haven't been *fine* since Deanna returned. And the closer she gets to leaving, the less fine you are."

Josh's fists clenched. Too bad he'd dropped off Austin, aka Mr. Big Ears, at his folks earlier. Because nothing put the brakes on a dicey conversation like a four-year-old.

"Then I'll be fine once she leaves and things get back to normal."

That got a smirk. "I seem to recall telling myself

something similar when I thought Mallory was going back to LA. Until I realized I was being an idiot of the first order, thinking there was nothing I could do to stop her."

Josh met his brother's gaze dead-on. "Only in my case, there isn't."

"You sure about that?"

"Her life's not here," Josh muttered as they walked out to Zach's truck, the dumb dog dancing around their legs. "I told you about that job offer, right?"

"You did." Seemingly in no hurry to catch up, Zach said behind him, "So you're good with Mallory's proposal?"

"Sure."

"Not hearing a whole lot of conviction there, buddy."

"It is what it is, okay? Although I'll tell you one thing—I'd give up the Vista like that—" he snapped his fingers "—if it meant…"

Damn. He couldn't even finish the sentence. Pathetic.

"She really hates it here that much?" Zach said. Almost kindly.

"Can you blame her?"

Under his cowboy hat's brim, Zach's face folded into a frown. "I know the place has some sketchy memories for her. But I'm guessing it's got some good ones, too. Memories she's afraid of owning. Because if she does that…" He shrugged.

For a good two, three seconds, Josh actually considered not taking the bait. However, since it wasn't like he could feel any worse… "And what memories might those be?"

"And you can't be that dense. It's not the *Vista* that

scares her, numskull. It's you. The ranch is only an excuse."

Josh gawked at his brother for several seconds before pushing out a dry laugh. "And how on earth did you come to this conclusion?"

"I didn't. But Mallory did. And Val. And I'd trust those two's intuition with my life. They're also of a mind that Deanna's not all that crazy about going back east, whether she'll admit that out loud or not. Only you haven't exactly given her a reason to stay, have you?"

Ramming his hands in his pockets, Josh stared out toward the house. "It's…complicated."

"So let's break it down into small bites. Does she even know you love her?"

"Dammit, Zach—" The dog danced out of the way when Josh spun around. "Loving a woman isn't enough to make her stay if she doesn't want to! And no *way* am I going there again."

A beat or two passed before Zach said, "So much for you telling everybody it was 'just a thing' between you and Jordan."

Josh grimaced. "I was feeling stupid enough as it was. Decided I'd rather have people mad at me than pity me."

"As in, Mom and Dad?"

"As in, anybody."

"Deanna's not Jordan, buddy."

"No kidding. Which is why I'm not even remotely interested in making the same mistake with her. Because nothing shuts down a woman faster than telling her you love her when that's not what she wants to hear.

And she's been through enough without me putting any more pressure on her."

His brother held Josh's gaze in his for far too long. "So you're just going to let her go."

And no jury in the land would convict him if he killed his brother right then. "Okay. Even if the whole here-or-there thing weren't an issue, even if I told her how I feel, she's made it more than clear she's got to figure stuff out on her own, that her problem is...how'd she put that? Looking for somebody to complete her."

"Because she's been hurt, idiot. By her dad, by Katie's father..." Zach shook his head. "For God's sake, Josh—the woman is probably *petrified* of being abandoned again. That whole *I gotta figure this out for myself* shtick? Oldest defense mechanism in the world."

"Oh, and like telling her that is the way to win her over? Dude. Not *that* stupid."

"And if you don't tell her *something*..." Zach squatted to pet Thor, then looked back up at Josh. "The animals I see who've been abused, the ones who're the most skittish—they're ones who need the most love. *And* the most patience. People are no different. Yeah, it's a risk, I get that. You might fail. She might leave anyway. You might even piss her off so much she'll never want to speak to you again. And hell, maybe she really does feel she belongs in DC, what do I know? But I do know if you don't put your ass on the line, you'll definitely lose her. Also, since I'm on a roll, here," he said, standing again, "being there for a woman isn't the same as trying to complete her. Not even close."

"Except if she doesn't see it that way—"

"Then make sure she does," Zach said, clapping Josh

on his shoulder before climbing back into his truck. But before he slammed shut the door, he said, "You really want to show her you're willing to let her make her own choices? Then make sure she's got all the information she needs to make 'em. Just be prepared—"

"To let her go. Got it."

Zach's eyes softened behind his glasses a moment before the old truck roared to life. "Showing a woman you love her enough to risk rejection? No better gift in the world."

Fists jammed in his coat pockets and his forehead crunched, Josh watched his brother drive away, his pickup bumping over ruts in the dirt road leading out to the main drag. Part of him—a pretty big part, actually—thought Zach was talking out of his butt, that what was all well and good in theory had nothing to do with the reality that was him and Dee. That, however, would be the part that didn't much cotton to accepting anything Zach—or anyone else, for that matter—had to say. Because Josh was pigheaded like that. As his parents regularly pointed out.

The other part, however—the part that'd reluctantly cozied up to adulthood along about the time Austin appeared—knew Zach was right, that there was no reward without risk. That nothing worthwhile came easy.

Or without being completely honest. With himself as well as with Dee.

He whistled for the dog and headed back to the house, ignoring the cold sweat trickling down his back.

After putting a sacked-out Katie in her crib, Deanna had gone out to the great room, where she plugged in the Christmas tree lights and lowered herself to the Navajo rug to sit cross-legged on the floor, stroking Smoky's silky fur as she stared up at the lit tree. Like she used to when she was little, letting herself become one with the pretty colors, the heady scent of fresh fir, the soothing, mesmerizing strains of familiar Christmas carols. There'd usually been a cat then, too, she thought, smiling at this one as he stretched a paw across her knee, his purr rumbling through her. Straw-colored, late afternoon light tumbled through the tall windows to tangle with the sparkling tree, and Deanna remembered how her mother would sit with her on the floor and look up at the lights, too…how the good days had been very good, how much Katherine Blake had loved the holidays, loved her…

How much Deanna *had* loved this house, the ranch, once upon a time. Just as Gus had said.

And the tears came. Copious and hard, the kind that made her chest hurt and her breath come in fitful, choking gasps. So hard, in fact, she didn't hear Josh come up behind her, let alone even react when he lowered himself to the floor, dislodging the cat before pulling her into his lap. Cradling her head to his smoke-scented chest, he pressed his lips to her hair, again and again, and Deanna's sobs only intensified, as she keened for everything she'd lost, everything that had been ripped from her…

Everything she'd been so afraid to grasp for fear of losing again.

And all she wanted, in that moment, was to stop pretending.

To not be afraid anymore.

And so, she thought as she clutched the front of Josh's shirt and brought their mouths together, she wouldn't be.

After his brain stopped sizzling from that *What the hell?* kiss—not to mention finding the poor woman in a pool of tears—Josh cupped Dee's face in his hands and held her back just far enough to see into her eyes. Water-logged and slightly crossed though they may have been.

"I don't understand."

"Me, either," she said, swooping in for round two. "Just go with it—"

Josh grabbed her hands. Definitely not how he'd imagined this playing out. Nor was he about to let himself be derailed. "And what, exactly, is this *it* I'm supposed to be going with?"

One thing about fair-skinned women, when they blushed, they blushed *big*.

He almost laughed. Granted, there would've been a time, not all that long ago, when his younger self wouldn't've questioned the turn of events, but would've gone with it, as she'd suggested. Eagerly. Not to mention gratefully. However...

"Not happening, honey," he said gently.

Dee froze, then clumsily shoved off his lap and to her feet, raking a hand through her straggly hair as she walked over to the nearest window, her arms tightly crossed. Cautiously, the cat writhed around her ankles, giving Josh the stink eye—because clearly this was all his fault—before warbling a series of hugely concerned *mrreow*s.

You okay, Human? You'll still feed me, right? Another glance in Josh's direction. *What the* hell *did you do to her? Fix it!*

"Sorry. I…" Dee blew out a breath. "Sorry."

Braving the cat's glare, Josh came up behind Dee to turn her toward him, kiss her forehead. "Come here," he said, steering her toward the nearest sofa, where she collapsed beside him, still strangling her rib cage. Until the cat jumped on her lap again, clearly daring Josh to pull a fast one. Not to mention Thor, who crept into the room, took one look at the cat and tiptoed out again.

Dee scrubbed at her cheek, folded her arms again. "And now that I've made a total fool of myself—"

"That wasn't a rejection, honey."

"Really."

"Okay, I wasn't rejecting *you.* What I was rejecting was the temptation to go down a path I never want to again. Because the last time a woman said something similar to me I ended up a daddy. Not that I'm not crazy about my son, but the next time I become a parent—if there is a next time—I'd like to have an actual say in the matter. And since I don't have any protection and I'm guessing you don't, either…" She grunted. "It's called being practical, honey."

Although she didn't seem inclined to move out of his arms. So there was that. Whatever that was. "And speaking of practical…" Josh reached out to pet the cat, who shot him a *You gotta be kidding me?* look that made him think better of it. "You only gave birth a month ago—"

A pause preceded, "I figured we could be careful?"

Now he did laugh. "Trust me—after all this time of wondering what it'd be like to get naked with you, *careful* is the last thing I'd want to be. Except for the part about making more babies, I mean. So you want to tell me what this is really about? Because I'm also not partial to being used to salve whatever wounds you're looking to salve."

Dee sat up so fast the cat shot off her lap and stalked off, only to stop a few feet away to lick his mussed fur.

"I would never do that! Especially…" Blushing again, Dee looked away. "Especially not to you."

"Even though you're going back east in a few days? I presume, never to return?"

She faced him again, her mouth twitching. "Wow. You sound kind of…pissed."

And with that, he was. Monumentally pissed. Pissed like no man in love had probably even been in the history of the world.

"Damn straight, I'm pissed. And you know what?" Josh surged to his feet, sending the poor cat streaking from the room. "What I said before, about being careful? I'm done with that. Done with tiptoeing around letting you know how I feel, because I…hell, I don't even know why anymore. Because it's like Zach said, how can you make a choice if you don't have all the options—"

"You were talking about this with your brother?"

Josh smacked away the interruption. "He brought it up, it's what this family does, in case you haven't noticed. But he's right. What's the worst that can happen if I admit I want you to stay? That, hell, I want to marry you, and be Katie's daddy, and for you to be Austin's mom? You'd tell me to go screw myself, and you'd leave anyway. Which you have every right to do, don't get me wrong. But at least…"

Josh pointed at her, only to realize his hand was shaking. Right along with the rest of him. "But at least you'd *know*." He gulped down the next wave of shakes. "At least I would've been up front with you, instead of pretending…of pretending everything's okay when it isn't. Pretending I'm okay with the idea of losing you when I'm anything but." He lowered his hand, his heart beating so hard his chest ached. "At least you'd know I loved you enough to let you go. But if…*if*…"

Swallowing again, he let his gaze melt into hers. "I don't know if what I have to offer is even remotely enough for you. I'm never gonna be anything but a country boy, never gonna like the opera or the ballet or any of that fancy stuff you do. But whatever I am…" He shoved out a breath. "At least you'd have all of me. Everything. Until my dying breath, swear to God. Because the one thing I'm good at is keeping promises. And if you truly hate the Vista, if you really can't shake yourself loose from whatever's haunting you about it, we can still sell it. Because no property, not even this one, is worth losing you over. I can promise you that, too."

From down the hall came Katie's fierce little cry. It seemed to take Dee a moment to hear her before she broke their gaze and got up to go to her child, not seeming to care that Josh followed her. He stopped at the doorway to the baby's room, listening to Dee coo to the softly babbling baby as she changed her diaper and apparently soggy sleeper. When she was done, she lifted her infant daughter to her chest and faced Josh again, a tiny crease wedged between her eyebrows, and Josh released a sorry-assed laugh.

"What am I saying? Your dream job…jeebus. I can't ask you to sacrifice that for, what? A life out here in the sticks—"

"No. You can't. And I won't let you."

By now his throat was so tight he felt like he was trying to swallow a baseball. Especially when she walked past him with the baby and back down the hall, where she curled up in the corner of the sofa to feed her kid. Without even thinking, he went to the kitchen to get her a glass of water.

"Thanks," she said quietly when he handed it to her. She drank half of it before setting the glass on the end table, then smiled for her daughter, noisily sucking away. Josh sat on a nearby chair, tightly gripping the arms. After a moment, Dee looked up, letting her gaze sweep over the room.

"When your life is based on lies and half-truths," she said quietly, "it tends to… I don't know. Contaminate what *is* true? What…" Her gaze touched his, a small smile on her lips. "What was good and pure and lovely. But then, if you're very lucky…" She smoothed her fingers across Katie's chick-fluff hair. "Something, or someone—or several someones—opens your eyes, and you see through all the muck to what was real all along. That the sweet memories always win out over the bad ones. If you give them that chance. And sometimes, if you're very, *very* lucky…"

Watery eyes lifted to his. "A very *special* someone comes along—or back along—who helps you trust again. Who makes you believe. Not in fairy tales. But in truth." She smiled. "In yourself. Even if you're not sure you can do that. Because it's scary."

Josh did some fast blinking himself. "It is for everybody, honey."

A moment passed before she nodded, then sighed. "I don't hate the house, Josh. Or the ranch. Or Whispering Pines. I never did, really. Any more than my mother did, I realize. What I hated was being lied to in the name of 'protecting' me. Of people making decisions for me instead of asking me what I might've wanted. Needed. Because leaving me out of the loop left me vulnerable and naive." She snorted a soft laugh. "*Un*-protected, actually. Which I doubt was my father's intention. Although it was probably my aunt's," she said, her mouth yanked flat.

"Your aunt—"

"Later," she said, then sighed. "But it was the lies, the *secrets*, that were so stifling, even if I didn't understand that until a little bit ago. Not the place. What I'd like to do now, though…" Another sweep of the room preceded, "is reclaim what was taken from me. Including…" She smiled at Josh. "You."

Josh hesitated, his heart thundering in his chest, before moving from the chair to squat in front of her, taking Katie's tiny hand in his. "Even if that means your father wins?"

Dee's laugh floated up to the beamed ceiling. "I suppose I'll have to cede this one to him," she said, and Josh pushed himself up to palm her cheek and kiss her, her mouth soft and yielding under his. Then he leaned back, and what he saw in her eyes made hope burn in his chest, glittering and bright.

"But that job…?"

Her mouth screwed to one side, she looked back at the baby. "It would be perfect. For someone else."

"You sure?"

"I need…" Her eyes shut for a moment as she hauled in a breath. "To push myself past what's safe. Because *playing* it safe hasn't exactly been a winning game plan."

"And why do I get the feeling there's more behind those words than you're saying?"

Laughing, she cupped the baby's head and said, very softly, "You know that old gift shop on Main Street that's for sale? It would be perfect for a gallery. Not that I have any clue how I'd go about financing it, but…simply the thought of it, that it'd be *mine*…"

By now Josh's heart was pounding so hard he could hardly hear his own thoughts. But the one he *did* hear…

Dee's brow creased when Josh pushed himself up to sit beside her on the couch, tugging over a nearby ottoman to prop his boot on the edge.

"Okay, what's with the grin?"

"I bet between us we could swing a half-decent down payment." He smiled into her startled gaze. "Whaddya think?"

Now her eyes nearly popped out of her head. Only to immediately squint. "And that wouldn't be you trying to buy me, would it?"

He actually laughed. "Even if that were possible— since you're the last person on earth who could be bought—we're talking a piece of property, honey. Hell, you can make it a loan, if that makes you more comfortable. But when I said everything I have, or am, is yours… I meant it."

Dee turned away, staring toward the tree. "You'd really be willing to risk it? On me?"

Chuckling, Josh swung his arm around her shoulders to tug her and the still nursing baby closer. "Trust me, laying my butt on the line with you like I just did? That was far scarier than investing in your new gallery could ever be."

Her breath actually hitched before she said, "*Our* new gallery."

"Oh, no—that's all yours. I'll stick with horses and rodeos, thank you. Since what I know about art you could write on a gum wrapper."

Several moments of silence passed before she said, real softly, "No one's ever…" Then she shook her head, and Josh kissed her hair, and she knuckled away a tear before shoving out another choked little laugh.

"I suppose this means I have to marry you now," she said, and Josh's heart banged against his ribs hard enough to hurt. "Since I doubt anyone's ever shacked up at the Vista before."

"And God forbid the ghosts talk smack about us."

Her chuckle rumbled through him. "God forbid."

"But *only* if you want to. No pressure."

"Got it." Then Dee looked up at him, her eyes all shiny. "What was always true still is, you know."

"And what's that?"

"That I love you," she said softly. "That I *trust* you. That you'll always be my best friend."

"Same goes," Josh whispered as the dog stuck his head back in the room, cautiously wagging his tail.

Chuckling, Josh smacked his leg to bring the dog closer. "Merry Christmas, sweetheart," he said, more content than he'd ever been in his life. "Or should I say, *Marry* Christmas?"

Dee groaned, then laughed so hard Thor got on his hind legs to shove his face in hers, making sure she was okay.

"You ready?"

Sitting beside Josh in his SUV, both kids strapped in their car seats behind them, Deanna blew out a breath, then nodded. Next year, he thought, they'd do Christmas Eve at their house—a thought that still, less than twenty-four hours after Deanna agreed to marry him, sent a thrill racing up his spine. But tonight they were all gathering at his parents' place, and it would be crazy and loud and a trial by fire for the girl whose childhood had been so lonely and quiet most of the time. But if she was truly opting for this life, best she know what she was really getting into.

He leaned over and kissed her, her lips cold and smooth even though the truck's heat had kicked in almost as soon as they'd left the ranch. Once she'd told him about her and Gus's conversation, when she'd learned about her mother's mental health struggles, her aunt's role in her father's sending her away, a lot of things made sense that hadn't before. For both of them, but especially for Dee. And Josh was well aware that it wasn't going to be a walk in the park for either of them, watching her feel her way through to the other side after all the crap her family, in some misguided effort to shield her from her own pain, had actually dumped on her to deal with later. At the same time, that she trusted him enough to do that…

Well. You really couldn't put a price on that.

Austin naturally ran off to play with his cousins the moment they entered the cozy little house, filled with the traditional New Mexico Christmas Eve scents of roasting turkey and spicy enchiladas and posole. Val appeared out of nowhere to claim Katie, who was taking in the sights and sounds with big dark eyes and pursed lips.

"Auntie time," his twin's wife said with a wink, as if she knew. Then again, knowing Val, she probably did.

Still in their coats, Josh took Dee's hand and led her into the jam-packed kitchen, filled to bursting with Talbots. Or soon-to-be Talbots. And immediately the chattering and laughter ceased, all eyes turning to them. Expectantly, Josh thought.

Then Dee took a deep breath and said, "I'm staying," and Austin popped up again out of nowhere and said, "An' she's gonna be my mom! For real!" and all *hell* broke loose.

In the best possible way.

Several minutes later, after the poor woman had been hugged within an inch of her life and Josh's back had been slapped so hard he was sure he'd have bruises, he tugged his fiancée into a back bedroom to kiss the stuffing out of her. Then she smiled up at him and whispered, "Thank you for loving me," and he saw so much promise in her eyes he almost couldn't stand it.

But he'd manage, he thought, pulling her into his arms with a big old grin on his face.

Epilogue

Several weeks later

Dude definitely hadn't been kidding about not being *careful*, Deanna thought with a satisfied smile as she gradually came awake in the new king-size bed in the house's master bedroom.

The bedroom she now shared with the warm, naked man in whose arms she'd awakened. The man responsible for that satisfied smile. The man who'd finally banished the ghosts from this house—her thoughts—forever. Or at least, was helping *her* banish them.

Dee lay in the silence of the deep winter morning, still gray and soft and velvety, cherishing the moment. The peace. The…*knowing*. That she was safe, and loved, and right where she belonged. Where she'd always belonged, if she were being honest. And where her daughter would grow up cocooned in love, in laughter and shenanigans, surrounded by family.

Thank you, Daddy, she thought, blinking back the suggestion of tears. Whatever mistakes her father might have made—even from the best of intentions—in the end, he got it right.

So right.

From his dog bed in the corner, Thor whup-whupped in his sleep, probably disturbing the cat, who'd taken to cozying up to the mutt, much to the dog's shock. It'd be a good hour before the kids woke up—Katie had been sleeping through the night for weeks, God bless her, in Dee's old room, now girlified within an inch of its life. Although her wicked, wicked mother-in-law had said not to get used to it, the next one probably wouldn't. A thought that pushed a silent chuckle from Deanna's chest. Not that she and Josh were in any hurry to add to their brood—they'd only been married a week, for heaven's sake, a no-frills justice of the peace affair with a reception at Annie's—but maybe next year...

She snuggled closer, breathing in Josh's scent, reveling in his solidity, his *there*ness. It'd been a crazy few weeks, including her returning to DC long enough to close up her apartment, arrange for shipping stuff here she wanted to keep, sell off what she didn't. Enduring an endless evening with her aunt and uncle to show off Katie, practically choking on the rampant disapproval, that clearly her aunt's plan to *rescue* Deanna had backfired so spectacularly. Then again, once Emily's wedding was over, she doubted she'd ever see them again. No reason to, really.

And, since the sale to Mallory was no longer an

option—not that her future sister-in-law seemed at all unhappy about that—Josh instead offered to rent her part of the spread for her therapy facility since so much of the ranch was underutilized, anyway. And those funds would go into the kids' college funds, as well into the gallery, which Deanna planned on opening in the spring—

Josh stirred, then yawned and stretched before pulling her closer, his early-morning beard haze tickling her neck, his fingers skimming the slim gold band on her finger before finding their way to her no-longer-leaking breast, hallelujah.

"Mornin', wife," he murmured, his voice thick with sleep as he thumbed her nipple, making her toes curl.

"Morning, husband," she whispered back, turning into a mass of tingles when Josh gave her an impish grin.

"How much time we got?"

"Enough," she said, laughing when he disappeared beneath the covers to stoke fires that, to be honest, didn't need all that much stoking. And she melted at his touch, his tenderness, the message behind them both— *I'm not goin' anywhere, darlin'*—breathing out a sigh of pure contentment when he slid inside her, filling all her empty spaces…and she saw, in his eyes, bright in the silky, filmy light, *home*.

"I love you," she whispered, and he grinned.

"Oh, just wait," he said, and she laughed, thinking, *I am a lucky, lucky girl.*

* * * * *

April Arrington grew up in a small Southern town and developed a love for movies and books at an early age. Emotionally moving stories have always held a special place in her heart. April enjoys collecting pottery and soaking up the Georgia sun on her front porch.

Visit April at Facebook.com/authoraprilarrington.

Books by April Arrington

Home on the Ranch: Tennessee Bull Rider
Home on the Ranch: Tennessee Homecoming

Harlequin Western Romance

Elk Valley, Tennessee

A Home with the Rancher

Men of Raintree Ranch

Twins for the Bull Rider
The Rancher's Wife
The Bull Rider's Cowgirl
The Rancher's Miracle Baby

Visit the Author Profile page
at Harlequin.com for more titles.

THE RANCHER'S MIRACLE BABY

April Arrington

Dedicated to Patricia B. of Alabama.

This writing life is tough. Knowing you're on the other side of the page changes everything and helps me make it to The End. You are a treasured reader, and the world is a great deal more beautiful with you in it.

Thank you for your sweet messages
and for always reading.

Chapter 1

Tammy Jenkins had managed to outrun a lot of things in life. But this had her beat.

"If you're on the road, we urge you to take shelter immediately." The truck's radio crackled, and static scrambled the urgent male voice coming through the speakers. "...summer outbreak...multiple tornadoes spotted. We've received reports of funnel clouds touching down in Leary County, Georgia. The most recent... forming... Deer Creek community."

Deer Creek. Tammy gripped the steering wheel tighter, recalling the crooked green sign she'd passed a few miles back. The bent edges and bullet hole through the center had obscured some of the letters, but the words were legible enough.

A high-pitched neigh and sharp clang split her ears. She glanced in the side-view mirror and cringed as the trailer attached to the truck rocked to one side, squeaking and groaning.

"It's okay, girl," Tammy called out. "I'll find somewhere to stop soon."

Razz, her barrel-racing horse, had experienced her fair share of close calls. And just like when they were about to take a tumble in the arena, the mare sensed danger approaching.

Tammy looked past the trailer and studied the darkening horizon behind them. The wall of black clouds gathered momentum, increasing in size and staining the sky. It swallowed up the dying light of the late-afternoon sun, and a green hue bled through the inky darkness. Thick grass lining both sides of the isolated road rippled with each powerful surge of wind.

Sour acid crept up the back of Tammy's throat, parching her mouth. She jerked her eyes forward, refocused on the road and slammed her foot harder onto the accelerator. The engine rumbled, and the broken yellow line splitting the paved highway streamed by in a blur.

"No need to panic," she said, nodding absently. "It's July. These storms blow over faster than they appear. I'll just have to outrun it before it gets started."

She grinned. If there was one thing she was good at, it was racing. Heck, she didn't have a gold buckle in the glove compartment and over three hundred grand in her savings account for nothing. And there hadn't been a cloud in the sky this morning when she'd left Alabama and crossed the Georgia state line. Chances were, she and Razz would reach their destination earlier than planned.

Her smile slipped. She just wished she'd stayed on

the busy interstate instead of cutting through a back-woods town. Especially one that was eerily similar to her rural hometown without a soul in sight.

But the empty road she'd taken was a shortcut. And loneliness had driven her to do what it had always done—made her act before thinking.

A second round of strong kicks rocked the trailer again and reverberated against the metal walls. The clouds looked darker than ever in the rearview mirror.

Calm down. She straightened and glanced at the trailer. Razz couldn't hear or understand her, but talking to the horse would at least keep Tammy from freaking out.

"We'll pull over somewhere, ride it out and be at Raintree Ranch before you know it, Razz." Tammy forced a laugh, seeking comfort in the sound of her own voice. A strategy she'd been forced to adopt as a child and still utilized at twenty-five. "Jen will be so glad to see you."

Her strained words fell into the empty cab and put a sinking feeling in her stomach. Lord, she wished Jen was with her now, sitting in the passenger seat and teasing her about speeding. A former barrel racer and Tammy's best friend, Jen Taylor had always made traveling the rodeo circuit feel like home. But a year ago, Jen had gotten engaged, retired from racing and settled on Raintree Ranch in Georgia. And for the first time in eight years, Tammy no longer felt like she belonged on the circuit.

Instead, she felt alone. More alone than she cared to admit.

"Suck it up, girl," Tammy muttered, studying the highway. "There's no bawling on Sunday, and there are too many things to be grateful for. Think about taffeta and veils. Flowers and cakes. Rings and vows."

Jen's wedding was worth a bit of bad weather, and with it only a month away, Tammy was determined to be the best dang maid of honor on earth. After scoring another big win in the arena, she'd left the circuit to help Jen finalize seating arrangements, accompany her to a final wedding gown fitting and plan the most fantastic bachelorette party ever known to woman. All in preparation for the bright future awaiting Jen.

A future that included a husband, a home and, eventually, the many children Jen planned to have. Babies Tammy had been asked to serve as godmother to and hoped to shower with love one day.

Tammy's smile returned, her spirits lifting. Her best friend was getting married. Starting a family. "Babies," she whispered.

Fat raindrops splattered against the dusty windshield in quick succession, then stopped as abruptly as they'd begun. Tammy flipped the wipers on, wincing as the rubber jerked noisily over the glass, smearing brown streaks of dirt in her line of vision. A vicious clap of thunder boomed against the ground beneath them and vibrated her sunglasses on the dashboard.

The angry storm wasn't just gaining on them—it was gnashing at their heels.

"It's not that bad, Razz," she said over the rumbles of thunder. "Just a little wind and rain."

Her eyes flicked over the empty landscape surrounding her. There were weeds, trees and fields but no houses or cars. There were no people. No signs of life. And nothing but static left on the radio.

Tammy swallowed hard, mouth trembling. "We need to pull over."

That was what the guy on the radio had said. That was what all news reporters blared in warning as tornadoes approached. It was safer to stop and get out of the vehicle. But the idea of lying facedown in a ditch with nothing but jeans and a T-shirt separating her from the elements was too terrifying to imagine. And there was no way she could leave Razz in the trailer. She needed to find shelter for the mare. A stable or barn. Anything that would give Razz a stronger chance of survival than just running.

"There's got to be something soon." She peered ahead and willed the truck faster up the hill. "We'll just…"

Her voice faded as several white balls tumbled across the road several feet ahead. Some bounced over the pavement and rolled into the grass. Others flew through the air sideways, never touching the ground. Dozens of them. One after the other.

Baseballs…?

She shook her head at the foolish thought, a panicked laugh escaping her. There were no kids playing outside in this weather. And there were no baseball games nearby—

One struck the windshield, punching a hole through the glass and leaving a jagged web of cracks. Tammy stifled a scream and glanced at the passenger seat. Her chest clenched at the thick ball of ice wedged between the door and the seat.

She gritted her teeth and faced forward, blinking rapidly against the wind stinging her eyes through the gaping hole in the windshield. "Everything's okay, Razz."

Her voice pitched higher as she shielded her face with one hand. "I'm gonna get us somewhere safe."

The pounding kicks from inside the trailer intensified as hail hammered the truck and trailer. Razz cried out, the sound primal and fierce, and the trailer took a sharp swing to the left.

Tammy grappled with the steering wheel, fighting the wind and managing to redirect the truck's path. Mercifully, the hail stopped, and she sped over the crest of the hill and down the other side.

Two dirt driveways appeared ahead, one on either side of the road and framed by a line of trees. There were no houses visible, but both roads had to lead somewhere. And wherever they ended, there had to be a better chance of shelter there than on the barren highway.

"Which one?"

Tammy hesitated, eyeing each entrance and catching sight of a wooden fence lining the dirt road on the right. A fence was promising. It meant a house might follow and, hopefully, people.

"Right." She shouted the word, demanding her stiff fingers loosen their death grip on the wheel long enough to make the turn.

She slammed her foot on the accelerator again, turning her face to the side as a fresh surge of rain flew through the busted windshield, smacking against her cheeks. The truck bounced over the uneven ground, jerking her around in the cab and slinging her bottle of soda from the low cup holder to the floorboard.

Tammy ducked her head, rubbed her wet face against her soggy shirtsleeve, then braved the lash of the rain again to scrutinize the end of the driveway.

There was a house, a truck…*and a stable*.

"Thank God," she whispered, jerking the truck to a stop. "We're going to be okay, Razz."

Tammy laid on the horn, then shoved the door open with her shoulder, forcing it out against the wind. No one emerged from the house, and there was no movement outside.

Please. Oh, please let someone be here.

"Help!" She pounded her fist on the horn twice more before jumping out of the cab.

Her boots slid over the slick mud of the driveway, and she gripped the hard metal of the truck, forcing her way through the violent gusts of wind to the trailer.

Razz jerked her head against the open slats. Her dark eyes widened in panic, stark against the black and white markings surrounding them.

"I'm right here." Tammy strived for a calm tone as the spray of wind and rain whipped her bare neck and arms. "I won't leave you."

She ducked her head and continued, making it to the back end and grabbing the latch on the gate. There were deep dents and dings where the hail had hit, making it difficult to pry the door open.

Razz cried out and thrashed against the walls of the trailer. Each panicked act from the horse sent a wave of dread through her.

"I know." Tammy jerked harder at the handle, the bent metal cutting into the sensitive flesh of her palms. "I'm gonna get you out, I promise."

A strange stillness settled around the truck, and the lashing rain stopped. She froze, her hand tightening around the latch.

Moments later, a distant rumble sounded at her back, the rhythmic roar growing louder with each lurch of her heart. Tammy slowly turned and peeled the wet strands of her hair from her eyes with shaky fingers.

There it was. A towering funnel, churning less than a mile away across the landscape, lifting above the hill she and Razz had just traveled over and bearing down on the other side of the road. Its snakelike outline widened with each passing second, growing in size and tearing across the landscape opposite her.

She stood, transfixed, as her eyes tracked its powerful spin. Trees hid its base, but large chunks of debris lifted higher into the air with each second, floating on the outskirts of the black spiral before hurtling to the ground.

The jagged objects were too big and solid to be bits of vegetation. They flipped and twirled like confetti and loose pieces of paper, but they looked firm and heavy. Definitely man-made.

"Oh, no." Tammy's strangled whisper sounded foreign even to her own ears.

Broken beams of wood. Fragmented sections of brick walls. All pieces of a home. There'd been a house at the end of the other driveway, too. And, possibly…*people*.

Her heart stalled. *"No…"*

The trees standing at the base of the twister bent, touched the ground, then disappeared into the black swirl of wind. A fierce chorus of cracks and growls erupted into the air, and the furious churning of wind howled across the field.

Tammy squinted in confusion when the sidetracking motion of the tornado stopped. It was odd. There *was* movement. Large chunks of debris still twirled with the powerful twister, lifting and lowering with each roar of wind. But, somehow, it was standing still.

How could—

Her muscles seized. It wasn't standing still. The twister had shifted its path and was heading across the field again. In her direction.

She spun back to the trailer and jerked on the latch violently. "Help! Please!"

The wind swept away her cry, her lungs burning as Razz's kicks rocked the trailer.

Tammy squatted low and yanked harder on the handle, her heart hammering painfully. She needed to run to the house. But to leave Razz without a chance—

"Please." She pulled harder, her arms screaming in protest.

A shrill noise erupted at her side. Something flashed in the air—flat and silver—then slammed into her temple, knocking her to the ground.

Tammy blinked hard, a sharp pain slicing through her head and a flash of light distorting her vision. Wetness trickled down her cheek.

Touching a trembling hand to it, she stared at the dark sky above her and noted the absence of rain. The white spots dancing in front of her eyes cleared, and she pulled her hand from her face and held it up. Red coated her palm.

"It's just blood, Razz," she whispered amid the mare's cries, studying the black clouds through the gaps in her spread fingers.

A hard blow to the head. That was all. Something

her father had doled out on a daily basis by the time she'd reached sixteen.

A large shape shifted, moving above her and obscuring the dark clouds. Tammy lowered her palm and her gaze locked with a pair of stormy gray eyes.

A man stared down at her, his broad shoulders and muscled girth blocking the wind. He had tanned skin and black hair sprinkled with silver. The striking mix as deep and rich as the storm overhead.

His big hands reached for her.

"My horse needs help," she rasped, scrambling back.

His piercing gaze cut to the trailer as Razz's kicks and desperate cries strengthened. He swung around, gripped the bent latch and wrestled the gate open. A moment later, Razz burst out of the trailer with disoriented jerks.

"Get," he shouted, smacking the horse's rear.

Razz leaped and took off, galloping out of sight.

"Come on." He yanked Tammy to her feet, tucked her tight to his side and ran across the front lawn toward the house.

Tammy pumped her legs hard, keeping up with his powerful stride and ignoring the nausea roiling in her gut.

The massive surge of wind grew stronger at their backs, and their boots slipped repeatedly on the slick grass. They stumbled up the front steps to the door and fell to the porch floor as the vicious growl of the tornado drew closer.

This is it.

Tammy squeezed her eyes shut, the concrete pressing

hard against her cheek and disjointed thoughts whip-
ping through her mind.

She wouldn't make it to Jen's wedding. Wouldn't hug
or kiss Jen's children one day. And would never get the
chance to have babies of her own. It would remain the
foolish dream it'd always been. The kind that belonged
to a woman who'd never been able to trust a man with
her body or her heart. Unrealistic and unattainable.

"Keep moving." The man's brawny arm tightened
around her back as he forced his way to his knees.

Tammy looked up, her eyes freezing on his face. The
strong jaw, aquiline nose and sculpted mouth belonged
to a stranger. But at least she wasn't alone.

The thought was oddly comforting, and when she
spoke, her voice remained steady despite the horrify-
ing possibility she acknowledged.

"We're not going to make it."

The hell they weren't.

Alex Weston balled his hand into a fist, pressed it to
the porch floor and shoved to his haunches. He steadied
himself against the strong surge of wind, then reached
down and pulled the woman up with him.

She was soft—*and strong*. The slight curves of her
biceps were firm underneath the pads of his fingers, and
she'd matched his pace as they'd sprinted to the house.
But she was slender and light. So light, each gust of
wind threatened to steal her from his grasp.

"Keep moving," he growled, ignoring the panicked
flare of her green eyes and forging ahead.

Alex shoved her forward and pressed her against the
wall of the house. He jerked the front door open and

helped her inside, but before he could follow, the wind caught it, ripping it wide-open to the side and yanking him around with it. The sharp edges of brick cut into his back.

Wet grass and dirt sprayed his face, and he spat against it, struggling to maintain control of the door and his panic. He squinted against the bite of wind and peered across the front lawn. The tornado barreled across the driveway toward the house, sucking up the wooden posts of the fence and spitting them out. The wood sliced through the air with shrill whistles, scattering in all directions and stabbing into the ground. Each jagged plank a deadly missile.

His eyes shot to the open field, which was bare and vulnerable in the path of the twister. He'd just released the horses from their stalls when the woman had driven up. The stable walls were sturdy but no match for the violent storm the weather forecasters had warned against. He'd hoped the horses would have a better chance of surviving if they were free to run. But he had no idea if it'd been the right decision. Was no longer even sure if he would survive the massive twister.

"Hurry."

It was a breathless sound, almost stolen by the wind. The door jerked in his grasp as the woman leaned farther outside, pulling hard on the edge of it.

A high-pitched screech filled the air, and a piece of metal slammed into one of the columns lining the front porch. Adrenaline spiked in his veins, pounding through his blood and burning his muscles. He renewed his grip on the door, and they yanked together, succeeding in wrenching the door closed as they staggered inside.

"This way." Alex grabbed her elbow and darted through the living room, pulling her past the kitchen and down a narrow hallway in the center of the house.

A wry scoff escaped him. His first guest in nine years—other than the Kents living across the road—and he was manhandling her to the floor.

She dropped to her knees, and Alex covered her, tucking her bent form tight to his middle and cupping his hands over the top of her head. They pressed closer to the wall as the violent sounds increased in intensity, filling the dark stillness enfolding them. It was impossible to see anything. But the sounds...

God help him—*the sounds*.

Glass shattered, objects thudded and the savage roar of the wind obliterated the silence. The house groaned, and the air hissed and whistled in all directions.

Alex's muscles locked, the skin on the back of his neck and forearms prickling. His blood froze into blocks of ice, and his jaw clenched so tight he thought his teeth would shatter.

The damned thing sounded as though it was ripping the house apart. Would rip *them* apart.

Bursts of panicked laughter moved through his chest. This was not how he'd planned to spend his Sunday evening. He'd expected a long day of work on his ranch, a whiskey and an evening spent alone. That was the way it'd been for nine years, since the day his ex-wife left. The way he wanted it. He preferred solitude and predictability.

But there was nothing as unpredictable as the weather. Except for a woman.

"It'll pass." The woman's strained words reached his

ears briefly, then faded beneath the ferocious sounds passing overhead. "It'll pass."

Hell if he knew what it was. For some reason, he got the impression she wasn't even speaking to him. That she was simply voicing her thoughts out loud. But something in her tone and the warm, solid feel of her beneath him, breathing and surviving, made the violent shudders racking his body stop. It melted the blocks of ice in his veins, relieving the chill on his skin.

He curled closer, ducked down amid the thundering clang of debris around them and pressed his cheek to the top of the woman's head. Her damp hair clung to the stubble on his jaw, and the musty smell of rain filled his nostrils. Each of her rapid breaths lifted her back tighter against his chest, and the sticky heat of blood from the wound on her temple clung to the pads of his fingers.

"Yeah," he said, his lips brushing her ear as he did his best to shelter her. "It'll pass."

Gradually, the pounding onslaught of debris against the house ceased. The violent winds eased to a swift rush, and the deafening roar faded into the distance. Light trickled down the hallway, and the air around them stilled. The worst of it couldn't have lasted more than forty seconds. But it had felt like an eternity.

"Is it over?"

Alex blinked hard against the dust lingering in the air and lifted his head, focusing on the weak light emanating from the other room. "Yeah." He cleared his throat and sat upright, untangling his fingers from the long, wet strands of her hair. "I think so."

She slipped from beneath him, slumped back against the wall and released a heavy breath. "Thank you."

Her green eyes, bright and beautiful, traveled slowly over his face. His skin warmed beneath her scrutiny, his attention straying to the way her soaked T-shirt and jeans clung to her lush curves and long legs.

He shifted uncomfortably and redirected his thoughts to her age. She looked young. Very young. If he had to guess, he'd say midtwenties...if that. But he'd never been good at pinning someone's age. Just like no one had ever been good at guessing his.

The dash of premature gray he'd inherited made him look older than his thirty-five years. And, hell, to be honest, he felt as old as he probably looked nowadays.

She smiled slightly. "That's pitiful, isn't it?" She shook her head, her low laugh humorless. "A cheap, two-word phrase in exchange for saving my life."

A thin stream of blood flowed from her temple over her flushed cheek, then settled in the corner of her mouth. The tip of her tongue peeked out to touch it, and she frowned.

"Here." Alex tugged a rag from his back pocket and reached for the wound on her head. "It's—"

Her hand shot out and clamped tight around his wrist, halting his movements. "What're you doing?"

He stilled, then lowered his free hand slowly to the floor. Damn, she was strong. Stronger than he'd initially thought. Even though his wrist was too thick for her fingers to wrap around, she maintained control over it. And the panic in her eyes was more than just residual effects from the tornado.

"You're cut." He nodded toward her wound, softening his tone and waiting beneath her hard stare. "You can use this to stop the bleeding."

Her hold on his wrist eased, and her face flooded with color. "Th-thank you."

She took the rag from him and pressed it to her head, wincing at the initial contact, then drew her knees tightly to her chest. He studied her for a moment and touched his other palm to the floor, noting the way she kept eyeing his hands.

"I'm sorry that rag's not clean," he said. "I get pretty sweaty outside during the day." He remained still. "I'm Alex. Alex Weston."

"Tammy Jenkins." She held the rag up briefly. "And thank you again. For everything."

"You've thanked me enough." Cringing at the gruff sound of his voice, he stood slowly and stepped back, his boots crunching over shards of glass. "We better get outside. I need to check the damage to the house before I can be sure it's safe to be in here."

"The house across the road," she said softly, peering up at him. "Did someone live there?"

"Did someone live…" His heart stalled. Dean Kent, his best friend and business partner, lived there. Along with his wife, Gloria, and their eleven-month-old son. "Why? What'd you see?"

"I think it hit that house, too," she said, dodging his eyes and shoving to her feet. "I can't be sure how bad, but it looked like…"

Her voice faded as his boots pounded across the floor, over the porch and down the front steps. The heavy humidity clogged his nose and mouth, making it difficult to breathe, and the frantic sprint made his lungs ache. He jumped over several small piles of debris, registering wood planks, buckets and tree limbs.

He stopped at a twisted pile of metal and absorbed the damage around him. Trees were down everywhere. Some were split in half, the remaining jagged halves stabbing into the air. His stable was in shambles, but, thankfully, the main house seemed somewhat sturdy.

It appeared as though the twister had only side-swiped his house. But Tammy's tone had suggested Dean's house had been hit head-on.

Alex darted toward his truck, but the massive tree lying over the tailgate would take time to move. Precious time he didn't have.

Tammy, breathless, jogged up behind him. "Alex—"

"Do you have your keys?"

She patted her front pocket absently, her wide eyes focused over his left shoulder. "Yes. But they won't do you any good."

He spun and stifled a curse at the sight of her truck and trailer overturned in the mud. Though the worst of the storm had passed, dark clouds still cloaked the sky, and several large drops of rain hit his cheeks and forehead. Another storm approached.

Alex gripped a thick tree limb and hefted himself over the trunk, scrambling over broken branches and shards of glass. He ran as fast as his legs would allow, his boots pounding into puddles of water and mud splashing up his jeans.

A power line was down and crisscrossed the road in a snakelike pattern. He jerked to a halt and stiffened at the sound of feet sloshing over wet ground behind him.

"Wait." He threw out his arm and glanced over his shoulder.

Tammy skittered to a stop, her boots slipping over

the mud. Her chest rose and fell with heavy breaths as she surveyed the downed power line.

Alex stood still, each heavy thump of his heart marking the seconds ticking by. *To hell with it.* Dean and Gloria were on the other side. He stepped carefully over each curve of the tangled line until he reached the opposite side of the road.

To his surprise, Tammy followed, her boots taking the same path as his. He waited for her to reach him safely, then they ran the rest of the way to Dean's house.

"Dear God..." His voice left him, and his frantic steps slowed.

There was no longer a two-story house. Just a foundation filled with fragmented brick walls, massive piles of wood, shredded insulation and broken glass. There were no movements and no voices. Only the distant rumble of thunder and random plop of raindrops striking the wreckage filled the silence.

"Dean?" Alex winced. His shaky voice barely rose above the rasp of the wind. He cleared his throat and tried again. *"Dean!"*

No answer. He took a hesitant step forward, then another until he reached the highest pile of rubble, visually sifting through splintered doors, broken window frames and loose bricks. Dread seeped into his veins and weakened his limbs. He began walking the perimeter, struggling to stay upright and fighting the urge to collapse on the wet ground.

Maybe they weren't home. He nodded and kept moving. They might have driven the twenty miles to town to get groceries and could still be there. He rounded what used to be the back of the house and scanned the heaps.

That was what it was—they weren't home. *Thank God.*

"They weren't here," he called out, turning and starting back toward Tammy. "They—"

He froze. The toe of a purple shoe stuck out beneath a toppled, broken brick wall.

Those dang shoes of yours are gonna blind me one day, Gloria.

Alex began to shake. How many times had he heard Dean tease his wife about her purple shoes? The bright ones she liked to run in every morning after they'd fed and turned out the horses?

It's not my shoes that are blinding you, baby, she would chide Dean. *It's my beauty.*

"Gloria?" Alex hit his knees and touched the laces with trembling fingers. He could still hear her laugh in his head. Joyful and energetic. *"Gloria."*

There was no answer. He gripped the edge of the bricks and heaved, barely registering Tammy dropping to his side and lifting with him. They wrestled with the weight of the brick wall, and he counted off, directing Tammy to shove with him in tandem until they managed to shift it. Huge chunks crumbled away, and the largest section broke off to the side, revealing Dean and Gloria underneath.

Lifeless.

"No." Alex shook his head, tuning out Tammy's soft sobs. "This is the wrong one. This is the wrong damned house." He shot to his feet, choked back the bile rising in his throat, then threw his head back to shout up at the dark sky. *"You got the wrong one, you son of a bitch!"*

The storm should've taken his house. It was an empty shell. A pathetic structure that would never shelter children or a married couple—his infertility had seen to the former and his ex-wife had ensured the latter. He wasn't a father or a husband. Hell, he wasn't even a man in the real sense of the word. And there was no bright future to look forward to in his life.

"It should've been me, you bastard," he yelled, his voice hoarse and his throat raw.

Not Gloria. Not Dean. And not... *Brody.* His stomach heaved. Not that beautiful boy who'd just learned to walk. The son Dean had been so proud of and whom Gloria had smothered with affection.

"Alex?"

He doubled over, clamping a hand over his mouth and trying not to gag.

Tammy moved closer to his side. "I hear something, Alex."

He glanced up. Tears marred her smooth cheeks, mingling with the dirt and rain on her face. "They're gone," he choked. "There's no one."

"No." She shook her head. "Listen."

Alex heard it then. A faint cry, no louder than a weak whisper, swept by his ear on a surge of wind. He couldn't tell if it was an animal or a human. If it was a final cry of death or a declaration of life. All he knew as he scanned the wreckage in front of him was that he was terrified of what he might find.

Chapter 2

Tammy tilted her head and strained to pinpoint the soft cries escaping the demolished house in front of her. They were muffled and seemed to emanate from a stack of rubble next to...

She stifled a sob, tore her eyes from the couple lying in front of her and pointed at a high pile of debris. "There," she said.

For a moment, she didn't think Alex would move. He remained doubled over beside her, silent and still. But when a fresh round of cries rang out from the rubble, he shot upright, scrambled toward the towering mass in the center of the demolished home and began heaving jagged two-by-fours out of the way.

The broad muscles of his back strained the thin, wet material of his T-shirt as he flung the debris away. He jerked to a stop when he reached a ragged portion of a wall—the only one left standing. A battered door dangled from its hinges and barely covered an opening.

Tammy stepped to his side, hope welling within her chest. Other than a hole having been punched through the upper corner, the door looked relatively untouched. Just like the plastic hanger sitting on the ground in front of it. And the healthy cry of a child reverberated within.

Alex reached out and gripped the doorknob, the shine of the brass dulled by mud and bits of leaves. The door squeaked as he pulled it out slowly, then propped it open. The dim light from the cloudy sky overhead barely lit the interior.

A young child huddled on the ground against the back corner. He stopped crying and looked up, his red cheeks wet with tears. The denim overalls and striped shirt he wore were damp, too.

His big brown eyes moved from Tammy to Alex, then his face crumpled. A renewed round of cries escaped him and echoed over the ravaged landscape surrounding them. Chubby hands reached up toward Alex, the small fingers grasping empty air.

Tammy gasped, her chest burning, and glanced at Alex.

He didn't move. He stood motionless amid thick planks of wood and pink insulation. The increasing gusts of wind ruffled his hair and a stoic expression blanketed his pale face.

"Alex?"

Throat aching, Tammy hesitated briefly, then knelt and scooped up the boy. His thin arms wrapped tight around her neck, and his hot face pressed against her skin, his sobs ringing in her ears.

"Alex." She spoke firmly and dipped her head toward the boy at her chest. "What's his name?"

Alex blinked, eyes refocusing on her, and whispered, "Brody."

Tammy smoothed a palm gently over the boy's soft brown hair. "We're here, Brody." Her chin trembled, and she bit her lip hard before saying, "We're here now."

She stepped carefully over a large portion of the roof, the tattered shingles flapping in the wind and clacking against the rafters.

"Don't let him see," Alex rasped.

He moved swiftly to block the couple behind them, then cleared a safe path to the grass.

Tammy walked slowly behind him, swallowing hard and concentrating on his confident movements. His brawny frame seemed massive above the razed house, and under normal circumstances his towering presence would have set her nerves on edge. But she didn't feel the usual waves of apprehension. Only a deep sense of gratitude. And she found herself huddling closer to his back with each step, the boy in her arms growing quiet by the time they'd reached the road.

Alex stopped and held out his hands, slight tremors jerking his fingers. "Let me have him."

Tammy nodded and eased Brody into his arms. Alex squatted, set Brody on his feet, then ran his palms over the boy's limbs. He examined him closely.

"Nothing's broken," he said, his strained voice tinged with wonder. "There's not a scratch on him."

Brody whimpered and took two clumsy steps forward, bumping awkwardly between Alex's knees and settling against his broad chest. He laid his head against Alex's shirt and gripped the material with both hands.

"I know, little man." Alex dropped a swift kiss to the top of Brody's head before pressing him back into Tammy's arms. He spun away and started walking. "We better get him to the house. More clouds are rolling in."

Tammy looked up, her lids fluttering against the sporadic drizzle falling from a darker sky, then followed Alex. They took a different path than before, moving farther up the road before crossing to avoid the downed power line. The dirt drive leading to Alex's house had transformed to slick mud, and what was left of the late-afternoon light died, giving way to night and leaving the ravaged path cloaked in darkness.

Tammy swiped a clammy hand over her brow when they finally reached the front lawn. It seemed like the longest walk she'd ever taken. Her arms grew heavy with Brody's weight as she waited outside for Alex to check the house and make sure it was structurally sound.

"Razz," she called softly, cradling Brody's head against the painful throb in her chest and peering into the darkness.

Closing her eyes, she shifted the baby to her other hip and listened for the sound of hooves or neighs but heard neither. Only the rhythmic chirp of crickets, the faint croak of frogs and a sprinkle of rain striking the ground filled the empty land surrounding them.

Her legs grew weak, and a strange buzzing took over, assaulting her senses and mingling with the remembered images of Brody's parents lying among the rubble.

"You can come in." Alex stood on the front porch, holding a camping lantern. The bright light bathed his handsome features and highlighted the weather-beaten foliage littering the steps below him. "It's safe. Just be careful of the glass."

Safe. Tammy pulled in a strong breath and held Brody tighter as she made her way inside. She hadn't felt that way in a long time. Not a single corner of the world felt safe anymore, and she never stayed in one place long enough to find out if it was.

"We should probably get him out of those wet clothes." Alex gestured toward the dark hallway and turned to close the door behind them.

The door frame had been damaged by the storm, and he kicked the corner of it with his boot repeatedly until it shut. Tammy walked slowly down the hall, feeling her way with a hand on the wall as they drifted out of reach of the lantern's light and arrived at the first door on the left. She fumbled around to find the doorknob, then twisted, but it was locked.

"Not there," he bit out.

She jumped and glanced over her shoulder. Brody lifted his head from her chest and started crying again.

Alex winced and looked down, cursing softly. "I'm sorry," he said, easing awkwardly around them and moving farther down the hall. "I don't use that room. And the windows are blown out in the guest room." He opened a door at the end of the hall and motioned for her to precede him inside. "But you're welcome to this one."

She took a few steps, then hesitated at the threshold, an uneasy feeling knotting in her stomach as she scrutinized his expression. He'd sheltered her during intense events, and she truly believed she'd seen him at one of his weakest moments back at the demolished home. But...he was still a stranger. One who obviously cared for Brody but refused to hold the boy. And she'd learned a long time ago that a kind face could mask a multitude of evils.

Alex slowly reached out and rubbed his hand over Brody's back. "I'm sorry," he repeated gently. "From the looks of your truck, you're not going to be able to drive it tonight. Power's out. Landlines and cell service are down, so we can't make any calls, either. I did mean what I said. You're welcome to use this room tonight."

His expression softened, and his tempting mouth curved up at the corners in what she suspected was supposed to be a smile. But it fell flat, as though he rarely used it, and he turned away.

Broken. Tammy swallowed hard past the lump in her throat. His body was agile, solid and strong. But his smile was broken.

She straightened and followed him into the room, trying to shake off the strange thought—and the unfamiliar urge to touch him. To comfort a man. They both arose from the intensity of the day's events. And the loss he and Brody had suffered was enough to evoke sympathy from even the hardest of hearts.

"I pull from a well, so there's no running water." Alex crossed the room and riffled through the closet. Hangers clacked, and clothing rustled. "I have some bottled water on hand that I can put in the bathroom for you." He held up a couple of shirts and a pair of jogging pants. "It wouldn't hurt for you to put on some dry clothes, too. These will swallow you both whole, but they'll at least keep you comfortable while the others dry out."

Tammy looked down and plucked at her soggy T-shirt and jeans. Brody squirmed against her, squinting against the light Alex held.

"I'll wait in the kitchen," Alex said. "If you don't mind seeing to Brody?"

At her nod, he placed the clothes and lantern on a dresser, then left, calling over his shoulder, "I'll take the wet clothes when you're done and lay 'em out to dry."

"Thank you," she said.

But he was gone.

The white light glowing from the lantern lit up half of what seemed to be the master bedroom, and the dresser cast a long shadow over an open door on the other side of the bed. The room definitely belonged to Alex. If the absence of feminine decor hadn't hinted strongly enough, the light scent of sandalwood and man—the same one that had enveloped her as Alex had covered her in the hallway—affirmed it.

Brody made a sound of frustration and rubbed his face against the base of her throat.

"Guess it's just you and me for now." She cradled him closer, closed the door, then grabbed the lantern from the dresser. "Let's get cleaned up, okay?"

It took several minutes to gather what she needed from the bathroom and strip the wet clothes from Brody. He grew fussy, wriggling and batting at her hands as he lay on a soft towel on the bed.

"Mama." He twisted away from her touch and tears rolled down his cheeks. "Mama."

"I know, baby," Tammy said, scooting closer across the mattress. "I'm so sorry." She strained to keep her voice steady and forced herself to continue. "I'll be quick, I promise."

She hummed a soft tune while she worked, hesitating briefly after removing the diaper and cleaning his bottom, then grabbed one of the T-shirts Alex had provided.

"This will have to do for now," she said, folding the cotton shirt into a makeshift diaper around him and tying knots at the corners. "I'll get something better soon."

He rubbed his eyes with a fist, and his thumb drifted toward his mouth. Tammy caught it before it could slip between his lips, then wiped it clean with a damp washcloth. His face scrunched up, and he fussed until she released it.

"There," she whispered, bending close and placing her palm to the soft skin of his chest. His heart pulsated beneath her fingertips. "Does that feel a little better?"

Brody blinked slowly, his eyes growing heavy as they wandered over her face. He returned his thumb to his mouth, and his free hand reached up, his fingers tangling in her hair, rubbing the damp strands. He grew quiet, drifted off, and his hand slipped from her hair to drop back to the mattress.

A heavy ache settled over Tammy and lodged in her bones. Being careful not to wake him, she stood and gathered several towels from the bathroom. She rolled each one and arranged them on the bed around him as a barrier.

Keeping a close eye on him, she changed out of her wet clothes and into the dry ones Alex had provided. Her mouth quirked as she held the jogging pants to her middle to keep them from falling. Alex had been right. The pants were at least three sizes too big, but she folded the waistband over several times and tied a knot in the bottom of the T-shirt to take up some of the slack in both.

When she was finished, she pulled her cell phone from the soggy pocket of her jeans and tried calling Jen. But there was no service, just as Alex had said. Sighing, she turned it off, gathered up the wet clothes and lantern, then made her way down the hall, drawing to an abrupt halt in the kitchen.

Alex stood by the sink, tossing back a shot glass and drinking deeply. He stilled as the light bathed his face and the bottle of whiskey in his hand.

A trickle of dread crept across the flesh of her back and sent a chill up her neck. The sight was nothing new. Her father had adopted the same pose every morning and every night. For him, each day began and ended with a bottle, and she imagined it was still that way, though she hadn't laid eyes on him in eight years.

The desire to run was strong. It spiked up her legs and throbbed in her muscles, urging her to drop everything and take off. Even if it meant walking twenty miles in the dark to the nearest town.

"I brought the wet clothes," Tammy said, shifting from one foot to the other, her boots crunching over shards of broken glass. "I can lay them out if you'll just tell me where—"

"No." He set the shot glass and bottle on the counter, then held out his hand. It still trembled, and the light from the lantern couldn't dispel the sad shadows in his eyes. "I'll take care of them. Thanks."

The calm tone of his voice eased her tension slightly, and she handed the clothes over before returning to the bedroom to check on Brody. She set the lantern on the nightstand, then trailed a hand over his rosy cheek, closing her eyes and focusing on his slow breaths.

His soft baby scent mingled with that of Alex's, still lingering on the sheets. Uncomfortable, she kissed Brody's forehead gently, then slipped away and stood by the window. She parted the curtains, and the glow from the lantern highlighted her reflection in the windowpane.

"He sleeping?"

Alex's broad chest appeared in the reflection behind her, and she stepped quickly to the side and faced him. "Yeah."

"Thanks for seeing to him," he said, looking at Brody.

Tammy nodded. "He…he's been asking for his mama."

He watched the baby, his mouth tightening, then took her place at the window. A muscle ticked in his strong jaw as he stared at the darkness outside.

Tammy fiddled with the T-shirt knotted at her waist. "I'm sorry about Dean and Gloria."

Alex dipped his head briefly, then turned away, shoving his hands in his pockets.

"Did you know them well?" she asked.

"Yeah." He dragged a broad hand over the back of his neck, his tone husky. "We all grew up together. Dean and I've been best friends since second grade. And Gloria and Susan—" His words broke off, and his knuckles turned white, his grip tightening around the base of his neck. "Dean helped me build this house. And I helped him build his."

Tammy stilled, her palms aching to reach out and settle over his hard grip. Ease the pain in some small way. She focused on his words instead, wondering who Susan was and why he'd clammed up so abruptly after mentioning her.

His wife, maybe? This was a big house for a single man. But she hadn't seen any women's clothing in the closet or feminine toiletries in the bathroom.

"Is Susan—"

A steady pounding drummed the roof and bore down on the walls of the house. Fat drops of water splattered against the windowpane, and steady streams began flowing down the glass.

"It's raining again," he said, releasing his neck and placing his palm to the window. His biceps flexed below the soggy sleeve of his shirt. "I don't know when emergency services will make their rounds out here. We're so far from town." His whole body shook as he stared straight ahead. "I can't leave them out there alone," he choked. "Not like that."

He shoved off the window and strode swiftly to the door.

"Alex?"

He paused, gripping the door frame and keeping his broad back to her.

Tammy blinked back tears and gnawed her lower

lip, wanting so much to help but feeling useless. "What can I do?"

He glanced over his shoulder, his voice thin. "Stay here and take care of Brody until I get back?"

She nodded. "Of course."

He left and the rain grew heavier, the sound of water pummeling the house filling the room. Rhythmic tings and plops started in the hallway as water leaked from the ceiling and hit the hardwood floor.

Shivering despite the heat of the summer night, Tammy moved slowly to the bed and sat down. She watched the empty doorway for over an hour, waiting to see if someone who knew Alex would walk in. A wife or girlfriend. Maybe a family member or friend. Anyone who cared enough to brave the weather, make the drive to Alex's ranch and check on him.

But no one did.

Eventually, the day became too heavy to carry, and the tears she'd struggled to hold back ran down her cheeks, the salty taste seeping into the corners of her mouth. She gave in and lay on the bed, curling into a ball near Brody and placing a comforting hand on his small shoulder.

She thought of Brody's parents and Razz in the dark, in the rain. She thought of Brody. And Alex...

His distinctive scent grew stronger as she silenced her sobs in the pillow and realized that, for the first time, she'd found two people who were more alone than she was.

"I'm real sorry, Alex."

Alex forced a nod as Jaxon Lennox, a paramedic and

old classmate from high school, joined his colleague and lifted a second gurney into the back of an ambulance. The white sheet covering Dean flapped in the early-morning breeze.

Stomach churning, Alex spun away from the sight and studied the ruins of Dean's house. The rain from last night had soaked the wreckage, leaving deep puddles of dingy water on the piles of broken wood and battered bricks.

Alex had remained at Dean and Gloria's side all night until emergency services arrived in the early-morning hours. He'd been unable to bring himself to leave. The scene blurred in front of him, and he blinked hard, balling his fists against his thighs to keep from dragging them over his burning eyes.

The ambulance doors thudded closed, and Alex stiffened as footsteps approached from behind.

"I spoke to the sheriff. He said he'd contact a social worker this morning about the baby," Jaxon said. "Probably Ms. Maxine."

Alex held his breath and tried to suppress the heat welling in his chest and searing his cheeks. Deer Creek was a tiny community by anyone's standards, and everyone knew Ms. Maxine. Most everyone also knew Ms. Maxine had served as Alex's social worker from the time he'd turned five until he'd aged out of foster care at eighteen. She'd attended his high school graduation and his wedding. And had been the first guest at his and Susan's housewarming party eleven years ago, with an armful of gifts in tow.

Ms. Maxine was one of the brightest spots of a naively hopeful past that he wanted to forget.

"Sheriff said she should be at your place this afternoon to collect the child. I told him about that overturned truck at your place, too, and he said he'll send someone out as soon as he can." Jaxon sighed. "Wish we could've gotten here sooner, but things are so crazy right now. That storm was a monster, and it damaged a lot of houses, though this was the worst I've seen so far. Listen, I know you and Dean were close, and if you need anything…" His voice trailed away. "Well, you know where I am."

"Thanks," Alex said, barely shoving the word past his lips.

It'd be more polite to turn around and offer his hand or try to dredge up a smile, but he couldn't manage either. The expression of pity on a person's face was something he'd become unable to stomach.

The heavy presence at Alex's back disappeared, then a second set of doors slammed shut. An engine cranked, and the ambulance drove away, sloshing through the deep mudholes left in the dirt driveway of Dean's property.

Alex stared blindly at the rubble before him, frowning as the sun cleared the horizon. It blazed bright, tingeing the scoured landscape in a golden glow and coaxing the birds to sing in ravaged trees. There wasn't a single cloud marring the deep blue of the sky.

His skin warmed, and his soggy shirt and jeans clung uncomfortably to him. The damp band of his Stetson began to dry against his forehead, turning tight and stiff.

It was a hell of a thing—the sun rising on a day like this. The damned thing shouldn't have the nerve.

He scoffed and shook his head, squeezing his eyes hard enough to clear them, then started sifting through the mess on the ground for anything worth saving. A dented microwave, filled with muddy water, was lodged between broken staircase rails and a cracked cabinet door. Two recliners and one sofa were overturned, and the cushions were twisted within a tangle of curtains, sheets and wood beams. The remnants of a smashed crib littered a large, heavy pile of broken bricks.

Alex flinched, his boots jerking to a stop. This shouldn't have happened. Dean had walked the line all his life, married a good woman and had a healthy baby boy. This house should still be standing with their small family safely in it.

"I'm sorry, Dean," Alex said, plucking a bent nail from the ground and cringing at the tremor in his voice. "I should've built it stronger."

He gritted his teeth, flung the nail into the distance and kept moving, carefully investigating each stack of wreckage and methodically collecting the few scattered remains that might be of use. He shoved a few unbroken jars of baby food, several intact juice boxes and a half dozen dry disposable diapers into a stray trash bag. One hour later, he started back to his ranch, wanting nothing more than to guzzle a bottle of whiskey, collapse onto his bed and escape into oblivion.

But that wasn't a possibility. A woman and baby were still on his ranch—whatever little there was left of it—and he had to remain hospitable for at least a few more hours. Then they'd both be on their way and he'd have the comforting silence of privacy back.

The thought should've been a welcome one. But the

relief he felt at their expected absence was overshadowed by a pang of loss. One that was accompanied by the warm image of Tammy's bright green eyes and the remembered feel of Brody's small, grasping fingers against his chest. All of which were ridiculous things for a man like him to dwell on.

Shrugging off the unwanted sensation, Alex picked up his pace and searched each empty field he passed for any sign of his horses. He'd made it past the downed power line and across the road when a sporadic pattering sounded behind him. It continued with each of his swift strides, then stopped abruptly when he stilled, a soft whine emerging at his back.

He glanced over his shoulder. A puppy—Labrador, maybe?—stood frozen in place, his yellow fur dark with mud and grime. The dog's black eyes widened soulfully, then he ducked his head and took up whining again.

Alex turned, then eased his bag to the ground. "Where'd you come from?"

The pup wagged his tail rapidly, then rolled belly up and wiggled. The leaves clinging to his matted fur and the pine needles stuck to his paws were an indication that he might have spent the night in the woods.

Alex lowered to his haunches and rubbed a hand over the puppy's thick middle before checking the rest of him for injuries. The dog was healthy, unharmed and looked to be about seven or eight weeks old.

"You belong to Earl, buddy?" he asked, scratching behind the pup's ear.

Old Earl Haggert bred and sold Labs. Could be one of his. Earl's place was about a mile up the road, and it was possible the dog might've wandered that far. With the storm they'd had yesterday, it seemed like every-thing had been displaced.

The dog stopped whining, licked Alex's fingers and nuzzled a wet nose into his palm.

Alex grinned, a soothing heat unfurling in his veins. "Well, hell. What's one more?" He stood, picked up his bag and started walking again. "You might as well come on." He patted his thigh with his free hand. "You can stay today, and I'll get you back to Earl tomorrow."

The dog followed, bounding forward with as much gusto as his short legs would allow.

"But it's only fair I warn you that there's not much to my place anymore." Alex slowed his step until the pup fell into a comfortable pace at his side. "Not after that tornado. My stable is shot, the fences are busted and my horses are missing. Got a damaged roof and broken windows all over the house. 'Bout the only thing not ruined was my bed, and a woman and baby are piled up on that."

The dog yelped up at him, and Alex cocked an eye-brow.

"I know, right? Only thing worse than all that is a man talking to himself." He grimaced, gripped the bag tighter and increased his pace again. "That's a damned shame in itself."

Alex clamped his mouth shut and forged ahead.

Rhythmic thuds echoed across the ravaged field as they drew closer to his house. He stopped a few feet from the end of the driveway, the dog skittering to an awkward halt against his shins.

Tammy pushed a wheelbarrow from one side of the front lawn to the other, pausing every few feet to pick up a broken tree limb and toss it into the cart. The wheels squeaked with each shove, and the contents clanged every time it bumped over uneven ground. Brody tottered close at Tammy's side, his brown hair gleaming in the sun. He followed her lead, bent to grab a stick and stumbled.

"Whoa, there." Tammy stopped the wheelbarrow and steadied him with one hand. She waited as he fumbled around in the grass, then straightened and held out a twig. "Good job," she praised, pointing at the wheelbarrow. "Can you put it in the cart?"

Brody stretched up on his tiptoes, flung the wood into the wheelbarrow and squealed.

"Nicely done," Tammy said, clapping.

Brody smiled, smacked his hands together awkwardly, then waddled toward another stick. Tammy laughed, her face lighting with pleasure.

The rich sound traveled across the front lawn and vibrated around Alex, sending a pleasurable tingle over his skin. He tried not to stare as she chased after Brody, her long brown hair falling in tangled waves over her shoulders and her slim legs moving with grace. They wore their clothes from last night and, though dry, her jeans and Brody's overalls were wrinkled and stained with mud.

But even weather-beaten, she and Brody were a beautiful sight. The kind he'd imagined years ago when he'd hammered shingles onto his newly constructed roof and set the windows in their frames. He'd spent the last free hour before his wedding looking through the glass pane of the kitchen window at the front lawn, envisioning

Susan and the children they'd planned to have playing, laughing and living well.

Tammy's and Brody's energetic movements across the green grass breathed a bit of life into that old fantasy, conjuring it to the forefront of his mind and coaxing it past the tight knot in his chest. And it stung just as much as it soothed.

Alex averted his eyes and scrubbed the toe of his boot over the dirt.

"Hey."

He glanced up at the sound of Tammy's voice. She'd stopped following Brody and studied him closely, her gaze traveling over his face.

"I found the wheelbarrow out back and thought I'd make myself useful," she said, tucking her hair behind her ears and brushing a hand over her rumpled T-shirt. "Brody's been crying for his parents. I thought taking him outside and keeping him busy might help. Hope you don't mind. And I found a banana and cereal in the kitchen that I gave to him. The paramedics stopped by a couple of hours ago, and I sent them in your direction. Did they make it to you okay?"

He nodded, swallowing the thick lump in his throat, and gestured to the white bandage covering her temple. "How's your cut?"

Her fingers drifted up and touched it as though she'd forgotten it was there. "Oh, it's fine. I told them it was nothing, but they insisted on patching me up anyway." She waved a hand in the air, then shoved it in her pocket. "They checked Brody out, too, while they were here. He's just like you said. Not a scratch on him."

Brody stood behind her, holding a stick out with a

chubby hand and staring at the dog snuffling around in the dirt at Alex's heels. The boy's eyebrows rose, and his mouth parted. He pointed his free hand at the pup and shouted.

The dog poked his head between Alex's ankles. He eyed Brody, then bounded across the grass and leaped for the stick Brody held, knocking the boy down in the process.

Brody plopped down on his backside and sat, stunned, for a moment. His brown eyes widened and a wounded expression crossed his face before he took up crying.

Alex froze, a strangled laugh dying in his throat and escaping him in a choked grunt. Years ago, he'd seen Dean hit his butt in the same position with an identical look on his face. Except Dean had been twelve years old and the cause of it had been the kickback from a shotgun. One he'd swiped from his dad's gun cabinet and used without permission, accidentally shooting out a window on his dad's truck.

Dean had insisted he'd outgrown his BB gun, but he hadn't been too grown to shed tears that day. He'd taken one look at that shattered glass and cried, "My dad's gonna kick my ass good for this one!"

Of course, his dad hadn't. He'd fussed a great deal but had been relieved that Dean and Alex hadn't been injured. That they'd emerged from what could've been a deadly incident without a scratch on them. Like Brody.

A boy who would grow up without ever knowing how great a man his father had been.

Alex dropped his bag, turned his back on the trio

and stifled a guttural roar, the rage streaking through him almost uncontainable.

"Oh, it's all right, Brody." Tammy's soothing words quieted the baby's sobs. "You're okay, and there are a lot more sticks where that one came from." There were shuffling sounds, then she asked, "This little guy a friend of yours, Alex?"

He glanced over his shoulder to find her kneeling on the ground, petting the dog and hugging Brody to her side. Her eyes met his, and the smile on her face melted away, a concerned expression taking its place. The kind he knew all too well.

Unable to answer her, he spun away, stalked up the front porch steps and entered the kitchen. He went straight to the cabinet, grabbed a bottle, then upended it, drinking deeply. The fiery liquid burned a trail down his throat and lit up his gut, forcing him to set it down and gasp for breath.

He watched through the window as Tammy got to her feet and took a hesitant step toward the house. She stopped, frowned up at the front porch, then walked away. The squeak of wheels rang out and the consistent clang of sticks being thrown into the cart resumed.

Alex gripped the edge of the counter and closed his eyes. She probably thought he was a crazy, selfish bastard. And to a certain extent he was. But how could he explain it? How could anything he might say help her understand?

He was truly grateful that Brody had survived the storm and that Tammy had escaped without serious injury. Last night as he'd grieved at Dean's side, he'd even thanked heaven that he, himself, had managed to emerge from yesterday's carnage still breathing. That he wasn't buried beneath the broken walls of his house being pummeled by rain.

But no amount of gratitude would ease the anger of knowing that death had stolen Dean and Gloria. Or change the fact that, sometimes, life could hurt like hell.

Chapter 3

A body rests easier after doing the right thing.

Alex stood on the front porch and waited as Tammy finished changing Brody's diaper on the grass, recalling the words Ms. Maxine had repeated to him a thousand times over the years. Ones she'd spoken when he'd gotten suspended from middle school for smoking, then reminded him of when he'd returned to his foster parents' house after sneaking out for a weekend party binge as a teen.

It was a phrase he'd grown to know well. And one he'd strictly adhered to after mending his ways and proposing to Susan.

But there were some things a man couldn't control.

He adjusted the bag of cookies under his arm and gripped the can of soda in his hand tighter, hoping the toothpaste he'd rubbed over his teeth masked the whiskey on his breath. Abstaining from the bottle between the hours of five in the morning and nine at night was a rule he'd taken pride in for nine years. But, surely, his grief from losing his best friends excused today's slip.

Only, his shortcomings were easier to deal with—and accept—when there were no witnesses to them.

Alex winced and rolled his shoulders to ease the tight knot at the base of his neck. He couldn't stay holed up in the kitchen all afternoon, tossing back shots, while Tammy cleaned up the front yard and took care of Brody. The only thing left to do was pull his shit together and at least be hospitable. It was what any gentleman would do. And he still knew how to be one. Even if it'd been years since he'd put his good manners into practice.

A little longer. That's it. Make them comfortable for a few more hours, and soon Ms. Maxine would whisk Brody away to a new home and the wrecker would cart Tammy and her overturned truck back to the highway. Then he could curl up with a bottle for hours and grieve in private.

Alex nodded curtly and eased his way down the front steps to Tammy's side. "Figured you might be thirsty," he said, handing the soda to her as she knelt next to the baby. "Power's still out, so it's warm. Sorry about that."

"Thanks." She lifted Brody to his feet, then took the soda and popped the top.

Her slim throat moved as she drank deeply, drawing Alex's eyes to the flushed skin of her neck and upper chest. The dog climbed onto her knees and jumped to lick the can. She pushed him away with her free hand, causing the collar of her T-shirt to slip to one side. It revealed a faint tan line below her collarbones that contrasted sharply with the ivory complexion of the upper swell of her breast.

Alex had a sudden urge to trail his lips across her warm skin and breathe in her sweet scent. He peeled his gaze away, ignoring the heat simmering in his veins, and caught her eyes on him. She lowered the can, straightened her shirt with her free hand and pushed to her feet.

Ah, hell. A gentleman didn't ogle a woman, and this was becoming a habit.

Cheeks burning, he cleared his throat and gestured to the trash bag on the ground nearby. "I see you found the diapers. There's some baby food and juice in there, too. Not a lot. But enough to get him through at least one more day."

Something tugged at his jeans, and a frustrated squeal erupted. He looked down, finding Brody attempting to climb up his leg, his small arm stretched out and tiny fingers grabbing for the bag of cookies under Alex's arm.

Tammy laughed. "I don't think he's interested in baby food. Looks like he'd much rather get a hold of those cookies."

A soft breeze ruffled Brody's hair, and the boy blinked wide, pleading eyes up at him. The brown strands and deep chestnut pools were the same shade as Dean's, and his small cries were impossible to resist.

Alex's chest constricted so tight he could barely breathe. "A social worker is coming for him," he rasped, reminding himself as much as informing Tammy. He handed a cookie to Brody, then smoothed his knuckles across the boy's soft cheek. "And someone's arranging to have your truck and trailer hauled to the body shop in town. Don't know how long it'll take to fix 'em, but power will probably be restored in town first. You'll have a better chance of reaching a friend or family member sooner there."

She nodded absently, and her gaze drifted to the empty field behind him. "I looked for Razz this morning," she said softly. "I couldn't find her."

"Your horse?"

"Yeah." Those emerald eyes returned to his face. "Do you think she survived?"

He grimaced, then watched Brody mouth the cookie and spin in awkward circles to avoid the puppy leaping for the treat. "Can't say for sure."

Chances were, her horse was gone along with all of his. God help him, he didn't want to lie to her. But he didn't want to see pain engulf those beautiful features, either.

"She might've made it," Alex said, squinting against the sharp rays of the sun and scanning the landscape. "There's a chance she's huddled up somewhere with mine."

Though he wouldn't bet what little money he had left on it. And he didn't even want to think about how much it'd cost to put this struggling ranch back in working order.

"How many do you have?" she asked.

"Ten."

"You board them?"

"And breed them." He turned to study a field behind him. "Mainly for ranch work. I try for blue roans, since

they've brought in the most over the past two years."
His throat tightened. "Dean was my partner."

Brody yelped and reached for a second cookie. Alex
gave him another, then held the bag out to Tammy. She
took a cookie and turned it over in her hand, staring at
it with a furrowed brow.

"I know the storm was bad," she said. "But Razz is
fast." She glanced up, a hesitant smile appearing. "She's
the best barrel horse on the circuit."

So, she raced. Alex surveyed the slim but strong
curves of Tammy's arms and legs more closely. No wonder she'd held her own through yesterday's nightmare.
The few rodeo riders he'd known were a tough lot. Full
of grit and fight.

He'd never taken to the circuit life, though he'd tried
it once years ago, riding bulls one summer in his early
twenties. It was fun, brought in a decent amount of cash
and provided an outlet for his reckless streak. But then
he'd started missing Susan and realized he wanted her
more. Wanted a wife and home. A family of his own.
And he'd decided it wasn't fair to keep Susan waiting.
That he should return to Deer Creek, settle down like
Dean and do the right thing.

His jaw clenched. If he'd known then how much
he'd end up disappointing Susan, the right thing to do
would've been a very different choice.

"I'm hoping she dodged the worst of it."

Alex blinked and refocused on Tammy's face, his
stomach dropping. "What?"

"Razz," Tammy clarified, studying him again. "She
might have outrun the tornado, and if she managed to
survive, then maybe your horses did, too." Her atten-

tion drifted to Brody, and her smile widened. "After all, this little guy came out of it okay."

Brody grinned, his mouth laden with crumbs, and stretched his arms out to Tammy. She slipped her cookie in her pocket, lifted him up and cradled his head against her chest.

"Yeah, he did," Alex murmured, his eyes clinging to the gentle embrace of her arms around Brody and the slow sway of her body as she rocked him.

The movements were calming, and Brody soaked it up, his eyelids growing heavy and his breaths slowing. Her brown hair slipped over her shoulder and rested against Brody, the wavy locks sharing the same chestnut tones as those of the baby.

She was a natural at comforting a child and, had Alex not known better, he would have assumed Brody belonged to her. It would be the easiest thing in the world to mistake the two of them for family. For mother and son.

An ache streamed through Alex's limbs, making his palms itch to reach out and tug them both close. To hold them in a protective embrace, feel the steady pulse of their hearts and draw strength from their solid presence. To imagine, just for a moment, that he belonged, too. As a man and a father…

But that would be a mistake. He stiffened and turned away. He'd been abandoned as a child and had struggled to fit in with each of the three foster families he'd lived with as a youth. He'd had to fight his damnedest to establish enough stability in his life to offer Susan the promise of a secure future filled with family and happiness. Things he'd failed to deliver, wrecking Susan's dreams along with his own.

No. Nature knew what it was doing. He wasn't built to be a family man—it wasn't in his DNA to be a father—and he was foolish for even entertaining the fantasy.

"Someone's here."

Tammy's words were joined with the faint churn of an engine and the slosh of tires through mud down the driveway. A compact car eased over the hill, maneuvered around various piles of debris and drew to a stop several feet behind the fallen tree blocking the path. The door opened, and an older woman stepped out, wisps of gray hair escaping her topknot in the soft breeze.

Alex caught his breath, smothering the urge to run into her arms and seek comfort like he had as a boy. Instead, he placed the bag of cookies on the ground, took off his hat and waited.

A sad smile dispersed the soft wrinkles lining the woman's face as she made her way over. "Oh, Alex." She wrapped her arms tight around him, standing on the toes of her high heels to whisper in his ear, "I'm so sorry about Dean and Gloria."

A low cry dislodged from Alex's throat and pried its way out of his mouth. He coughed, closing his throat against another sob, and tucked the top of her head gently under his chin. "Thank you, Ms. Maxine."

He gave in to the moment, closing his eyes and squeezing her close. The familiar scent of her perfume arose from her clothing, and the sweet aroma took him back years. All the way back to when he was a dumb kid and the only bright spot in each day had been her forgiving smile and unconditional support. Ms. Maxine was the closest he'd ever come to having a real mother. His mother had abandoned him at an early age. And from what little information Maxine had available to share with him, his father had never been in the picture.

"I'm so thankful that you're okay." Maxine pulled back and cupped his face with her palms as she scrutinized him. "I think a shave, a wholesome meal and a good night's rest are in order." She smiled. Bright and sincere. "Though even without that, I think you're more handsome now than you were the last time I saw you."

He ducked his head, his neck and chest warming. It'd been years since he'd last seen her. Hurt and anger had knotted in his gut the day Susan left, and he'd pushed everyone away, including Maxine. He'd avoided her calls and visits. Had never been able to face the possibility of seeing disapproval in Maxine's eyes. But there wasn't a trace of disappointment in her expression.

Just sympathy and kindness.

Alex reached up, cradled her thin wrists gently in his hands and managed a small grin. "Nah. I've just gotten old."

"Old?" Maxine scoffed. "You've got years ahead of you before you qualify as being old." She chuckled, patted his cheeks, then gestured toward his hair. "No, my dear boy. You've just got a touch of silver fox in you."

The dog yelped and squirmed its way between them, his tail thumping against Alex's leg as he gnawed on the toe of his boot.

"Well, hello." Maxine bent and scratched the dog's head, then leaned to the side, her eyes straying to Tammy and Brody. "And who do we have here?"

Alex stepped to the side and swept an arm toward the pair. "Ms. Maxine, this is Tammy Jenkins. The tornado forced her off the road yesterday."

Maxine nodded toward the overturned truck and trailer on the other side of the driveway. "I see that. I'm Maxine Thompson and it's very nice to meet you, although I wish it were under different circumstances." She held out a hand, which Tammy shook. "I'm sorry about your truck, dear. But don't worry. The sheriff asked me to relay to Alex that he's arranging for it to be towed to Sam Bircham's shop. Sam's the best mechanic in town, and he'll have it as good as new before you know it. They're overwhelmed right now, though, and he asked me to let you know it'll be a while before he can get to it. If you need to send a message to a family member or friend, I'd be happy to pass it along to the sheriff when I return to town. He'll make sure it reaches them."

Tammy smiled, rearranging Brody on her hip as he straightened in her arms. "Thank you."

"And this must be our beautiful Brody." Maxine rubbed the baby's arm and sighed as he burrowed his face back into Tammy's chest. "What a sweet boy." Her voice lowered. "How's he doing?"

"As well as can be expected," Tammy said, kissing the top of Brody's head.

Maxine looked the pair over, then flashed a tender smile before saying, "I see he's taken to you, Tammy. It's so good of you to look after him during this difficult time."

Alex felt a small smile emerge on his own face, the pleased glow in Tammy's cheeks provoking it. She and Brody were such a beautiful sight.

"Oh, it's no trouble," Tammy said, blushing. "He's a joy."

Maxine made a sound of agreement, her eyes moving from Tammy to Alex and back again, then wrapped her hand around Alex's elbow. "Will you please excuse us for a minute?"

Tammy nodded, and Maxine tugged Alex several feet away to stand facing the field. The dog followed, bumped into the back of his leg, then started snuffling around the grass.

"How are you, Alex?" Maxine asked, peering up at him.

"Fine." Alex dodged her watchful eyes and gestured toward the field. "I'll be better if I manage to find my horses in good health and get the business going again. But without Dean…" He sucked in a strong breath and replaced his hat on his head. "I think this ranch may have reached the end of the line."

"Oh, I wouldn't say that." Maxine shifted at his side, her sleeve brushing his arm as she swiveled to survey the house and stable. "There may be some damage," she continued, facing him again, "but your foundation is strong. With time and a little elbow grease, this place will breathe again."

Alex's mouth tightened as he scanned the demolished fences, ravaged trees and barren paddocks. Ms. Maxine meant well. But that'd be a lot easier said than done.

"I worry about you," Maxine added softly. "Hiding out here all by yourself for so long."

"I'm not hiding—"

"Yes, you are." The firmness in her voice forced him to meet her eyes again, the blue depths earnest behind her glasses. "You're not a quitter, Alex. Never have been." She glanced at Tammy and Brody, then stepped closer to his side. "If I asked for a favor, would you humor me?" she asked. "For old times' and an old woman's sake?"

Alex stiffened, acutely aware of Tammy's curious stare and the dog chewing on the toe of his boot. "Depends."

"How long is Tammy staying?"

He shrugged. "Just till the wrecker gets here, I imagine. She's a barrel racer and is probably itching to get back on the circuit already."

Maxine sighed. "Dean didn't have a will, and I know he lost his father a few years ago. I've left messages for his half brother in Boston, but it may be a while before I hear back. Do you know of any family Gloria might've had that I could contact for Brody?"

Alex shook his head. "Not that I know of. Gloria's mother remarried and moved to California years ago. She was never big on keeping in touch. That's one reason why—"

He stilled his tongue. No need to drag Maxine through the mud he, Dean and Gloria had lived through in their lives and point out how it'd glued them together. Besides, nothing stayed a secret for long in Deer Creek, and he'd be willing to bet she already knew most of it anyway.

Maxine frowned. "Everything's a bit chaotic in town what with all the damage from the storm. If I take Brody now, I'll have to place him in a children's home near Atlanta until I'm able to find a suitable foster family. I can't bring myself to take Brody so far from home just yet. Not when there's a possibility of him being cared for by someone he already knows."

Alex stilled, an unpleasant prickling sensation snaking up the back of his neck. "What are you getting at?"

"Would you be willing to take Brody in until I can finalize a permanent placement for him?"

He held up a hand. "Ms. Maxine—"

"It wouldn't be for too long," she interjected. "Just for a little while. Brody's been through such a traumatic experience and he knows you."

"Yeah, he knows me," Alex sputtered, a stabbing pain ripping through him as an old wound reopened. His eyes flicked over Brody as he snuggled against Tammy's chest. "But that doesn't make me a fit guardian."

"It would only be temporary, and I'd be in this with you. Judging from that overturned truck, that young lady's not leaving Deer Creek anytime soon. She'll need somewhere to stay. I know it's not good to assume…" Maxine hesitated, nodding pointedly in Tammy's direction. "But I think if you asked, you might get more help than you'd ordinarily expect."

The surprised expression on Tammy's face made it clear she'd heard every word. It also made Alex's heart slam rapidly against his ribs.

Open the door of his battered house and washed-up life to a baby and stranger?

"Hell, no," Alex muttered, stumbling back and shaking his boot to dislodge the pup. "And you're right about the assuming thing. When you assume, you make a pair of asses out of—"

"Language, Alex."

He bit his tongue. That was a familiar tone. Her no-nonsense one. "Sorry," he mumbled. "But it's a bad idea."

"If you won't do it for me, will you do it for Dean?" Maxine asked softly.

Alex winced, a hollow forming in his gut. Damn. She wasn't pulling any punches.

"I'm sorry, Alex. I wish none of this had happened," she whispered. "But it did. And, sometimes, the best way to take your mind off your own pain is to help alleviate someone else's. Please do this for Dean. And for Brody. It's just for a little while."

Alex dropped his head back and closed his eyes, flinching as the dog growled playfully and bit into his boot harder. "And what am I supposed to do with a baby and a woman?"

"Where the baby is concerned," Maxine said, "it'll come to you. As for the woman…"

At her prolonged silence, he opened his eyes and faced her. Her mouth stretched slowly into a grin.

"Well, as for the woman…" She winked. "If I have to explain that to you, you've been hiding out from civilization for longer than I thought."

A stifled laugh came from Tammy's direction.

Lord, help him. He spun on his heels and stalked off, the dog yipping and biting at the hem of his jeans along the way.

"Alex," Maxine called. "A body always rests easier after—"

"Doing the right thing," Alex grunted back, waving the words away with his hand.

Only, it was the damnedest thing. None of this felt right. None of it at all.

Tammy silenced another giggle with her hand, watching Maxine shake her head as Alex stomped off.

Good grief, she was being rude but couldn't help it.

A constant stream of laughter bubbled in her belly at the sight of Alex stumbling over the small puppy at his feet, his muscular frame jerking awkwardly to avoid stepping on the animal.

"He barks a lot but never bites."

Tammy lowered her hand, still laughing. "What?"

Maxine chuckled, too, and walked over. "Alex. He may come across as a mean ol' grouch, but he's just a big teddy bear underneath. You just have to be patient enough to get past it all."

Tammy's laughter died out, and she shifted from one foot to the other as Maxine smiled at her. Her arms trembled beneath the weight of Brody's sleeping form, and the familiar trickle of trepidation crept into her veins. The other woman had a kind face and pleasant personality, but her wise eyes saw too much. And there were so many things Tammy didn't want anyone to ever see. Most especially, her constant fear of men. It made her feel weak and vulnerable.

"I see he's drifted off," Maxine murmured, smoothing a hand over Brody's back. She held her hands out, palms up. "Would you mind?"

Tammy shook her head. "No, not at all."

She passed Brody to Maxine, then helped settle him comfortably within her arms. Brody pulled in a noisy breath, then nuzzled his cheek against Maxine's neck as he settled back into sleep.

"He's so precious." Maxine kissed the top of his head, then grinned. "I hope you didn't mind me pushing you out on a limb earlier with Alex. I'm just hoping you might consider helping him out and tending to

Brody while you wait for your truck to be repaired. You seem to be a natural with kids."

Tammy lifted a shoulder briefly, her belly warming. "Oh, I don't know. Brody is easy to love, and I've always wanted a houseful of children."

The smile on the other woman's face dimmed. "Do you have children, Tammy?"

"No. But someday…"

Tammy tensed, the words trailing away as she wondered for the millionth time how she'd ever have a family if she couldn't manage to trust a man.

"It's just me right now," Tammy added, shoving her hands in her pockets. "I was actually on the way to help my best friend with her wedding plans when the storm hit. She's getting married next month."

Maxine's face brightened. "Oh, how exciting. Weddings have always been my favorite event. Alex had a beautiful—" She stopped short, and her mouth flattened. "Well, that's not for me to discuss."

Tammy hesitated, sneaking a peek at Alex's broad back as he disappeared into the stable on the other side of the property. The dog scuttled in after him. "Is Alex married?"

Maxine looked down and rubbed small circles over Brody's back, her tone sad. "He was at one time. But not now."

Tammy dragged her teeth over her bottom lip. "Does he have any family?" She hurried to add, "I don't mean to pry, but I couldn't help but wonder when no one came to check on him last night."

The other woman nudged her glasses up with a knuckle and shook her head. "Alex has been alone a long time. That's one reason why he has trouble accommodating guests." She smiled. "But I think it'd do him good to have Brody around for a bit. It might help him get over losing Dean and allow him to find a bright spot in all of this." She hugged Brody, her expression lifting. "And this young man is definitely a bright spot."

Tammy laughed softly. "Yes, he is."

Maxine walked over to her car. "I brought some supplies for Brody and, once the news spread this morning, a few ladies from my church went to the Red Cross setup in town and fixed a few plates of food for y'all. It's nothing special but should get you through today and tomorrow. And, hopefully, power will be restored soon."

Maxine retrieved her keys and started to unlock the trunk, but Tammy stalled her, saying, "Why don't you let me get that for you?"

"Thank you." Maxine handed over the keys. "There are three boxes, and they're rather heavy. You might want to ask Alex to lend you a hand. I'll take Brody inside." She headed toward the house. "Where should I set him down for a nap?"

"Alex let us use his room last night."

Maxine nodded, then made her way up the front porch, tossing over her shoulder, "Remember what I said about Alex. Don't let that grouchy facade fool you."

Tammy opened the trunk, then jingled the keys in her hand, listening to the birds chirp as her skin absorbed the warmth of the sun. A soft breeze whispered over the tall grass in the field, ruffled through her hair, then scattered leaves around on the front porch. Even with the visible damage from the storm, the grounds were peaceful and welcoming. She could only imagine how beautiful the ranch would be fixed up.

If she did manage to find Razz, the spacious fields would be a perfect place for the mare to spend a few calm days before returning to the circuit. Her stomach churned at the thought of leaving without knowing what happened to her racing partner. Even if the worst had happened, she'd rather know than not. And the thought of Alex struggling to restore his ranch and take care of Brody alone made her ache.

Staying would interfere with her plans to spend the month with Jen, but once she explained the situation, surely her best friend would understand. Plus, she couldn't go anywhere until her truck was fixed. According to Maxine's estimation, finding a placement for Brody would take two or three weeks at the most. That would still leave one week to help Jen prepare for the wedding.

Decision made, Tammy shoved the keys in her pocket, shut the trunk and headed for the stable Alex had entered. The scent of honeysuckle lingered on the air and calmed her nerves, spurring her boots across the thick grass to the cool, shaded entrance. The steady pound of a hammer clanged from inside.

"Alex?"

She knocked on the wide door. Debris from the storm had battered the shine off the wood, and the hinges squeaked as she shoved it farther to the side. The pounding stopped, and the clicking of claws against hardwood rang out, echoing around the empty building as the puppy barreled around the corner.

"Hey, buddy." Tammy petted the dog, then went inside, scanning the line of stalls gracing opposite sides of the building.

It was a large structure by anyone's standards, built for forty horses with twenty stalls on either side. She nudged bits of broken wood and twisted metal out of the aisle with the toe of her boot. Scattered patches of sunlight dotted the littered floor, and she looked up, eyeing the jagged holes in the roof.

"Not a pretty sight, is it?"

She stopped. Alex emerged from a stall at the end of the aisle, carrying a set of broken stall bars, which he leaned against the wall.

"It needs some work," she said.

He grunted and rolled his thick shoulders. Dust clung to his jeans and T-shirt, casting a gray haze over his brawny build beneath the speckled sunlight. "That's an understatement."

"Maxine brought some supplies for Brody." Tammy watched the puppy lap water noisily from a metal bowl on the floor, then took a hesitant step forward. "I started thinking that her idea might not be such a bad one."

Alex took his hat off and hung it on a broken stall post. She caught herself focusing on the thick waves of his hair and the way the rich, dark strands contrasted with the dusting of silver. Her fingertips yearned to trail through them, and she balled her hands into fists at her sides to fight the urge.

"I mean, you saved my life," she continued. "The least I could do is stick around for a little while and help you in return."

He didn't answer. Or ask. Just turned his head and stared at the disarray of the stable.

"You'll need an extra hand with Brody around," she said. "I'm used to hard work, and I wouldn't mind taking care of Brody and helping out wherever I can. I could help you look for your horses, and hopefully we'll find Razz, too."

Alex looked at her then, his dark five o'clock shadow rippling as his jaw clenched. His eyes were haunted, and exhaustion lined his features.

Tammy rolled her lips and pressed them together hard, trying her best to ignore the flutter in her belly and the odd desire to move closer. To lean against the muscular wall of his chest and wrap her arms around him.

"You'd be doing me a favor, too, you know? If I do find Razz, she'll need a calm place to rest before I take her back out on the road. And I *will* find her. She's a strong horse, and I can't leave without at least knowing—" She cleared her throat and gestured toward the empty stalls. "I can help you get the stable back in working order in exchange for you boarding Razz for a while. Then, maybe by the time my truck is repaired, Brody will have a new home and Razz and I will move on. It's a win-win situation for us both."

A heavy sigh escaped him. "I guess you have a point," he said, approaching. "And a deal."

He held his hand out, the big, tanned palm tilted in an open invitation for hers.

Tammy tensed, a tight knot forming in her throat. *Teddy bear.* She uncurled her fist and rubbed her hand over her jeans, recalling Maxine's words. *He's just a big teddy bear.*

"Deal," she whispered, slipping her hand into his.

His palm was rough with calluses, but his long fin-

gers wrapped around her hand, encompassing it in caressing warmth. He squeezed gently, and a delicious
shiver of longing traveled through her. The kind of longing that made her want to slide her hand up his wrist,
smooth her fingers over his thick biceps and cup his
chiseled jaw. To see his tempting mouth stretch into a
smile. A real one.

"Now you'll have to figure out what to do with me,"
she teased. "Seeing as how I'm just a woman and all."

His dark brows rose, and his mouth twitched. His
lips parted, revealing white teeth and deep dimples. A
low rumble escaped him, the sound rich and sincere. It
swept through the hollow interior of the stable and the
empty space within her, filling both with joy.

"It's not broken."

His laughter trailed away, confusion marring his features. "What?"

Tammy froze, realizing she'd voiced the thought
aloud. "Your mouth," she mumbled. "I... I mean your
smile. I thought it looked broken yesterday when..." She
tugged her hand free of his, face burning as he stared
at her. "It's nothing."

He watched her for a moment, then lowered his head
and leaned in, stopping when she took a step back. His
gray eyes traveled over her face, and that small spark of
desire reignited within her. It rushed through her veins,
prompting her to lift her chin and present her mouth in
an invitation of her own.

Alex moved closer, his familiar scent surrounding
her as his warm lips brushed softly across hers. Her
eyes fluttered shut, and she breathed him in, savoring

the tenderness of the moment. Wanting to hold on to it. Wanting, for the first time, to hold on to a man.

But the moment was over.

The heat of his presence faded, and her eyes sprang open.

"It's not broken, baby," he murmured, easing away. His relaxed expression vanished, and a frown took its place. "But a lot of other things are."

The dog whined and leaped at Tammy's knees, his small body banging against her shins. Seeking a distraction, she knelt on weak legs beside the puppy and stroked his soft fur. The rapid thump of her heart made her catch her breath and her fingers trembled. All sorts of emotions she'd never felt before swirled in her belly and swelled within her chest.

"It's not a good idea to get attached to that dog."

She looked up. Alex stood at the other end of the aisle, watching the pup.

His eyes shifted to her, and his voice softened. "Or Brody, for that matter. The wind that blew the three of you in here is gonna carry you all away just as fast in different directions."

Alex reentered the stall, and the steady pounding of a hammer resumed.

"Maybe," Tammy whispered. Her lips still tingled from his kiss, and she touched her fingertips to them, smiling as the puppy snuggled against her middle. "But we're here for now."

Chapter 4

Alex firmed his stance in the bed of his truck and swung the ax hard, grunting with satisfaction at the sharp crack of wood beneath it. The busted branch flopped to the side and slid off the back of the truck's tailgate to the ground. Each scrape of bark against metal left more scratches than the truck had already suffered, but prying the vehicle free and clearing the fallen tree from the driveway was more important.

He and Tammy had worked on it yesterday afternoon after Maxine had left, then resumed early this morning after searching for the horses, spending the majority of the day continuing their efforts. With no power and no sign of the horses, there wasn't much left to do but keep busy and hope for the best.

"I think it's safe to say you'll have enough firewood

for the winter," Tammy said, looking up at him. She grabbed the thick end of the branch and dragged it off the driveway toward the large pile of limbs behind her. "Maybe three winters after you chop up the rest of the downed trees."

She dropped the branch, puffed a strand of hair out of her flushed face, then beat her gloved hands together. Dust billowed out, and she coughed, squinting against the low-hanging sun as she surveyed the fields before them.

Alex followed her gaze and cringed at the jagged line of broken trees on the other side of the grounds. It'd take at least a week to haul off all the fallen limbs. Hell, it'd taken all afternoon to chop up the few in the driveway, and they still weren't finished.

Though, he couldn't say Tammy hadn't pulled her weight. More than that. She'd chopped, heaved and hauled almost as much wood as he had today. And she hadn't complained once.

"Can we get it off the truck now?" Tammy asked, eyeing the tree trunk wedged over the tailgate in front of him. Sweat glistened on her forehead, and she dragged the back of her arm across it. "I know it's big, but we could tie a rope around it and with the two of us pulling—"

"No." Alex shook his head, his eyes drifting to the smooth curves of her lips. "It's too heavy for dragging and too thick for an ax. We'll need something stronger to cut it up first."

Her hopeful expression dimmed, and her mouth drooped, making him want to lean over, dip his head and place kisses at the corners. Coax and tease until they softened under his. Like yesterday…

Damn. He tossed the ax into the bed of the truck,

swung his leg over the tailgate and hopped down. What the heck was wrong with him? Here he was, a grown man, fixating on a barely there kiss from hours ago with a woman he hardly knew. A woman he'd continued thinking about as he'd fought for sleep last night crammed on the living room couch while she and Brody occupied his bed.

But he guessed that was what nine years of self-imposed celibacy would do to a man. One touch of her soft palm against his made him ache to feel more. A chaste peck on the lips made him long to explore her mouth to see how sweet she tasted. And an entire day of working alongside her, her lithe movements brushing against him and her rapid breaths close to his ear, kept those unwelcome desires smoldering in his blood.

He jerked his gloves off, then scrubbed a hand over his face, the sharp scent of sap and pine invading his nostrils. It was just comfort his body was seeking. Something to take his mind off the fact that he'd no longer have Dean and Gloria in his life and how much that hurt.

The last thing he needed to do was get tangled up with a young barrel racer who'd hightail it back to the interstate in a couple weeks. No matter how much her long legs, soft curves and soul-searching eyes tempted him to—

Hell, he needed some space. Needed to stretch his legs, fill his lungs with fresh air and clear his head.

"No, Brody." Tammy tugged off the baggy gloves he'd loaned her and jogged across the driveway to the lawn.

Brody stood on one leg in the portable playpen Maxine had provided, holding on to the top edge and attempting to lift his other leg over it. The dog ran in circles around the structure and barked as the boy climbed. Each sharp yelp from the puppy prompted a frustrated wail from Brody.

"I know," Tammy soothed, lifting Brody out of the playpen and setting him on his feet. "That thing gets old after a while, doesn't it?"

The dog pounced playfully, springing into the air and nipping at the short sleeves of Brody's shirt. Tammy nudged him off, but the pup persisted, knocking into Brody's knees and causing the baby to stumble backward.

"'Bout time I take that dog back to its owner," Alex said, jumping at the chance to get away for a little while.

Tammy straightened the small baseball cap on Brody's head—another gift from Maxine—and pulled him closer to her side. "You know where he came from?"

"I've got a pretty good hunch. There's a man about a mile up the road that sells Labs. The dog probably wandered off from there. And he might have a chain saw I can borrow to break that tree up into manageable pieces." Alex threw his gloves onto the pile of wood, grabbed a flashlight from the glove box in his truck, then whistled to get the dog's attention. "Come on, boy. Let's go for a walk."

The dog joined him, and they made it three feet before Tammy called out, "Wait."

Alex stopped and closed his eyes, barely smothering a groan. "Yeah?"

"We're coming with you."

No. Alex jerked his chin over his shoulder and shook his head. "It's better if y'all stay here. You and Brody could both use the rest."

"I've put Brody down for two naps today, and he's been cooped up in that playpen for the past hour so we could work. He needs some time to play and get some exercise or he won't sleep a wink tonight."

Alex gritted his teeth and tapped the flashlight against his thigh. "Look, it's two miles there and back. That's too much for a child Brody's size, and it'll be dark by the time I head home. It'll be faster if I go by myself. Besides, if you stay here, you can keep an eye out for the horses in case they come wandering back."

"Or," Tammy stressed, eyes flashing, "if we go with you, I can help you look for them while we walk. And when Brody gets tired, I'll carry him." She straightened and took Brody's hand. "I'm sorry. I don't mean to be an aggravation, but it's been two days since I've seen Razz. I can't just sit here and twiddle my thumbs when I could be out looking for her. If I do that, I won't be able to sleep tonight, either."

Her chin trembled and his irritation faded, a sudden surge of sympathy warring with his good sense. It must've shown on his face, because the tension on hers eased and she smiled.

"Please, Alex."

Ah, hell. Just the sweet way his name rolled off her tongue was enough to tip the scales.

"All right," he grumbled. "But stay close and stick to the trail. We're taking a shortcut that goes near the creek, and there are usually snakes."

"Thank you." She held up her pointer finger and rushed to the front porch, then up the steps. "Just let me grab a couple things real quick. You mind watching Brody for a sec?"

Alex sighed. No need to answer. She was gone.

Brody stood silently, staring up at him with a bemused expression. The crooked tilt of the boy's eyebrows was so similar to Dean's. Lord, how that lifted his heavy heart and shot a bolt of pain through him at the same time.

Alex frowned. *He's not Dean. And he's not staying.* He knew he should keep his distance, but his arms yearned to pick the boy up and hug him close.

"So," he said, taking a hesitant step toward Brody and holding out his hand. "Ready for this walk? It's a mighty long way for a little man like you."

Brody blinked, blew a raspberry, then took off across the grass, babbling. The dog sprang after him, ears and tail flopping. The pair zigzagged across the lawn and into the backyard before Alex managed to round them up.

Fifteen minutes later, they were well on their way up the dirt road. Alex toted the small bag Tammy had packed with diapers and juice, and Tammy guided Brody along the path, keeping him clear of the high grass and deep creek on one side. The sun was strong, hanging low against the horizon, heating their backs and casting a golden glow over the path.

Tammy stopped twice to whistle for her horse, give Brody juice and wipe the baby's rosy cheeks with a damp washcloth.

"If it's too much, we can go back," Alex said. "I can make the trip tomorrow morning."

"No, we're fine." Tammy smiled down at Brody. "Aren't we?"

The baby squealed gibberish, then toddled faster up the road after the frolicking puppy.

"The man we're going to see," Tammy said, stooping to steady Brody as he stumbled over a pothole. "What's his name?"

"Earl Haggert." Alex paused, scanned the path for snakes and wondered how much more he should say. "He goes by Old Earl."

Tammy laughed. "Old Earl? He actually asks people to call him old?"

He shrugged. "His age never seemed to bother him."

Nor did other people's reactions to him.

Alex winced, recalling the first time he and Dean had encountered Old Earl. They'd been nine years old and heard the rumors circulating around school that Old Earl's property was haunted. That the old man himself was a monster to be feared. And he and Dean had accepted a dare to slip through Earl's fence, spend the night in his hay field and swipe one of his hand-carved wolves from the front porch as proof they'd been there.

Only, Old Earl had caught them sneaking up the front steps, and the sight of his damaged face was so unexpected that they'd screamed their heads off and run.

Alex ducked his head, his face burning. The tales of devils on Earl's land and the darkness of the night might have heightened his and Dean's fright, but being young and stupid was no excuse for their rude, insensitive reaction to the man. Neither he nor Dean had been able to face Earl since then.

As kids, they'd been too afraid. As adults, they'd been too embarrassed.

He'd hate for Tammy to be caught off guard like he and Dean had and risk offending Earl. Old Earl was a good man who just preferred to keep to himself. Something Alex definitely understood and respected.

"Earl is…" He hesitated, searching for the right words. "Well, he's got—"

"Is that the place?"

Tammy pointed at a house on the right. The front yard was littered with tree limbs but immaculate otherwise. Wooden crafts lined the railings of a spotless front porch, and wind chimes tinged together with the gentle breeze, filling the air with a harmonious tune.

"Yeah, that's it," Alex said.

The pup dashed across the front yard and up the porch steps to scratch at the door. Brody immediately waddled after the dog.

Tammy halted Brody with a gentle hand, lifted him into her arms and whispered over his head, "It's going to be tough to separate these two. You know that, right?"

Alex nodded curtly, his chest aching as Brody squirmed in her arms and reached for the dog.

The door opened, and a deep voice bellowed, "Well, look who finally decided to swagger home."

A bulky figure, clad in denim overalls and a plaid shirt, walked onto the porch and petted the pup. Thick scar tissue wound around his forearms in red and white patches and encased his broad hands.

Alex quickened his step, edging in front of Tammy and Brody as the elderly man approached. "Hey, Earl."

Earl straightened, held out his hand and smiled. "Alex. I haven't seen you in a month of Sundays."

The disfiguring grooves on one side of Earl's face were deep and discolored. Each cluster of burn marks denoted the horrors of the house fire he'd survived years ago. The damaged web of skin marred his jovial expression and produced an uneven tilt to his facial features.

Alex took Earl's hand and lowered his gaze, a prickling sensation spreading through him. It was an odd mixture of respect, admiration and guilt that he always experienced around Earl. Respect and admiration for the other man's bravery and good-hearted, forgiving nature. And guilt from his embarrassing childhood encounter.

"I thought this pup might be yours," Alex said, gesturing toward the Lab as he sat on the wide toe of Earl's boot. "Figured it was time he found his way home."

"Yep, Scout's mine," Earl said. "Don't matter how I fence him in, he manages to escape. That storm scared off a lot of my dogs, but I've managed to round up most of them. Glad to see you made it through okay." Earl frowned. "Maxine stopped by yesterday and told me about Dean and Gloria." He shook his head, his eyes sad. "Damned shame."

Throat closing, Alex managed a stiff nod and stepped slowly to the side. "Earl, this is Tammy Jenkins and Brod—"

"Brody," Earl interrupted softly, easing down the stairs. His step faltered, however, when a frightened expression crossed the baby's features. "Hey there, fella."

Brody's face crumpled, and he turned, burying his forehead against Tammy's throat and balling his fists into her T-shirt.

Alex cringed and rubbed his hands over his jeans. "Brody just—"

"He's just tired, is all," Tammy chimed. "It was a long walk." She climbed up the two stairs to reach Earl, her bare arm brushing Alex's, and she smiled. "It's nice to meet you. I'm Tammy."

"The barrel racer, eh?" Earl's expression brightened at her nod, and he gestured toward the bandage on her temple. "Maxine told me that twister tore you off the road. Bet you gave it a run for its money, though."

Tammy laughed. "I tried." Her laughter trailed off, and her voice grew heavy. "But some things you can't outrun. I'm just glad I'm still breathing, you know?"

"Yeah," Earl murmured, meeting her eyes and nodding. "I know."

Alex stilled. Something passed between Tammy and Earl. An understanding? Shared emotion? He wasn't sure. But it hung on the air between them, lifting the corners of their mouths into resigned smiles as they exchanged a look.

Then Tammy spoke and the moment was over.

"If it hadn't been for Alex, I probably wouldn't be here." She turned her attention to him, and her smile widened. "He saved my life."

Those beautiful eyes lingered, traveling over his face, then down to his chest and arms, soft and appreciative. Pleasure fluttered through Alex, easing through the numbness under his skin. It'd been so long since a woman had looked at him like that. With approval and subtle—Lord help him—*wanting*.

He grunted and tore his gaze away. She was so young and susceptible. Too young to recognize what a hollow, broken man he was. And too susceptible to an attraction born out of gratitude.

"She's exaggerating," he said, waving a hand in

Earl's direction. "I just happened to be in the right place at the right time."

"Watch that, son," Earl chuckled. "If there's one thing I've learned in life, it's to never brush off a compliment from a woman. Those come few and far between for some of us."

Alex ducked his head, feeling like more of a heel than ever. Tammy's sweet compliments, pretty face and bright smile were things he imagined Earl had stopped encountering years ago after he sought seclusion in his isolated home. And Earl deserved them more than he ever would.

Alex sagged with relief when Tammy changed the direction of the conversation.

"I take it you didn't have much damage from the tornado?" Tammy asked.

Earl shook his head. "Nope. Just some broken branches and a roughed-up hay field."

"That's good," she said, eyeing the porch. "Because it'd be a shame to lose all these beautiful crafts. Do you make them yourself?" At Earl's nod, she jiggled Brody gently in her arms and pointed at a wooden dog balanced on the porch rail. "Look, Brody. Do you know what that one is?"

Brody lifted his head and looked at the figurine, darting sideways glances at Earl.

"Need a hint, baby boy?" Earl asked, grinning. "It makes a sound like this…"

Earl barked. Well, howled, really. He did his darnedest to imitate the wooden bloodhound, but his voice cracked and a coughing spell overtook him, doubling him over. A chorus of muffled barks escaped the closed front door, and Scout yipped, then gnawed at his boot.

"Dagnabbit, Scout." Earl shook his leg, laughing and waving his arms in circles as he stumbled. "You bite more than any dog I've come across."

A high-pitched cackle split the air. Brody threw his head back against Tammy's shoulder, his small chest jerking with powerful giggles. Tammy joined him, struggling to keep Brody in her arms as he squirmed and reached for Scout.

Alex smiled, his breath catching at the sheer joy on the baby's face.

"Oh, you like dogs, eh?" Earl spun and opened the front door, and four more puppies streamed out to nip playfully at Scout's ears. "Put that boy on his feet, Tammy, and we'll have some fun."

And it *was* fun. More fun than Alex had experienced in what seemed like forever. The sight of Earl, Brody and Tammy bumbling around on the front porch, chasing pups and tripping over their own feet, had him chuckling. He sat on the top step and watched, reminiscing over the fun he and Dean used to have as kids.

Alex closed his eyes. How damned wonderful it had felt back then. To be young and have his best friend.

When the trio lost their breaths from exertion and laughter, Earl coaxed Tammy into a rocking chair, set Brody in her lap, then brought out sandwiches and glasses of sweet tea. Alex sipped his drink on the porch steps and tried not to stare at Tammy's graceful movements as she carefully tipped her glass to Brody's lips, wiped the baby's mouth and laughed at Earl's tall tales. They enjoyed each other's company for over an hour and, soon, the golden glow of the setting sun faded and night arrived, bringing with it a full moon that cast a white light over the front porch.

"It's a beautiful night," Earl said, setting his empty cup on the porch rail. "And a long walk home for y'all." He nodded at Alex. "How 'bout a hayride back? I loaded up a few bales on the trailer last week. Just haven't had time to haul 'em off for sale. Bet Brody would like it, and it'd save you another long trek."

Alex glanced at Brody. The baby snuggled deeper into Tammy's embrace, slipped his thumb into his mouth and blinked heavily.

"You want to, Alex?" Tammy asked, studying his face.

Alex tightened his grip on his glass. The gentle plea in her eyes and the exhausted child in her arms made it impossible to refuse the request.

After helping Earl secure the pups inside the house, Alex joined him at the shed while Tammy waited with Brody on the porch. Alex asked to borrow a chain saw, and after loading it up, he hooked the hay-laden trailer to Earl's truck.

"I think that's good," Earl said, tugging on the chains of the hitch.

Alex nodded and moved away.

"You ever gonna look me in the eye, son?"

Alex stopped. His cheeks warmed beneath Earl's scrutiny. He pressed his palm to the hard metal of the truck and turned his head, forcing himself to meet Earl's gaze.

"You only live a mile down the road, and I rarely see

you," Earl said. "You still holding on to the past? 'Cause I don't hold grudges, and I ain't mad at you. Never was."

Alex cringed. "I know."

"No. You don't." Earl sighed and tapped a blunt finger against his damaged face. "When a person has trouble looking, it's usually because they're more uncomfortable with themselves than they are with me. Either that, or they've never encountered a hardship like the one I sport. With you, I suspect it's the former." He frowned. "You and Dean were good boys, Alex. And you've grown into a good man. You got nothing to be ashamed of."

Alex swallowed hard, his tongue clinging to the dry roof of his mouth. "I'm not ashamed."

"Yeah, you are," Earl stressed. "You're ashamed of something." He looked away, peering across the moonlit lawn toward the front porch. "As for that young gal, she didn't bat an eyelash when she got a good look at me. Not like most people." He nodded. "I think she's seen something a whole lot uglier in her life than that tornado. And she don't seem to be ashamed of nothing." The corner of his mouth curled up into a small smile. "A man can't help but admire that."

A breeze rustled through the tall grass, and an owl hooted in the trees behind them.

"Night's calling," Earl said. "Better get a move on."

He walked away, climbed into the driver's seat, then revved the engine.

Alex stood still for a moment, absorbing the vibrations of the truck's motor beneath his fingers. "I'm not ashamed," he whispered.

But his voice shook, and the words didn't ring true.

His wrist tingled where Tammy had forcefully stilled it two days ago in the hallway of his home, and a bead of sweat trickled down his cheek. He wiped it away with the back of his hand and wondered if Earl was right.

And if so…what kind of ugly had Tammy seen?

Something about a clear night sky had always been soothing to Tammy. Maybe it was the shine of the moon or the way the glittering space stretched on endlessly, as though it could swallow up any problem. No matter how big that problem might be.

Tammy tilted her head back for a clearer view of the stars, shifted to a more comfortable position on the hay bale and cradled Brody closer to her chest. Goodness knew she'd encountered her fair share of problems in the past forty-eight hours. A wrecked truck and trailer. She was already a day overdue at Raintree with just a brief message that she was okay having been sent to Jen via the sheriff's office. To save the battery, she kept her cell phone powered off with the exception of an hour in the morning, afternoon and evening, hoping service would return so she could call Jen. It hadn't. Which added to her troubles.

But not finding Razz was, by far, the worst of them.

The thought made her chest burn, the pain fueling her fears of never finding her racing partner. No—her family, really. She'd never been able to trust many people as implicitly as she trusted Razz. Every time she entered the arena with the quarter horse, they were dependent upon each other for success and survival. And she never doubted Razz to deliver either.

"Y'all all right back there?"

Earl's shout barely reached the back of the trailer, but the wave of his broad hand from the truck's window signaled he was checking on them. Just as he had twice since pulling onto the dirt road and heading toward Alex's ranch.

"Yeah," she called back, holding Brody tight with one arm and waving with the other.

The engine rumbled, and the truck moseyed along the path, bumping gently over uneven dirt and crunching over rocks. A tendril of hair blew across her face and caught on her eyelashes for the umpteenth time. She blinked and brushed it back, tucking it behind her ear.

"Too much wind?" Alex eased to the edge of the hay bale facing her and gestured toward the baby in her lap. "There's enough room in the cab for you and Brody if you'd like to sit in there."

"No, thanks. It's a warm night and he's already knocked out." She smiled. "The fresh air will do him good."

The moonlight highlighted Alex's chiseled cheekbones and strong jaw. His gray eyes seemed more mesmerizing than ever beneath the soft glow of the night sky. Tammy dragged her eyes away and looked up again, savoring the pleasure spiraling through her as she recalled the brief kiss from yesterday. Focusing on the tender way his mouth had touched hers was a welcome distraction from her worries about Razz. And her body continued to clamor for more of his attention despite the familiar whisper of caution that always arose when she was around a man.

"I was wondering why you..." Alex cleared his throat. "Well, why you didn't..."

"Hmm?" Tammy prompted, refocusing on Alex. "Why I didn't what?"

He propped his elbows on his thighs and scooted closer, twisting a straw of hay between his knees and asking in a low voice, "Why didn't you ask about Earl's scars?" He frowned and averted his gaze, focusing intently on the hay in his hand. "That's usually the first thing most people ask after meeting him."

"I'm not like most people." She smiled gently as he glanced up. "And I didn't think it'd be polite to ask."

His brow furrowed, and he hesitated, casting a glance at the truck's cab, then asking quietly, "But aren't you curious?"

The soft, sexy rumble of his voice and the moment of shared confidence sent delicious shivers over her skin, and she found herself wanting to coax him into further conversation. "Why?" She leaned in, raised an eyebrow and whispered, "Are you itching to tell me, Mr. Gossip?"

An affronted expression crossed his face. "No." He blinked, shook his head and sat back. "Not at all. I just wondered."

Her mouth twitched. He must've noticed it and the flirtatious gleam in her eye, because his lean cheeks flushed and he pressed his lips together as though trying to fight a smile. It got the better of him, though, and spread across his face, denting his dimples and casting a boyish look to his face.

"Point taken." He chuckled softly. "I've been duly chastised."

She laughed with him, stopping when he did. He looked away and stared at the dark clusters of trees lining the dirt road. The trailer squeaked over a pothole, and a sad silence filled the space around them.

"Does it really matter how he got them?" she asked, settling Brody more comfortably against her middle. "Earl seems like a nice man. Better than most of the ones I've known."

Alex returned his attention to her, and the intense curiosity in his handsome face made her squirm uneasily on the hay bale.

She straightened and held his gaze. "We all have scars, Alex. It's just that you can't always see them."

Her mouth twisted. She had scars of her own, too. Except she'd been luckier than Earl. There were no visible marks on her body or residual physical pain from the frequent beatings she'd endured beneath her father's fists. But there were still wounds inside. Ones that had formed every time her mother had closed her eyes and walked away, ignoring Tammy's cries for help and choosing her husband over her daughter.

Tammy winced and studied Alex more closely, her eyes drifting over his broad shoulders, chiseled biceps and muscular thighs. He was well built and attractive with no physical flaws she could see. And no one could doubt his loyalty and genuine concern for his friends. Heck, he'd risked his own safety to help her, and she was nothing more than a stranger to him. But his guarded demeanor hinted that something hid beneath his skin.

What could have driven him to choose to be alone for so long, as Maxine had put it?

"The scars you can't see are usually the worst," Tammy whispered, hugging Brody close and resting her chin on top of his soft hair.

Alex's chest rose on a strong breath, his mouth opening and closing as he met her stare. For a moment, she thought he'd speak, but he didn't. Instead, he nodded, then looked silently at Brody for the remainder of the ride.

A few minutes later, they arrived at Alex's ranch. Earl brought the truck to a stop in the backyard and Alex hopped off the trailer.

"Here," he said, reaching out. "Hold on to Brody and I'll help you down."

Tammy stood, embraced the baby more securely and stepped to the edge of the trailer. His strong hands wrapped around her waist, then eased her down.

Her heart tripped in her chest, making her breath hitch, and she gasped as her boots fumbled over the ground.

"Okay?" Alex asked.

His warm palms lingered on her sides, caressing almost, as he waited for her to get her balance.

"Yes." She tried to ignore the heat and appealing scent of his strong frame as he released her. "Thank you."

The truck door creaked open, and Earl stepped out, his bulky figure outlined in the moonlight. The house cast a shadow over his profile as he approached and the undamaged side of his face became more prominent.

"I expect it's time to tuck that baby in for the night," Earl said, arriving at Tammy's side and rubbing a hand over Brody's back. "As young as he is, though, he'll be raring to go again as soon as the sun comes up."

Tammy laughed and kissed Brody's forehead. He slipped deeper into sleep, his thumb slipping from his open mouth and falling to her chest. "He keeps us on our toes, that's for sure."

"Noticed on the way in that you got your fair share of downed trees." Earl glanced at Alex, then nodded toward the house. "How's your roof?"

Alex sighed. "Needs work. The stable was hit the worst, though."

Tammy's stomach sank, and she scanned the dimly lit land, wishing Razz would somehow miraculously appear.

"I'm available if you need help," Earl said. "How 'bout I swing by in the morning and help you get the tree off your truck? Then we could tackle that roof of yours. My joints have been acting up all day, and that's usually the first sign of rain coming." He smiled. "I could be here at daybreak and, together, I think we could have your truck and roof in good shape by dark."

"Thanks," Alex said, nodding. "I'd appreciate that."

Earl returned to the truck, hopped inside and revved the engine. "I'll be back in the morning with the chain saw. Y'all get that baby a good night's rest, okay?"

"We will," Tammy shouted over the engine.

Brody shifted against her, rubbed his face against her throat, then nuzzled his cheek onto her breast. His small fingers dug deeper into her T-shirt, squeezing rhythmically until a snore escaped and he drifted off again.

Her heart turned over in her chest. She kissed his forehead and cradled him closer. The weight of him in her arms filled some of the emptiness inside her, and she stood still under the full moon and bright stars, absorbing the peace.

"Both of you need a good night's rest."

Tammy started at the gruff sound of Alex's voice. He reached out slowly and covered her hand with his on Brody's back. Her skin danced beneath the warm weight of his broad thumb as it swept gently across her wrist.

"Follow me?" he asked softly.

The tender light in his eyes and gentle smile made every inch of her eager to follow. She pulled in a deep breath and nodded.

He led the way into the house, guiding her carefully up the front porch steps with a flashlight he pulled from his pocket, then drew to a halt in the kitchen.

"Wait here a minute, okay?"

She did, watching as he disappeared around the corner and listening in the dark kitchen as he rustled around in another room. Light pooled onto the kitchen floor again as he reappeared, motioning with the flashlight toward the hall.

"First door on the left," he said, his fingers rubbing over something in his palm.

She proceeded down the hall, then stopped in front of the door. Her hand lifted toward the doorknob but froze in midair. "I thought you never used this room."

The familiar heat of him drew close to her back, and his soft breath tickled her neck. He eased a brawny arm around her and slid a key into the lock. "I don't," he whispered. "But I'll make an exception for Brody."

The lock clicked, and he shoved the door open. He swept the flashlight over the interior of the room, highlighting baby blue walls, a wooden chest, a rocking chair, a changing table and…a crib. Every item was pristine and arranged in a welcoming semicircle.

She swung her head to the side, stilling as her lips

brushed the rough stubble of his jaw. Heart pounding, she fought the desire to nuzzle her cheek against his skin and asked, "Why do you have—"

"Nothing was damaged in here," he said, voice husky. "The crib sheets are in the chest, and once you get Brody settled, you can have my room to yourself for the night."

"But, Alex—"

"Not tonight, okay?" He lowered his head, his mouth moving against her temple and his broad palm settling on her hip. "Let's just get some rest. We all need it."

Of its own accord, her body sank back against his. She fit perfectly, his wide chest and muscular thighs cradling her as though she belonged there. A peaceful tenderness welled inside her, quieting that inner voice of caution and strengthening so much it filled her eyes, blurring her vision.

Alex pressed the flashlight into her palm at Brody's back, his fingers trembling. "Good night."

He left, and moments later, a cabinet thudded, then glass clinked. She imagined him standing at the kitchen sink, taking shots as he had the first night she'd arrived, and wondered why a man who kept such a careful distance from children would've invested so much in the future of having one.

Her throat tightened as another thought hit her. Had he lost a child? Was that why he was no longer married?

Tammy clung tighter to Brody, wanting, more than anything, to wrap her arms around Alex and hold him just as close.

Chapter 5

"There are a few things in life a woman just needs."

Tammy stopped sweeping the front porch, propped her hand on her hip and leveled what she hoped was a stern expression on Brody. But it was difficult to keep her frown in place when he looked up at her from the top step and grinned. His tiny feet inched their way down to the next step despite her ten thousand requests to stay put. The same requests he'd ignored throughout the morning as she'd cleaned the house while Alex and Earl worked on the roof.

Clearly, the comfortable slumber in the crib last night had replenished his energy.

"Say, for instance," Tammy continued, "I'd kill for a hot shower right now." She dragged her fingers through her dingy hair, the tangled, straw-like strands making her cringe. "And a huge bottle of conditioner."

Three days without power or running water didn't
make for the best beauty regimen. She dipped her head,
eyed her rumpled T-shirt, then frowned. Of course, the
fact that the tornado had flung her overnight bags from
her truck, leaving them pinned beneath the overturned
trailer in the mud, hadn't helped matters, either. She'd
spent over an hour sifting through soaked shirts and
underwear for a decent outfit after the wrecker hauled
away her truck.

Brody smiled wider, gripped the edge of the bricks
with both hands and shimmied down to the next step.

"A cheeseburger would be great, too." Her mouth
twitched as he stretched the toes of his sneakers toward
the next one. "One piled with bacon and a big side of
onion rings. You know, the whole shebang. Unfortunately, there's no chance of that."

Brody slipped to the lowest step and glanced up at
her, his shoes only inches from the grass.

"But what I need most of all," Tammy said, propping
the broom against the porch rail, "is for a certain little
boy to listen to me when I tell him no."

Brody turned his head, pointed at the front lawn and
squealed as a golden ball of fur darted across the grass.

"I know you want to play with Scout."

Good grief, did she know. When Earl arrived at first
light, Scout had shown up shortly after, having followed
Earl's truck to the ranch, and had remained underfoot
ever since. Apparently, Brody's love for the puppy was
reciprocated.

"But," Tammy added, "I can't finish sweeping this
porch and chase after you and Scout at the same time,
now can I?"

Brody grinned mischievously and scooted to the edge of the step.

"Don't do it." Tammy took a slow step forward, smiling as he stood. "Don't. You. Do it…"

Brody cackled and took off, his jeans and diaper swishing with every step.

Tammy darted down the steps and chased him around Alex's truck, which Earl and Alex had freed from the fallen tree. Scout joined Brody in the chase, and Tammy continued to play along, stumbling over the dog and laughing.

"That's it, Brody," Earl called out from the roof. "Give her a run for her money."

Tammy caught Brody, hugged him to her middle and looked up. Alex and Earl stood on the roof, shading their eyes from the sun and chuckling down at them. Alex's T-shirt, soaked with sweat, clung to his muscular frame and sent a wave of wanting over her.

"Don't encourage him, Earl," Tammy said, forcing her attention from Alex to the other man. "I've already had to—"

A strong buzzing started in Tammy's back pocket. She froze in place, then scrambled to pull her cell phone free of her sweaty jeans. The red battery at the top of the display indicated the charge was almost depleted, but was it finally receiving calls? The lit screen displaying "Jen" in the center proved it was. Hallelujah!

"It's working," Tammy shouted. She kissed Brody's cheek, then jumped up and down, waving the phone in the air. "We have cell service! That means the power may be back on soon."

Alex and Earl exchanged an amused glance, then

made their way to the ladder and started climbing down. Tammy swiped the screen and squealed hello into the receiver.

"Oh, thank heavens. I've been worried sick about you." Jen's voice held equal amounts of frustration and concern. "Every time I've called, your phone has been off, and you haven't answered any of my text messages."

"I couldn't," Tammy said, a relieved laugh bursting past her lips. "Cell service has been out and the land-lines were down. There was no power because of the tornado—"

Jen gasped. "Are you all right? The sheriff sent word that you were okay, but I needed to hear your voice."

"I'm fine. But my truck took a beating."

"The storms have been all over the news the past couple of days. Colt said he didn't think you normally took that route, but after the sheriff called, he went out of his mind worrying about you."

Tammy winced. Colt Mead, Jen's fiancé and Tammy's cousin, had answered Tammy's call for help years ago when her father's beatings had become too severe to endure. Colt had picked her up the same day, and they'd eventually ended up on the rodeo circuit, where Colt began bull riding. After they met Jen, the three of them had toured the circuit together for years until Colt's father was killed in a tragic accident. Colt left the circuit to take care of his younger sister and asked Jen to help him temporarily. But *temporary* turned into permanent after Colt and Jen fell in love, then decided to retire and settle down at Raintree Ranch to raise Colt's sister.

"Please tell Colt I'm fine," Tammy said, grabbing un-successfully at Brody's waistband as he toddled away.

"I'm stuck here for the moment, since my truck isn't drivable, but I made it through okay."

"Where are you? We'll come get you." There were scuffling sounds on the other end of the line. "Just tell me the address and we'll leave right away."

"No, please wait. My battery is about to die and I don't have long, so please listen for a sec, okay?" Tammy gripped the phone tighter and hustled across the lawn, chasing Brody. "How are plans for the wedding coming? Is everything working out?"

"Everything's going well," Jen said. "I've got more than enough help and my mom is in wedding planner heaven." Her laugh was brief. "It's just that Colt and I miss you."

"I miss you, too. But would you mind if I stayed and helped someone out for a couple of weeks, then came to Raintree a bit later? I promise I'll be there in time for the rehearsal dinner. There's no way I'd miss it." She caught up with Brody, wrapped an arm around his waist and halted him before he reached a pile of debris by the driveway. "It's just that someone helped me out and I kind of owe him a favor."

Brody whined and strained in her hold, wiggling against her chest and jostling the phone.

"What was that?" Jen asked.

"The favor." Tammy released Brody, allowing him to run across a safer part of the grass, then followed him to the other side of the lawn. "The storm was bad, Jen. It did a lot of damage. Razz is missing, and it left a little boy orphaned. It would've done me in, too, if it hadn't been for Alex."

"Alex?"

"That's who I'm staying with while my truck is fixed. And until I find Razz. I can't leave until I know what happened to her." She cleared her throat to erase the shakiness from her voice. "Besides, Alex saved my life, and the least I can do is help him out."

Tammy watched as Brody plopped onto the grass with Scout and quickly filled Jen in on what had happened, cringing each time the low-battery signal dinged across the line.

"So it's just the three of you staying out there?" Jen asked. "Are you sure this Alex is trustworthy? I mean, you just met him."

"I know. But he's different."

Tammy dragged her teeth over her bottom lip and sneaked a glance at Alex. He walked up the front steps, flipped the porch light switch on, then eyed the fixture. When it didn't illuminate, he looked in her direction and shook his head, smiling sadly.

Tammy turned away, face heating, and lowered her voice. "*I'm* different with him. And after what we went through…" She pulled in a deep breath, searching for the right words. "I don't know how to explain it, but I think I'm safe with him."

"Sounds like he's made quite an impression."

"He has." Tammy smiled, her belly fluttering as she recalled his gentle kiss and touches. "He's a good man, and I owe him." She pressed the phone tighter to her ear, waiting for Jen to speak. When she didn't, Tammy asked, "What is it? You're never this quiet."

"I'm just thinking."

"About what?" Tammy pressed. "You can always be honest with me."

Jen remained silent for a moment, then said, "I know how difficult it is to be on the road alone, and I'm sorry Colt and I left like we did. We're still family, and there's always a place for you at Raintree if you get tired of the circuit." She sighed. "This is really none of my business, but I love you like a sister and you've been through so much. Please don't take this the wrong way, Tammy, but could how you met Alex have affected the way you see him?"

Her stomach tensed. She focused on the jagged line of trees on the other side of the grounds. "No. He *is* different. He's a good man."

"I'm not saying he isn't," Jen said hastily. "And I'm glad he helped you. But that doesn't obligate you to him in any way. Of course, I'll support you in whatever you choose to do. I just worry about you staying in the middle of nowhere with a stranger. And I worry about you getting too attached too fast and getting hurt. Could you please just think about it? For me? Just ask yourself if you think about this man the way you do because Colt and I are no longer with you. And, well, without Razz…" She hesitated. "Is it because you feel alone?"

Tammy closed her eyes, cheeks burning and throat thickening. "I—" Her voice broke. She opened her eyes and tried again. "I don't…"

Two thick figures moved between the broken trees across the field.

Tammy squinted against the sharp rays of the sun, stilling as identifiable shapes emerged from between the stripped branches. Two muzzles appeared, then broad necks, long legs and tails.

"I'm sorry, I've got to go," Tammy whispered, cutting the call and shoving the phone in her pocket.

She watched silently as the two horses cleared the tree line and ambled into the center of the field. They stopped and stood motionless, side by side. The distance and glare of the sun made it impossible to decipher the color of their hides.

"Razz?" Tammy lifted a shaky hand to her mouth and whistled around her fingers.

The horses didn't respond. She took a jerky step forward.

"Easy." Alex's broad palm touched the small of her back, his voice soft. "We don't know which horses they are or what state they're in. Let me check them first."

"I'm going with you," she said.

Alex frowned. "Tammy—"

"Let her go," Earl said. "She knows what she's up against. If one of the horses is hers, she has the right to do what needs to be done if necessary."

Tammy flinched, her stomach churning. She didn't know what she'd do if she found Razz mortally wounded. But she couldn't stand the thought of never knowing what happened to her.

Earl walked to Brody's side and petted Scout. "Y'all go ahead. Brody and I will wait here."

Brody smiled up at Earl, babbling and pointing at Scout's rapidly wagging tail. Tammy's eyes lingered on Brody, and she drew strength from the boy's bright expression before meeting Alex's solemn gaze.

"Ready?" he asked.

Tammy nodded, and they walked slowly across the field. As they approached, Tammy scrutinized the horses' mud-slicked hides for Razz's black-and-white pattern. The thick sludge coating the majority of their bodies made it difficult, but she managed to discern a broad black-and-white marking on one horse's chest.

"Razz?"

Eyes swollen, both horses remained motionless with their ears meekly back and tails still. Though she didn't respond, the horse on the left was definitely Razz.

Tammy stepped forward. "Hey, girl."

Razz flinched and stepped back. The horse on the right followed suit, pressing close to Razz's side. The sun dipped lower at their backs, and the wet streaks of tears on the mare's cheeks glistened. Bright patches of blood mixed with the mud on both horses' hides, denoting gashes and punctures on their shoulders, hips and legs.

Tammy held her breath, stifling a sob, and clenched her fists at her sides. She didn't know what was worse—the days spent not knowing where Razz was at all, or finding Razz so badly wounded that she'd be forced to put her down.

"She's been hurt so much," she whispered, throat tightening.

Alex's warm palm enveloped hers and squeezed. "We don't know anything for sure yet." He waited until she looked up, his gray eyes kind and reassuring. "Let me take a look at her, all right?"

Unable to speak, she nodded. Alex released her hand and moved slowly toward Razz. He spoke softly, his voice low and gentle. Tammy couldn't make out the words, but the tone was enough to help her catch her breath and unfurl her fists.

It seemed to have the same effect on Razz. She stood still as Alex approached and continued to stand motionless as he cupped her cheek gently, allowing him to stroke her jaw.

Alex continued to murmur in a soft tone and Razz responded, lowering her muzzle and nudging Alex's forehead with her own. Alex praised her, then began checking her injuries, moving slowly from her head to tail and carefully examining her wounds. He repeated the process with the second horse and returned to stroke Razz's neck.

"The other horse is mine," Alex said. "Razz and Sapphire are hurt pretty badly." He smiled. "But they're gonna be okay."

"How do you know for sure?" Her voice pitched higher, tremors coursing through her limbs. "What if there's more damage than you think?"

His smile slipped, and his handsome features gentled. "If that's the case, we'll cross that bridge when we get to it. But from what I can tell, their wounds will heal."

Hot tears scalded her cheeks, and she blinked rapidly, eyes darting over Razz's wounds. "Are you sure?"

"Tammy, look at me." Alex moved into her line of vision, his deep voice calm but firm. "Razz is going to be okay." He reached out and cradled her jaw with his palm, his thumb wiping a tear from her cheek. "We'll make sure of it."

Tammy's shoulders sagged with relief, and she managed a shaky smile.

"Help me lead them to the stable?" Alex asked, stepping back.

Tammy wiped her face with the back of her hand and cleared her throat. "Of course." She eased past Alex and crossed to Razz's side. "Hi, girl," she whispered, touching the mare's shoulder.

Razz dipped her head and took a step closer.

"I told you I wouldn't leave you." Tammy slipped her arms around Razz and pressed her cheek against the horse's neck.

She breathed in the familiar scent of her racing partner, her chest swelling with joy and a fresh round of tears trickling down her face to mingle with Razz's. After a few moments, Razz made a soft sound of pleasure, and Sapphire moved close for soothing pats, too.

Tammy laughed and glanced at Alex. "You're right. I think they're going to be okay."

Alex smiled, his charming dimples appearing, and nodded.

That flutter in her belly returned, unfurling and spreading through her in a rush of pleasure. There he stood. Broad and muscular. Gentle and protective. A tower of tender strength in another seemingly hopeless situation, providing things she hadn't known she needed. Understanding and reassurance. Support. And every inch of her body wanted to press against his, wrap around him and hold on tight.

Is it because you feel alone?

Tammy stilled, Jen's words flitting through her mind. She studied Alex, her eyes traveling over his handsome face, the warmth of his expression and his solid presence.

Maybe. Maybe she did feel alone. But at least she *did* feel when she was with Alex. She felt more alive than she had in her entire life. She wanted Alex so much that the dance of desire beneath her skin overrode her fears and insecurities. And singing Brody to sleep in the nursery last night had made her dream of a home and children of her own almost…*tangible*.

She wasn't ready to let those feelings go. Not yet.

Tammy released Razz, walked over to Alex and wrapped her arms around him. She hugged him close, pressing her body to his and savoring the strong throb of his heart against her breasts. "Thank you."

Alex applied one last strip of tape to the gauze on Sapphire's leg wound, then sat back on his haunches in the stall. "There, gorgeous. Now you can rest."

Sapphire looked down at him and released a soft breath, her swollen eyelids blinking heavily.

Alex grimaced, then reached up and stroked her leg. After he and Tammy had settled the horses into the two least damaged stalls, Earl had driven ten miles to contact the nearest vet. It'd taken almost the entire afternoon for the vet to tend to Razz's and Sapphire's most severe injuries, and Alex and Tammy had taken over the more minor ones after he'd left.

It'd been an exhausting process for all of them. Most especially Brody, whom Earl had taken inside two hours ago to keep entertained. But it was worth it to know Razz and Sapphire would heal and could finally rest easy for the night.

"I've never seen such a perfect blue roan." Tammy entered the stall, then knelt at his side, her green eyes roving over Sapphire.

Alex couldn't stop the proud smile spreading across

his face. A thorough washing had highlighted the blue sheen of Sapphire's hide and powerful build. And though he was a long way from recouping his losses, Sapphire's return kindled a spark of hope within him that, perhaps, more horses had survived.

Tammy curled her slim fingers around his knee and smiled up at him. "Sapphire is beautiful."

He studied her, absorbing the pink flush in her cheeks, the tempting curve of her soft lips and the trusting adoration in her gaze.

Hell, *she* was beautiful.

The press of her soft curves as she'd hugged him hours earlier had eased through the thin cotton of his T-shirt and still lingered on his skin. Her embrace had heated his blood and stirred long-buried desires to life, making him feel as though he was important to someone. A part of something. As though he belonged.

Damned if those yearnings hadn't begun to hinder his good sense. And their talk of scars yesterday had tempted him to imagine she might be different. That maybe she looked for what a person had rather than what a person lacked.

Even so, it was a bad idea to get tangled up with a woman who was leaving soon, and it'd be even worse to take advantage of her hero worship.

His stomach dropped. That was all it was. Hero worship. The kind he hoped would stay solid until she left, obscuring his flaws and hiding them from her forever. Then, at least, he'd remain a man in Tammy's eyes.

His mouth twisted. Unlike with Susan.

Alex pressed his palms flat against the floor, the shavings poking between the gaps in his fingers as he fought against gripping Tammy's hip, tugging her tight to his side and covering her mouth with his own.

"She's got a strong heart," he said, tearing his eyes from Tammy and glancing up at Sapphire. "Sapphire and Razz were in better shape than I thought they'd be after being gone for so many days. Sapphire knows the land. She must've led Razz to the creek for water, then found her way home and brought Razz with her."

"I'm glad she did."

Tammy leaned in closer, her soft breath tickling his ear and her small hand warming his skin through the thick denim of his jeans.

Heart skipping, he shoved to his feet and glanced in the neighboring stall. "Razz settling down okay?"

"Yeah." Tammy stood, too, then shoved her hands in her back pockets. The action pulled her T-shirt tight against the full curves of her breasts. "She's already drifting off."

Alex averted his eyes. "A full belly, good doctoring and a comfortable place to rest…" He shrugged to relieve the tension in his shoulders. "They'll probably sleep for a day or two straight."

Tammy laughed. "I'm kind of wanting that, too." She dragged a hand through her dark hair, wincing as her fingers tangled in the wavy strands. "I'd give anything to soak in a bubble bath, then wallow around on a soft bed in an air-conditioned room."

His eyes shot straight to her long legs, curvy hips and ample breasts, the idea of her sprawled on a bed, soft and welcoming, fanning that spark of desire into flame.

She held up a hand and smiled. "Not that your bed

isn't comfortable. As a matter of fact, I've enjoyed sleeping on it."

Ah, hell. His bed. A fresh set of images flashed through his mind. Ones that made his body tighten uncomfortably. Alex dragged a hand across the back of his neck and cleared his throat, heat searing his face.

She laughed, the full-bodied sound echoing around the stall. "Did I embarrass you?" Her expression was full of surprise. And, oddly enough, delight. "Because embarrassing you wasn't what I was going for." Seemingly emboldened, she stepped closer and placed a hand on his chest. "Though it's nice to know I affect you in at least one way."

Her gentle teasing made his heart trip, the tender flirtation prompting him to recall what his life had been like years ago. When he didn't balk at stripping himself bare, holding a woman close and letting her in. When he enjoyed exploring the depths of her heart, searching for her secrets and sharing his. Back when he believed himself to be solid. And whole.

"One way?" Before he knew it, his hand drifted around her back to settle between her shoulder blades, and his head lowered, his mouth moving against the soft skin of her temple as he whispered, "You have no idea how many ways."

She pulled in a swift breath, her green eyes darkening as she slid her hand up and wove her fingers through his hair. Her touch was confident, but she trembled against him as though unsure.

He froze, her potential uncertainty yanking him back to reality. He was a far cry from the man she thought he was. And he was experienced enough to recognize the dangers of her youthful naïveté and hesitation. If they took this any further, they'd both walk away empty. This was *not* a good idea.

"Tammy." He released her hip, tugged her hand from his neck and stepped back. "This isn't—"

"Alex?"

Earl's faint call came on the heels of the creak of the stable door.

Grateful for the interruption, Alex slipped out of the stall, trying to ignore the wounded look in Tammy's eyes and fighting the urge to return and scoop her into his arms.

Brody ran down the center aisle of the stable with Scout nipping at the laces of his sneakers.

Earl followed at a much slower pace, then stopped, sighing deeply. "Y'all finished doctoring those horses?" At Alex's nod, Earl tugged a rag from his pocket and dabbed at his forehead. "Good." He gestured toward Brody. "I've been trying to entertain that rascal for a while now, and I've run out of things to keep him occupied."

The baby cackled, then dropped to all fours, attempting to crawl between Alex's legs.

"Hold up, buddy." Alex bent and lifted Brody to his feet. "You can't crawl around on this floor. There's still too much junk lying around."

Brody wiggled against his hands and scowled up at him. Something green speckled his cheeks and forehead. It also clung to his hair and caked the front of his overalls. Scout bounced at Brody's side, licking at the stains with each jump.

"Why is he green?" Tammy knelt beside Brody,

nudged Scout away and wiped Brody's cheeks with the hem of her T-shirt.

"Oh, that'd be the peas," Earl said. "He got hungry and I tried to feed him some of that jarred baby food I found in the kitchen. But that didn't work out too well." He wrinkled his nose. "Neither did the diaper changing."

Brody released a frustrated squeal, batting at Tammy's hands as she scrubbed at his food-splattered face.

"I think he just got to missing y'all." Earl walked over, kissed Brody's head, then headed for the door. "I gotta get home and let the rest of the dogs out while there's still an hour of daylight left." He paused, glanced around the stable, then looked at Alex. "Need some more help tomorrow? I could help you spruce up a bit in here."

Alex smiled. It'd been so long since he'd had company besides Dean and Gloria. Earl had been a huge help in more ways than one, and he'd enjoyed the other man's wild tales and crass jokes throughout the earlier part of the day. He was already looking forward to working with him again. Not to mention he could definitely use the help—though he couldn't afford to pay very much.

"I'd like that," Alex said. "But you've got to let me pay you."

Earl held up a hand. "No need for that. We're friends."

"I know, but—"

"I tell you what." Earl pointed at Scout. "You take that pup off my hands for a while, and that'd be payment enough. It'd be nice not to have my feet chomped on for a few days, and I think Brody would enjoy having him around."

Alex laughed. "Sounds good."

Earl waved goodbye to Tammy, then left, whistling.

"Oh, what a sweet mess." Tammy giggled as Brody forced his way past her attempts to clean his face and hugged her neck. His legs lifted restlessly as he attempted to climb into her arms. "That creek you've been talking about…" Tammy stood, lifting Brody and settling him on her hip. "Is it deep enough to wade in?"

"Yeah." Alex smiled as Scout started gnawing the hem of Tammy's jeans.

"Deep enough to bathe in?" Tammy frowned and shook her leg as Scout growled.

Alex nodded.

"Good. I think it's time we all cleaned up, and since there's still no power, we'll just have to hunt running water down at the creek." She grinned and started for the door. Scout slid along with her, his teeth latched on to her jeans. "I'll grab my conditioner, then you can lead the way."

An ache bloomed in his lower belly. A creek and bathing meant a wet, tempting Tammy.

He spun away and shut the door on Sapphire's stall, taking longer than usual to secure the latch. "I'll take you down there, then leave you to it."

Her footsteps halted. "I'm going to need your help, Alex. Brody is a mess, and I can't wash my hair and hold on to him at the same time. And trust me, another bird bath in the sink with bottled water isn't going to get the job done."

Alex glanced over his shoulder. "Then I'll bathe

Brody here and put him to bed while you clean up. Give you some peace and quiet for a while."

Tammy shook her head. "I think Brody would prefer us all to go together."

And spend the last hour of daylight fighting to keep his hands off her? *Hell, no.* He planned to go inside, extinguish his lust with a shot of whiskey, then crash on the couch. Alone.

"Brody's too young to care either way. I'm staying here."

Her eyes narrowed, and she squared her shoulders.

Ten minutes later, Alex stood, arms crossed, with his back to the creek and scowled at the feminine pair of jeans draped over a bush. The shiny stitching on the back pockets seemed to wink at him as the sun dropped close to the horizon, forcing him to recall just how well Tammy's curves filled out the denim.

"Okay," Tammy called over the rush of the creek. "Brody is fresh and clean again."

Water splashed, then twigs snapped. Scout scuttled by, stopped to shake his wet fur, then stretched out on the grass.

"Would you take Brody, please, so I can wash my hair?"

Alex tensed, the soft, melodic sound of her voice sending excited shivers up the back of his neck. Lord, how he wanted her lying next to him on a bed, her teasing words whispering across white cotton sheets and tickling his ear—

Brody shouted, the sharp sound causing Alex to jump.

"He wants to go back into the water," Tammy said. "Do you mind?"

Alex grunted, then reached up with both hands, tugged his shirt over his head and tossed it on a pile of towels on the ground. Turning, he closed his eyes and thrust his arms out.

Tammy laughed. "I appreciate the fact that you're a gentleman, Alex, but I'm wearing a bra and underwear, which covers more than most swimsuits nowadays." Her wet fingertips tapped his forearm. "You're going to have to open your eyes to hold on to Brody properly."

Reluctantly, he did. He tried his damnedest to keep his attention above her collarbones, but his eyes strayed anyway, snagging on the thin material of her bra. It was the same shade of green as her eyes and plastered to her breasts, leaving little to the imagination.

God, help me.

"You…uh…" Tammy's voice faltered, squeaking slightly. Brody squirmed against her. "Are you going to wear your boots in the water?"

Alex refocused on her face. Her eyes left his boots, lingered over his jeans-clad hips, then lifted to his bare chest. A blush snaked down her neck, and her mouth parted enticingly, bringing a smile to his face.

"Nope." His mouth quirked, and he had a sudden urge to test how far her bravado would stretch. "Not gonna wear my jeans, either."

He pulled off his boots and socks, unbuttoned his jeans, then reached for the zipper.

She watched until it rasped halfway down, then her eyes darted skyward, looking everywhere but at him. "Just let me know when you're ready for Brody."

He laughed, finished removing his jeans, then reached for the baby. "Here, I'll take him."

She held Brody out, her eyes still avoiding him.

"I appreciate you trying to protect my virtue and all," he teased, "but I'm wearing boxers."

Tammy laughed, then met his eyes as she handed Brody over. "Your virtue's safe with me. For the moment."

Alex raised an eyebrow at her mischievous expression, then waded into the creek with Brody. He spent the next few minutes distracting himself from Tammy's graceful movements as she bathed by holding Brody at a safe height in the water while the baby kicked and babbled.

Alex smiled. "So you like water, huh?"

Brody squealed and slapped the surface. A spray of water hit Alex in the face, stinging his eyes. He grimaced. Brody cackled and bounced harder in Alex's arms, the sheer joy in his face so reminiscent of Dean's fun-loving nature.

"Your daddy liked the water, too." Alex smiled, an ache returning to his chest. "We used to go swimming out here every summer." He swallowed hard, his throat burning. "Those days were the best ones of my life."

Brody stared up at him, his gaze drifting from Alex's forehead down to his chin, then he reached up and tugged at Alex's hair.

Alex laughed and drew Brody closer. "Yeah. We were a lot younger then, and I didn't have all this gray."

He gently untangled Brody's fingers from his hair, then examined the baby's hand as it nestled within his own. Brody's palm was so small against his, but the tiny fingers curled tight around his thumb and squeezed, proving there was more strength in that little body than he might've initially guessed. The firm tug traveled up his forearm, across his shoulder, then seeped into his chest, blurring his vision.

"I know you miss your daddy as much as your mama. Your daddy was a good man," Alex whispered. "One of the best."

He didn't know how long he stayed still in the water, studying the color of Brody's eyes, the shape of his nose and the playful expressions that flitted across the baby's face. All he knew as Brody's small chest lifted against his rhythmically was that Brody was breathing. He was strong and alive. And every beat of that baby's heart meant that, in some small way, Dean would go on living, too.

"Alex?"

He blinked and dragged his eyes from Brody. Tammy sat at the edge of the creek with a towel wrapped around her, watching him with a concerned expression as the last bit of daylight began to fade.

"Are you okay?" she asked softly.

"Yeah." He stilled at the husky note in his voice, realizing the wetness coating his cheeks was no longer creek water. He scrubbed a hand over his face. "I'm fine."

Brody resumed splashing and babbling.

"I think the power's back on," Tammy said, gesturing toward the field behind her. "I can see a light over in the direction of the house. I think it's the porch light you turned on earlier." She hesitated. "Are you ready to go in?"

Alex looked down at Brody, peace settling sweetly inside him as the baby laughed and splashed in the water. Then he looked at Tammy, savoring the gentle tone in her voice and the patient tenderness in her eyes.

He smiled. "Not yet. Would you mind if we stayed a little longer?"

"Not at all." She returned his smile, hugged her knees to her chest, then whispered, "I'd like that a lot."

Chapter 6

A sweet satisfaction existed in hard work. The kind Alex never failed to appreciate.

"Feels good, don't it?"

Alex lowered his glass of iced tea, stretched his legs out across the porch steps, then smiled up at Earl. "Sure does."

Earl laughed, then tipped his glass up and drank heavily, the clink of ice mingling with his contented groan.

One perk of the power coming back on was being able to enjoy a cold drink in the late-afternoon sun. And after a week and a half of repairing the stable, caring for the horses and clearing fallen trees from the field, Alex had every intention of soaking it up.

Apparently, Scout did, too. He ran from one end of the newly cleared field to the other, stopping to snuffle and roll around in the grass every few feet.

Alex chuckled, propped his elbows on the top step behind him and closed his eyes. His T-shirt clung to his sweat-slicked back and his jeans had become stiflingly hot, but, hell, what did that matter after all he'd accomplished over the past few days? The steady progress in reparations to the ranch had returned a sense of control to the day. And each newly restored section of the stable and fields, however small, made him think he actually had a say in what the future held for him.

Which was the exact opposite of how he'd felt after attending Dean and Gloria's funeral last week. That had been one of the longest days of his life and he'd been anxious to get back to the ranch with Tammy to resume a sense of normalcy. And help Brody find the same.

A squeal pierced his eardrums, then a small body climbed over his shoulder and onto his chest, almost dislodging the glass from his hand.

"Brody, wait."

Alex caught the baby with one arm and held his iced tea up with the other as Tammy ran up behind him. "Aw, he's all right." He sat up, cradling Brody to his midsection and tipped his drink toward him. "You want some of this, too, little man?"

Brody babbled, reached out and tugged the glass toward his mouth.

The sun glinted off the glass, and Alex squinted up at Tammy. "Is it okay for him to have some?"

"I put a lot of sugar in it, so it's not good for his teeth." Tammy grinned. "But I don't think a little will hurt."

Alex smiled, admiring the pretty blush in her cheeks and playful sparkle in her eyes, but he wasn't sure he agreed with her comment. He'd spent only a little time at the creek with her and Brody last week, but that brief hour had been enough to keep the image of her tempting mouth and soft curves reemerging behind his eyelids each night despite his attempts to sleep in the recently restored guest room.

She'd managed to slip farther past his guard than he'd realized, and the thought should've prompted him to keep his distance. Instead, he found himself wanting to spend more time with her. Wanting to enjoy more of her feisty banter, warm laugh and gentle flirtations.

Brody fussed, and Alex glanced down, tipping the glass carefully to the baby's lips and helping him sip the tea. Brody grinned, licked his lips and reached for more.

Tammy laughed, bringing Alex's eyes back to her. He wasn't sure if the way she'd helped him heal with Brody last week was the cause of the lingering gratitude he had for her or not. But he wanted to keep her as smiling and content as she was now, without a trace of the fear or panic that had shadowed her expression when she'd first arrived.

"Looks like Ms. Maxine is making the rounds again today." Earl nodded toward the driveway, where a small car eased up the path, dust particles dancing in the sun behind it.

Alex set his glass down, stood with Brody in his arms, then walked over to greet Maxine.

"Now, isn't this a sight?" Maxine chimed as she exited the car and shut the door. "I guess you figured out how to handle a baby after all, hmm?"

Alex smiled. Maxine beamed up at him, then leaned in and kissed Brody's cheek. Brody patted her cheek, then pointed toward Scout in the field.

"We were just having iced tea," Tammy said, walking up with Earl. "Would you like a glass?"

"Oh, no, thank you, Tammy. I can only stay a minute. I've got business to tend to but thought I'd stop by and give you this." She held out something square, which was wrapped in a white cloth. "Sam at the auto body shop found it this morning when he was working on your truck. He thought you'd like to keep it safe while your repairs are being finished."

Tammy took it and removed the cloth, revealing a cracked glass case with a gold buckle mounted inside. World Champion was etched across the top edge of the glass in elegant script.

Alex stilled, securing his grip on Brody as the baby leaned over and grabbed at it. "You won at Vegas last year?"

Tammy smiled, her fingers drifting slowly over the large words. "*We* won at Vegas." She nodded toward the stable. "I told you Razz was fast."

"Well, what do you know?" Earl poked his head over Tammy's shoulder for a better look at the medal, then winked at Alex. "You had a celebrity in the house all this time and didn't even know it."

An uneasiness settled in Alex's gut. *World champion. Celebrity.* They were stark reminders of the differences in his and Tammy's lifestyles. And an even more unwelcome reminder of how little they knew about each other.

He forced a tight smile and tried to shrug off the awkward tension knotting between his shoulder blades. Had the traumatic experiences of the past weeks clouded his judgment more than he'd thought? Was the newfound connection he'd begun to feel with Tammy no more than misplaced grief?

Hell, he should've been more worried about himself falling prey to a compulsive attraction rather than Tammy.

"…update."

Alex refocused on Maxine. "I'm sorry, what did you say?"

"I said, I also stopped by to give you an update on Brody's situation." Maxine reached out and brushed a wisp of hair from Brody's forehead. "I finally got in touch with Dean's half brother, John Nichols, and explained the situation." She frowned. "I didn't realize how little he and Dean had to do with each other, and I'm not sure he'll come forward. John just turned twenty-one and got engaged. He and his fiancée agreed to think it over and will let me know in a week or two if they're willing to take responsibility for Brody. If he doesn't let me know by then, I'll need to take Brody to the children's home in Atlanta."

Alex stiffened, his arms tightening around Brody. What a fool he was. He'd known this was only temporary, so this wasn't a surprise. But it didn't dull the pain throbbing in his chest at the thought of Brody leaving. Or quell the panic that arose at the thought of losing the last connection he had to Dean.

"But Brody will stay here for now, right?" Tammy curved her hand around Alex's biceps, staring at Maxine as though pleading for confirmation. "With us?"

Maxine remained silent as she scrutinized Tammy's face, then glanced at Alex. "Yes," she said, a small smile appearing. "Brody will stay with you for now."

Tammy's relieved breath whispered across Alex's neck. Alex shifted Brody to his other hip, then took Tammy's hand in his own, threading his fingers through hers and tugging her close to his side.

"There's one more thing I discovered when I was completing paperwork for Brody," Maxine said, her smile growing wider. "His first birthday is at the end of next week. Saturday, to be exact. Thought I'd let you know in case you wanted to plan something special for him."

"Oh, that's perfect, Alex." Tammy grinned up at him. "With the power back on, I could make Brody a birthday cake. One of those little individual ones with lots of colorful icing. And we could blow up some balloons and get party favors—"

Alex laughed, gesturing with their joined hands toward the fields surrounding them. "And where exactly do you plan on rounding all this stuff up?"

Tammy fell silent, frowning and biting her lip.

"The grocery store in Deer Creek reopened a few days ago," Maxine said. "I'm sure you'll find most of what you need there. But you'll want to get there soon. From what I hear, the lines are stretching out of the front door, and they're already getting low on milk and bread."

Tammy's expression brightened, and she clutched the medal to her chest, her body practically vibrating against his with excitement. "How 'bout it? Want to take a trip to town?"

Not particularly. Alex rolled his shoulders and sighed. How long *had* it been since he'd actually shown his face in Deer Creek? Dean and Gloria had undertaken all the errands for the ranch, and normally he drove an hour in the opposite direction to get groceries in a different county.

He grimaced. Going to Deer Creek meant potentially bumping into old friends and classmates whose calls and visits he'd avoided for years. And he damned sure didn't relish the idea of carrying on conversations about what he'd been doing with his life since his split with Susan.

"Please, Alex. We need groceries anyway, and it'll be Brody's first birthday. He deserves to have a special day." Tammy leaned over and kissed Brody's forehead. "Don't you, handsome?"

Brody chortled, squished Tammy's cheeks with both hands and tugged her closer for more kisses. They both giggled, then glanced up at Alex with beaming smiles.

Aw, hell. The cute factor was off the charts. And he knew when he was beaten.

He chuckled. "When do you want to leave?"

It took longer than he remembered to drive into the city limits of Deer Creek, the distance seeming greater than usual. The houses and businesses in town had been damaged and there were a lot of downed trees, but the bulk of debris had been cleared from the roads, and the small business district of the community was bustling.

Maxine had definitely heard right. Two lines stretched out of the Deer Creek Market's front entrance, and the parking lot was packed.

"I think everybody and their brother are here restocking supplies." Alex eased his truck into a parking space and cut the engine. "Want to divide and conquer? Or bulldoze our way through there together?"

Tammy unsnapped her seat belt and lifted her chin.

"Bulldoze our way in together." She twisted and peered into the back of the cab. "That okay with you, Brody?"

The baby squealed and kicked his feet against the car seat.

Decision made, they wove their way through the crowd, snagged a shopping cart and headed straight for the dairy section. Tammy held Brody while Alex grabbed the last two gallons of milk and a carton of eggs. Diapers and baby food were next, then they eventually made their way to the cake mix aisle.

"Mind holding him for a sec?" Tammy asked, passing Brody to Alex, then bending to inspect the various boxes.

Alex settled Brody on his hip while Tammy picked out a box of cake mix and a can of icing, tossing them in the cart. He glanced around, noticing a few curious looks from other shoppers. He shifted from one boot to the other as Tammy browsed a small selection of pans.

She poked around the items on the shelf, then held up a cupcake tin in one hand and a large griddle in the other. "Which one?"

Alex bit back a laugh. "Have you ever baked a cake before?"

She grinned sheepishly, then shrugged. "There's a first time for everything, right?" Blushing, she added firmly, "I've decided to make this a summer of firsts."

Something in her eyes provoked a strong hunger within him. One that had nothing to do with food. He waved a hand at the cart. "Throw 'em both in there. We'll figure it out together."

Together. He held the word on his tongue, relishing the feel of it. Shopping together with a woman and a baby was definitely a first for him. A first he wouldn't mind repeating with Tammy and Brody for as long as current circumstances allowed.

"We're getting a lot of interested stares," Tammy whispered, eyeing a couple craning their necks for a better glimpse as they passed. "Do I look that out of place?"

Alex shook his head. "It's not you, it's me. It's been a while since I came into town. Deer Creek is small, and news travels fast." He winced. "I haven't been all that friendly to people lately."

"Yeah." She nodded, adopting a solemn expression. "They're probably afraid of you."

He frowned, heat snaking up his neck. "Afraid?"

"Well, you are a very manly kind of man," she said, eyeing his chest and arms. "Some people might find that intimidating." Her mouth twitched. "Except for me and Brody. We know you're just a big ol' teddy bear."

As if on cue, Brody yawned, blinked heavily, then laid his cheek against Alex's chest.

Tammy laughed. "See what I mean?" She froze, then threw her hands in the air. "Oh, I forgot the balloons. We can't have a party without those. I'll be back in a minute."

And she was off, rushing down the aisle and around the corner.

Alex chuckled under his breath, then bent his head to Brody's ear and whispered, "She's got a lot more energy than either of us right now, huh, little man?"

Brody rubbed his eyes, then stuck his thumb in his mouth.

Alex smiled, lingering close to Brody's hair and breathing in his soft baby scent. The light weight of

him in his arms was comforting—soothing, almost—
and he couldn't help but remember how happy Dean
had looked holding his son.

His chest tightened, a devoted pride swelling within
him. Was this how it had been for Dean? Was this how
it felt to be a father?

"Alex?"

He froze. The voice was soft. Barely discernible. But
he recognized it instantly.

He lifted his head, swallowed hard and turned.
"Susan."

She hadn't changed much. She still had the same
thick blond hair, bright blue eyes and clear complexion. The lines beside her mouth were a bit deeper, but
they just drew attention to her appealing smile. Time
had been good to her.

"I… I thought it was you, but…" Her hesitant words
trailed off, and she shifted restlessly behind her shopping cart as her eyes drifted down and hovered on
Brody.

Alex forced a smile. "It's been a long time."

"Yes," she said softly, looking up at him again. "It has."

"You look well."

"Thank you. So do you." She glanced down, cheeks
flushing. "I heard about Dean and Gloria. I'm so sorry.
I know I didn't keep in touch, but I still loved them."
Glancing at Brody, she bit her lip, then asked, "Is he their
son?" At Alex's nod, she continued, "It's so unfair for him
to have to grow up without them. I can't bear to think
of my girls having to go through something like that."

His throat constricted, and it hurt to speak. "You
have children?"

Susan nodded, smiling. "Three daughters. The oldest is six, and the twins are four. They're at home, helping their dad clean up the damage from the storm." Her voice weakened. "I remarried seven years ago."

"That's good. You always said you wanted a big family." He clutched Brody tighter, his voice hoarse. "I'm happy for you."

She tucked a curl behind her ear with a shaky hand, then adjusted her purse strap on her shoulder. "How about you? Still living outside town?"

Heat scorched his face. "Same place."

Her eyes glistened. "At…at our house?"

Our house. He gritted his teeth and looked away. It'd stopped being their house the day she'd asked for a divorce, crying for hours in his arms and saying she loved him but that a future without children of her own wasn't the life she'd envisioned. That adopting and being a mother to someone else's child wouldn't be enough.

And the hell of it was, he'd known it was coming. Had seen it solidifying in her eyes for months after they learned of his infertility. Before, their disappointment at being unable to conceive could be brushed aside, but once they'd discovered the possibility of a pregnancy was nonexistent, it was an issue they could no longer ignore.

"I'm sorry," she said. "I didn't mean to offend you. I thought you would've sold it after—" Her voice broke, and she moved closer. "It's just that I still think of it as our place, you know? I still think of how beautiful it was and how many good times we had." She stopped and refocused on Brody, her lower lip trembling and face paling. "I've wanted to call you for a long time. I wanted to tell you—"

"Found 'em."

Tammy's hip bumped against his. She tossed a pack of balloons in the cart, then glanced up, stilling as she noticed Susan.

"Oh." Tammy looked from Susan to him, then back again, her smile fading. "I didn't mean to interrupt."

"You're not," Alex said. His chest tightened painfully, and he struggled to soften the hard edge in his tone. "We're done. Aren't we, Susan?"

An uncomfortable silence ensued, stretching on for what seemed like an eternity, until Susan spoke, her voice strained.

"I just wanted to tell you that I wish things had turned out differently. That I'm sorry. For everything." She backed away. "You look good holding a baby, Alex." Her smile shook and she wiped away a tear, whispering as she left, "I always imagined you would."

Alex stood still and watched her walk away. A heavy weight settled over him, weakening his body and making his arms tremble beneath Brody. And he felt like a bigger failure than ever.

"Take him." Avoiding Tammy's eyes, he pressed Brody into her arms, then grabbed the cart and shoved it to the front of the store.

He managed to make it through the long wait at the checkout, pay for the groceries and load the bags in the truck without losing his composure. He even managed to crank the engine and drive in a straight line all the way back to the ranch.

But he couldn't manage to face Tammy. Not once.

Because he was too afraid to answer the questions that would inevitably come. And he couldn't stand to see the same look in her eyes that he'd seen in Susan's when she realized what a fraud he really was.

Tammy settled Brody in the crib, then kissed his forehead. "Sleep well, sweet boy."

He made a soft sound of contentment, his thumb sliding from his mouth as he drifted off. She slipped quietly from the nursery, pausing to pet Scout, who was asleep on the floor, then walked to the kitchen and peered out the window.

Night had fallen, and the bright moon spilled a soft white glow across the front porch, highlighting Alex's profile. He sat on the top step, his elbows propped on his knees and a liquor bottle dangling between his fingers. He had the same expression on his face that he'd maintained during the silent drive back from the Deer Creek grocery store.

Blank and unapproachable.

Tammy pulled in a deep breath and made her way onto the porch, shutting the door behind her. "Is it okay if I join you?"

His broad shoulders stiffened. He shrugged but didn't face her.

She smiled. "I'll take that as a yes."

Tammy eased down beside him on the step, laughing as she squirmed for a comfortable position. "You know, this porch would be a lot more welcoming with a couple of rocking chairs."

No response.

She motioned toward the dimly lit walls of the stable

in the distance. "Sapphire and Razz were doing well when I checked on them earlier."

Alex nodded and turned away, staring at the empty fields. The stubble on his jaw had darkened, and the thick waves of his hair curled slightly at his nape.

Her fingertips tingled, wanting to slip through the soft strands, slide beneath the collar of his black T-shirt and caress his warm skin. Smooth across the thick muscles of his back and feel the tension release from his brawny frame. Anything to return the charismatic smile that had brightened his handsome face that night in the creek.

"I just put Brody to bed. He went out like a light." She bumped his shoulder with hers and grinned. "Scout did, too. You're gonna have dog hair all over the nursery carpet tomorrow morning."

He shifted away from her on the step, his guarded expression so similar to the one he'd had when she'd first arrived. He hadn't spoken a word since Susan had walked away from him in the store.

Susan. Tammy's stomach tensed. The former wife whom Alex and Maxine talked around instead of about. A woman who could cast a shadow over Alex's entire day with just a brief conversation. Tammy clasped her hands together and pressed them between her knees, wincing as she recalled the woman's words.

I wish things had turned out differently.

There'd been no mistaking that, judging from the pretty blonde's tearful expression and regretful tone. It was clear Susan still had strong feelings for Alex. But did Alex feel the same?

Her chest stung, the question a more unwelcome one

than she'd expected. And one she'd give just about any-thing to settle for certain.

Hesitating, she gestured toward the bottle Alex held. "That stuff helping you feel better?"

He grunted, studied the bottle in his hand, then faced her. "You could say that."

Stomach churning, Tammy took a deep breath, then said, "My dad used to go through several of those things in a week, and it never seemed to solve any of his prob-lems." Her throat thickened, and she hugged her knees to her chest. "It just made him mean."

Alex frowned, his eyes roving over her face, neck and arms.

Her skin tightened in patches where old wounds had been inflicted. She squirmed and glanced down, half expecting blotches of bruises to resurface on her flesh. Which was ridiculous.

"What does it do to you?" she asked, cringing at the weak thread in her voice.

"The whiskey?"

She nodded.

The gray depths of his eyes gentled. "It helps me forget."

"Forget Susan?" She bit her lip. "I'm sorry. It's none of my business, but…"

"But you want to know," Alex murmured, glancing back down at the bottle in his hands.

"Yeah." She held her hand out, palm up, and nudged his knee with her knuckles. "We could talk instead. And it goes both ways, you know? You could ask me anything."

He hesitated, then handed her the bottle, a small

smile appearing. "Are you curious about Susan because you're jealous?"

The bottle slipped from her grasp, and she scrambled, catching it before it shattered against the brick step. "Really?" She laughed, hands shaking. "That's the first question you want to ask?"

"Yep." His smile widened. "You said anything."

Face heating, she set the bottle on the porch landing before answering, "Yes." Her heart skipped at the pleased gleam in his eyes. "I'm a little jealous."

He raised an eyebrow. "Only a little?"

"That's two questions," she said, giving him a pointed look. "It's my turn. What other jobs have you had besides ranching and breeding horses?"

"I made decent money bull riding years ago."

Her mouth dropped open. "You were a bull rider?"

He laughed. "Only briefly. And don't look so surprised. I may not have a world championship buckle, but I was able to hold my own when the occasion called for it."

"No. I mean, I wouldn't doubt that." Her eyes clung to the strong curve of his biceps, a delicious shiver running through her as she imagined his powerful frame striding across an arena. "It's just…" Lord, she was being rude. She tore her eyes away and took a deep breath. "It's just that I don't see you as the roaming type." She frowned. "Of course, I didn't think of my cousin Colt as the settling-down type, but that's what he went and did. He's managing a guest ranch in Raintree and marrying my best friend in two weeks."

Alex leaned back on his elbows, studying her. "You

don't seem as excited about that as I would've expected. Weddings are usually happy occasions for most people."

"Oh, it is." Tammy smiled, excitement coursing through her veins. "I can't wait to see Colt in a tux, and I know Jen's dress will be beautiful. They're perfect for each other, and I'm happy for them." She looked down, picking at a loose thread on the hem of her jeans. "It's just that Colt was my partner. He rode bulls and I barrel raced. We toured the circuit together for years."

"Years?" Alex peered down at her. "You must've left home at a young age."

"Yeah. When I was seventeen."

"How old are you?"

"Twenty-five. You?"

He gave a wry smile. "I've got ten years on you." His smile slipped. "Why'd you leave home?"

She hesitated. "Things were rough. We didn't exactly have a model family. I didn't feel like I fit in there, and I wanted out. Colt wasn't happy where he was, either, so we packed up and took off. We met Jen on the circuit. She barrel raced, too, and joined up with us. For the longest time, we were a family of sorts, until Colt's father died. Then he and Jen retired to raise Colt's little sister and start their own family. Now I'm the only one left traveling." She shrugged. "It gets lonely on the road."

"You don't like being alone?"

She glanced up, stilling at the somber expression on his face. "No. Not at all. Do you?"

He looked away. "I didn't use to. But I began to prefer it after Susan and I divorced."

"How long were you married?"

"Two years."

Tammy studied the toes of her boots. "What happened?"

He remained silent for a moment, then said, "There were things she wanted that I couldn't give her."

"What kind of things?"

He straightened, hands clenching around the edge of the step.

"Alex?" A bigger house? Money? Tammy shook her head and slid closer, the defeated slump of his shoulders making her heart ache. "You've built a beautiful home here," she whispered. "Invested in a business that would keep you close to raise a family and spend more time together." She covered his hand with her own and squeezed. "That's the kind of life I dreamed about when I was a girl. I never had any brothers or sisters, and I always felt alone. Before racing, all I ever wanted was a peaceful home and a big family of my own to love."

He closed his eyes, and a muscle in his jaw ticked.

"When you showed me the nursery the other night, I couldn't help but wonder if you might have lost a child—"

"No." He blew out a heavy breath then faced her. "I…" He made as if to continue, then dragged his teeth over his bottom lip, his eyes heavy and shadowed as they examined her face.

Throat aching, she asked, "Do you still love her?"

He blinked, his brow furrowing. "I fell out of love with Susan a long time ago. I've just been angry with the way things ended. With the fact that what we had wasn't enough for her. That *I* wasn't enough." He shook his head. "But it wasn't Susan's fault. She's a good person. She just wanted to be happy, and she did what she had to do to get there." His voice turned hoarse, his words strained as he repeated, "She's a good person."

Tammy cupped his face, the stubble on his jaw rasping against her fingertips. "So are you." Something heady and warm unfurled within her, dancing in her veins and urging her closer. "And you're so much more than just enough, Alex."

His eyes softened, and his throat moved beneath the heels of her hands on a hard swallow.

She leaned closer, wanting so much to prove it. To show him. To share at least a small part of the intense feelings he stirred within her. "I'm going to kiss you."

Cheeks heating, she cringed at the high-pitched uncertainty in her voice. *Great.* So much for a smooth approach.

His brows lifted, then a soft rumble of laughter escaped his lips. "Are you asking me, babe? Or telling me?"

The flirtatious tone of his voice untied the knot in her belly, and the intoxicating buzz in her veins flooded her senses, spurring her on. She moved across the step, straddling his thighs, and smiled down at him. "I'm telling you."

His mouth parted, and his gray eyes darkened as he whispered, "Well, hell. Have at it."

Head spinning, she closed her eyes and eased closer, her lips hovering a fraction of an inch above his, their rapid breaths mingling. His distinctive scent, sandalwood and man, enveloped her. Her belly heated, but her muscles tensed, her limbs turning cold and stiff.

It'd been so long since she'd taken a chance and allowed her body to be vulnerable to a man. And even then, the few fumbling kisses she'd dug up enough courage to enjoy had been fleeting at best. They were nothing like the kinds of kisses a man like Alex was probably used to.

Oh, God. What if her inexperience showed? What if she humiliated herself? In front of Alex, of all men?

"Tammy?"

She hesitated, squeezing her eyes tighter, and concentrated on the soothing sound of his voice. Her body trembled, and she struggled to relax. To let go and…

"Tammy." His voice firmed, his thighs shifting beneath her. "Are you afraid of me?"

Her eyes shot open. The teasing expression had left him, concern taking its place. "What?"

She looked down, finding her hands covering his on the step, flattening his palms hard into the brick at his sides. His fingertips were red beneath the heels of her hands.

"Are you afraid of me?" He peered up at her. "Because you've got to know, I'd never hurt you. Never." He shook his head. "Maybe I do look intimidating to some people, but—"

"No." She released his hands, placed hers on his chest and whispered just before covering his mouth with hers, "I'm not afraid."

She wasn't. Not one bit. Even when the tang of whiskey clinging to his lips touched her tongue, she forged past it. She slid her arms around his neck, pulled him closer and searched deeper for the man she'd grown to trust and admire.

And there he was. The intoxicating taste of him just as pure and potent as the liquor. But so much more exciting and addictive. She explored him fully, easing her tongue past his lips, threading her fingers through his hair and pressing her breasts against his hard chest.

He groaned, the deep rumble vibrating against her rib cage as his big, warm palms delved beneath her shirt, gliding up her back in caressing strokes. His teeth nibbled at her lower lip, the gentle pressure sending delicious shivers down her spine. His hands drifted lower, cupping her bottom and pulling her tight against his hips.

A cry of pleasure escaped her. Tammy leaned back and looked down, absorbing his tousled hair, passion-filled eyes and kiss-reddened mouth. There were no insecurities. No anxieties. And no fears. Just a strong desire to ease back into his arms and discover just how powerful this connection between them could become.

Tammy leaned closer and rubbed the nape of his neck with her fingertips. "You're so much more than enough, Alex." She grinned, her lips brushing his ear as she whispered, "And I'm always available if you need to forget."

His broad chest jerked with laughter. He smoothed her hair from her cheeks, eyes roving over her face, then his warm mouth claimed hers, each of his hungry kisses heightening her desire.

A weight lifted from her, lightening her chest and strengthening her limbs, and she felt stronger than ever. She no longer wanted to run. What she wanted, more than anything, was to stay right in his arms.

Chapter 7

"I may not be a decent cook," Tammy said, jerking on an oven mitt. "But I rock at icing."

Alex leaned into his elbows on the kitchen island and smiled, watching as she spun around and opened the oven to remove a pan of freshly baked cupcakes.

After three failed attempts at baking a cake and two additional trips to the Deer Creek Market for more cake mix, Tammy had finally accepted his suggestion to try making cupcakes for Brody's birthday party instead. And judging from the pleasant aroma filling the kitchen, he'd bet good money this batch was going to be...

She bent over, and the denim covering her curvy backside pulled tight, halting his thoughts and sending his blood south.

Damn. He stifled a groan and pressed his hands tight

to the table, his palms tingling with the remembered feel of her soft curves filling them. It'd been a week since he'd held her in his arms on the porch and over one hundred and sixty-eight hours since he'd thoroughly kissed her. Not that he was keeping count.

The decorative stitching on her back pockets vanished, and she faced him, tipping the cupcakes in his direction.

"...together with lots of icing."

He blinked, dragged his eyes up past her tempting breasts and focused on her face. "What did you say?"

"I said we could stack a few of these on top of each other and stick them together with lots of icing." She smiled. "Then it'd at least look like a cake. Wouldn't it, Brody?"

Alex glanced over his shoulder. Brody looked up from his seated position on the floor, grinned mischievously, then banged the wooden spoons in his hands on the metal pot between his knees. Scout barked and ran around him in circles.

"Do you think he'd like blue or yellow frosting the best?" Tammy asked, yelling over the racket.

"Both."

She cupped her free hand to her ear and tilted her head. "Blue?"

"Both," Alex shouted, laughing at the chaos filling his kitchen.

Lord, it felt good. So good to laugh and talk and kiss. To have life fill his home again. He hadn't realized how empty it'd truly been until Brody and Tammy had stepped inside it.

Brody, distracted by the shiny buttons on his overalls, stopped banging the pot, tucked his chin to his chest and started picking at his straps. Scout skipped over and started gnawing Brody's untied shoelaces.

"So you think we should use the blue *and* the yellow?" Tammy asked.

"Yep," Alex said, the sight of Brody and Scout widening his smile. There wasn't a cuter kid on the planet. "I think he'd like both."

"And you were checking me out earlier, right?"

"Yeah." Alex jerked upright. "Wait, what?"

"Busted." Tammy winked, green eyes twinkling. "Not that I mind. As a matter of fact— Ouch!"

She jumped, the pan falling from her hold and clattering to the table. One cupcake bounced out and rolled across the floor. Scout darted after it, trapped it with a paw and started chomping, his loud smacks filling the kitchen. Brody cackled and banged the pot again.

Tammy jerked the oven mitt from her hand, blowing furiously on her fingers. "Doggone thing was hotter than I thought," she said, waving her hand back and forth through the air. "Burned me right through the mitt."

"Let me see." Alex walked around the island and took her hand. Bright red blotches marred her fingertips. "Here."

He tugged her to the sink, turned on the faucet, then held her fingers under the cold stream of water. She relaxed and leaned against his shoulder, the soft scent of her shampoo releasing from her hair.

He firmed his hold on her wrist, fighting the urge to drift his fingers through the shiny waves, cup the back of her head and plunder the soft curves of her mouth. "Better?"

"Mmm-hmm." She tipped her head back and looked up at him, those beautiful eyes lingering on his lips, her cheeks blushing a pretty pink.

Alex turned off the water, then lifted her hand to his mouth, kissing her fingertips. Her mouth parted, and she pressed close.

I'm always available if you need to forget.

He squeezed her hand gently, realizing he hadn't sought comfort in a bottle since that night they'd shared on the porch. He hadn't felt the need for it. Because the trouble was, he didn't want to forget anything. He wanted to remember every moment he had with Tammy. Wanted to imprint the silky feel of her skin on his hands, memorize the delightful chime of her laugh and capture every sweet sigh against his lips. And he'd had only a few brief moments over the past week to savor a quick brush of his lips over hers. The immediate needs of the ranch had taken over, preventing anything more.

Last week, two more horses, Jet and Cisco, had wandered back to the ranch in poor shape, but the vet assured Alex they'd recover given time and attention. Tammy had worked as hard as he had to heal the animals and complete repairs over the past several days. They'd spent the majority of their time caring for Brody, rehabilitating Razz and Sapphire, and restoring the stable. And Brody was beginning to recover from the loss of his parents. He hadn't cried for them in several days and he smiled more than ever.

The more time Alex spent with Tammy and Brody,

the more precious they'd become. But like every valuable summer he'd spent with Dean, this one would eventually come to an end, too.

He winced, hoping their time together would last longer than he thought. Because, though he'd tried, he had difficulty envisioning his home without them. And he couldn't shake the nagging feeling that the privacy he'd craved in the past might become isolating after Tammy and Brody left.

He reached out and cradled her face with his palms, shaking off the invasive thought. He'd lived long enough to recognize an opportunity when it presented itself. Tammy was here. Right in front of him. He was going to enjoy whatever little time he had left with her and make damned sure Brody had a fantastic first birthday. The kind of birthday Dean would've wanted for his son.

Alex nudged Tammy back against the island and slipped a leg between hers. "I'm going to kiss you," he teased, angling his lips close to hers and raising his voice above Brody's banging and Scout's snuffles. He smiled, hoping the chaos didn't kill all the romance of the moment. "Right here, right now."

She laughed and half shouted, "Are you asking me or telling me?"

"Asking." He outlined her lips with his finger, a wave of need surging through him at the catch of her breath. "There's a sweet smell in the air and we've got a one-toddler band serenading us. I'm hoping that's enough to sway you."

Her green eyes softened. She wrapped her arms around his waist and tilted her mouth in invitation. "That's more than enough."

Something shifted in his chest. He touched his lips to hers, tasting and teasing, and the heat filling him intensified. It throbbed deep within him, overpowering the loud noises filling the kitchen and swelling with each of her soft sighs of pleasure.

It'd been so long since he felt it, he almost didn't recognize it. He'd forgotten how all consuming and disorienting it could become. But he knew exactly what that strong surge in his chest and deep pull in his gut meant.

He was falling in love.

He stilled, heart stalling. It'd happened so fast, he'd almost missed it. And it sure as hell wasn't a good idea. But Tammy had slipped right into his heart and had him thinking of her every day.

When he was tending to the horses and rebuilding fences, he dreamed of holding her. When he was hauling off broken limbs and replacing windows, he imagined kissing her. And he remained fixated on thoughts of her during the hours before dawn when, after tossing and turning in the guest room, he'd slip out to the stable to sand and reapply varnish to neglected rocking chairs he'd constructed years ago.

All so he could make Brody's first birthday as special for Tammy as it would be for him. So he could enjoy more precious moments with her, rocking beside her on the front porch and sharing more kisses. And, heaven help him, moments like the one last week—and now—made him wonder if what he and Tammy shared could be real. They made him hope that the future might hold something more for him.

You're so much more than enough, Alex.

Reluctantly, he lifted his head. "I've got a surprise for you."

Her eyes opened slowly, a dazed wistfulness filling her expression. "Does it involve more kisses?"

Alex laughed, pressed one more lingering kiss to her lips, then straightened. "Lord, I hope so." He released her and crossed the kitchen to kneel in front of Brody. "Wanna help me out, birthday man?"

Brody stopped banging the pot, dropped the spoons and clambered to his feet. He smiled, then ran into Alex's arms, babbling as Alex propped him on his hip and stood. Not to be outdone, Scout followed, slipping on the tiled floor and barreling into Alex's boots.

"All right, Scout. You can come, too." He stopped midstride and frowned at the pup. "So long as you don't chew on anything."

"What about me?" Tammy asked, rounding the island.

"Mind waiting here a minute? I need to set up the surprise first. It's a beautiful day. I thought I'd set up a folding table, too, and we could have the party outside."

She nodded, mouth twitching as she stood on her tiptoes and cut her eyes toward the window. "Sure. I'll just stay here and work on the cake."

Chuckling, Alex paused on his way out to close the blinds, tossing over his shoulder, "No peeking."

It was tough moving two rocking chairs from the stable to the front porch with an adventurous one-year-old and a frisky pup in tow. But he managed it. And the bright red bows he tied to the center slats brought out the cherry undertones in the dark varnish pretty damned well, if he did say so himself.

"Pfffttt."

Alex glanced down, biting back a smile as Brody blew raspberries and shoved one of the chairs, watching with wide eyes as it rocked back and forth.

"What? You don't like 'em?"

Brody pointed at the chair and squealed.

"Oh, I get it. They're too big, huh?" Alex smiled. "Well, don't worry, birthday man. I've got you covered."

Alex jogged across the front lawn with Scout at his heels, keeping a careful eye on Brody as he retrieved a third rocking chair from the bed of his truck. This one was much smaller. He carried it to the porch, set it down carefully between the other two, then lowered to his haunches, eyeing Brody closely.

He'd never made baby furniture before. And especially not in the short amount of time that he'd had to put this one together. The measurements could be way off.

"Wanna give it a try?"

He held his breath, his lungs burning as Brody toddled his way over, grabbed the tiny armrests and climbed up. The small chair tilted forward, and Alex grabbed it, holding it steady as Brody settled in the center.

It fit him perfectly. There was even enough extra space to ensure he could still enjoy it after growing several more inches. And Scout took full advantage, leaping into the chair and stretching out across Brody's lap.

Brody leaned forward, then sat back, rocking the chair. A wide smile broke out across his face, exposing his small teeth, and he giggled. The delighted sound morphed into full-blown laughter as he glided back and forth. The baby-fine strands of his hair ruffled in the warm afternoon breeze, and his chubby cheeks flushed with excitement.

Alex swallowed the tight knot in his throat. How many days did he have left with Brody? Maxine hadn't called with an update on the uncle's situation, and his heart broke at the idea of Brody not being claimed by a family member.

But when it came down to it…wasn't *he* family? He'd been Dean's best friend and had vicariously lived every monumental moment in Brody's life so far through Dean. And he'd helped Brody survive the most devastating time in his life *without* Dean and Gloria. Didn't that count for something?

Alex tightened his grip on the chair, hope swelling in his chest. When Maxine had first asked him to take Brody in, he couldn't imagine being able to scrape by as a decent guardian. But now, he found himself wanting the chance to try. If he was given a shot, he'd do everything he could to make sure Brody was provided for and protected. More than that. He'd make sure Brody knew he was loved.

Hell, he knew how it felt not to be wanted. He'd never had a real family of his own as a child, and after his failed marriage, Dean and Gloria had been the closest he'd ever come to having one as an adult. Dean and Gloria had loved and wanted Brody before he was even born—Brody had never known anything different—and it damned near broke Alex's heart to think Brody could possibly lose that feeling.

Alex gently covered Brody's hand on the chair with his. He'd never be a father in the truest sense of the word. He'd accepted that. But if he asked, could Maxine find a way for him to keep Brody? And if he had Brody, he might be able to give Tammy some of what she wanted. At least enough to make her happy and tempt her to stay.

Would life actually deal in his favor for once and give him another shot at building a home with a child who needed him? And a woman he loved?

The strength of emotion spearing through Alex made it difficult to speak. He brushed a kiss across the baby's forehead and whispered, "Happy birthday, Brody."

A soft gasp sounded. Tammy stepped onto the porch, her hand covering her mouth and her gaze fixed on Brody.

Alex bit back a grin. "You were supposed to wait."

Her eyes met his, glistening in the sunlight, as she lowered her hand. "I couldn't wait any longer. Not after hearing Brody laugh like that." She walked over and trailed her fingers over the back of one of the chairs. Her touch lingered on the decorative edges. "You made these?"

He nodded. "Two of them I made a long time ago. They were the only items in the stable that made it through the storm virtually untouched. They just needed to be refinished. I made Brody's over the past week."

She shook her head, smiling. "They're gorgeous, Alex."

Brody yelped, slapped his hands on his armrests, then babbled up at Tammy.

"I think he wants you to try it out." Alex stood and gestured toward the chair. "Go ahead."

She rounded the chair, sat down, then smoothed her

hands appreciatively over the armrests. Alex sat in the third rocking chair on the other side of Brody.

"Someone told me this porch would be more welcoming with rocking chairs," he said. "You think these fit the bill?"

Tammy leaned her head against the headrest and smiled. "They're perfect."

He eased back in his chair, the sight of pleased surprise on her face making the extra hours of hard work more than worth it. He pushed Brody's chair gently and helped him rock. Tammy did the same, and they sat for several minutes, enjoying the sight of Razz and Sapphire grazing in the green field, absorbing the beauty of the summer day and savoring Brody's enjoyment.

Alex closed his eyes, listening to Tammy's gentle teasing and Brody's responding laughter. How great it would be to end a long day of hard work like this. Hell, he could tough out any backbreaking project if he knew he'd see Tammy smile and hear Brody laugh at the start and end of each day. And what was most surprising was that the idea no longer felt out of reach.

"That's not Ms. Maxine or Earl, is it?" Worry laced Tammy's tone. "I told them we'd start the party at three, and it's only a little after one."

Alex opened his eyes and glanced at the driveway. Sunlight glared off a vehicle as it approached, and dust billowed out behind it.

"I haven't finished the cake yet," Tammy said. "Or put up the decorations…"

The growl of the engine drew closer.

"That's not Earl," Alex said, squinting at the approaching shape. "He comes in on the back road. It's not Maxine, either. She drives one of those compacts. That's a—"

"Truck," Tammy shouted, jumping to her feet, her voice pitching higher with excitement. "*My* truck." She darted down the porch steps and across the lawn, spinning back briefly to call out, "*And* Razz's trailer."

Alex froze. His boots glued to the porch floor, and his chair jerked to a halt.

Tammy ran to the driveway, waited until the truck stopped, then hopped onto the running board. Her breathless voice carried across the yard as she talked to the driver, her laughter ringing out occasionally.

Brody grunted and pointed at Tammy. His fingers curled in midair as if to pull her to him, then he looked up at Alex and frowned.

"I know," Alex mumbled, a hollow forming in his gut.

Tammy could go anywhere now. To her friends' ranch for the wedding, back to the circuit to resume racing and, eventually, to Vegas to win a new championship. The whole world lay at her feet. His battered ranch was merely a bedraggled speck on an otherwise pristine map. And it would be selfish and unfair to ask her to sacrifice her dreams.

His skin chilled. "Looks like summer may be over sooner than I thought."

A birthday just wasn't a birthday without a cake.

Tammy walked outside to the table Alex had set up, placed the colorful concoction she held in front of Brody and grinned. "The birthday cake has arrived."

Alex, Maxine and Earl, all seated around the table, clapped, then leaned in for a closer look.

Tammy laughed. Well, the iced-together cupcakes could pass as a cake. Of sorts. The lopsided lump was colorful, arranged into the shape of a number one, and she and Alex had even managed to write Happy Birthday, Brody, in green frosting, having mixed the blue and yellow for an added wow factor. Of course, due to limited space, the words squished together and ran slightly off the edges. But Brody didn't seem to mind. He dug his pointer finger deep into the *H* and cackled.

"Now, hold on a minute, birthday boy," Tammy teased, tugging his finger from the pile of heavily iced cupcakes. "We've got to sing first."

"Aw, let him have a taste." Alex reached across the table and scooped a bit of icing onto his fingertip.

Scout jumped at Brody's side, his ears flopping and black eyes emerging above the table as he struggled in vain to reach Alex's hand.

Brody stared at Alex's finger as it drew near. He latched on to it with both hands, brought it to his mouth and pulled off the icing. His brown eyes widened, then he licked his lips and squealed.

"What'd I tell you?" Tammy asked, smiling at Alex. "I rock at icing."

Alex laughed, then grabbed a napkin and looked down, his smile fading as he wiped his hands.

Tammy retrieved the yellow bib Maxine had brought and fastened it loosely around Brody's neck, then glanced at Alex. He'd grown quiet again. He'd smiled and played with Brody as they'd assembled the cake and put up decorations, but the flirtatious demeanor from two hours ago had dimmed. It'd started slipping away as soon as her truck had appeared in the driveway. And he'd become even more guarded since Maxine and Earl had arrived.

"All right, y'all," Earl bellowed, leaning forward in his lawn chair and sharing a smile with Maxine. "That boy's hungry. Let's do this on the count of three."

Earl counted them off, then everyone joined in for a less-than-stellar performance of "Happy Birthday." Scout howled. Brody's gaze darted over each of them, fixating on their mouths, and he bounced in his high chair, gurgling with excitement.

When they finished, Alex nudged the makeshift cake closer to Brody. "It's all yours, little man."

Brody looked down at the cake, smiled up at Alex, then dived face-first into it, his fists gripping the sides as he mouthed the icing. Clumps of blue and yellow frosting plopped onto the table as he jerked upright, giggling and flexing his cake-coated fingers.

His delight was infectious, and everyone laughed.

"Everything's beautiful, Tammy." Maxine smiled, gesturing toward the colorful streamers and balloons taped to the tablecloth. "You and Alex have really outdone yourselves."

"Thanks." Tammy shrugged, sat down and sipped her soda. "I just wish I had a better touch in the kitchen. The cake didn't turn out quite like I wanted."

"Oh, you did a fine job," Maxine said.

"Better than fine." Alex pinched off a piece and popped it into his mouth. "It's delicious."

Brody chortled, then reached up and patted Alex's face, smearing cake crumbs all over his jaw. Chuckling, Alex leaned over and placed noisy kisses on Brody's messy cheeks as the baby giggled and squealed. Alex pulled away and smiled, his strong jaw and sexy mouth speckled with icing.

Tammy's heart turned over. Gracious, he was handsome. And if she imagined it just right, she could picture what he'd look like as a groom at a wedding reception. She could see him patiently posing for pictures in a tux, feel the tender press of his hand on hers as they cut the cake and taste the sweetness of his icing-laced kiss as they shared the first slice.

Her grip tightened around the plastic cup in her hand, the icy condensation a shock against her hot palm. *A wedding.* Oh, Lord. Jen and Colt's wedding was next Saturday, which meant she needed to get back on the road first thing Friday morning if she wanted to make the rehearsal on time.

But that would mean leaving Alex and Brody. Her belly fluttered. Unless, of course, she asked Alex to go with her.

She smiled, the thought of walking in on Alex's arm warming her cheeks. What she wouldn't give to spend a romantic evening with him. To meet his eyes across the aisle, brush against him during a dance and kiss him freely again beneath the stars. And she didn't want it to end there.

Was this the same feeling that had lured Jen away from the circuit and into Colt's arms? Tammy studied Alex and Brody closer, her chest tingling at the happiness on their faces. It must've been, because as much as Tammy loved to race, she loved being with Alex and Brody more.

Love. Her heart skipped. She loved Alex. And fantasizing about marrying him and staying at the ranch permanently made her ache with need. She yearned to lie beside him at night and wake up next to him every morning. To have Brody with them every day so they could laugh and play and help him grow strong. And what she dreamed of most of all was to watch her belly swell with Alex's child.

Her breath caught as she studied him. Would a baby they made have his smile or hers?

"I'm so grateful to you both."

Tammy started at the sound of Maxine's voice, the soda sloshing over the rim of the cup and trickling down her wrist.

Maxine studied Brody, smiling as he laughed. "The two of you have really made this a special day for Brody." She placed a hand on Alex's arm. "Dean and Gloria would be so happy."

Alex's cheeks flushed. He grabbed a napkin and wiped the icing from his face. "I hope so." He cleared his throat, then asked in a low voice, "Have you heard anything more from Dean's brother?"

Maxine averted her eyes and picked at the cookie on her plate. "Not yet." She sighed. "John is so young. And he's just starting out in life. I'm not sure how willing he and his fiancée are to take on an instant family. Especially since he and Dean weren't close. He barely knew Dean."

"*I* knew Dean," Alex said. "And I know Brody."

Tammy stilled. The strained note in Alex's voice and determined look in his eyes made her long to hold him close.

"I know," Maxine said quietly.

"What will happen if John doesn't come through?" Tammy asked.

"The children's home in Atlanta would be the next step."

Alex propped his elbows on the table and leaned closer. "But what if someone in Deer Creek was willing to take him?"

Maxine hesitated, exchanging a glance with Earl, then said gently, "We're not there yet, Alex. We'll have to wait on John's answer first."

Alex moved to speak but turned back to Brody, remaining silent.

Tammy placed her cup on the table, her hand trembling as she studied the tight set of Alex's jaw. He'd grown so close to Brody. They both had. It was clear he was as uncomfortable with letting Brody go as she was, and his kiss earlier made her believe he might actually feel as strongly for her as she did for him. But it was hard to tell for sure.

Which left her with only one option—to cowgirl up and show him what she wanted. To prove to him how good they could be together and ask if the future she envisioned was the kind he wanted, too. And Jen's wedding would be the perfect opportunity to make her move. If he'd just let her stay long enough to persuade him into going with her.

Tammy straightened, her spirits lifting. "All right." She stood and rubbed her hands together, suddenly eager for a moment alone with Alex. "How about we help the birthday boy open a few presents?"

Two hours later, Brody was clean, happy and sprawled in his crib, snoring with abandon. Maxine and Earl had kissed Brody's cheek, said their good-byes, then left. Tammy and Alex waved as they drove away, then started cleaning up the party decorations and tossing away the clumps of cake Brody had dropped.

Or rather, what was left of it. Tammy grinned, spotting Scout asleep under her newly repaired truck. The pup had done a pretty good job of gobbling up every cake crumb that had hit the ground.

"I don't think you'll need to feed Scout for a while." Tammy laughed. "His belly is probably about to pop from all that cake."

Alex smiled and pulled the plastic tablecloth off the table. "I suspect you're right about that."

She grabbed a trash bag, peeled it apart and held it open as Alex shoved the tablecloth into it. "I wasn't expecting the auto body shop to deliver my truck. I thought they'd just call and tell me it was ready."

Alex's hands stilled, then he moved away, tilted the small table on its side and folded in the legs.

"They even gave it a good wash job before they chauffeured it out to me," she added.

"Sam always did go the extra mile. He's a good guy." Alex set the folded table aside and started gathering up bits of ripped wrapping paper off the grass. "And I'm sure you're eager to get back to racing."

He smiled, but it seemed forced and died quickly.

Tammy shrugged. "I guess." She tightened her grip on the trash bag. *Ask me. Please ask me to stay.* "Getting the truck back now worked out really well because Jen's wedding is next Saturday. So I won't have to bum a ride from you."

He walked over, tossed the wrapping paper in the

trash bag, then took it from her. "Why don't you take a break? I'll finish this up."

No hug. No kiss. Not even another attempt at a dimpled smile. He just turned and walked off.

Heart pounding, she stared at his broad back, watching him move farther away, then blurted out, "Can I stay?"

He stopped, the bag bumping his thigh as he stilled. "What did you say?"

"I asked if I could stay." Her voice shook, and she balled her fists at her sides. "With you and Brody. For just a little longer? I know that wasn't part of the deal, but I don't want to go just yet." Throat tightening, she forced out, "Can I stay until at least the end of next week? And then maybe…"

Alex dropped the bag, turned around and started toward her, his long strides fast and powerful.

"And then maybe we could—"

His mouth covered hers, silencing her words. His tongue parted her lips, his big hands cupped her face and his fingers speared into her hair. He filled her senses, his familiar spicy scent surrounding her and his warm, delicious taste sweeping across her tongue.

She wrapped her arms around his waist, slid her hands up to spread across his muscular shoulders, then tugged him closer. The hard length of his body aligned with hers, and she pressed against him, moaning softly.

He lifted his head and stared down at her, their heavy breaths mingling as his calloused palms caressed her nape.

"And then maybe we could all go to the wedding together," Tammy said, head spinning and body tingling.

"It'd be a shame for me to go alone, seeing as how I'm maid of honor and all."

A slow smile spread across his face, and he dipped his head, his facial stubble tickling her cheek as he kissed her more thoroughly.

She giggled breathlessly in between kisses. "Is that a yes?"

Alex smiled wider, his teeth bumping her lips gently as he whispered, "That's a hell yes."

Chapter 8

Tammy straightened in the passenger seat of her truck, tried to still her bouncing knees and peered at the sun-drenched road ahead. A dirt driveway emerged on the right, curving through an unending stretch of green fields.

"There it is." Tammy drummed her hands on the dashboard, pointed at the road, then smiled at Alex. "Right there. Raintree Ranch."

Alex laughed, his gray eyes teasing and hands sliding farther up the steering wheel. "Are you sure? We're about an hour earlier than we expected. Maybe the turn is farther down—"

"Nope. That's the turn." Tammy unsnapped her seat belt. "We just made good time." She twisted, stretched over Brody's rear-facing car seat in the back of the cab and tapped the toe of his sneakers. "Tell him to take the turn, Brody. We're ready to see Jen and Colt, aren't we?"

Brody looked up and grinned as her hair brushed his cheek, his nose wrinkling and baby teeth appearing.

Tammy spun back around and craned her neck as Alex turned onto the dirt path. A rustic wooden sign etched with Raintree Ranch appeared, making her heart pound. Familiar white fencing lined the fields on both sides of the road, and the white, multistoried guesthouse at the end of the driveway looked as welcoming as ever.

Gracious, she was excited to see Jen. Even though she'd heard her voice a thousand times over the phone, it'd been more than a year since she'd seen her best friend in person. And Jen was getting married. To Colt. *Tomorrow!*

"Oh, you're gonna love them, Alex." Tammy wrapped her hands around Alex's brawny arm. "Jen is so easygoing and fun. And Colt is—"

She bit her lip, her stomach flipping. *Overprotective.*

Alex glanced at her and smiled, then turned his attention back to the road. "Colt is what?"

"He's…" Guarded? No. Suspicious? Uh-uh. "He's my cousin."

Alex laughed. "I know."

"Yeah. But what I mean is, we've been through a lot together." She smoothed her thumb over Alex's biceps, concentrating on his warm skin below his sleeve. "So he worries about me, you know?" She shrugged. "Like any good cousin would."

"So what you're really trying to say is that I should be prepared for the third degree."

"No. Not at all." She pulled in a deep breath. "Just don't be surprised if he asks some questions." Her grip on him tightened. "And don't let him…" Oh, Lord. *Run you off.* "Just don't read anything into it, okay? Please?"

"Relax, Tammy." He squeezed her knee. "I can handle myself."

The tight knot in the back of her neck released, her shoulders relaxing and a smile stretching her cheeks. "I know."

And it felt wonderful. So wonderful to have him by her side and in her life. His strength and support made her feel secure in ways she never had before.

"That someone you know?" Alex asked, gesturing ahead as he drew the truck to a halt.

A tall woman ran down the front steps of the main house and darted across the front yard, her red hair streaming behind her.

"Jen!" Tammy shoved the door open, hopped out and ran.

"It's about time," Jen shouted, laughing.

"We're an hour earlier than I told you we'd be." Tammy winced as Jen hugged her tight, squeezing the air from her lungs.

"I know, but it feels like it's been years since I've seen you."

Tammy laughed as Jen's hair tickled her nose and her vision blurred. "It has. It's been a whole entire year." She pulled back, the tears rolling down Jen's cheeks making hers flow more freely. "I've missed you so much."

"Oh, you have no idea how much I've missed you." Jen dragged the backs of her hands over her cheeks, then smiled. "But you're here now."

Tammy grabbed her hands and squeezed, whispering, "And you're getting married."

Jen tipped her head back, her smile beaming as she squealed to the heavens, "I'm getting married."

"To me, I hope."

Tammy glanced over Jen's shoulder at the familiar deep voice. Her smile grew wider as Colt walked up and spun Jen around for a kiss. They shared soft whispers and a laugh, then Colt edged around Jen and wrapped his arms around Tammy.

Tammy closed her eyes and hugged him back, realizing she missed him more than she'd thought.

"I'm glad you're safe, girl," Colt said, easing back. "We were worried about you, and it's nice to finally have you here in one piece."

Tammy ruffled a hand through his blond hair, noting the relieved gleam in his blue eyes. "You think I'd let a silly tornado keep me from your wedding? I wouldn't miss it for the world."

Colt's eyes drifted over her shoulder. "Wanna introduce us?"

Tammy turned to find Alex approaching, Brody babbling in his arms. "Of course." She moved to the side, mumbling, "And I like him, so be nice."

Colt cocked an eyebrow, his grin turning mischievous. "When am I ever *not* nice?"

She gave him one last look of warning, then faced Alex. "Alex, I'd like you to meet my cousin Colt."

Alex smiled, adjusted Brody in his arms, then held out his hand. "Congratulations on your marriage."

"Thanks." Colt shook his hand. "And thanks for helping Tammy out. She told us you've been taking good care of her."

"She's done the same for me." Alex's eyes met hers,

the warm gleam in them sending a delicious thrill through her.

"Tammy!"

A door slammed, then a blonde girl, around ten years old, rushed over and barreled into Tammy's middle. Tammy hugged her close, then kissed the top of her head.

"And this," Tammy said, smiling at Alex, "is Colt's sister, Meg. Who," she teased, "I haven't seen in way too long."

Far too long, actually. Since before Meg and Colt had lost their father, prompting Colt and Jen to leave the circuit to take care of her.

"Guess what?" Meg asked. "I get to be the flower girl tomorrow. And…" She held up her hands and wiggled her fingers. "Me and Jen got matching French manicures."

"That's wonderful." Tammy studied Meg's bright expression and cheerful smile. Clearly, she was happy with Colt and Jen and it was good to see that.

"You brought a baby." Meg smiled, her blue eyes landing on Brody. "Oh, what a cutie," she crooned, easing over and taking Brody's hand.

Brody looked down at Meg and grinned as his brown eyes roved over her curls.

The rest of the introductions were made, and it wasn't long before Meg led Brody to the main house, holding his hand and laughing at his babbles the entire way.

"You decided not to bring Razz?" Jen asked.

"Yeah." Tammy studied the horses grazing in the fields. "She loves it here, but she likes it at Alex's ranch just as much. And since she's still healing, one of Alex's neighbors agreed to tend to her and the other horses for us while we're gone."

"Well, that's good." Jen smiled. "With so much family around, we have plenty of babysitters, so you and Alex can make this a sort of mini vacation. We set y'all up in two guest rooms in the main house. They're right beside each other, and if you need anything, don't hesitate to ask." She grabbed Tammy's arm and tugged. "But before you get settled, I want you to see the new house Colt had built."

"It's finished?"

"Yep." Jen laughed and pulled harder. "It's on a back lot, and I can't wait to show it to you. Colt and I just finished decorating Meg's room and found the most adorable bedroom suite. Oh, and I can show you my dress."

"Well, that officially counts me out, seeing as how I'm not allowed to see the dress before the wedding," Colt said, smirking.

"It's a surprise," Jen stressed. "I want to knock your socks off when you see me tomorrow."

"You already knock my socks off, baby." Colt winked. "And whatever you wear, you won't be wearing it for long, anyway."

Jen blushed bright red and grinned. Alex chuckled. Tammy smacked Colt's arm playfully. "Behave."

Colt laughed, then nudged Alex with an elbow. "I say we hang here and I'll give you a hand with the bags."

Alex agreed, and Tammy and Jen left them to it, then walked the long, winding path to the back lot. The grounds at Raintree Ranch were extensive, and the new two-story house with white siding contrasted beautifully with the lush green fields surrounding it. Jen led the way inside, then through a tour of both floors. Each room they entered was even more impressive than the one before.

"I love it," Tammy said, following Jen into the master bedroom.

"I was hoping you would." Jen paused at the threshold of the closet and smiled. "Colt and I miss you. We want you to feel at home so you'll visit more often. And one day, when you're ready to retire from the circuit, maybe you'll decide to stay?" She walked inside the closet, saying over her shoulder, "But no pressure or anything."

Tammy sat on the edge of the bed and rubbed her hands over her jeans. A month ago, she'd have seriously considered the offer. She might have even decided to stay after visiting for the wedding, since the thought of returning to the road on her own was so unwelcome. But she no longer felt alone. Instead, Alex's ranch had begun to feel like home.

"Okay. Please be honest and let me know exactly what you think."

Tammy looked up as Jen walked out of the closet, holding a dress in her arms. It was off-the-shoulder white satin and the intricate detail of the lace trim was eye-catching and ornate. Soft, oversize bows adorned the off-the-shoulder sleeves and waist, giving it a gentle, romantic air.

"It's fancier than I'd originally planned," Jen said softly, ducking her head to study the dress. Her long red curls spilled over the white satin, and her cheeks flushed. "But when I saw it, I just fell in love with it."

Tammy's throat tightened, and she blinked back tears. Jen looked every inch the beautiful, blushing bride.

"It's perfect," Tammy said. "Absolutely perfect."

Jen lifted her head and smiled. "I'm glad you think so, because I picked something out for you, too."

Tammy shook her head, laughing, as Jen darted back into the closet, then returned with a second dress. "You're the bride. You should be the one getting the gifts."

"It's a gift just having you here." Jen draped a Western-style teal bridesmaid dress over her lap. "I hope you're the same size you were last year, because that's what I went by. I thought it'd bring out your eyes, and you can wear a pair of my dressy boots if you want. They'll be more comfortable than heels."

Tammy smoothed her fingers over the soft material, the white embroidery around the waist blurring in front of her. "It's beautiful. Thank you." She glanced up. "I'm so sorry I haven't been here to help, Jen."

"Oh, don't worry about that." Jen sat beside her on the bed and leaned against her. "You were needed elsewhere, and I've had more than enough help. It's going to be a simple outdoor service with family and friends. It's what Colt and I both wanted. I'm just glad you called to say you were bringing Alex and Brody with you this weekend." She laughed. "I've been itching to lay my eyes on Alex and see if he's been treating you right. And I have to say, that man is easy on a girl's eyes. I can see why you're so attracted to—"

"I'm in love with him."

Jen grew quiet, a small smile appearing as her brown eyes examined Tammy's face. "I kinda picked up on that."

Stomach fluttering, Tammy looked down and twisted her hands together in her lap. "I'm going to tell him this weekend." She cleared her throat. "I'm crazy, right? I know we haven't known each other that long and it's hard to explain, but when I'm with him, I feel like I've come home. Like I finally made a right turn somewhere and I'm meant to be there." Her hands clenched tighter, her fingertips turning red. "I want Alex so much, Jen. I want to marry him. Have children with him. Grow old with him. Life has been rough on him, and I want to see him happy," she whispered. "I want to be the one who makes him happy."

Jen's hands covered hers, squeezing gently. "I need to ask one thing."

Tammy raised her head and bit her lip at the somber look on Jen's face. "What?"

"Does he make *you* happy?"

Tammy pulled in a deep breath, sat up straight and nodded. "Yes. More than anything."

Jen smiled. "Then that's all that matters."

Brody was officially in hog heaven.

Alex sat back in his seat and smiled as Meg, seated at a table in front of him, bounced Brody in her lap and sweet-talked him into another giggle. She hadn't let Brody out of her sight or her arms since they'd arrived at Raintree hours earlier. And the other five children seated at the kids' table seemed to enjoy Brody's company as much as she did.

"You're such a big, beautiful boy," Meg crooned above the happy chatter in Raintree Ranch's dining room.

She dipped another slice of strawberry in chocolate

sauce, then handed it to him. Brody brought the strawberry to his lips with both hands, then looked across the candlelit table at Alex and smiled a toothy grin. Something about the lift of the baby's eyebrows and smug expression hinted that Brody knew exactly what he was doing.

Soft lips touched Alex's ear. "Don't tell Meg, but I think Brody's milking this rehearsal dinner for all the chocolate he can get."

Alex laughed and turned his head, his lips brushing against Tammy's smooth cheek. "I think you're right about that."

She smothered a laugh and eased closer to his side at the head table.

The press of her breasts against his upper arm and the sweet scent of her skin sent pleasurable shivers up his spine. He raised his arm and settled it around her shoulders, leaning back to get a clearer view of her.

Damn, she was beautiful. And if the golden flicker of candlelight highlighting her deep green eyes didn't prove that fact, then the tempting curve of her smiling mouth did.

Unable to resist, he lowered his head for a quick taste of her. The hum of voices and clang of dishes in the background rose, and she moaned as he kissed her, prompting him to leave her lips and trail chaste kisses down the graceful sweep of her neck.

Her hands cradled the back of his head, and her fingertips smoothed through his hair, making his body tighten.

"What I wouldn't give to get you alone right now," she whispered, hugging him close.

"Hmm." He lifted his head, nipped her earlobe gently, then smiled as she shivered against him. "And what exactly would you do with me?"

She moved her hands to cup his jaw, her thumbs sweeping over his lower lip and those gorgeous eyes darkening. "Everything."

Sweet heaven. He dropped his head, rolled his forehead against hers and groaned. Why the hell did they have to have an audience? They'd had one earlier, too, during the wedding rehearsal outside. Tammy had looked so perfect at the end of the aisle, standing beside Jen and smiling as the sun set at her back. It'd taken all his control to keep from walking over and taking her into his arms. And even then, he hadn't been able to tear his eyes away from her.

"Excuse me."

The clink of metal against glass forced Alex to draw back to a respectable distance. He shared a regretful glance with Tammy, then focused on the dark-haired man standing at the other end of the head table. Dominic Slade. Alex remembered meeting him earlier.

After stowing the bags in the guest rooms, Colt had given Alex a tour of Raintree Ranch and introduced him to several of Tammy's friends, including Dominic. Dominic owned Raintree Ranch and was a former bull rider and traveling partner of Colt's. Everyone Alex had met had been kind and hospitable, and it was easy to see why Tammy loved this place so much.

The room grew quiet, and Dominic stopped tapping the wineglass. "As best man, I understand it's my job to give a toast and say a few words to the groom." He grinned. "And I bet Colt's shaking in his boots right now at what I'm about to say."

Scattered laughs filled the room, and Colt smiled, sitting back and curling an arm around Jen.

"No worries, though." Dominic bent and kissed the cheek of a pretty blonde sitting next to him. "My wife has given me strict instructions to keep it short and sweet." He straightened and faced Colt. "Colt, we spent a lot of years on the road together, and you've been a great business partner and even better friend."

Alex looked down, a heaviness settling in his chest. The moment felt so familiar. He could still see Dean standing in a similar pose, raising a glass and wishing him and Susan well the night before their wedding. Dean and Gloria had been so happy and hopeful. So certain the future held nothing but wonderful things for all of them.

Tammy's hand covered his, her fingers threading through his and squeezing gently. His throat thickened, and he focused on the contrast of her creamy skin against his tanned hand.

"The only thing in life as valuable as a good friend is family," Dominic continued, "and you've become that, as well. I couldn't be happier that you've decided to make Raintree Ranch your home." He raised his glass. "I wish you and Jen a life full of laughter and love." He chuckled. "And a houseful of rascals as wild as we were as kids." He gestured toward the children's table, his laughter trailing away and his smile wide as he said, "Because family is what it's all about."

Alex stiffened. He glanced up and studied Tammy's face. Her attention was fixed on the children, her eyes shining and her lips parting. She faced him then, and her hand tightened around his as she smiled.

He forced a smile in return, his gut churning.

Dominic raised his glass. "To Colt and Jen."

The other adults followed suit, sipped their drinks, then applauded. After dinner concluded, friends and family stopped by the head table to give their final congratulations before the big event. Tammy stayed close by Alex's side.

The sheer happiness on her face was a blessing, but the expectant adoration in her eyes was a curse. He cringed. He knew he should tell her. Had to at some point if what they shared turned out to be real and they decided to plan for the future. But the rich life of family, children and a thriving estate that lay ahead of Colt and Jen made his potential offer of a barren home and struggling ranch pale in comparison.

So much so, that even after Meg brought him Brody, the warmth of the boy's small hands hugging his neck couldn't fight the chill that had crept over Alex's skin.

One hour later, Alex stood on the front porch of the main house, holding Brody as he slept. The night sky was clear, the air was warm and the hum of nocturnal wildlife surrounded him. Tammy, Jen and Colt chatted at his side, enjoying a few moments of privacy from the crowd in the dining room.

Alex rolled his shoulders and ran a palm over Brody's hair, but the unease shrouding him refused to dissipate.

"A few of the ranch hands checked the tents earlier, and everything looks ready for tomorrow's reception," Colt said. "The food is well in hand, the decorations are up and there's nothing but sun in the weather forecast." He tugged Jen to his side and smiled. "All that's left is for you to show up, baby."

"As though I wouldn't," Jen teased, kissing his cheek.

Colt nuzzled her neck. "Why don't we just grab the preacher and do this thing now?"

"No way." Tammy poked Colt in the chest. "Jen's got a killer dress, and I refuse to leave here without seeing you in a tux. There's no telling when the opportunity will arrive again. Plus, Dominic and I have planned parties for both of you tonight. Separately," she stressed. "So say your goodbyes now."

Colt cast Alex a sardonic scowl. "You hear that, man? I'm being banished from my own home."

Alex laughed.

"You're not being banished from your home, Colt." Tammy shrugged. "Just to the opposite side of the ranch." She moved close and rubbed Brody's back. "That means you, too, Alex. Jen's mom is babysitting tonight so we can celebrate with Jen and Colt."

Alex stifled a grin. "Separately?"

"Yep. After the party, I'm going to sleep at Jen's new house." Her smile grew brighter. She raised to her toes and whispered in his ear, "Tomorrow night, however, is another story."

Alex's mouth longed to cover hers and he leaned closer, the tension in his muscles relaxing slightly. Resisting the urge to turn his head and kiss her, he passed Brody into her waiting arms, holding a hand to the baby's head until he snuggled securely against her chest.

"I'll see you tomorrow afternoon," she said before walking inside with Brody.

Alex watched her leave, then averted his eyes and smiled as Jen shared a long good-night kiss with Colt. Reluctantly, Jen left, too.

Colt sagged back against the porch rail, pressed his palm to his chest and winced. "Damn, I love that woman."

Alex laughed.

"All jokes aside," Colt said, leaning back on his elbows. "I love Jen more than I ever thought it was possible to love someone. I can't wait to watch her walk down that aisle to me tomorrow." He shook his head and sighed. "Tonight has a strange feel to it, you know? I'm excited and nervous and eager and afraid." He laughed. "I'm feeling damned near everything. It's just…bittersweet, somehow. Having something end and begin at the same time. You know what I mean?"

Alex nodded, recalling the way his hands shook and stomach rolled the night before his wedding to Susan. He'd had all the usual nerves he'd been told to expect. But, as it turned out, his worries regarding a successful marriage hadn't been entirely unfounded.

"Yeah," he said. "I know what you mean."

Colt straightened, his smile fading. "You've done this before?"

Alex glanced away and studied the fields in the distance, the light from the porch reaching the fences, then dying a few feet past them. "Once." His mouth twisted. "Obviously, it didn't work out."

"I'm not one to judge." Colt braced a hand on the white column at his side and dragged his boot over the porch floor. "I spent a lot of time on the road and wasted a lot of years on relationships that didn't matter. Took a long time for me to get it through my thick skull that settling down was what I really wanted."

The determined note in his voice brought Alex's eyes back to him.

"The thing is, despite all of what I'm feeling now, I don't have any doubts," Colt said. "Not a single one. I love Jen, and I know this is exactly what I want. And I know marrying her is the right thing to do. For both of us."

A knot formed in Alex's gut, tightening and twisting. He stood still and waited as Colt examined his face.

"Can I be straight with you?"

Alex nodded, shoved his hands in his pockets and rocked back on his heels. "Shoot."

"How old are you?"

"Thirty-five."

Colt tapped his thumb against the column, his eyes narrowing. "Tammy is twenty-five."

"I know."

"How well would you say you know her?"

Alex frowned. "What do you mean?"

"How much has she told you about her past?"

"Not much," Alex said. "But enough."

"Enough to know she's been through some stuff?" Colt pressed.

"Yes." Alex blew out a heavy breath. "Look, I get that you're watching out for her—"

"But you want me to mind my own business?" Colt grinned, but it faded. "Tammy has been my business since the day she called eight years ago and asked me for help. Said her dad was worse than usual and she was done. That she needed to leave. I drove for hours in the middle of the night to pick her up, and when I got there, he'd beaten her so badly she could barely walk to the truck on her own." His throat moved on a hard swallow, and he jerked his chin to the side, his knuckles paling against the column. "But she made it. She picked herself up and moved on." He shook his head. "We were both kids back then. Still teenagers. And I think just the fact that I showed up that day made me her hero." He dipped his head, his blue eyes firm. "That is, until you came along."

Alex flinched, a sharp pain shooting through his palms as his nails dug into them. He uncurled his fists in his pockets, his gut roiling.

"It's tough letting go of a gig like that once you've got it—being a hero and all," Colt said. "Tammy might be my cousin, but I love her like a sister. She's been running for most of her life, and when she does decide to stay put, I want to be sure she's getting the life she deserves. The very best. And that the man she settles with cares about her as much as I do."

Something strong waved through Alex. It pushed past his chest and escaped his mouth before he realized it. "I do care for her. I love her."

"Enough to do the right thing?" Colt held his gaze. "To make her happy? Whatever it takes?"

Alex nodded. "Yes."

He said the word. And he meant it. But he prayed, even as it left him, that luck would be on his side for once. That he'd actually have a shot at giving Tammy the future and happiness she deserved.

Chapter 9

"Smile."

Tammy knelt beside a table and squinted, eyeing Alex and Brody through the viewfinder of a disposable camera. Brody bounced in Alex's lap and grinned, his cake-coated fingers pausing on the way to his mouth. Alex looked up and smiled, bits of icing clinging to his lower lip where Brody had fed him wedding cake moments before.

Her heart turned over in her chest. *Perfect.*

"Hold it right there." She pressed the button, then nodded at the resulting click. "This one's gonna be a winner."

"You've said that after every picture you've taken over the past two hours." Alex laughed. "That thing oughta be running out of film soon."

Tammy shrugged and pushed to her feet. "Maybe.

But my boys love cake and I just captured the moment in all its glory. So this one will most definitely be the winner. I already gave Jen your address so she can mail them to us once they're developed."

She returned the camera to the table, then looked around, cheeks heating. Good grief, she hadn't meant to say that. Not yet. And especially not in the flippant way it'd come out, as though she knew he'd be okay with her staying with him longer. But she guessed tonight was as good a time as ever to follow through and tell him how she felt. As a matter of fact, she didn't think a more romantic opportunity could've possibly come along.

Jen and Colt's wedding had been perfect, and the reception was turning out to be just as impressive. Wooden tables, each draped with burlap and lace and decorated with full lilacs in mason jars, surrounded a wide dance floor beneath a clear tent. Softly lit chandeliers and strings of lights hung from the ceiling, and the setting sun cast a rosy glow over the interior, the colorful hues mingling with the starlight emerging overhead.

The hum of cheerful voices, laughter and clicks of cameras filled the elegant space. Tammy smiled. Jen had asked everyone to leave their phones and tablets behind and give their attention to one another instead. The only pictures taken were those by the photographer during the wedding and the ones guests snapped during the reception with the cameras Jen and Colt had provided at each table. As a result, everyone was focused on the happy couple seated at the head table and the ones they loved at their side.

Tammy closed her eyes and sighed. She was lucky enough to have the two people she loved most with her tonight. And it was high time to tell Alex how much she loved him. Tonight was an ideal opportunity.

"Perfect," Tammy whispered.

"That's true from where I'm sitting."

Tammy glanced over her shoulder at the deep rumble and found Alex's eyes roving down her back. An appreciative grin curved his lips and lit his eyes.

Lord, he was handsome. He'd discarded his jacket and tie long ago, and the top buttons of his blue collared shirt were undone, revealing a tantalizing glimpse of his muscular chest. His salt-and-pepper hair was mussed from Brody playing with it during the wedding, and the dark stubble covering his jaw had deepened throughout the afternoon, giving him an earthy and attractive air.

Tammy turned, pinched the corner of her teal skirt and cocked an eyebrow. "I take it you like my dress?"

His eyes traveled up over her chest to her mouth, then darkened. "I like everything."

His husky voice danced over every inch of her. She breathed in deep and held the warm summer air in her lungs for a moment before gesturing toward his lap. "Is there room for one more?"

His eyes sparkled and he moved to speak, but Brody beat him to it. The baby squealed and beckoned her with his messy fingers.

Alex laughed. "There's your answer."

Smiling, Tammy picked Brody up, sat on Alex's muscular thigh, then cuddled Brody to her chest. As she kissed his cheeks, the baby giggled, then poked his fingers against her mouth, thick crumbs of cake falling from his hands and into the V of her dress.

"No, thank you, Brody," she said. "I've had enough

cake." She studied the white icing and red punch stains on Brody's baby tie and slacks. "And I think you have, too." She looked at Alex and laughed. "It's gonna take a fire hose to wash him down tonight. I hope Jen's mom knows what she's getting into."

"Oh, she'll take care of it." Alex pulled them both closer, then ran a broad palm over Brody's shiny hair. "He'll be squeaky clean by the time we get him back in the morning."

His arms tightened around them, and his eyes dimmed.

Tammy studied his face, limbs trembling. She knew what he was thinking. The same thing she was. Brody would have a great time playing with the other children at a sleepover tonight, and it was guaranteed that he'd be back in their arms tomorrow. But what about the days that followed? How much longer would he remain theirs? She'd grown to love him and couldn't imagine life without him.

Her stomach lurched, and she forced her fears down, wanting so much to see Alex smile again.

"We might need to hose you down, as well," Tammy said, eyeing Alex's mouth and leaning closer. "You've got a bit of icing…right here."

His lips were soft and warm beneath hers, the icing melting on her tongue and mingling with his familiar taste as she kissed him. It was as wonderful as she imagined. He groaned, the sexy sound vibrating against her breasts and sending a delicious thrill through her.

"All right. I think it's 'bout time I took that beautiful baby."

Tammy reluctantly pulled away to find Nora Taylor, Jen's mom, lifting Brody from her lap.

"Looks like y'all need a little alone time," Nora said. "We've got a movie, toys and junk food ready inside for the kids, and I'll take great care of this little one."

She began soothing Brody as he whined and twisted, reaching for Tammy.

"Oh, it's okay, sweet boy," Tammy said, standing and kissing Brody. "We're right here and you'll see us in the morning."

Brody quieted down after Alex hugged and kissed him, then smiled again as Meg bounded over. She took his hand and cooed at him as they left the tent, and Brody was laughing before they made it outside.

Tammy forced her feet to stay still, but her heart screamed for her to follow and take Brody back. Her arms felt empty without him. As though a part of her was missing.

"He'll be okay." Alex's whisper tickled her ear and ruffled her hair. He took her hand in his, the gentle strength of his grip releasing some of the tension in her legs and easing her fears. "There's a space on that dance floor just waiting for someone to fill it. Care to dance with me?"

Tammy faced him, noting the sad look in his eyes and tender expression. She didn't know if the offer was an attempt to distract her from the loss of Brody or if he wanted to hold her as much as she longed to hold him. Either way, she'd take it.

"I'd love to."

He smiled, then led the way to the dance floor, taking her in his arms and swaying to the slow beat. She moved closer in his arms, her skirt rustling against his dress slacks.

Each of his movements surrounded her with a heady mixture of his cologne and masculine scent. Excited shivers chased through her. She closed her eyes, pressed her cheek to his chest and savored the strong throb of his heart through the soft cotton of his shirt. His hands drifted lower on her back, then stopped as they reached the curve of her bottom.

He chuckled, his chest vibrating beneath her cheek. "It's a shame we always have an audience."

She raised her head, her breath catching at the dark heat in his eyes. He smiled, then tipped his chin toward the other side of the room. She swiveled in his arms and sifted visually through the couples swaying in time to the music.

Jen and Colt watched them from the head table. They leaned against each other with their arms entwined. Jen had a dreamy expression on her face. Colt smiled, lifted his glass with his free hand and tipped it toward them.

Tammy's chest fluttered. Colt and Jen looked perfect together. Just as perfect as this moment with Alex felt.

She spun back to Alex, slid her arms around his waist and hugged him closer. "If you don't want an audience, why don't you take me to your room?" She met his eyes, smiled up at him, then whispered, "And make love to me? Because I can't think of a better way to end the day."

His chest rose on a swift breath, and his hands cradled her face. "Neither can I."

They left, easing their way through the maze of dancing couples, then crossed the dimly lit fields to the main house. The sun had set and the stars were out, lighting their way. Tammy held Alex's hand tighter as they climbed the front porch steps, then walked down the hall to his room.

Once inside, he toed the door shut behind them, crossed the room and turned on the lamp. He stood still beside it, his eyes heating as they traveled down the length of her. The soft light highlighted the strong curve of his jaw and the sculpted outline of his muscles beneath the fitted dress shirt.

Her belly quivered, nervous tension assaulting her, and the floor dipped beneath her feet. She reached out and placed a palm flat against the wall.

"Tammy."

Her eyes lifted to his, and she melted at the patient concern in his expression, a sudden lightness flooding her.

"This is your call." He shook his head. "We don't have to—"

"No." She smiled, then lifted each foot in turn, removing the dressy boots Jen had loaned her. "I mean yes. I want to."

He smiled, his voice soft as he slid off his tie and tossed it aside. "Then I'm yours. However you want me."

She walked over and unbuttoned his shirt, her fingers trembling as they brushed against his warm skin. Parting the material, she slid it over his broad shoulders and down his arms, letting it fall to the floor. She placed her hands on his wide chest, the sprinkling of hair tickling her palms, then ran them gently over his biceps, his back and, eventually, his muscled abs. They rippled beneath her touch.

A soft groan escaped him, and his eyes closed, his throat moving on a hard swallow.

He was beautiful. More beautiful than any man she'd ever seen. She bit her lip, a wave of heat moving through her as she took his hands in hers. They were so big her palms disappeared beneath his, but there was a gentle stillness in them. One that was protective and kind. As though they were at her bidding.

Her throat tightened, and her heart swelled in her chest, warming her eyes and blurring her vision. She rose to her tiptoes and touched her lips to his, her kiss gentle as she breathed him in and relished the pleasure on his face.

He deepened the contact, his tongue parting her lips and sweeping against hers. She closed her eyes and gave herself over to his kiss, vaguely registering him removing the rest of their clothing, then walking her backward. The soft corner of the mattress bumped the back of her legs as he guided her gently to the bed.

The warmth of his mouth touched her ankle, then trailed farther up the inside of her leg. His tongue flicked softly against her skin, sending shivers through her. She giggled, then looked down when he teased the back of her knee, her breath snagging at the sight of his dark head between her thighs.

He glanced up, and a slow grin spread across his face as he eased up her body and kissed her. He worked his way back down to her breasts, his attention lingering there. Each strong pull of his mouth overwhelmed her with new, exciting sensations and caused her grip on his shoulders to tighten. When he traveled lower, drifting his mouth across her belly, then lower still, her head dropped back and all thoughts left her.

He rolled away briefly, palmed his wallet from his discarded pants, then returned. He knelt between her thighs, then hesitated, frowning at the protection in his hand.

"Tammy, I…" A flush spread over his face and neck, and his hand shook slightly.

"Wait." Heart slamming against her ribs, she lifted up on her elbow and covered his hand with hers, the foil package cool against her palm. "I guess I need to tell you before we go any further that I've—" Her throat closed, and she swallowed hard, wishing she knew what he was thinking. Wishing his body was still covering hers. "I've never done this before." She laughed, her cheeks burning. "If for no other reason than so you'll be aware. But I don't want you to stop. You make me feel so much. So many things I never knew I could feel."

His eyes shadowed, and he began to pull away.

"Please, Alex," she whispered, hooking an arm around his neck and tugging him back over her. "Please don't think. Just feel."

She kissed him, pouring her soul into it, hoping he could feel what she felt. Could understand how much she loved him.

He closed his eyes and touched his forehead to hers. A muscle ticked in his jaw. "I don't want to hurt you."

She cupped his face and brushed her thumbs over his mouth, loving him more than she'd ever thought possible. "You won't," she whispered.

And he didn't. There was no pain. If anything, she felt safer and more loved than she ever had in her life.

He joined his body to hers and moved tenderly, filling her completely, body and soul. The emotions he stirred within her grew so strong they broke free, overtaking them both and spilling down her cheeks.

Afterward, he stilled above her, his heavy breaths dancing over her breasts and ruffling her hair as he stared down at her. His cheeks glistened in the low lamplight, and the same wonder and surprise overwhelming her was reflected in his eyes.

Tammy drew in a shaky breath and wrapped her arms tighter around his muscular back, wanting to hold on to the moment. Wanting to hold on to what she'd never had before.

This is how love should feel.

She smiled, her heart tripping when he returned it. His face creased with pleasure, and they laughed softly. She drifted her fingertips through the tears of joy on his face, losing herself in his warm eyes and glimpsing the beautiful possibilities that awaited them. A home filled with love and laughter. And children. Lots of children. Babies with his beautiful smile who would feel as safe and loved in his arms as she did.

It was the perfect moment to tell him. Absolutely perfect.

"I love you."

Alex tried to still the tremors rippling through his limbs at Tammy's words. His body was sated, his mind clear, and his heart strained to hold itself together, the longing welling within it threatening to make it burst.

She'd given him such a gift. One he'd never be able to return. And the sweet words she'd just spoken stoked the fire in his belly, sending a fresh wave of desire through him and urging him to take her again.

She was so beautiful lying there beneath him, cheeks flushed, hair tousled and eyes soft.

He moved to speak, but his throat closed with emotion. His biceps shook on either side of her and his hands curled tighter into the sheets.

"You don't have to say it." Tammy reached up, her fingers fumbling over his lips as her smile widened. "I know. I just want to tell you that I'm willing to make an honest man of you."

He laughed and shook his head, his arms almost giving way beneath him. He rolled to his back before his strength completely left him and tugged her with him, holding her close.

She propped her chin on his chest, her soft breasts pressing against his abs, and drifted her fingers through his hair. "I want to share my life with you."

God, how he wanted that. He wrapped his arms around her and lifted her farther up his body. Her hair spilled over her shoulders and cascaded around his face as he kissed her, her sweet scent filling his senses and the taste of her kiss lingering on his tongue.

"I want to help you rebuild your business." Her green eyes traveled over his face as she smoothed her fingers over his jaw. "I want to rock beside you in those beautiful chairs every day. I want to grow old with you. I want to hold you and kiss you every night."

He grinned and kissed her again, pulling back when she moaned softly. Lord, she was gorgeous. He had no doubts she'd grow only more beautiful over the years. But he, on the other hand…

Alex chuckled. "I'm ten years older than you. Years down the road, after I lose my touch, will you still hold and kiss me? Dentures and all?"

She laughed. "Especially then. Because I have a feeling I'll love you even more, if that's possible." Her eyes softened on his face. "I love you, and I want to make you happy."

He glided his hands in circles across her smooth back. His palms rasped against her soft skin, and his chest swelled with hope at the future she described. He needed so much to hear her say it. To hear her tell him a life together was all she wanted. That it'd be enough.

"This goes both ways," he said, staring into her eyes. "What would make you happy?"

"Hmm." She smiled. "A home with you."

His chest expanded, filling with relief, and he squeezed her tighter.

"And babies," she whispered.

He froze.

"Lots of beautiful babies," she continued, "with your dimples, strength and stubbornness." She laughed. "I want a houseful of rowdy boys that look like you and a couple of feisty girls that look like me."

He held her gaze and fought to keep his smile in place, his chest aching.

She frowned as she studied his expression, her words becoming hesitant. "Do you want that?" Her lips trembled. "Do you want me?"

His throat tightened, and his lungs burned. He hugged her close, eased her cheek to his chest and tucked her head under his chin. "Yes." He struggled to breathe. "I want you."

He winced, the pain streaking through him almost unbearable. He wanted her. More than he'd ever wanted anyone or anything in his life. Loved her more than he'd ever loved anyone before.

But she'd given him so much more than he'd ever be able to give her in return. How the hell could he take even more? Especially when he couldn't give her what *she* wanted?

His gut burned. He ached to tell her, but his throat locked and the words died on his tongue, the thought of her looking at him differently too much to bear. What could he possibly offer her other than an empty house and a future filled with regret?

"I love Brody, too."

He stilled as her soft whisper swept over him.

"I wish he was ours," she added, her warm lips moving against his skin.

Alex clenched his teeth. Brody *was* theirs. They loved Brody as much as he imagined any biological parents could love a son. And the three of them had become a family. *His* family.

Alex closed his eyes and kissed the top of her head, her hair soft against his cheek. He'd drive to Deer Creek first thing when they returned to the ranch Monday. He'd see Maxine, convince her that Brody belonged with him and ask her what he had to do to make it happen.

He couldn't give Tammy a child of her own. But he'd do everything in his power to give her Brody. And he hoped like hell he and Brody would be enough.

Chapter 10

"Go ahead, Brody." Alex smiled. "Throw 'em a big handful."

Brody looked down at the oats and seeds filling his tiny palm, glanced up at Alex, then pointed with his free hand at the large pond on Raintree Ranch's front lot. "Dat."

"Ducks," Alex said, gesturing toward the dozens of multicolored birds dunking their heads underwater and ruffling their thick feathers. "Those are ducks and they're hungry. Go give 'em some breakfast."

Brody blinked up at him, forehead creasing, then stepped slowly to the edge of the pond. Alex followed, squatted on the thick green grass at Brody's side, then guided his hand forward, sprinkling the food into the water with a soft splash.

He brushed the baby's brown bangs out of his wide eyes as he stared at the ducks. "If you stay really quiet," he whispered, "they'll come grab it."

As if on cue, three ducks on the fringe of the group craned their long necks in their direction, then swam over. They skirted around the floating seeds, then dipped their heads and started eating.

Brody gasped. His brows lifted, and his mouth curved into an O of surprise. He grabbed Alex's forearm and whispered, "Dat."

"Ducks."

Brody turned Alex's hands over and scowled at his empty palms.

Alex chuckled. "I don't have any more." He turned and pointed behind him. "But Tammy does."

Brody's eyes followed the direction of his hand to where Tammy sat on the grass. He took off, running toward Tammy as fast as his short, chubby legs would carry him.

Tammy held up a plastic bag filled with seeds and waved, urging Brody on. When he reached her, she tipped the bag and poured more seeds into Brody's hand.

Alex admired the gentle way her hand cupped Brody's and the soft smile she gave as she spoke. It was so similar to the one she'd had this morning when he'd drifted kisses over her cheeks and forehead as she slept beside him. Full of love and adoration.

Her eyelids had fluttered open beneath his lips, and she'd tugged his head down to kiss him back. Her soft curves and warm kiss woke him up better than a strong cup of coffee ever could. But he'd had a hard time leav-

ing that bed this morning. So had she. One night with
her in his arms wasn't nearly enough, but they'd both
been anxious to see Brody and spend their last day at
Raintree Ranch together. They'd started touring the
ranch right after a big Sunday breakfast, showing Brody
the animals and enjoying his reactions to them.

"Get ready," Tammy said, helping Brody turn without spilling his handful of seeds. "He's restocked."

She laughed as Brody toddled over, and a rush of
pleasure swept through him at the sound.

"Dat," Brody shouted, stopping at Alex's side.

More ducks had glided over—at least a dozen swam
around the edge, pecking the water for more food.

Alex smiled and put a finger to his lips. "You've got
to be as quiet as you can—"

"Dat!" Brody slung his hand forward, scattering
seeds over the ducks, and squealed.

The ducks scattered, darting wildly in different directions. Brody stopped yelling, pointed at the fleeing
animals, then frowned up at Alex. A wounded question
formed in his big brown eyes. "Uh-oh."

"That's what happens when you're not quiet around
them." Alex picked Brody up and tickled his ribs.
"We've got to work on your finesse, son."

Brody giggled and squirmed, then threw his arms
around Alex's neck and hugged him.

Son. Alex closed his eyes and rubbed Brody's back.
In his heart, that was exactly what Brody had become.

"I wish I still had that camera from last night."

Alex glanced over to find Tammy smiling at them,
her knees to her chest and her chin resting on them. Her

cheeks were flushed from the heat of the morning sun, and freckles were scattered along the bridge of her nose.

"Nah." He laughed. "You've taken more than enough pictures this weekend."

He crossed to her side and bent, pressing kisses across her cheeks, then down her neck as she tipped her head back with a soft sound of pleasure.

A buzz in his back pocket intruded, and he pulled away with a groan, lowering Brody into her arms. "Hold him for a sec, please? Earl promised he'd call with an update on the horses."

Alex tugged his phone out and took the call, grinning as Brody smooshed Tammy's cheeks and ran his tiny hands through her hair. "Hello."

"Alex. It's Maxine."

His grip tightened on the phone. Several possibilities as to why Maxine had called formed in his mind. But one stood out more than the others.

The sounds of Tammy's and Brody's laughter grew louder, and he turned, focusing on the pond water as it rippled in the warm breeze.

"Are you there, Alex?"

"Yeah. I'm here."

"I hate to call so early in the morning," she said. "Especially when you're out of town. But it was necessary, and I think you know why I'm calling."

His gut roiled.

"John got in touch with me last night." She sighed, the soft sound whispering across the line. "He and his fiancée have decided to take Brody."

Alex clenched his teeth, a pain shooting through his jaw. Last night while he'd made love to Tammy and imagined himself part of a family, his dream was being dismantled by Dean's sorry-ass brother in Boston. A man who hadn't given two thoughts to Dean when he was alive and thought he had a claim to Brody now.

Hell, no.

"He can't have him." Alex winced at the sharp sound of his voice. He regrouped, striving for a calmer tone. "Maxine, I understand John is blood, but I knew Dean. And I know Brody. He's been happy with me and Tammy." He balled his fist at his side. "Brody belongs with me. It's what Dean would've wanted."

"I know that's what Dean would've wanted had he known what was going to happen." Her voice softened. "But he didn't know, Alex. He didn't plan for anything like this. And John is Brody's family."

"The hell he is." Alex shook his head, his chest burning. "I'm the closest thing Brody has to a family. He's *my* family—" His voice cracked, and he sucked in a ragged breath. "Maxine, please. If there's anything you can do…"

"I'm so sorry." Her words shook. "We both knew this was temporary. I was hoping things would turn out differently, but they didn't. We have no choice. You have to bring Brody back now. John is coming to your place this afternoon to pick him up."

The peaceful scene before Alex blurred, the green field bleeding into the pond. A hollow chasm unfolded inside him, and every dream he ever had fell right through it.

"Think of Brody, Alex." Maxine's tone turned firm. "I know it hurts to lose him, but he'll be going to a good home. And whatever John and Dean's relationship may or may not have been, by all accounts, John is a good man who is doing what he feels is the right thing. He's promised to take good care of Brody. You, of all people, know how precious finding a permanent placement is, and I know you love Brody. So please try to make this transition as easy as possible for him."

Everything turned numb. His chest, his body, his skin. But he managed to speak. "We'll leave right away."

He cut the call, shoved the phone in his pocket, then flexed his hands, trying to dislodge the stiffness and collect his composure.

"They're taking Brody, aren't they?"

Alex turned, the weak thread in Tammy's voice bringing his eyes to hers. The shadows in her expression and the blissful, unaware grin on Brody's face as he bounced in her lap shot a stabbing pain through him. And he wondered how in the hell he could feel nothing—*and everything*—at the same time.

"Yes."

The drive back was silent, except for Brody's sporadic chatter and giggles from the back of the cab. Alex drove as slowly as possible on the highway, ignoring the cars speeding by and trying to hold on to every last second he had left with Brody. He glanced in the rearview mirror every few minutes, catching a quick glimpse of Brody's shoe kicking the back seat or his tiny fingers lifting as he played. And he tried to make it last forever.

But the miles continued to pass, and when they arrived at the ranch, the late-afternoon sun glinted off an unfamiliar sedan parked in front of the house.

"Is that them already?" Tammy straightened. Her hands gripped the edge of her seat, and her voice hardened. "They'll just have to wait. We haven't packed his things or had a chance to…"

She turned away and looked out the passenger window, her shoulders shaking.

Alex reached out and covered her hand with his, forcing himself to say the words that needed to be said. "He's going to be okay, Tammy."

She faced him. Tears welled over her thick lashes and spilled down her cheeks. "Without us?"

He nodded, his stiff neck protesting the movement. "Without us."

After parking the truck, Alex waited as Tammy removed Brody from his car seat and cradled him to her chest. They walked to the front porch to find Earl standing on the top step with Scout stretched out at his feet. A man and a woman each sat in a rocking chair, visibly anxious.

"Ah, here they are now." Earl nodded at Alex, his smile not reaching his eyes as he whispered, "Hope you don't mind. Maxine called, said they were leaving her office to come out here and asked if I'd hold down the fort with them until you got back."

"Thanks." Alex stepped past him as the couple stood. "John?"

The man moved forward, brushed a blond curl from his forehead and held out his hand. Alex shook it and forced a polite smile. He looked so young. And nothing like Dean.

"It's nice to meet you, Alex." John gestured to the woman who now stood beside him. "This is Becky, my fiancée."

Alex greeted her, then made the rest of the introductions, his throat thickening more with each word. Brody grew frustrated and wiggled in Tammy's arms, straining to get down.

"We've had a long trip," Tammy said, setting Brody on his feet. "He hasn't had a chance to stretch his legs."

Brody scrambled off, climbed into the small rocking chair and leaned forward, smiling as it rocked back, then picked up a steady rhythm. Scout darted over, leaped into his lap and propped his chin on Brody's knees.

Alex flinched, his skin growing clammy. "I need to pack some of Brody's clothes. And there's a few toys he got for his birthday that he'll want to take with him." He turned and walked toward the door, needing privacy. Needing to be alone. "Tammy will fill you in on what he likes and doesn't like."

Alex made his way to the nursery, praying his legs didn't give out beneath him. It took half an hour to pack a few bags for Brody. Alex's hands shook as he folded small shirts and pants, then packed diapers and toys. When he finished, he stopped on the threshold and took one last look around.

Years ago, he'd stood here after receiving the news of his infertility. Right in this same damned spot, feeling like a failure and less of a man than he ever had. But back then, he didn't have a face to the loss. The children he and Susan had planned to have were just bits of imagination. Hazy thoughts, at best.

But *this*. Losing Brody…

Alex choked back a sob. Then he stepped into the hallway and slammed the door shut. And the hell if he'd ever step foot in that room again.

A few minutes later, Earl said a gruff goodbye to Brody, then left, ambling toward his house. Alex waited by the car with John and Becky, his chest aching as Tammy knelt in front of Brody's rocking chair, speaking softly to him. Brody smiled up at her as she picked him up, then walked over.

"He likes to play in water," Tammy whispered. She kissed Brody's cheek as he nuzzled his face against her chest. "Do you have a swimming pool?"

"No." Becky smiled. "But my mother does. She lives down the road from us."

"That's good." Tammy rubbed a hand over Brody's back. "He likes long baths, too. And dogs. He loves dogs."

"We'll take good care of him," John said, opening the back door and holding his arms out. "It's time for us to get going. We have a flight to catch."

Tammy nodded. She bit her lip and leaned over to pass Brody to John. "This is John, Brody. He and Ms. Becky are going to take good care of you."

Brody lifted his head, looked up at John, then back at Tammy. His brow creased with confusion. John reached out, and Brody shrank back, hiding his face in Tammy's throat and issuing short cries of panic.

Alex gritted his teeth. His hands clenched at his sides as Tammy tugged at Brody's arms and tried to coax him into going to John. Brody refused, his wails growing shriller.

"It's okay, Brody," Tammy said, wincing as Brody's fingers tangled in her hair and pulled. Her eyes welled with tears, and she glanced at Alex helplessly, her voice breaking. "He won't let go."

Grimacing, Alex moved close and took Brody's hands in his. He gently unwound Brody's fingers from Tammy's hair, then forcibly removed him from her arms. Brody stiffened and cried out, the sound piercing Alex's ears and cracking his heart.

"It's okay," Alex whispered against Brody's ear as he passed him to John. He inhaled Brody's soft baby scent, holding it in his lungs and imprinting it on his heart. "You're gonna be okay, Brody."

John and Becky scrambled to get Brody settled in his car seat and shut the door. Brody sobbed louder, the sound echoing within the car.

"Thanks for taking care of him," John said hastily, climbing in the driver's seat.

Becky gave a pained smile, then slid in the passenger seat. The engine turned over, and they pulled away, dust billowing up behind the car as they disappeared down the driveway. Scout followed for several feet, barking, then eventually turned and darted into a field to snuffle around in the grass.

It was quiet for a few moments. Then Tammy's sobs broke the silence, filling the emptiness surrounding them.

Alex pulled her to him, wrapping his arms around her and holding her tight. Her fists dug into his back and her hot tears scalded his throat, each of her cries cutting deeper into his chest.

And he knew, without a doubt, that he could no longer offer her the family she dreamed of and deserved. That he could never truly make her happy.

He closed his eyes as her sobs grew louder. God, he couldn't go through this again. He couldn't let Tammy stay with him out of a sense of duty like Susan had, only to see her smile fade and regret haunt her eyes. He wouldn't be able to survive it. He loved her too much.

Enough to do the right thing? To make her happy? Whatever it takes?

He cringed. At least he could do the right thing this time, the only thing he could do to ensure she had a shot at getting the future—and happiness—she deserved. And the longer he put it off, the harder it would be.

Alex waited until she grew quiet again, the shudders sweeping through her body easing and her hold on him loosening. He eased back and lifted her chin with his knuckle, swallowing hard at the trails of tears on her cheeks and feeling completely dead inside.

"This is the end of our deal, Tammy."

Tammy blinked, her eyes hot and gritty, and tried to fight her way out from under the pain of losing Brody. Tried to focus on Alex.

He stared down at her, his expression grim and his eyes empty.

"What did you just say?"

His hands moved, cupping her jaw, and his thumbs brushed over her cheeks. "I said this is the end of our deal." His chest lifted on a sharp inhale. "It's time for you and Razz to leave."

A laugh burst from her lips. She cringed at the bitterness of it and grabbed Alex's wrists, tugging them away from her face. "I'm going to forgive you for this later," she said, blinking back a fresh surge of tears. "Because I know you're hurting right now. And I know that's where this is coming from." She shook her head.

"But for now, we're going to go inside, crawl in bed together and cry. And when we can't cry anymore, we're going to get up, take a shower and wash this day away. Then we'll start over. Together."

He pulled away and rubbed his hands over his jeans. "I don't have another fresh start in me."

Tammy balled her fists, her legs weakening. "Look, these past few hours have been a nightmare for both of us. But this pain won't last forever. It'll pass. It'll blow over and we'll survive it."

"No, we won't." He dragged a hand over his face and looked away, his wide shoulders sagging. "I can't give you what you want."

"You're not making sense, Alex." She scrubbed the back of her hand over her cheeks. "I told you what I wanted last night. I want you. I want—"

"A home with me?" He faced her, his gray eyes piercing. "And children?"

"Yes." Her throat ached, and a heavy weight pressed on her chest. "We may have lost Brody, but there'll be other children once we recover from this." She pressed her palms to his chest, searching for the strong throb of his heart. "We'll make them together. As many as we want."

His muscles tensed beneath her touch, his expression darkening. "I can't give you children."

Tammy froze. "What?"

Alex covered her hands with his and searched her face. "That's why Susan left. It's what I couldn't give her." His eyes narrowed as he stared down at her. "If you stay with me, that nursery will remain empty. You'll never be able to get pregnant. You'll never be able to give birth to your own baby, and you'll never see yourself reflected in a child." His boot scraped across the ground as he shifted, squeezing her hands hard. "Can you honestly tell me that's what you want? That just having me would be enough?"

The ground warped beneath her, and her head spun, the pain streaking inside her becoming more intense. She closed her eyes and pulled her hands away, pressing them tight to her middle.

Her mind raced, and she scrambled to focus. To comprehend what he was saying.

They'd never be able to have children. Would never have babies with Alex's smile or her eyes. Would never be able to watch them grow and know they'd left a small part of themselves behind in the world.

She'd never have the family she'd longed for as a girl. And Alex would never hold a son of his own.

Her stomach heaved. It was almost too much to conceive.

"There's nothing for you here, Tammy." His tone turned hard as she opened her eyes. "Nothing but an empty house and beat-up land. You saw it the day we met." His lips twisted, warped and empty. "I'm broken."

Your smile. I thought it looked broken...

Tammy's hands flew to her face and covered her mouth, her teeth biting her lip. "Oh, God. I wish I'd never said that to you." The sharp tang of blood touched her tongue, and she swallowed hard, her cheeks flaming. "I didn't mean it." She shook her head and her hair fell into her eyes, obscuring him. She pushed it back and reached for him. "It's not true."

He stepped back, shoving his hands in his pockets and jerking away.

"This thing between us…" He frowned. "It's a result of circumstance. If we hadn't gone through what we did—" He winced. "If I hadn't helped you like I did and if we hadn't found Brody, you'd have left long ago. You'd have seen me the same way you saw every other man."

"That's not true," she repeated. "I love you and you love me. I know you do." She widened her stance and dug deep, keeping her words solid and firm. "We both have ugly pasts, Alex, and we may not have the future we wanted. But we can build one that'll be ours. What we make of it. And it can be beautiful—"

"Nothing can be built here," he bit out. His eyes drifted toward the road. Toward the wreckage of Dean and Gloria's house. "This place doesn't breathe. Everything just dies."

"Brody and Razz didn't." Tears streamed down her face. "And neither did we."

His attention returned to her, and his expression softened, the pain etched into his features making her heart bleed.

"My chance for happiness has passed," he whispered. "My dreams died years ago. But you're so young, you still have a shot at yours. I won't take away your chance to be happy. I won't give you a future filled with regret." He flinched. "You'll fall in love again and you'll have children. You'll build the home and family you've always wanted. And you'll be happy."

"Not without you." She held her breath, fighting off

a sob. "I don't want any of that if it means losing you. I know you want me, Alex. I know you love me."

"Then let me do the right thing." He walked over, cradled her face with his hands and touched his lips to her forehead. "Let me let you go."

"Alex—"

He dipped his head and took her mouth, his kiss deep and gentle. She wrapped her arms around him and held as tight as she could, but he slipped away, moving toward the house.

Soon, he'd be gone. Just like Brody.

"You're not doing this for me, Alex," she called out as he walked away. "You're doing this for yourself because you're afraid. You've been so worried about my fears, but you're the one who's afraid. You're afraid to take a chance and trust me. Afraid to believe that you're enough. But there's no way I can prove that to you. You have to believe it yourself before you can ever accept it from me."

He didn't respond. Or look back.

"Alex." She shook where she stood, struggling to stay upright as he made his way up the front porch steps. "You said you'd never hurt me."

He jerked to a halt, his broad back stiffening.

"This hurts." Her throat closed, and she forced herself to speak, hoping he'd cave. "It hurts so much. More than anything else ever has."

His head dropped forward as he half turned. The line of his muscular profile sagged, growing weak and defeated as he repeated her own words, his voice strained. "It'll pass."

He entered the house, closing the door behind him and effectively shutting her out.

Tammy stood still until the sun began to set, the darkness creeping over the silent fields and enveloping her. And there was nothing left to do but leave.

She went inside and packed her bags, then she hooked up her trailer and loaded Razz. She climbed into the driver's seat, revved the engine, then drove down the winding driveway until she reached the paved road.

The headlights flooded the land in front of her as she stopped the truck, casting shadows over Dean and Gloria's crumbled home. She looked to either side of her, but the fading fringes of light didn't reach very far, leaving the road dark and indistinguishable in each direction.

Her hands tightened around the steering wheel, and she closed her eyes, knowing the circuit was waiting for her on one end of the highway and Colt and Jen at the other. But neither destination seemed right. And neither path felt the same as it had before.

She didn't feel the same. Her heart, broken into jagged pieces, stabbed sharply within her chest. Her arms felt awkward and empty without Brody. Even her body felt different, Alex's tender touches and movements from last night still lingering deep inside her.

Tammy opened her eyes, hot tears scalding her cheeks, and realized Alex was right about one thing. Like every painful event in her life, this one would pass, too. Only this time, she didn't want to move on. And she had no idea which way to go.

Chapter 11

"Finishing up early tonight?"

Tammy scraped the shovel across the stall floor, shook out the clean shavings, then dumped the last bit of manure in the wheelbarrow beside her. Sweat trickled down her cheeks and back. She dragged her arm across her forehead, glanced at the man standing in the entry of the stall and smiled.

"Yeah." She propped the shovel against her hip and tugged her gloves off. "This is the last one. I've already done the rest."

She shoved the worn gloves in her back pocket, rolled her head from side to side to stretch her aching neck and laughed. The *rest* included the other fourteen stalls that were on her job detail as a hand for Red Fox Ranch in Jasper, Georgia. Sixty-five acres and a steady stream of horses to board guaranteed her consistent work and pay.

"I've just finished, too." The man grinned and propped his arm on the stall door. "I was thinking about driving into town and getting a beer. Maybe shooting a few rounds of pool. Care to join me?"

Keith Brinson was a ranch hand, same age as Tammy, who'd flirted with her every night since she'd arrived a month ago. He was blond haired, blue eyed and handsome. And harmless enough.

"I'm standing next to a cart of manure, am sweaty as a pig and probably stink to high heaven." Tammy cocked an eyebrow. "And you're still asking me out?"

"Yep." His blue eyes drifted over her briefly, then returned to her face. "Doesn't matter when I catch you. You're always beautiful."

She dipped her head and smiled. Keith was a good man. One of those rare gentlemen who still knew how to treat a lady. A woman would be lucky to grace his arm.

Her smile slipped, stormy gray eyes and deep dimples intruding into her thoughts. Just as they had every day over the past month since leaving Deer Creek.

Keith wasn't for her. Her heart still belonged to Alex. Always would.

"Thank you, Keith, but—"

"But you'd rather not." He winced good-naturedly. "I kinda figured that, since you've turned me down every time I've asked." He shrugged. "You taking Razz out tonight, as usual?"

She nodded, glancing toward the open stable doors. It was a beautiful late-September night. "It's cool out and she loves an evening stroll."

That had become Tammy's favorite part of the day, too, since she'd retired from racing and settled in at Red

Fox Ranch. She no longer felt the need to run or dreaded being alone. Instead, she enjoyed sitting on the tailgate of her truck in an empty field, watching Razz frolic and gazing at the stars. It helped her feel closer to Alex somehow. Made her think there was a chance he was outside, too. Maybe sitting in one of the rocking chairs on his front porch, looking up and thinking of her…and Brody.

An ache formed in her chest. The same one that returned every time she thought of Brody. It was fruitless, really—thinking of him like she did. But she couldn't help but wonder where he was and what he was doing. If he was happy and safe.

Tammy sighed and eased past Keith, saying good-night as she made her way to Razz's stall. She guessed that was what being a parent was like—worrying about your children when you weren't with them. And that was how she still felt about Brody. He still belonged to her and Alex. No matter where he was or who was taking care of him.

A half hour later, she sat on the tailgate of her truck in Razz's favorite field and tipped her head back, taking in the moonlit sky above her and wondering if Brody still thought of her. If he still thought of Alex and missed them both.

She lifted her hip, pulled her phone from her back pocket, then dialed the same number she'd dialed several times since Alex had sent her away. It didn't ring. Just went straight to Alex's voice mail as usual.

"Hey. It's me again." She licked her lips and shifted on the tailgate. "You know if you get tired of these messages, you ought to answer your phone at least once and tell me to bug off." She laughed, the sound thin and weak even to her own ears. "It'd save us both a lot of…"

Grief. She cringed. That was the word she was going to say, but it didn't fit. Being apart from Alex hurt no matter what the circumstances. And grief didn't quite cover it.

"Anyway, I thought I'd let you know in case you do decide to call that I'm going off the grid for the weekend starting tomorrow." She swung her legs, watching as her boots skimmed the top of the tall grass. "I'm driving to Raintree to visit Jen and Colt for a couple of days, and she wants my full attention. She said she has news she wants to share in person. I'm thinking she's probably going to tell me that she's adding to the family." She stopped swinging her legs and gripped the hard metal edge of the tailgate. "Just in case you're wondering, I'm happy for her. And I don't envy her." She pulled in a strong breath. "But I do still miss you. And I still love you."

She thought of saying goodbye. Thought of telling him this would be the last time she called. But her heart wasn't ready for that yet. So she cut the call and laid the phone beside her, wishing she could let go of Alex as easily as he had let go of her.

"Looks like it's just us again tonight, girl."

Razz tossed her head, her shiny mane rippling under the starlight, and trotted off, taking full advantage of the energetic thrill buzzing through the cool breeze in the air.

Tammy sighed and managed a small smile. Summer was definitely over.

A clatter started at her side, and she glanced down. Her phone vibrated harder, skipping across the tailgate. She snatched it up.

"Alex?"

Silence greeted her, then, "Tammy?"

Her shoulders sagged at the sound of a female voice. "You got her. Who's this?"

"It's Maxine."

Tammy hopped off the tailgate. "Maxine? Is everything okay?"

"Well, I hope so," she said. "I've been trying to reach Alex for several days now, and I can't seem to get him to answer the phone or return my calls. And he didn't answer the door when I stopped by." She blew out a breath. "I know he's there. Earl told me he walked over several times to lend a hand with the ranch, but he said Alex barely speaks."

Tammy's stomach churned. "But Alex is okay otherwise?"

"Yes, of course," Maxine said. "He's just being more stubborn than usual."

"Tell me about it," Tammy muttered under her breath.

"What was that?"

"Nothing. What can I do for you, Maxine?"

"Are you still in Georgia?"

"Yeah," Tammy said. "Jasper."

"Good." Maxine cleared her throat. "Actually, Brody is the reason I'm calling."

Tammy froze, a chill sweeping over her skin. "Brody? What's happened? Is he okay?"

"He's fine," Maxine said hastily. "There's no need to worry. It's just that John called last week and said he and Becky were having a tough time adjusting." She paused, the silence rankling Tammy's nerves even more. "I think it was just too much too soon for them. They were ready for marriage but not for a family. Not yet. And John felt awful about it. He said they thought about giving it more time but that they just aren't ready to be parents."

Tammy reached out and gripped the edge of the truck bed, her heart thumping painfully in her chest.

"I was hoping to get in touch with Alex, but since I couldn't reach him, I thought I'd give you a call." Maxine breathed deep over the phone. "Brody is staying at the home in Atlanta and needs to be placed with a foster parent. We have several options for him, but I couldn't help but think of you." Maxine hesitated. "I know things didn't work out with you and Alex, but I know you love Brody. And since you took such good care of him before, I thought—"

"How soon can I have him?"

Maxine laughed. "Slow down. Are you still touring or do you have a permanent place to stay?"

"Yes." Tammy shook her hand and tried to collect her scattered thoughts. "I mean, no, I'm not touring. And I do have a permanent place."

She winced, a pang of discomfort dimming her excitement. She'd prefer to return to Alex, but considering the circumstances, Raintree Ranch would do just fine. Colt and Jen had made it clear over the past weeks that she was more than welcome.

"You'll have to start as a foster parent," Maxine said. "Then after some time, you can apply for adoption. I'll draw up the paperwork tonight and pull a few strings first thing in the morning. Can you make it to Atlanta before three tomorrow?"

Tammy smiled, tears welling onto her lashes. "I'm already on the way."

By one o'clock the next afternoon, after a pile of paperwork and a background check, Tammy stood in the waiting room of the Atlanta children's home, wringing her hands and waiting for Brody to arrive.

"What if he doesn't remember me?" Tammy paced and eyed the closed door to the corridor.

"Relax, Tammy," Maxine said from her seated position across the room. "Everything will be fine."

"But it's been a whole month since I last saw him. He probably won't—"

The door creaked open, and Tammy spun around, clamping her mouth shut. A woman walked in with Brody in her arms. His eyes were heavy, and he looked around the room slowly, as though he'd just woken up from a nap.

"Brody?" Tammy held her breath, her lungs burning as his head swiveled in her direction.

Brody blinked, then his eyes widened, recognition dawning on his face. He squealed and reached out to her, wiggling in the woman's grasp. She set him on his feet, and he toddled over as fast as his little legs would go, his smile bright.

Tammy knelt and opened her arms, catching him as he barreled into her middle. She picked him up and hugged him close, closing her eyes as he laid his head on her chest and sighed contentedly. She breathed him in, savoring the feel of him in her arms and the comforting weight of him over her heart.

"I'm here, Brody," she whispered. "I'm here now. For good."

Tammy smiled, her broken heart beginning to heal. Alex might not allow her to love him, but she would still be able to love Brody.

A body rests easier after doing the right thing.

Head pounding, Alex groaned and covered his eyes

with his hand, avoiding the nagging phrase and struggling to slip back into oblivion. "That's a damned lie."

The pounding grew louder and more painful. He flinched and tried to find a more comfortable position, the wood of the table hard and cold against his cheek.

"Alex?"

More pounding.

"I know you're in there, and if you don't open this door in the next three seconds, I'm gonna kick the damned thing down."

Earl. That was Earl yelling—and pounding.

Alex grunted and cracked his eyes open to peer through the part in his fingers. Sunlight poured through the windows and flooded the kitchen, glinting sharply off the empty glass bottles littering the floor.

"One."

Alex laid his hands flat on the table, shoved himself upright and scrambled to his feet.

"Two."

"I'm coming."

His throat was so dry his words cracked. Which was a hell of a thing, since he'd drunk enough whiskey last night to drown a cow.

"Thr—"

"I said I'm coming."

He stumbled his way to the front door, unlocked it, then jerked it open. The sun scorched his eyes, and he shrank back, squinting and trying to bring Earl into focus.

Earl eyed him from head to toe, then frowned. "You look like hell, son."

Alex scoffed. "Thanks."

Undeterred, Earl shoved past him, clutching a small

bundle under his arm, and walked into the kitchen. He stopped in the center of the room and glanced around. "And this room looks worse."

Alex dragged a hand over his face and sighed. "Well, hell, Earl. You think all these compliments can wait until at least after noon?"

"It is after noon," Earl said, kicking a bottle and watching it spin off with a clang. "It's two o'clock, in fact. You've slept half the day away and who knows how many others since you've holed yourself up in here."

Alex rubbed his temples. "I've just needed some time alone."

"I know." Earl nodded. "I've been tending to your horses while you've had plenty of it over the past month. Helped any, has it?"

Alex winced. No. It hadn't. He'd cut his phone off, ignored his messages and avoided visitors, hoping to return to the status quo. But he missed Tammy and Brody more now than he had weeks ago. And the solitude was no longer comforting. It was just damned lonely.

Earl harrumphed. "It's about time you stop wallowing around in this self-pity of yours and do something productive."

"I'm not wallowing," Alex said. "I'm just…"

"Hiding?"

"No." Alex scowled and shoved his fists in his pockets. "I've been trying to do the right thing."

Earl's eyes narrowed. "By tossing Tammy out?"

Alex flinched. "I didn't toss her out. I asked her to leave."

"Why?"

Alex yanked out a chair with his boot, then sat down and rubbed his forehead.

"Not gonna tell me, huh?" Earl shrugged. "Doesn't matter why. Just tell me this—does it feel right?"

Alex's head shot up, a sharp pain shooting through his neck. "What did you say?"

"Does it feel like you're doing the right thing? 'Cause from where I'm standing, it sure as hell doesn't look like it."

"You don't know anything about it," Alex said, ducking his head at the intense gleam in Earl's eyes and focusing on the rumpled edge of his collar instead.

Earl nodded. "Maybe not. But I know you miss Tammy." His eyes softened. "And Brody. I also know what you're doing now isn't doing you a bit of good."

Alex sighed and sagged back in the chair. "Then what would you suggest I do?"

"Well, for starters, you can get your ass up, drink a pot of coffee and check your mail."

Earl grabbed the bundle from under his arm and threw it. It slammed into Alex's chest and bounced into his lap. A large manila envelope slid off the top of the stack. Alex grabbed it before it fell to the floor.

"Then," Earl continued, "you can clean this mess up and come check on your horses." He smiled. "After that, I might consider inviting you over for supper. You're pretty decent company when you're not hungover."

Alex's mouth quirked. He gathered up the stack of mail, dropped it on the table and started sifting through bills.

"That's the spirit. I'm coming back to check on you to be sure you make it to the coffee." Earl chuckled and headed for the door. He paused on the threshold and turned back, hesitating. "You know, I spent a lot of years alone. I was fine on my own and never needed anyone. Only thing is, I never thought about whether or not someone might need me." He sighed. "I know it hit you hard when Susan left, so I can imagine it was scary letting Tammy in like you did. But the way I see it, if you did decide to take a chance with Tammy and things fell apart, well, it couldn't hurt any worse than it does now, could it?"

Alex froze, his stomach sinking at the words.

The door thudded shut on Earl's exit, and Alex blinked, refocusing on the manila envelope in his hand. It was addressed to him and Tammy.

Alex's hands shook as he studied the postmark. It'd arrived three weeks ago from Raintree, Georgia. Mrs. Jen Mead was listed on the return address. He turned it over, opened it and dumped out the contents.

Dozens of pictures slid across the table, scattering in different directions. All of them had been taken at Jen and Colt's wedding, and every single one of them had Brody in it.

He slumped into a chair, thumbing through them. There were so many. A few he remembered taking of Brody with Tammy as the baby smiled up at her or hugged her neck. All the rest were of him and Brody.

Alex smiled, recognizing the camera angle from when Tammy had knelt in front of them to take the picture or stood over them, cajoling bigger smiles. Even the winner—as Tammy had dubbed it—was there. Brody, the spitting image of Dean, sat on Alex's lap, grinning, his hands covered in icing and frozen halfway to his mouth.

Alex's gut churned, and he looked away, his gaze snagging on a small note among the pictures. He plucked it from the pile and read it.

Hi, Alex.

Colt told me I'm overstepping my boundaries by writing to you. And I know Tammy will kill me if she ever finds out. But heck, I've always gone for broke and I want Tammy to be happy. So here it is—you screwed up. Big-time. And if you're as smart as I think you are, you'll make it up to Tammy. Sooner rather than later. Because she's a wonderful woman who deserves the best. And after seeing the two of you together, I know without a doubt that you *are* the best. She shines when she's with you. Go see her, talk to her and you'll understand. (But please don't feel obligated to tell her that I wrote you. Did I mention she'd kill me if she ever found out?)

Alex laughed, the paper shaking in his hand.

I've enclosed pictures from the wedding. I promised to mail them to Tammy, but I'm hoping you'll pass them along to her instead. I took the liberty of enlarging one. Colt took it, and it was my favorite. It's proof you're a handsome man, Alex. And I've never seen Tammy happier.
Jen

Alex glanced over the pictures covering the table, then retrieved the manila envelope and felt inside, finding a larger picture. He tugged it out and laid it on the table.

Brody wasn't in this one.

A wave of heat swept through Alex, blurring his vision. He blinked hard and studied the picture closer.

Tammy stood on the dance floor in her teal dress, her arms around his waist and her face tipped up toward his. Her eyes were on him, bright and beautiful, and her smile was gentle. His hands cradled her face as he looked down at her, his smile just as wide as hers and both of their expressions full of love.

Alex stilled, remembering it clearly. It was the moment after Tammy had asked him to take her to his room and make love to her.

...I can't think of a better way to end the day.

He smiled, wet heat streaming down his cheeks as he whispered, "Neither can I."

God, she was beautiful. And *happy*. So damned happy. *Because of him.*

He held his breath and trailed a finger over her smile. She hadn't been happy in that moment because of Brody. Or because of another baby. She'd been happy because she was with him.

And he was a lucky bastard.

Alex exhaled, then let out a burst of laughter.

"Aw, hell. You didn't dive back into the liquor instead of the coffee, did you?"

Alex spun in his seat, steadied himself with the back of the chair, then scrubbed a hand over his face. Earl stood in the doorway, a look of trepidation crossing his face while Scout nipped at his ankle.

Alex shoved to his feet, shook his head and smiled. "I'm a lucky bastard."

He stopped, suddenly afraid. Just as Tammy had said. He'd focused more on what he couldn't give her than what he could. What he *could* do was love her better than any other man walking the earth. Loving her felt right. Instead, he'd sent her away, believing he wasn't enough.

"And I'm a dumb bastard," he spat, scrambling to regroup.

Earl's eyebrows rose, lips twitching. "I won't argue either point with you."

"You mind if I take a rain check on that dinner tonight?" Alex scooped the pictures up, tidied them back into the envelope, then began picking the empty bottles up off the floor. "I need to straighten up, see about the horses, then take off."

"Where you headed?"

Alex paused, clutching the bottles to his chest. "Wherever Tammy is."

Earl smiled. "I'm all for that. But you're not going anywhere until you drink some coffee, shower and shave. Otherwise, she'll unhook you and throw you right back in the pond."

Alex laughed, a weight lifting from him. "I've got to find her first."

Earl gestured toward the cell phone sticking out from underneath a pile of trash on the table. "Why don't you start by giving her a call?"

He did. But she didn't answer. It rang several times, then kicked to voice mail. He couldn't leave a message. What he wanted to say needed to be said in person.

She'd left him messages, though. He played each one several times as he cleaned up, shaved and packed a bag. She'd called so many times, asking him to pick up or call back, and she'd ended each one with the same phrase.

I still love you.

Lord, he hoped so. He hoped she still loved him despite him acting like a crazy, selfish bastard. And if she didn't, he'd do anything he damned well had to do to earn it back.

The last message was from three days ago and she'd mentioned visiting Jen at Raintree Ranch. It was the best lead he had, so he started there. He asked Earl to tend to his horses for a few more days, threw his bag in his truck, then headed out, taking the straightest shot he could to Raintree.

The sun was just beginning to set when he arrived. He drove past the main guesthouse to Colt and Jen's house on the back lot, hoping Tammy was still there. He turned onto the driveway, and his headlights illuminated Tammy's truck and trailer parked at the end of it.

His heart lurched. He parked the truck, hopped out and strode up to the front door, running his clammy palms down the sides of his pant legs. He hesitated, then raised his fist and knocked, his knees shaking when footsteps approached.

The door swung open, and the welcoming smile on Jen's face melted away, a cool expression taking its place.

"Hi, Jen."

"Alex." She propped a hand on her hip. "What can I do for you?"

"I'm here to see Tammy."

"Oh, really?" Her eyes narrowed, swept down his frame, then back up again, her gaze lingering on the slight tremble of his hands at his sides. "What for?"

Alex winced. "I screwed up. And I want to make it

up to her." He swallowed the tight knot in his throat.
"Please, Jen."

A slow smile spread across her face. "It's about time."
She turned her head to the side and shouted, "Tammy,
get your cute butt down here. You have a guest."

Alex smiled, mouthing *thank you*.

"You're gonna pay me back," Jen whispered, pointing a finger at his chest and grinning. "You better have
that matron of honor position on lock for me."

He nodded, and she left. Footfalls sounded down the
stairs, then he heard a murmur of voices from inside. He
looked down and dragged a boot over the porch floor,
trying to calm his nerves. A pair of boots appeared in
front of his, smaller and feminine.

Alex looked up, his heart aching at the guarded look
on Tammy's face. "Hey."

She crossed her arms over her chest, her full breasts
lifting and her tempting mouth firming.

Every muscle in his body strained to reach out and
pull her close. He shifted his stance and cleared his
throat. "I needed to see you. I needed to tell you I'm
sorry."

Her beautiful eyes flashed. "For what?"

"For ending things the way I did and not having more
faith in you. For not being even half as brave as you've
been." He sucked in a deep breath. "See, the thing is,
everyone keeps thinking it's me who rescued you. But
you're the one who rescued me. And I want to return
the favor."

She stayed silent, her expression softening.

"I want to offer you a deal." He stepped forward and
looked down at her, the warmth radiating from her soft

curves making him long to lean closer. "I can't give you children. And I can't—"

His voice broke, and he looked away, fighting back the wave of grief washing over him.

"I can't give you Brody," he forced out, flinching. "But I can give you my heart. Every corner of it." He faced her, peering into her eyes. "I can give you a life full of love, laughter and time spent together. I love you. I want to marry you and share my life with you. I want to rock beside you on the front porch every day and hold and kiss you every night. And I swear I'll love you better than any other man ever could. Every day. For the rest of our lives."

Her lower lip trembled. "You want to kiss me every night? For the rest of our lives?"

He nodded, leaning closer. "Yes."

She smiled, small and shaky, and tears escaped her lashes. "Dentures and all?"

He laughed, his own eyes tearing up, and cradled her face in his hands. "Yes."

Tammy's smile faded. She uncrossed her arms, then wrapped her hands around his wrists. "I can only accept on one condition."

Alex straightened, his heart pounding. "Anything."

She sighed. "I come with a lot of baggage, and you have to agree to take it on, too."

"I will." He dipped his head and kissed her, eager for the sweet taste of her again. She melted into him, and at her soft moan, he lifted his head and whispered, "Whatever it is."

She smiled, then slipped out of his arms. He immediately followed, reaching for her as she turned her head and beckoned someone with her hand.

"Come on," she said, laughing.

A familiar cackle rang out. Alex stopped and turned his head to the side.

Brody, clad in baby jeans and a T-shirt, ran toward them, hair flopping and diaper swishing with each step.

Alex sank to his knees and held out his arms. "Brody?"

Brody's brown eyes lit up as he spotted Alex. "Dat!"

He darted over, wrapped his arms around Alex's neck and squealed, his legs lifting restlessly in a demand to be picked up.

"John and Becky changed their minds." Tammy smiled softly as Alex stood with Brody in his arms. "It wasn't the right time for them." She stepped forward and touched his forearm. "But I think it's just the right time for us."

Alex pulled her close and wrapped them both in his arms, laughing and crying at the same time. "It's the perfect time," he whispered. "Just perfect."

Tammy hugged him back, kissed Brody's cheek and asked, "Can we go home now?"

Alex nodded, his heart full to bursting. "Yeah. We're going home."

Brody laid his head on Alex's chest, right over his heart. Alex kissed Tammy again and held his family in a protective embrace, savoring every moment. And he knew he was right where he belonged.

* * * * *

SPECIAL EXCERPT FROM

H HARLEQUIN®

SPECIAL EDITION

*In the small Texas burg of Rambling Rose, real estate
investor Callum Fortune is making a big splash.
The last thing he needs is any personal complications
slowing his pace—least of all nurse Becky Averill,
a beautiful widow with twin baby girls!*

*Read on for a sneak preview of
Fortune's Fresh Start
by Michelle Major, the first book in
The Fortunes of Texas: Rambling Rose continuity.*

"I didn't mean to rush off the other day after the ribbon cutting," he told her as they approached the door that led to the childcare center. "I think I interrupted a potential invitation for dinner, and I've been regretting it ever since."

Becky blinked. In truth, she would have never had the guts to invite Callum for dinner. She'd been planning to offer to cook or bake for him and drop it off at his office as a thank-you. The idea of having him over to her small house did funny things to her insides.

"Oh," she said again.

"Maybe I misinterpreted," Callum said quickly, looking as flummoxed as she felt. "Or imagined the whole thing. You meant to thank me with a bottle of wine or some cookies or—"

"Dinner." She grinned at him. Somehow his discomposure gave her the confidence to say the word.

He appeared so perfect and out of her league, but at the moment he simply seemed like a normal, nervous guy not sure what to say next.

She decided to make it easy for him. For both of them. "Would you come for dinner tomorrow night? The girls go to bed early, so if you could be there around seven, we could have a more leisurely meal and a chance to talk."

His shoulders visibly relaxed. "I'd like that. Dinner with a friend. Can I bring anything?"

"Just yourself," she told him.

He pulled his cell phone from his pocket and handed it to her so she could enter her contact information. It took a few tries to get it right because her fingers trembled slightly.

He grinned at her as he took the phone again. "I'm looking forward to tomorrow, Becky."

"Me, too," she breathed, then gave a little wave as he said goodbye. She took a few steadying breaths before heading in to pick up the twins. *Don't turn it into something more than it is*, she cautioned herself.

It was a thank-you, not a date. Her babies would be asleep in the next room. Definitely not a date.

But her stammering heart didn't seem to get the message.

Don't miss
Fortune's Fresh Start *by Michelle Major,*
available January 2020 wherever
Harlequin® *Special Edition books and ebooks are sold.*

Harlequin.com

Looking for more satisfying love stories
with community and family at their core?

Check out **Harlequin® Special Edition**
and **Love Inspired®** books!

New books available every month!

CONNECT WITH US AT:

Facebook.com/groups/HarlequinConnection

 Facebook.com/HarlequinBooks

 Twitter.com/HarlequinBooks

 Instagram.com/HarlequinBooks

 Pinterest.com/HarlequinBooks

ReaderService.com

**ROMANCE WHEN
YOU NEED IT**

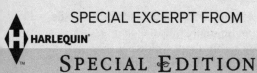
Mackenzie Wallace is back and wants excitement with her old crush. She hopes there's still some bad boy lurking beneath the single father's upright exterior. Dan Adams isn't the boy he was—but secrets from his past might still manage to keep them apart.

Read on for a sneak preview of the next book in the Gallant Lake Stories series,
Her Homecoming Wish,
by Jo McNally.

"There's an open bottle of very expensive scotch on the counter, just waiting for someone to enjoy it." She laughed again, softly this time. "And I'd *really* like to hear the story of how Danger Dan turned into a lawman."

Dan grimaced. He hated that stupid nickname Ryan had made up, even if he *had* earned it back then. Especially coming from Mack.

"Is your husband waiting upstairs?" Dan wasn't sure where that question came from, but, to be fair, all Mack had ever talked about was leaving Gallant Lake, having a big wedding and a bigger house. The girl had goals, and from what he'd heard, she'd reached every one of them.

"I don't have a husband anymore." She brushed past him and headed toward the counter. "So are you joining me or not?"

Dan glanced at his watch, not sure how to digest that information. "I'm off duty in fifteen minutes."

Her long hair swung back and forth as she walked ahead of him. So did her hips. *Damn.*

"And you're all about following the rules now? You really have changed, haven't you? Pity. I guess I'm drinking my first glass alone. You'll just have to catch up."

He frowned. Mackenzie had been strong-willed, but never sassy. Never the type to sneak into her father's store alone for an after-hours drink. Not the type to taunt him. Not the type to break the rules.

Looked like he wasn't the only one who'd changed since high school.

Don't miss
Her Homecoming Wish *by Jo McNally,*
available February 2020 wherever
Harlequin® Special Edition *books and ebooks are sold.*

Harlequin.com